Advance Praise

"Richly immersive, the story grabbed me from the start and never let go. It's rare for novels to be set in the mid-Republic [of ancient Rome], let alone about the Vestal Virgins, but Alvear rewards us in spades. It's common for a sense of place to be lacking in historical novels, or at least for it to be patchy in its execution. Not so with *The Cleansing*. I thought it was excellent, and very evocative, and its main character Mia, a feisty and determined heroine."

– Ben Kane, international bestselling author of the *Hannibal of Rome* and *Spartacus* series

"*The Cleansing* is all at once a shocking true story, a searing courtroom drama and a scathing indictment of religion in politics. Alvear writes an all too timely tale of female independence and the price far too often paid when a woman refuses to be blamed for the wrongs of others in the face of religious persecution."

– Kate Quinn, *New York Times* bestselling author of *The Alice Network*, *The Diamond Eye* and *The Rose Code*

"Few authors bring the ancient world to life with such clarity. In *The Cleansing*, Alvear exposes the ruthless calculus of power and superstition in ancient Rome with devastating impact. Gripping, this is historical fiction that dares to confront our darkest human impulses.

Bold, brutal, and bittersweet—a powerful and unflinching portrait of a woman caught in the wheels of a cruel empire."
  – Stephanie Dray, *New York Times* bestselling author of *Lily of the Nile, My Dear Hamilton,* and *Becoming Madame President*

"'What is then is now,' a philosopher once said, and Alvear shows how true that is in this shocking true story. She shows how expectation of behavior is still controlled by society, religion, and family. What has changed? This haunting tale of slaughter, fire, and the dangers of state sponsored superstition is more relevant than ever."
  – Rob Cain, host of *Ancient Rome Refocused* blog and podcast Enter

"Gripping and unflinching, *The Cleansing* breathes life into the haunting true story of a Vestal Virgin scapegoated for Rome's greatest military loss. Alvear turns a forgotten footnote of history into a fierce, page-turning indictment of purity culture—both ancient and enduring. I highly recommend this powerful and timely read!"
  – Eliza Knight, *USA Today* and international bestselling author of *Confessions of a Grammar Queen* and *The Mayfair Library*

"Although *The Cleansing* begins on a battlefield full of men, the flesh, bone and soul of this story belongs to Mia, one of Rome's Vestal Virgins. This brilliantly crafted novel inspires introspection and reflection even as its plot races onward, keeping the reader in thrall. It remains fiercely and disturbingly relevant in the modern world."
  – Sophie Perinot, bestselling author of *Medici's Daughter, Ribbons of Scarlet,* and *A Day of Fire.*

The Cleansing

The Cleansing

A Novel of Ancient Rome
Based on a True Story

Victoria Alvear

HYPATIA
PRESS

Published by Hypatia Press in the United Kingdom in 2026

ISBN: 978-1-83919-634-8

www.hypatiapress.org

Content warning: this true-to-the-period tale contains scenes of ancient Roman religious practices involving blood/animal sacrifices. Also includes slavery, military battle, capital punishment, and rape (not depicted), as well as suicide and suicide ideation.

She said "there is no reason"
And the truth is plain to see
…One of sixteen Vestal virgins
Who were leaving for the coast
…But she smiled at me so sadly
That my anger straightaway died
…Her face at first just ghostly
Turned a whiter shade of pale

Procol Harum
"A Whiter Shade of Pale"

For Bruce, Matthew, Aliya, and Ian

Roman Forum
Republican Era

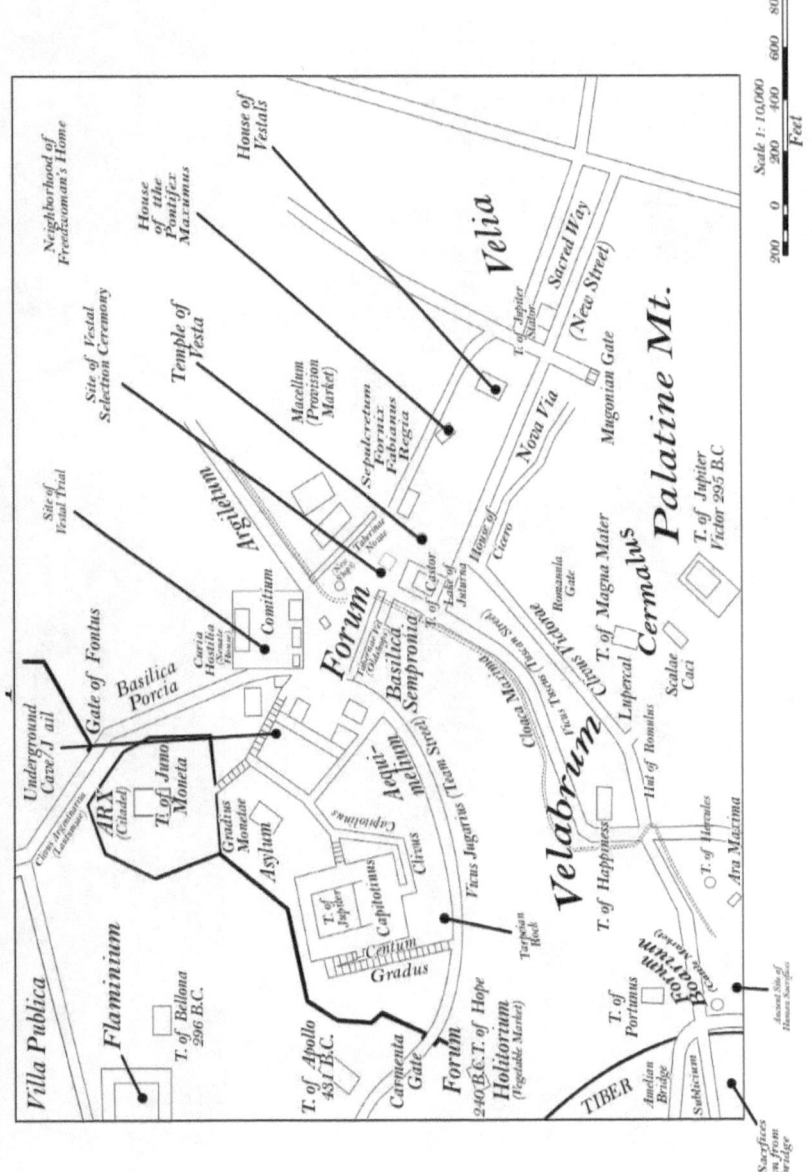

Scale 1: 10,000

Feet

Villa Publica

Flaminium

T. of Bellona 296 B.C.

Neighborhood of Freedwoman's Home

House of the Pontifex Maximus

House of Vestals

Site of Vestal Selection Ceremony

Temple of Vesta

Site of Vestal Trial

Macellum (Provision Market)

Sepulcretum Fornix Fabianus Regia

Velia

Sacred Way

(New Street)

Nova Via

Magonian Gate

Argiletum

Comitium

Curia Hostilia (Senate House)

Forum

Basilica Sempronia

Basilica Porcia

T. of Castor

House of Cicero

Lake of Juturna

Romania Gate

T. of Magna Mater

T. of Jupiter Victor 295 B.C.

Palatine Mt.

Cermalus

Gate of Fontus

Underground Cave,Jail

ARX (Citadel)

T. of Juno Moneta

Gradus Monetae Asylum

T. of Jupiter

Capitolinus

Clivus

Aequi-melium

Vicus Jugarius (Teem Street)

Vicus Tuscus (L) Street)

Cloaca Maxima

Lupercal

Scalae Caci

Hut of Romulus

T. of Hercules

Ara Maxima

Velabrum

T. of Happiness

Carmenta Gate

T. of Apollo 431 B.C.

Forum Holitorium (Vegetable Market)

Centum Gradus

240 B.C.T. of Hope

Tarpeian Rock

Forum Boarium (Cattle Market)

T. of Portunus

T. of Hercules

Sublicium

Aurelian Bridge

TIBER

Ancient Site of Human Sacrifice

Angel Sacrifices Thrown From this Bridge

The Battle at Cannae (216 BCE)

Attius figured he would be either dead, maimed, or a hero at the end of their march. He preferred the latter. He would settle for deeply injured if he must. As long as he got back to Rome. To Mia. But the reality hit hard: the Carthaginian general Hannibal had defeated Rome's forces twice before.

It will be different this time.

Attius gripped his shield, reminding himself that never before had any city-nation assembled a fighting force of this magnitude. Eighty thousand Roman warriors in total, including cavalry and auxiliary fighters. Rome outnumbered the Carthaginians by more than half. The earth shook with the thunder of their advance.

We will crush them.

The pounding pace of the march picked up. The air was thick with the reek of sweat, leather, and fear. All of Rome's best men kicked up clouds of dust so thick they stung Attius' eyes and coated his ragged throat. Hannibal had cut off access to the river and he, like all of the Romans, hadn't had a drop to drink in two days.

Attius' heart lurched as the plains of Cannae echoed with screams, clashing metal, and shrieking horses. The fighting had begun. But which flank? Being deep in the center meant his vision had narrowed to the circle of brothers marching beside and in front of him.

"Where are they?" someone on his left muttered. At that pace, they should have already hit Hannibal's front line. Yet nothing stopped their advance. Rumors whipped through the mass of warriors like wind rippling over wheat fields.

They're retreating. Hannibal's middle is collapsing. They're running!

Hope and excitement hit the unit as one and their march turned into a jog, and then a run.

Go, go, go!

Was it possible that Hannibal's dreaded Gallic barbarians were actually running scared? Attius had the sudden sense of floating above his body, looking down at the mass of advancing Romans. He didn't find himself in the endless rows of anonymous warriors and imagined trying to describe the experience to Mia. A childhood memory flashed through his mind as he ran: the two of them, so young, watched ants stream over the ridges of a fallen log as they squatted under a sycamore.

"What are all those little Myrmidons thinking?" he'd muttered.

"Nothing," Mia had said. Her face, like his, had been inches from the tiny tramping army. Inches from his own. "Ants march until they die."

Attius murmured a silent prayer. *Let me survive this.* He imagined Mia laughing, "Who are you praying to?" she'd ask, grinning. "You don't believe in the gods!" The fighter on his left barreled into Attius and the shock brought him fully back into his body. Numidians—Hannibal's elite cavalry—must have broken through their left flank.

The pace slowed to a walk as they were pushed into each other from both sides. Shields clanged, leather creaked, shoulder guards scraped flesh, metal studs on their fighting boots dug into rock.

"What in Pluto's prick is happening?" Attius muttered.

"It's not Pluto's prick I'm worried about," his friend Marcus, on his right, spat through gritted teeth.

A second massive surge from the left had them ricocheting off each other's shoulders like iron nails in a box. Still, they pushed on. Nothing was stopping their forward lurch.

That is a good thing, surely.

Sounds swelled around them: horses screaming, swords clashing, men bellowing. The air was heavy with the scent of copper. The whirling dust became shaded with red mist. New whispers made Attius' heart drop.

"It's a trap."

"They've got us surrounded."

"We're going to die here."

They were being pushed together closer and closer without advancing, like children marching in place. But where was the enemy? Gasps and curses filled the air.

Attius was squeezed from all sides.

No. No. Please. They must be wrong.

Whispers of *I can't breathe* swirled around him.

They stopped advancing all together. *This can't be happening,* Attius thought. *This couldn't be happening!* He and Marcus both cursed their generals. They'd been marched into yet another of Hannibal's traps. How many times would their leaders underestimate the North African general? Insulting commanders was punishable by death but they were going to die anyway.

Attius' heart pounded in his ears. Men roared in helpless rage. Why, *why,* hadn't Mia run away with him when he had offered? He'd had everything planned. Nobody would have ever found them! But now he was going to die—another anonymous body thrown onto the sacrificial altar of Rome's arrogance. The soldier behind Attius pushed his shield into him and Attius kicked back like a horse in a too-small stall.

Air, air, I need air.

3

A wave of panic seemed to hit everyone at once. Despite being trained to never turn his head on a march, he looked at Marcus, as if he could confirm this was really happening. His friend's grimace, the whites of his eyes, made his insides curdle.

They couldn't even lift their arms in the crush, let alone fight if the enemy broke through. He pressed even harder against the men in formation in front of him, as others pressed on his back. Grunts and curses flew through the air.

Attius pushed harder. He had to break out. He needed air. He had to fight. He needed to *do* something.

The crush was maddening. A sudden opening and Attius' feet slipped. Not mud. Blood. Bits of flesh. Severed limbs. Slick organs. He stepped on something round, the nails in his boot scraping flesh, and knew without looking it was a head. Enemy or friend?

Bellowing in the strange guttural sounds of Celtic Iberian, Gaulish warriors pressed in from all sides. Hannibal's most vicious fighters were coming closer, cutting them down, limb-by-limb, man-by-man.

Desperate, Attius climbed over writhing bodies. Unmoving bodies. To stay still was to die. He had to keep moving. Where was Marcus? From the corner of his eye Attius spied him clambering over a fallen cohort, his friend's face a mask of horror. Attius placed his knee on something slick and warm as he boosted himself up and over. If he could only stand, he might be able to get above the fray. To see what was happening. To breathe air that wasn't thick with the scent of blood and death.

A giant long-haired Celt plunged through the red mist, snarling at Attius in a strange language. As if from far away, Attius felt the sting of sharp metal cut into his defending arm. Where was his shield? Time slowed. The man bared his teeth. Bits of gore clung to the edges of the man's enormous mustache. Attius crouched and thrust his gladius straight for the heart, but the man had fought Romans before. He blocked his strike. In that moment, another legionnaire threw himself at the man with the blond braids, and the big Celt lost his balance. Attius thrust his sword deep just below the ribs. A spray of blood covered his arms as he pulled his slippery gladius out to use again.

Another long-haired Celt came flying at him. Attius tried to dodge but wasn't fast enough. A stinging sensation on his thigh and he stumbled onto the slickness beneath him. Time slowed as he fell. The Celt's sword missed him but caught Marcus. Hard. His friend's helmet flew off his head, in a burst of red.

"No," Attius cried, crawling to help his friend. But Marcus disappeared under the swell of bodies. The bearded Celt, without even turning in his direction, smashed his heavy, curved shield into Attius' helmet.

Ringing pain and a strange quiet enveloped him as he fell to the ground. The edges of his vision glowed red. Bodies twitched underneath him. Hobnailed soldiers clambered over him, their spikes piercing his flesh. Every step stole his breath. The world shrank to nightmarish sound. Flesh gutted to bone. Men gurgling last breaths. The panting of attackers. The howls of the downed.

He had to help Marcus. But why couldn't he move? A great winged beast had sunk its talons into him. It sucked his strength. Stole his breath. A single thought flashed through his mind before more bodies fell over him... *Mia.*

Chapter One

Six Weeks Later
Mia, Priestess of Vesta
Ides of October

On a crisp fall morning on the field of Mars, three sharp trumpet blasts shattered the crystalline blue of the sky. I imagined the firmament's jagged shards plunging toward us to rend our flesh the same way so many Romans had rent their clothes and hair in grief after Cannae.

And so began the rite I dreaded the most every year—the ritual of the October Horse.

When the trumpets' shrill ringing melted away, the quiet was disorienting. The milling crowd stilled as one, like grieving statues before the face of Medusa. When the priest of Mars, the god of war, held up his arms, all turned toward him, as if he could explain the unexplainable—how it was possible to lose fifty thousand of our best Roman men in one day.

Including Attius.

The familiar stabbing pain of loss stole the air from my body, but I dared not show it. As one of Rome's six Vestal virgins, priestesses of Vesta, the goddess of the hearth, I could never let on that I grieved for one man in particular. I grieved *all* of them. And I had to perform this grief with great dignity. No ululating, no rending of clothing or hair, no ashes on my face. With the prospect of Hannibal's invasion an ever-present fear, we Vestals had to project the illusion of quiet calm.

But on the inside, I roared until all of Rome's seven hills crumbled into dust. Still I managed to hold on to my demure virgin's closed-lipped smile.

The wooden risers upon which we stood creaked as the Pontifex Maximus, the head priest of Rome and the man to whom we Vestals reported, climbed to the top tier of our viewing station, reserved for the most powerful in Rome. Cornelius Lentulus, with his downturned mouth, thick neck, and protruding belly, had always looked to me like a toad waiting for prey to wander near its slimy tongue. His tall, white pontifical hat only emphasized his lack of neck.

Our very own frog priest.

The lower risers teemed with Rome's senators in their best ceremonial togas. They looked especially old and frail in the bright, fall light—a constant reminder that nearly one hundred of our stronger, younger senators also died on the fields of Cannae. Did their hunched toga-ed shoulders hint at their shame for living while so many good men died?

The College of Priests, nineteen leaders representing Rome's oldest gods, settled on the risers above us, reeking of myrrh, spikenard, and frankincense oils. Perhaps they thought the gods would find them by scent alone.

On the field below, the priest of Mars signaled the charioteers to steer their two-horse teams to the starting line. In keeping with the ancient roots of this rite, the horses had been selected for their bravery on the battlefield. The racers, dressed in the ancient costume of woven chest plates and grieves, rode old-fashioned wicker war chariots.

The horses, sensing the competition and excitement, snorted and stomped in the cool air, their gleaming flanks rippling with anticipation.

Another blast of the trumpets sent the horses into wild galloping. Even in times of mourning, Romans could not resist a good race and the field erupted with cheering. Instead of following the heads of the horses though, my gaze lingered on the clouds of dust they kicked up behind them. *Keep running. Save yourselves!*

But they never did.

A heavily pregnant woman on the risers below us turned to speak to a friend and for a moment, my heart leaped. Prisca! But no, it was not my best friend. The woman below wore black and Prisca had no need for mourning colors. Her husband managed to escape Hannibal's death machine without a scratch. Why he and his plummy officer friends escaped while so many good men like Attius died was yet one more mystery the gods never bothered to explain.

Memories flooded in of all the times Attius begged me to run away with him, from my duties as a priestess, to create a life of our own somewhere far from Rome, living off the land, hunting and playing in the woods like we used to as children. He would be Orion to my Diana.

My heart squeezed at the innocence of our dreams. Of how tempted I was, not just to escape with him, but to break my vows and love him physically. But I never succumbed. In exchange for maintaining my purity, the gods promised safety for Rome.

We did our part. So why were we on the brink of annihilation?

Every day we heard ever more terrible details about how our best Romans died.

The Senate verified as true one story that seemed too gruesome even for Mars himself: when the Carthaginians returned to the battlefield to collect their dead, they pulled a living Numidian warrior—

one of Hannibal's mercenaries—out from under a pile of dead bodies. A Roman had fallen over the enemy warrior during the fighting. As more and more of the dead piled on top of them, neither could move. With arms and legs trapped, the Roman, in a frenzy of rage and frustration, used the only weapon he had left—his mouth. He chewed off the Numidian's nose and ears before he died atop him. The mutilated Numidian, pulled out from under his dead attacker, lived to tell the tale. The idea that Attius may have suffered in a similar way made my spine twist with horror.

May his death have been quick. I knew it was ridiculous to pray for something after the fact, but what else could I do?

Floronia, my fellow priestess, elbowed me. She had remarkably sharp bones. "You are frowning again," she whispered, bringing me back to the field. The thunder of the racing horses and the screams of the crowd flooded in with an almost physical force.

Breathe. I adjusted my expression into a mask of impassivity. A projection of blank calmness, like the statues of the deathless gods, provided comfort and hope to the people of Rome during times of crisis. Surely if the priestesses were calm, and composed, all would turn out well for us.

A cry went up as the chariots made their final turn. The wooden risers shook and trembled as people stomped their excitement. The rite of the October Horse marked the end of the fighting season and was meant to honor the dead and cleanse our surviving warriors and the city of the taint of human blood and foreign enemies. But what sense did it make to mark the end of the fighting season when Hannibal could march on Rome at any moment? Were we tempting the fates and insulting the gods by holding this celebration? But what else were we to do? The auspices were clear—the sacred birds flew to the right, which meant we had to proceed with the ritual.

The crowd roared as the winning chariot crossed the finish marker. Floronia and I released a breath at the same time. Had there been no clear winner, or had there been a terrible crash, the people would have fallen into yet another panic, claiming it a sign of impending doom.

The priest of Mars and his attendants unleashed the right-hand horse of the winning team and paraded the proud victor up and down the track for all to see. The gleaming, sweating war horse pranced in joy, head and tail high.

I leaned into Floronia. "Let us leave now," I urged under my breath. "The carriage is ready for us."

She moved her head in a barely perceptible shake. "You know we cannot until the throw."

We had this conversation every year and every year the answer was the same: *Not yet.* An old dread compelled me to ask anyway.

Only a rope—decorated with colorful flags—separated us from the huffing, sweating horses and the oiled, cursing charioteers. The colored flags whipped in the wind, a blur of reds, greens, blues, and whites. On the other side of the field, rose the path up to the Capitoline Hill. The bright yellow leaves of the sycamores and myrtles lining the paths flashed in the sun like the golden coins we threw into the air for Janus and Mercury—the gods of wealth and prosperity—on the new year.

A barefoot young man jogged into the center of the field. He was dressed like a warrior of old in a vest of braided leather rather than today's more common iron mail shirts. The red plume of his helmet rippled in the breeze. He held out an ancient spear to the priest of Mars for inspection. Even from my vantage point I saw this "warrior" was too young. The smoothness of his limbs gave him away. Normally, the warrior with the most kills performed this rite. Or at least one of our strongest warriors. But all of Rome's champions were dead. The only viable candidates for spear thrower were an aging veteran or one of Cannae's survivors—like my friend Prisca's husband—but the latter were tainted with the stink of defeat. So the priest of Mars picked a young recruit destined for our new legions as a symbol of hope and cleansing.

The sun glinted off the metal edge of the ancient spear stained with the blood of countless October Horses. The field hushed as the young man took one, two, three furious running steps before hurtling the ancient weapon with surprising viciousness toward the uncomprehending horse.

Run. Please. Now.

The throw landed true—cleanly and deeply into the animal's arched, muscular neck. The horse staggered and half-reared in surprise. I suppressed the shudder that instinctively wavered up my spine at every sacrifice, even after all these years.

"Now we may leave," whispered Floronia and the two of us descended the risers and headed for the carpentum, the enclosed carriage ready to speed us to the Forum. The other Vestal priestesses stayed behind to witness the next part of the rite as we rushed back to the Forum. Our carriage driver whipped the two city-horses into a run, throwing us back onto our wooden seats. Speed was essential. We had to arrive at the altar before the next part of the rite began. As with all our religious rites, no mistakes were tolerated lest we angered the gods.

Floronia and I did not speak. We were too busy holding onto the wooden planks of our seats during our pell-mell ride back to the Forum. So much for the dignity of our order. We looked like stuffed thrushes bobbing in a cage. Floronia and I exchanged a silly grin. It was a good thing the carriage was entirely sealed. We never wanted any Roman to see us in such undignified postures, let alone grinning. Smiling in public was forbidden for us Vestals, lest men misconstrue our good humor as an invitation.

Still, it was better than staying with the other Vestals who had to witness the next part of the ancient rite. After the slaying of the October Horse, the priest of Mars would cut off the beast's tail and phallus. He would then wrap the two symbols of virility and strength in an ancient warrior's cape said to be worn by Romulus himself. Then a swift runner would take the bundle to the Regia's altar, where Floronia and I would wait for him to oversee the next part of the rite. Blood from the October Horse had to anoint the altar. And we two Vestals had to bear witness to sacralize the rite.

As our carriage careened toward the Forum, the roar of excitement from the field chased us like a dark cloud. The runner had likely received his precious cargo and had set off in a sprint.

Floronia breathed out. "We should make it in plenty of time," she said over the clatter of iron wheels on cobblestone.

"May the gods make it so," I uttered out of habit, despite how much I hated what was to come next.

Chapter Two

I knew the moment our carriage turned onto the Via Sacra leading to the center of the city. The smell of animal waste from free-roaming dogs, the squeals of pigs escaped from pens, the sweat of countless working men and women, the calls of food vendors, the squawking of chickens—it always brought me back to the bewildering, overwhelming experience of seeing Rome for the first time.

When I was just six, pater brought mater and me from our farm outside of Capua to the city. I believed that we had come for a short visit to see where pater worked as he represented Capua as senator. If I'd known it was going to turn into a life sentence, I would have tried to hide with the pigs in the pen.

I hated Rome from the moment we passed through the Capuan Gate. After the lush lands, endless skies, and crisp country air of our farm and vineyards, Rome seemed like a descent into Pluto's caverns. Every building was covered in black soot. Acrid smoke hung over the entire seven hills like a beast protecting its kill: bodies burned in pyres outside the city walls, bakers fed immense ovens, priests burned sacrifices at crossroads, and hungry families squatted over small fires in the streets to cook whatever scrap of food they could find. Smothered under a blanket of smoke, Rome reeked of burning flesh, animal waste, poverty, and despair.

I'd wailed my disgust, begging to return to our farm. As always, I was slapped and told to be good. Nothing in all of the years since changed my perception of the city. Only now the slaps came from the most powerful priest in Rome, the toad-like Pontifex Maximus and the Virgo Maxima, the head priestess of our order.

There had been one blessing at least: pater had arranged for Attius' family to move to the city with us, a demand he could make as powerful patron to Attius' father, who had no real choice in the matter. Despite the trauma of the move, at least Attius and I had each other. He hated Rome and missed the country as much as I had. We knew no one else in the city, so we spent nearly every day together, boxed inside one or the other's small courtyard, recreating our adventures in the woods and being yelled at for refusing to wear shoes.

The first argument we ever had on the day we met would haunt and taunt me throughout the trajectory of the rest of my life. If only I'd seen it as the warning it was.

**

Sixteen Years Before
At the Farm Outside Capua

Attius had been dragged by his mother to visit us, as was proper since we were their neighbors and the most powerful family in the region. "Be nice, Attius," his mater said. "Say hello and go play with your new friend."

He crossed his arms. "But I don't want to play with a girl," he whined.

His mother laughed nervously and glanced at my elegant mother. "You will because her father is a senator and your father's patron," she said in a low tone into his ear. "Do. You. Understand?"

Attius sighed as she pushed him toward me. "Yes, mater." His head drooped so low his chin grazed the top of his tunic.

"Can you shoot an arrow at a pine cone from twenty paces, because I can," I challenged.

His head popped up. "You have a bow?"

Of course I had a bow! Our farm manager, an Etruscan named Larce, had made one for me from one of the fallen elms on our property. And I used it every day to honor my favorite goddess, Diana the Huntress.

We raced to the woods, Attius kicking off his fancy sandals to join me in barefoot bliss. After we went a few rounds, I declared myself the winner, thanking Diana for guiding my arrows.

Attius dropped onto his backside under the shade of an umbrella pine. He gave a disdainful grunt. "Don't bother. My pater says the gods aren't real."

It was the first time I'd ever heard such blasphemy. I turned, drew an arrow, and aimed at his face.

"Take that back," I said. How dare he insult the goddess? Didn't he know how the goddess of the hunt punished those who disrespected her?

Attius scrambled up, putting a hand out in front of his face like a shield. "Wait, what are you doing?"

"Take it back," I repeated.

"Take what back?"

"Say, 'the gods ARE real,'" I commanded. He rolled his eyes, but eventually and resentfully complied. That was the first of many arguments between us about the existence and nature of the gods.

"Why does your pater say that about the gods," I asked, taking a step back from him and pulling the bow into my chest. I had never imagined people could have those thoughts. It was terrifying but also strangely exciting.

Attius shrugged and looked around as if checking for eavesdroppers. "Don't tell anyone!"

"Why?"

"Because I'll get in trouble," he said. "My mater told me never to repeat my father's words," he said, pulling at the top of his dark curls so that they stood up like tufted feathers. "Especially when we visit Rome. She and pater get into big fights about it. She thinks the gods are angry at us because of what my pater believes. And that's why my uncle and cousin died fighting the Iberians."

***

It was the first time I had heard anyone suggest that the gods punished some people merely for not liking what they said. It was bad enough that my nurse and my mater told me I angered the gods whenever I misbehaved. But I also had to worry about what I said or thought?

The horror of that possibility was deeply disturbing. At only four years old, I could barely manage my impulses, let alone my thoughts. Attius had handled the impossibility of it by following in his pater's footsteps. He rejected the entire premise.

But my family was different. Both my parents were extremely conservative and pious. We honored the gods and performed all rites with devoted precision. Every day, our altars had been filled with the highest quality offerings—the most beautiful flowers, the sweetest dates, our finest oil, the first bites of our beautifully prepared meals.

The gods knew this, mater had claimed. And that was why the gods rewarded us with such an abundance of wealth and power. The conviction of my parents' beliefs overrode the strange claims Attius made.

Still, his words had disturbed me. I didn't shoot him with my arrow that day, but every time I saw him after that, I pretended to. Then we would chase each other until we both fell onto the soft, green ground laughing and clutching our stomachs.

Stop thinking about the past, I told myself for the thousandth time, but it was useless.

Especially now that grief for Attius had merged with my longing for the other life I was meant to have, that I was sure I *would* have—with Attius in the country—had Pater not brought me to meet the head priest of Rome.

Fourteen more years of this, just fourteen more empty, rite-filled, joyless years and I will be free of my thirty-year Vestal obligation.

The jerk of the cart's sudden stop meant we'd reached the Regia. A sharp sting pierced my thumb as I scrambled out of the carriage. Had I gotten a splinter? No time to check. We dodged the horses as they clomped and stomped in irritation at having to stop. Clearly, they wanted to keep running at speed, a rare treat for them inside the city.

Trying to keep our dignity intact, we rushed to take up our positions next to the sacred altar. As we straightened and smoothed our robes, I imagined, once again, that we looked like plump, white birds settling ruffled feathers. We took a calming breath and locked in our expressions of pious impassivity.

While everyone watched the empty road for the runner carrying the horse's tail and phallus, I inspected my thumb. No splinter but there was a small cut where a bubble of blood had collected. Thankfully, no blood splattered onto my white Vestal dress. The people would have found that distressing and alarming. Surreptitiously, I tore off a small piece of fabric hanging from a faded old garland and pressed it hard against the cut to staunch the flow. I stuffed my wrapped hand inside the folds of my stola so that I appeared tranquil and dignified, as required. In these heightened times, the mob would interpret my cut as a terrible omen and panic.

A distant roar echoed from the Campius Martius, letting us know that the ceremonial fight for possession of the horse's head had begun. As per tradition, the priest of Mars oversaw the beheading of the horse and tossed the immense stallion head into a crowd of men representing two districts—the Sacrivites and the Suburites. The two groups fought for ownership of the head. Whoever won possession of it earned the right to mount the gory trophy in one of two sacred places—at the pillars in the Forum near us in the Regia if the men from the Sacra Via region won or at the ancient Mamilian Tower on the edge of the Subura if the Suburites won.

The scrappy Suburites—the poor folk from the Subura—tended to win this tussle. They were more likely to get violent. It was not unheard of for one or two men of each camp to die—from knifing or from being trampled in the melee—during the contention for the head. The winners were typically easy to spot—they were the men covered in blood and gore as they hoisted the captured head to mount on the winning wall, roaring with pride. Today's tussle over the horse's head was a war of old men.

Still, I hoped the head ended up on the Mamilian Wall rather than a stone's throw from where I lived in the Forum. I dreaded walking by the stinking, moldering horse head covered in buzzing flies. Then the surprisingly delicate and sad skull every day until the next October Horse rite.

We straightened and raised our chins when the runner finally arrived. Scattered applause greeted the young man. Chest heaving, eyes wide, the sprinter lurched toward the altar. Like the spear thrower, this one was also concerningly young—barely a teen.

We are a nation of boys and old men now.

The approaching teenager smelled of sweat, horse blood, and panic. He stopped before us, gasping and wide-eyed. Had he forgotten what he was to do next? I caught his eye and discretely motioned him to stand before the sacred altar. When he didn't move, I gave him an encouraging smile—keenly aware of the risk. Smiling at young men was extraordinarily dangerous for one such as me.

"Breathe," I whispered when he finally approached the altar. The knob in the boy's throat worked as he held the soaked, wrapped cape out to me. But Vestals cannot touch sacrificial blood.

I whispered, "Unwrap the cloak and hold up the tail and phallus for all to see." He scrambled to obey, relieved to have someone guide him.

The smaller than usual crowd cheered half-heartedly at the sight of the young runner holding proof of the October Horse before them. Already the crowd thinned as word spread that the Suburites won the horse's head. People set off in small groups to witness the nailing of the head onto the ancient and crumbling Mamilian Tower. Once its blood dripped over the dark layers of previously won heads and the October Horse's head was adorned with a crown of bread, the wine drinking would commence.

As instructed, the boy held the severed specimens over the altar. Blood from the sacrifice had to drip onto the altar to show that the gods had accepted the sacrifice. But nothing happened. My heart hammered in my ears. He must have pressed the wrapping too hard while he ran. A quick glance at the crumbled cape at the boy's feet confirmed this—it was sodden. Why would the priest of Mars depend on such a young and inexperienced child for this? He had clearly held the prize too tightly—confirmed by his sopping tunic—and now there was no blood for the altar.

The crowd grew disconcerted as low murmurs flew around us. Floronia and I exchanged glances. We could not let the fear escalate. The Senate had recently passed a law forbidding women from crying and wailing in public. The aim was to contain the expression of grief after Cannae, as if a law could enforce that. But if the mob lost itself in a frenzy of grief and fear, violence was sure to follow. Women would be arrested. And we would be blamed.

"Squeeze the phallus," I whispered to the teen. His face colored, but he obeyed, surreptitiously squeezing the limp phallus to milk droplets for the altar. The long, fleshy tube—a strangely colored mix of deep black and lurid pink—released nothing.

The rustling and murmurs increased. Something had to be done. "Block me from view," I whispered to Floronia.

I stood beside the young man and instructed him in an undertone to thrust the tail and phallus up even higher into the air with as much drama as he could manage. And to widen his eyes in an exaggerated manner as he stared at the sacrifice. It was an old magician's trick—as long as he was fervently staring at the tail and phallus, all eyes would follow his gaze.

No one would be watching me.

Floronia gave me a worried, wondering look when I stepped toward the altar. She widened her arms as if in prayer, the panels from her white stola blocking everyone's view. I unwrapped the piece of fabric covering the cut on my thumb and squeezed hard. Nothing.

Was the cut too clotted? Finally, I squeezed with all my might and felt the sting of renewed flow. Three fat droplets of bright red blood fell from my thumb onto the ancient, pitted marble altar.

My racing heart and near panic gave me additional strength so I squeezed even harder and managed another round of juicy drops before I rewrapped my hand and slipped it inside my stola.

"Behold," I cried in my most commanding priestess voice. "The gods approve, for there is blood!"

With my unwrapped hand I pointed to the fresh droplets of blood. A great sigh of relief was expelled all around me, especially by the boy-runner, who looked as if he were about to weep.

Even if people complained that they hadn't seen the blood fall, they could not argue with the evidence before their eyes: fresh blood on the altar. The crowd was appeased.

Chants of "The beast's blood has cleansed us! The gods are happy! The proof is on the altar," echoed all around us. Floronia instructed the young man to place the tail and phallus on a two-tiered, sieved, metal tray, which we walked to the Temple of Vesta and placed directly into the goddess' sacred fire for roasting. A huge burst of flame, along with the thick odious scent of burning hair and flesh, erupted with a dark burst and the people cheered.

Later we would collect the ashes that fell from the sieve to make sacrificial cakes for the Parilia next April to appease the Pales, the gods of protection for flocks and herds.

Only Vestal priestesses were allowed into the inner sanctum of our circular temple, where Vesta's eternal fire burned. We kept the wide, bronze doors open so those who had gathered at the bottom of the temple steps could witness the burning of the sacrifice.

Fabia, the elder virgin tending the fire that day, sang the hymns of purification. Once the offering had been completely consumed by fire, the ceremonial public aspects of the rites were complete. With no apparent mishaps, thank the goddess. Slowly, the crowd dispersed. As was custom, Floronia and I stood beside the massive bronze fire cauldron, awaiting the transformation of sacrificed flesh to ash. We watched as plumes of smoke—thick with the mingled scents of burnt hair, incinerated flesh, and cloying incense—roiled upward and through the oculus, the wide circular opening atop our small domed temple.

After sundown prayers, I finally found a moment to collapse onto my pillowed couch in my private consulting room. Inside the House of Vestals each Vestal had her own small space where we met with supplicants seeking counsel. The older Vestals—including the elderly Virgo Maxima—catered to supplicants from the patrician class, decorating their rooms with pretty frescoes, silken pillows, and alabaster end tables.

I took a different approach, seeking to emphasize warmth and comfort, especially as I made a point to invite people from all classes to consult with me on how to create harmony with the gods in the home. When the Maxima learned that a growing stream of plebian supplicants had been seen coming to the House of Vestals to consult with me, she had become apoplectic. It was not done! The ranks of the wealthy and working classes never mixed!

Fortunately, I had graduated into my second decade of service and she could do nothing to stop me (I had checked the laws). The Maxima was sure I did this only to anger her. I hadn't, but it was certainly an unexpected boon nonetheless.

Sighing, I dissolved onto a mountain of pillows, aware that my posture was most unbecoming given that I'd carelessly splayed my legs. It always amazed me that as a lifelong virgin, I was expected to provide wise counsel to women struggling with issues I knew nothing about. Images of the women who had sought me out before Cannae flitted through my mind—of the young wife who sobbed because her husband purchased a young male slave and left her bed entirely for him. Of another who was beaten regularly by a cruel husband, even while pregnant. Of the matron who sobbed over how her stepchildren hated her.

All I could do was listen and suggest they make special sacrifices to Vesta in the hopes of creating peace and harmony in the home. And when they returned complaining nothing had changed, that they continued being raped or beaten or abandoned by their husbands, I fell back upon our standard response: "The goddess must not have accepted your offering. You must try again. And make a bigger sacrifice this time."

After Cannae—where so many of these same men died—supplicants came to me wracked with guilt, convinced that they were somehow to blame for their deaths. They had begged the goddess to remove their pain, hadn't they?

Hadn't they?

It was my job to remind them that they asked only for safety and peace, not for the deaths of their men. What happened on the battlefield had nothing to do with them. Still, many women found a way to blame themselves. Self-blame, I was beginning to understand, was the purvey of the powerless. As painful as it was, blaming themselves gave them the illusion of control.

Floronia burst in and flopped onto a couch across from me. She hugged a pillow tight to her chest.

"Mia, what were you thinking?" she asked in a whisper. Despite being promised complete privacy in our individual consulting rooms, we always had the sense of being watched by the Maxima's minions. We learned to speak in whispers even when it appeared no one was around.

It took a moment for me to understand she was referring to the bloodletting at the altar during the October Horse rite. "It all worked out in the end, did it not?"

"But... but to use your own blood! At such an important rite. Aren't you scared?"

"Of what?"

23

Floronia stood and paced, twisting her hands. "I do not know. Of upsetting the fates. What if your actions bring Hannibal to us even sooner?"

A pang of fear gripped my belly, but I pushed it away. I had done nothing wrong. "My friend, the Senate's informers report that Hannibal's army is still in the midlands—"

"But what if they are wrong? What if Hannibal is on his way to burn us down as we speak?"

"Why would our informers lie?"

Floronia shrugged. "All I know is that everyone is genuinely scared."

"People always focus on the worst possible scenario," I reminded her. "We know better and can keep them calm."

Floronia shook her head. "We do not know much, that is the problem."

"Floronia, you are not… not going to tell the Maxima what I did, are you?"

Her eyes widened. "No, of course not. We all suffer when she goes into her rages. Besides, we would be forced to perform the entire rite again from the beginning and it is too late for that. The panic would be too great."

"Then why do you remain so agitated?"

"You sacrificed your own blood," she hissed. "What if the gods rain down their wrath upon you? Or upon *me* for not stopping it?"

Her genuine fear made my chest constrict. We had spent our entire lives desperately trying to avert the rage of the gods. The problem was that we never could guess what enraged them or when. They always managed to find something that displeased them. It was our job to anticipate and deflect their rage and disappointment, and that was what I'd done, yes?

I saved the rite.

Why would that anger the gods? The Sibylline Books said only that blood must adorn the altar to please the gods. And I ensured that.

"My friend," I said gently, masking my own disquiet. "Me using my own drops must be the gods' will or it wouldn't have happened that way, don't you see?"

I disliked relying on this antiquated circular reasoning—the gods approved of our actions because if they had not, *they would not have allowed it*—but I did not know how else to calm Floronia's nerves. I half expected her to scoff at my attempt—despite our constant use of it with worshippers—but she accepted it gratefully.

Why should she be any different than the rest of us? During troubled times, we all sought reassurance. We pined for someone—anyone—who would authoritatively promise us all would be well.

"You should purify yourself just in case," she warned.

"Of course," I said, smiling at her. "I will walk through the temple fire's sacred smoke three times before I retire. I promise. All will be well."

For a moment, I even believed it myself.

Chapter Three

The Forum was dark and silent when I paused at the steps of our small circular temple. The unearthly shine of a sickle moon drew my eye and I stared at it with ancient longing, as it was the mark of Diana, the goddess of the hunt, ruler of the wild woods. I couldn't help but wonder what I'd done to insult the goddess that she would send me to serve silent Vesta instead of running free in the woods like her.

Entering the temple was like walking into a living wall of heat and light. At least in the cooler months it was bearable. In the summer, the heat seared the breath from my chest and stewed me alive in my white woolen robes. No matter the season, we always had to appear in public covered from head to foot in the heavy, body-hiding layers of our priesthood.

The fire crackled and hissed, throwing its evermoving light and shadow against the painted walls and shining columns of the temple's interior. The elder Vestal on fire watch nodded at me and I nodded back. Sitting up on her backless stool near the sacred cauldron where she could be seen by the public, she went back into her open-eyed trance, a sleep-like trick we all mastered to appear attentive. Any late-night supplicant driven to leave a sacrifice on the goddess' altar in the courtyard facing us would be reassured by her seemingly unwavering attention on the sacred fire.

The fire was crucial to Rome's well-being. As long as Vesta's fire flared vibrant and strong, the gods would continue to protect us. If the fire went out, the gods would remove their protection. Since we did not understand why the gods abandoned us at Cannae, it was imperative that we kept the fire vibrant and strong at all times as proof it was not because of our laxity by the fire that caused the gods to abandon us.

And of course, the only other outrage that might have caused the gods to turn on us was unthinkable. We were all beyond reproach. None of us would have dared. Especially during difficult times. Ours was a world of women. We never met privately with any man—even fathers, brothers, or uncles. We never allowed ourselves to be alone with men. Only the pontiff was allowed to meet with us privately and the Maxima always made sure to attend those meetings too.

From a low table, I grabbed a handful of tiny lumps of dried orange-brown resin gum from the Boswellia tree—one of many offerings available to us—and tossed them into the fire. A burst of smoke and scent exploded and I waved the smoky tendrils—rich with the sweet-citrusy scent of what the Greeks called Frankincense—toward my body and around my form in an age-old dance of purification.

Being smoked was so familiar to me by now I could do it without thought, waving my arms in slow, graceful arcs from the bottom of my feet to over my head and back down again. The fragrant smoke moved over my entire body in a dance of cleansing. The breath from Vesta's fire removed the pollution and impurities of any mishaps or mistakes I had knowingly or unknowingly made. It was but one of many purifying rituals I performed daily as a priestess of Vesta. I'd been purified so much and so often it was a wonder I hadn't gone as transparent as fine Egyptian glass.

What made me so particularly polluted was never adequately explained to me. After years of beatings, I learned to stop asking.

The rituals of cleansing began the moment I was chosen to serve Vesta at just six years old. The Maxima—a horrifying crone to my child's eyes that terrible day—hated me upon sight. She had wanted Vesta to select one of the older, milder girls who, in her estimation, were more obedient and malleable. Vesta, to her eternal horror, had picked me, a prickly girl from the country.

And so the endless purifications began. On that first day, my six-year-old self was dragged terrified and screaming inside the House of Vestals, a dark and gloomy chamber that reeked of mold and decay and the fug of old women.

The Maxima, followed by the other priestesses, had hustled me into a dark bathing room where I was thrown, clothes and all, into a stone tub of cold sacred water. The Maxima held my head under as I thrashed and screamed. Giant plumes of bubbles shot from my nose and mouth. When the old woman finally dragged me up, I coughed and sputtered and wailed, which only incensed her more. Didn't I know virgins were meant to be gentle, quiet, and mild? But I was a farm girl with hardened calluses on my feet and fingers itching to dig in the dirt. I was meant to serve Diana, the goddess of the hunt, the strong one, not the silent maiden who demurely sat by the fire!

"Let me go, you witch," I screamed through chattering teeth. An attendant removed my sodden dress and dried me with a thin, useless towel. I was the daughter of a senator. I would tell on her and then she would suffer!

The old Maxima had apparently never been spoken to by anyone in such a manner, let alone a child, and her face turned purple with rage. She slapped me down hard, the sound of my bare bottom hitting the wet stone echoed in the gloomy chamber that smelled of stale oil and sweat.

"Why are you doing this?" I wailed when I caught my breath.

"Because you are polluted," my new jailer said through clenched teeth.

Floronia, then a young teenager, stood behind the Maxima, head down as if she were embarrassed or ashamed and I did not understand why. Floronia was the only kind face in the circle of Vestals and their ladies, and it scared me that she was twisting her hands.

"You must be cleansed of your foulness. Understand this now," the Maxima continued. "Your body is not your own, not any longer. You are a vessel of the gods. If you do not remain pure, the gods will punish all of Rome with terrible tragedies—famine, war, pestilence. Do you understand?"

No. I did not. I was six! But over time it became clearer and clearer: I was tainted, impure, polluted. And it was the Maxima's job to elevate and purify me and cleanse me in order to be acceptable to the gods. "Because," she said again and again, "as you go, Rome goes."

If I failed in some way—if I didn't remain a virgin (though I did not understand what that meant at that time), or I let the fire in the temple go out—disaster would befall us all. As I grew into adulthood, the pressure of such a message weighed me down like Earth crushing Atlas' shoulders. When I wasn't docile, quiet, or obedient—which was often, to be sure, in those early days—I was told I endangered the lives and well-being of countless innocent people. My body, my femaleness, was disgusting and dirty and had to be purified constantly to please the gods. At the same time, I learned my body was no longer my own. I was the property of Rome and the means by which the gods determined Rome's worthiness of protection.

The pressure of such a message—delivered daily by a furious Maxima and later, by the Pontifex Maximus himself—sunk deep into my bones.

Although I could not articulate it at such a young age, there was a part of me that rejected that reasoning. How could I or any one of my sister priestesses *possibly* have that much power? One mistake by one of us and the gods would send destruction, starvation, and pestilence? But any time I pushed back on this belief and questioned how my small body could possibly be that powerful, I was drowned in a tidal wave of shaming and purification.

Still, my questions and doubts persisted, though I learned to hide them well. But after Cannae? None of us let the fire go out. None of us broke our vows. So why did the gods abandon us? Nothing made sense. And the loss of Attius had opened up such a pit of despair, I did not have the wherewithal to try to make sense of it. I had only enough energy to carry out my duties with the blank-faced obedience demanded of me.

When I finished purifying myself with smoke, I rinsed my hands with sacred water poured from a delicately spouted, ancient, bronze vessel. As a priestess of Vesta, I was forbidden to touch ordinary water. We were only to touch water collected from one of the six sacred springs around Rome. So sacred were we, a man who touched us was put to death. Both ideas—that I was deeply polluted and had to be cleansed constantly, while at the same time being so pure that a man who touched me had to die—never quite made sense to me. But like everything else with my priesthood, I learned to stop asking why this should be so, and obeyed to avert the tragedy of causing harm to the land and our people.

The fear that it *could* be true kept me obedient. Why would I do otherwise if the lives of innocents were at stake?

Restless, I wandered to the back side of our inner temple. The inner sanctum was where we housed the ancient Palladium, the smooth black stone in the shape of the goddess Pallas Athena that fell from the sky long ago in Troy. According to legend, Aeneas brought her from Troy and ever since, she's served as Rome's most sacred emblem of our righteous rule over the land. Within her niche she gleamed a deep purple-black, heightening the sense of her primal majesty and other-worldliness. If our fire jumped the hearth and consumed the Temple, we were to save the Palladium before saving ourselves. As long as the Palladium survived, Rome was protected.

I stared at the relic, trying to understand. Here she was, untouched. Perfectly preserved. Still, Rome had not been protected. What had I missed? What sacrifices did the gods not accept? Our streets ran with the blood of countless animals as we beseeched the gods to protect us from Hannibal—chickens, doves, dogs, cows, bulls. None of it mattered. Why? The question nagged at me—an incessant demand to understand why Cannae happened, how it happened, and how we could prevent its tragedy to consume us all in a fireball of destruction at the hands of Hannibal and his army.

With my eyes still burning from the resin-soaked smoke, I bent my head to make obeisance to the goddess. I tamped down the rage that threatened to overwhelm at every turn, how I wanted to scream: *You failed us. You did not keep us safe from Hannibal's brutality! You didn't keep Attius safe even after I made daily sacrifices to you.*

Of course, I swallowed the rage back, not willing to give the gods any further excuse to hurt us. I drifted to the cabinet displaying the sacred relics of our priestess history. Three ancient priestesses had been almost put to death for impieties, but they had been saved by miracles and here was their proof.

The first box contained a faded patch of fabric once belonging to a Vestal named Aemilia who had accidentally let the fire go out. She was about to be put to death for the outrage when a piece of her dress touched the dead ashes. The hearth burst into flame again. The goddess saved her from certain death.

Next was a piece of rope used by Claudia Quinta to prove her piousness. During a brutal war, the Sibylline Books required that a statue of the sacred mother goddess from the East be brought to Rome

31

for worship. Unfortunately, the ship carrying the statue got stuck on a sandbar. People panicked over the meaning of such a bad omen. Nothing the sailors tried made any difference. Claudia Quinta took matters into her own hands. She grabbed a rope from the ship's prow, tied it around her waist, and calmly pulled the ship to safety.

Finally, I lifted the lid of the box containing the green-coated, bronze sieve of a Vestal named Tuccia. She'd been accused of incestum with a man, breaking her vow of chastity. At her trial, she demanded a test to prove her innocence and carried water in this very sieve all the way from the Tiber to the Temple without spilling a drop. It was one of our priesthood's most famous miracles.

Despite warnings to never touch the sacred objects, a surge of impetuous defiance moved me to lift the relic out of its ancient, warped box. There. A strange glimmer.

Curiously, I poked a finger through one of the mesh-like openings but met resistance. Odd. I brought my face closer to the center of the sieve and a strange orange light flared for a moment, then disappeared when I moved my head slightly.

What in Vesta's name?

With shaking hands, I ran the tip of my forefinger over the surface again and again to confirm what I saw. Impossible. And yet, irrefutable.

I stifled an ugly laugh. A nearly invisible piece of glass covered the holes of the sieve. I did not know glass that thin could be made, yet there it was, covering every tiny opening of the ancient copper mesh.

There had been no miracle.

Tuccia had tricked the religious court into believing she'd performed an act of the goddess. And it had worked. It had saved her life. My mind raced with questions. Did the Maxima know? What about the pontiff? Were the original religious leaders in on the sleight of hand? They must have been. Then they stowed it here in the back of the temple and instructed us never to touch it.

So much for the story of the exceptional purity of Tuccia, the Vestal virgin who performed a miracle.

An image of Attius' grinning face wavered before me. How he would have laughed over this discovery. "See," he would have said. "It's all theater. The gods do not exist. You are in service for thirty years to an imaginary ghost." I easily imagined his shining eyes as he praised the smart priestess. "What boldness, what brilliance, what ingenuity. Tuccia the Miracle Maker!"

A familiar ache welled in my chest as I remembered—for the thousandth time today—that we'd never laugh together again.

With a sigh, I replaced the sieve and returned to the central fire, relishing the familiar blast of heat on my face. A new thought gave me pause. Why had Tuccia been accused of impiety in the first place? More than anyone, we Vestals knew how difficult it was to step outside the bounds of our service. We were never unobserved, never alone with a man, never unsupervised by the pontiff's priests. Had something like the loss of the Battle of Cannae taken place? Was that why she needed to employ trickery?

As I left the temple, I wryly noted that that trick had worked. She'd not been buried alive for her crime. But why had it taken a miracle for men to believe she was innocent?

Chapter Four

The tang of frankincense lingered on my body, even after I slipped out of my Vestal raiment. My lady, Ketet, who everyone else called Tarpeia because the Maxima demanded a Roman name, slowly undid the six braids that all Vestals must wear under our Vestal head covering. I sighed at her gentle ministrations.

"In my land, we used the resin you burned to make the khol we painted around our eyes," she noted.

"How?" I asked. The resin lumps we used were an orange-brown color, not the deep black that the Egyptians were famous for using.

"We charred the resin until it blackened," she said. "Then we mixed it with galena powder from black rocks."

"Oh it must smell nice then."

She laughed. "Only when the duck fat we used to spread it was fresh. When it was turning... well, it made my eyes water and my grandmother would tut-tut about the cost the entire time she repainted the black lines around my eyes. Once she redid it five times before she gave up and ordered me to stay home and not attend the festival of Isis. Painting our eyes was required for religious ceremonies so I learned quickly to tolerate the smell and the itch."

"Why did your eyes need to be painted to attend?"

"Because it was disrespectful to the gods to serve them or visit their temples on festival days unless we were cleansed, perfumed, oiled, and painted." Under her breath she added, "Perhaps my reluctance to honor them when I was young, is the reason the gods punished my family."

Ketet's ancestral Egyptian coastal village had been sacked. The invaders killed everyone she loved. They then threw her and her little sister into a cage to be sold as slaves. Which was how she ended up here.

Did the gods of her land punish their people with tremendous suffering for such small mistakes too?

A sudden memory—our farm manager, a kindly Etruscan named Larce, crouching to look into my sobbing face. "The gods are not swayed by the tantrums of little girls," he had said with calm seriousness. I did not remember why I had come to him, only that my nurse accused me of angering Jupiter and that the god would smite us all. Even the baby pigs in the pen!

"I do miss the oil of blue lotus that was plentiful," Ketet continued. "Your traders in Rome claim what they sell in your markets is real, but it is nothing more than old oil mixed with jasmine and blue tansy. The day I find real Egyptian lotus oil in Rome you will know, for I will douse myself in it so thoroughly, your eyes will run and your nose will bleed."

Once all my braids were out, Ketet massaged my scalp, trying to pat down the way my curls sprung up, still separated into the six sharp divides carved into my scalp after all these years. Vestals have worn the six braided style since time immemorial. So associated with us was the style that all Roman brides now wore the six-braids during their wedding in honor of both Vesta and their virginity. In many ways, we six Vestals were brides too—brides of Rome, receptacles of Rome's purity and well-being.

"When I am retired, we will travel and you will show me the glory of your beloved land," I offered.

Sometimes Ketet responded with enthusiasm. Other times, like that night, she said, "I will never see Egypt again. Why should I go back when the pharaoh's men did not protect my village."

Everyone in Ketet's family—her two brothers, her parents, and grandparents—had been slaughtered before her eyes. She and her little sister were shoved into cages to be sold as virgin sex slaves to brothels in Rome. Her sister died from fever in her arms. She was all alone in the world until I selected her to be my handmaiden. Every night she thanked Isis for leading her to me, so that she lived a protected life, forever untouched by the savagery of men. She was obligated, like me, to live a chaste life. She could not marry or take a lover while in the House of Virgins. Even after all these years, she was still haunted by the trauma of watching groups of men rape her mother and grand-mother to death.

She and her little sister were made to watch lest they misbehaved, for the invaders planned on getting good coin for two pretty little vir-gins in the slave markets. Ketet sometimes whispered that it was the deadness of her mother's eyes as they abused her that made her swear to never be touched by a man. And that Isis finally listened to her prayers when I selected her to serve me as a virgin handmaiden.

"I have brought your favorite drink," Ketet said, leaning over to hand me an earthenware cup from the wooden tray shoved amidst the rubble of combs and pins covering the table.

"Mmmm, thank you," I said, relishing the bite of citron water sof-tened with rose hips. She helped herself and we clinked cups. I forgot how thirsty I became after tending the fire.

"Something is on your mind," she said.

Thinking of Tuccia's sieve, I asked, "Do you believe in miracles?"

Ketet raised one eyebrow and put her cup down. Her unbound hair—thick and black and straight—fell like a curtain over the side of her face as she leaned forward. "There are many miracles in my faith," she pointed out. "The biggest being that Isis reassembled her husband's murdered body and then breathed life back into him. Are you asking if I believe this literally or metaphorically?"

When I didn't answer, she added, "I used to believe it literally. But now I think they are stories meant to awe us and promise us answers to the unknowable. What makes you ask this?"

I told her about the trick of the sieve and how often Tuccia's "miracle" was relayed in story and song. Even dance. How all of Rome venerated her. Yet it was all based on a lie.

She nodded then chuckled. "Who can say what the real miracle was—perhaps it came in the moment the goddess whispered the idea into Tuccia's mind and she committed to acting on it."

Attius would have said something similar. Still, I was not sure I agreed.

"What is troubling you about this?" she asked. "We often talk about the nature of religion as theater, do we not?"

True. Part of my training had been to control all of my facial expressions to convey peace and calm and safety to the people, no matter what storm of emotion was raging within. Learning that Attius died at Cannae tested my ability to maintain my composure, yet it had held.

I had seen the terror that came when any one of us virgins expressed too much emotion. After our defeat at Lake Trasimene nearly two years prior—where we lost 15,000 men to Hannibal—the Vestal Fabia learned that her favorite nephew was among the dead. Most of our warriors were lost to the bottom of the dark, cold lake—slaughtered like eels in a barrel after Hannibal trapped them. Unable to recover their bodies, we could not hold the proper burial rites, which panicked the people. Rumors swirled that countless households had been visited by the dripping ghosts of bloodied young men who begged their loved ones to perform the rites so they could rest.

To assuage the grieving, the Maxima had devised a public rite in the Forum that would serve to purify all those whose bodies could not be retrieved. This communal funeral rite would ensure that every lost man could rest in peace. We each had to sing a psalm of honor for every lost warrior whose body had not been found. When it came time to sing for her nephew, Fabia folded into herself sobbing and could not complete her song. The people took that as a sign of impending disaster which caused great chaos and panic throughout the grieving city.

It took two days of exaggerated purifying rites on the exact spot she lost control—songs of cleansing and animal sacrifices—to allay the people's fear so that the communal burial rites could resume. Maintaining my affect at all times seemed like a small price to pay to keep the peace. It certainly meant less work for us in the long term.

"Are you worried about the blood on the altar at the October Horse?" Ketet whispered. "That was a bit of timely theater."

I took another long drink. "According to the Sibylline Books, blood on the altar satisfied the requirements of the rite."

Ketet chuckled. "Some might say it was a miracle that you cut your hand in such a way that you were *able* to save the rite."

"And around and around we go again," I said smiling. These conversations with Ketet always came with the added pang of longing for the way Attius also challenged me when we spoke about the nature of the gods.

After Ketet blew out the oil lamp and retired to her sleeping couch, I found myself unable to sleep and soothed myself with imagining how Attius would react to the events of the day. The look of mock horror on his face he would give me when I told him how I instructed the boy to squeeze the horse phallus to obtain the blood we needed. Then how he would laugh at how I solved the problem. Dreamily, I imagined telling him about my discovery of the sieve's secret.

"See," he would murmur. "It's always been a lie."

As I drifted off to sleep, he came to me again as he had the last time I saw him, shining and beautiful and forever lost to me.

***

Two Years Before

Waiting at the secret grove for him as I had promised, I looked up at the lotus tree at the center of the forbidden wood. It was here, on my first day of being selected to serve Vesta, that my hair was shorn to the skin and where all of the white-clad priestesses hung my long tresses on the sacred tree's gnarled, twisted branches. The priestesses sang strange discordant songs of sacrifice while my strands danced in the wind, caught in the claws of the Ancient One.

Attius snuck into the grove years later to find me and I was sure that Diana led him to it, for the grove would not be used again until a new Vestal was selected and her newly-shorn hair draped upon the sacred tree's branches. No one ever entered for fear of the goddess' retribution. Adjacent was the Spring of Egeria, where I regularly gathered the sacred water for our rites, so it never raised eyebrows that I often entered the grove to "commune" with the goddess. It became our private, secret wood.

The last time we met there, he'd told me he was joining the legions. I had begged him not to—he had a right to join the cavalry as an equite and serve in the officer ranks—but he had insisted that joining as an infantryman was the only way to escape the clutches of his mentor-patron, who had succeeded in convincing Attius' father to delay his manhood ceremony, effectively trapping him to continue serving the abusive man. But Attius had excitedly explained that the Senate had just passed a law that allowed a youth to be declared a man by his military commander if he joined as a foot soldier. Attius had found a way to circumvent the rules that kept him trapped in Rome.

Suddenly, a large silver and white dog crashed through the underbrush of the private grove and I smiled. Attius had brought his beloved dog. I knelt and hugged the goofy beast as it whined with joy at our reunion. "Silly boy," I murmured. "Silly boy."

When I stood, I staggered back in shock. A strange man stood before me. It took a moment for me to understand that it was Attius, completely transformed. He wore the rough red tunica and caligulae, military boots, of a soldier. His hair was shorn. Gone were the boyish curls I had so loved. Attius grinned and embarrassedly rubbed the back of his head.

"You have done it, then," I whispered.

"Yes," he said. "I leave tomorrow for training at a fort near Neapolis. I wanted to say goodbye. And… and to ask if you could watch him while I am away," he added, nodding toward the dog.

"He can't stay with your family?"

"I would feel better if I knew he were with you." He bent on one knee and embraced his dog. "You will take care of her for me, yes?" he whispered to the dog.

I could not take his dog! How would I explain to the Maxima? My only hope was Zena the cook. The ratter in the kitchen had died. She might be convinced to claim him. She loved all animals, didn't she?

When Attius stood again, I could barely catch my breath. Without his long curls, Attius looked older, more serious, and more beautiful in a different way. The change was both fascinating and frightening. I wanted to run my fingertips over the planes of his new face, to cup his neck where his curls used to gather, to press him tight to me and never let him go.

It was as if someone was carving a deep hollow in my chest. I wanted him—I wanted our life in the woods together—I wanted, wanted, wanted but was denied everything.

"Mia mine," he whispered. "Let me hold you before I go."

He reached out to pull me to him but out of habit, training, and terror whenever I was near a man, I stepped back. His eyes widened and he looked at me questioningly. "I may never be touched by a man," I said. Yesterday he was a boy. The legality of his new designation as a man meant he could be killed for touching me. And I could bring down the wrath of the gods upon us all. I could not, would not, risk anything happening to him. To all of us.

He blinked and tilted his head. "Mia, it is not true. How can you bel—?"

"No, do not," I interrupted. We had been over this many times. Every day for years it had been beaten into me that I would bring ruin to Rome if I were touched by a man. I could not bear the weight of the possibility that even a chaste hug could mean disaster for him or Rome.

A great swell of grief drew my hands to my mouth. I wanted to blurt out that I'd made a terrible mistake, that I should've listened to him and agreed to run away when we weren't at war and the cost of my disobedience wasn't so high.

Attius smiled sadly. "Nothing bad will happen if we touch. I am no different today than I was yesterday."

I shook my head. He was a man now. The Sibylline Books were clear on this. I could not risk it.

With sudden clarity, I saw his life unfold before me. He would fall in love with a beautiful local girl he'd meet on his marches and forget all about me. Worse, he might be killed in battle. The idea of a world without Attius made my chest shatter like glass. As did the realization that I had already lost him—either to a new life without me or to death on the battlefield.

I could stay in the grove no longer or I would burst into tears. "I will say a special prayer for you at our sundown ceremony," I said, backing away, pulling the dog by the collar with me. "For the gods to keep you safe."

Attius raised his hand to pull at the top of his curls as he'd always done when confused or frustrated, but they were no longer there, so it hovered awkwardly for a moment. He looked at me with a beseeching expression. "I had hoped... I wanted to hold you one last time."

I shook my head. "You must leave," I said. "It is not safe."

And then I ran, the dog nipping my heels with joy as if it were all a new game.

***

In my dreams, I was skin to skin with Attius in the woods, surrounded by golden light and the sighs of rustling leaves. If I had broken my vows with him, then his death and the deaths of all the best of Rome at Cannae would have at least made some sense. The pain of knowing I withheld myself from him and *still* the gods punished us had me questioning everything the Order ever pummeled into me. But I dared not ever express such doubts aloud, lest the gods heard my doubts and impudence and punished us even more.

Chapter Five

In the morning, I sighed with relief at the quiet. No protests in the streets, no women arrested for breaking the law of crying or wailing in public, no demands for a repeated rite. I had gotten away with saving the October Horse ritual.

All that was left to do was to sift through the ashes of the remains we burned the day before to remove bits of horse hair or flesh. Only then could we store the sanctified remnants in the penatus—the storage room for sacred objects at the temple. There we also stored the collected blood of the October Horse and preserved it with vinegar and sharp spices. We would use both in a special sacrifice to welcome the new year on the kalends of Martius.

The brick kitchen was set off from the main house and was my favorite place within the compound. Zena the cook greeted me warmly. "Good morning, Mia," she fairly sang, smiling so wide her eyes disappeared into slits. Her headcloth was a faded rust color, showing the splattered stains of cooking no amount of washing removed.

"Where is the dog?" I asked looking around. Zena, thankfully, had gladly accepted Attius' dog when he'd left for the legions. That it was his dog was my secret. That she accepted the new pet without question made me love her all the more.

"The guard at the gate asked to keep him with him this morning," she said. I nodded. Attius' dog was shared among all. His goofy, good nature lightened even the most distressed heart.

Zena chopped fresh basil and rosemary for the savory bread that was her specialty. I breathed in deep the sharp green tang that filled the room as her knife moved with unnatural speed while I worked.

After I sealed the sanctified ash container with wax, Zena pointed with her head to the salt barrels. "The sacred salt container is looking a bit low," she pointed out.

As with so many other sacred rules, only Vestal priestesses were allowed to touch the sacred salt and flour we used to make the mola salsa cakes that were broken over the heads of every animal before state sacrifices.

"Do you mind getting the mortar and pestle for me?" I asked, staring doubtfully at the aging salt barrel. It used to be full to the rim with chunks of crystal. Not anymore.

Carthage had been a main supplier of the precious mineral but once Hannibal invaded, all trade with our enemy stopped. As a result, we used lesser quality stuff from the salt flats near Ostia. Even that was running low—I had to dig deep into the barrel to find a decent looking crystal. Noticing the speckles of dark mineral still running through it, I said a little prayer asking Vesta to forgive us for using this less than perfect sample.

I ground the salt crystals into powder to the soothing rhythm of Zena's percussive chopping. Zena's warmth and kindness always reminded me of Larce, our farm manager in Capua. From the moment I could toddle, I followed him around like a shadow as he worked on the vines, checked the pens for the animals, or repaired fences. His weather-worn, dark face always broke into a grin at the sight of me. He often explained every step of the love and care he poured into the land as he worked. How I wanted to grow up and "be" him!

44

Flashes of memories spun in my head as I worked. Of the sunlit rows and rows of grape vines and how they seemed to disappear into the horizon as the sun set. The smell of the wet earth after a rain. The lowing of my favorite cow when she heard me coming. Larce's leathery fingertips pressing gently on gnarled vine trunks as if checking for a heartbeat.

Once I came to him after I'd been smacked and yelled at for running too quickly near the altar of our household gods. I'd accidentally knocked over the carefully arranged altar in honor of Ceres, the goddess of all that grew. Every year we begged for her help in making our farm fruitful. My carelessness caused the first little pomegranates of the season to tumble to the ground, bruising them and making them unfit for the goddess. Honey and oil went flying everywhere. Both my nurse and my mater were furious and fretted over what it meant that I'd been so careless. Would the farm be visited by root rot or grain rust or any other evil because I'd angered the goddess? When I pointed out that we'd cleaned it all up and replenished the offerings, my nurse grew angry.

"You made our household gods cry with your bad behavior," she said. But when I approached the small bronze statuettes of our Lares, I saw no tears. The little statues held the same expression they'd always had—joyful celebration with a touch of impishness. Each young man held overflowing cornucopia, their little bronze cloaks swinging behind them. Their small eyes, inlaid with tiny pieces of white ivory and black stone, seemed to shine with mirth and goodwill. I even checked the large snake painted on the wall underneath the small pediment. Its eyes were dry too.

Yet both my mater and my nurse insisted I had made our statues—and our gods—cry. The discrepancy between what they claimed and what I saw with my own eyes—the dry faces of our Lares—left me confused. Were they lying? But why would they lie? They were grownups, so it had to have been that they could see these things in a way I could not.

And so when they claimed that my transgressions would punish us all—including the innocent animals outside—the weight of my actions, even if I had not meant to cause harm or chaos, left me feeling despondent. The seeds of self-blame were carefully planted and nurtured by the people I loved most and then, later, by the Maxima and the other priests who held sway over my life.

It was this self-blame that had always rankled Attius the most. "How could you possibly be that powerful?" he would ask. "How could anyone?"

Gentle Larce always said something similar. How often he soothed me by insisting, "The gods are not swayed by the tantrums of little girls."

Crouching on one knee to look me in the eye, he had added once, "Little Domina, since I do not know the minds of the gods, I focus only on what I can control, like planting at the right time, watering, and fertilizing. If something goes wrong, I do not wonder about the gods, but look at what actions I can take. Do you understand?"

No I did not but I was soothed nonetheless. It was only years later, during my lessons as a Vestal, that I understood Larce was not merely an extraordinary farmer, but a natural philosopher. I came to hear his calm, plain-speaking voice in the writings of the Greek philosopher, Zeno of Citium.

"Finished?" Zena asked, grinning, as I stretched luxuriously with relief after sealing the replenished container of sacred salt.

That was when we heard the voices, the sounds of arguing. Zena and I exchanged a look. Her eyes widened in surprise at what I detected as well—a male voice. Inside the House of Vesta? Impossible. No man was allowed into our inner sanctum. My heart dropped when I recognized the voice of the Pontifex Maximus. All of us priestesses, including the formidable Virgo Maxima, reported to him. He alone had the ability to enter our space with impunity.

Not to mention beat us if he declared it necessary.

He rarely came into our compound. We always went to him in the public house adjacent to ours. Something important must have happened. The Maxima's voice also echoed angrily. A pit of dread opened in my stomach. Did someone report my sleight of hand yesterday? Will we be forced to repeat the October Horse rite because of what I did?

But the ides was yesterday—and the October Horse rite always took place on the ides. It would be impossible to repeat it. Unless they deemed my crime sufficient to warrant it. But who could have seen me drip blood from my finger? Surely someone would have made an outcry in the moment, not the day after!

With a quick nod to Zena, I rushed out of the kitchen and headed to the House, ready to explain that I considered it my duty—under the circumstances—to do what was necessary to keep the people of Rome from panicking. Not having enough blood to anoint the altar would have been disastrous. They had to see that.

"There she is," the Maxima said, pointing at me with one gnarled finger. I had seen her perform countless, quiet "adjustments" at rituals to maintain the peace. So why was mine so problematic?

The round-faced pontiff and the Maxima stopped before me. The head priest took a deep breath and for a moment I imagined the excess skin on his neck swelling like a toad's throat. "You, Opimia Pansa, priestess of Vesta, must come with me for you are to be formally charged with the crime of impiety," he thundered.

"How can you call what I did impious?" I cried, locking my knees and straightening my back.

They must not have expected that reaction for the pontiff and the Maxima exchanged surprised, confused glances.

"I ensured the rite went smoothly," I continued. "You yourself ordered us to make sure the rite succeeded—to calm the people and distract them from their grief."

The pontiff blinked several times.

"No one saw," I rushed on. "I instructed the runner to hold the tail and the phallus high above him and to stare at it, which drew everyone's eyes." I held out my hand and showed them the scabbed injury from yesterday. "I must have cut it when I scrambled out of the carriage. When no blood dripped from the sacrifice, it seemed godsent for me to use my own blood to reassure the people and complete the rite!"

They continued staring at me as if I were speaking another language. Fear drove me on.

"And everything went as smoothly as we could have hoped afterward." I gestured behind me to the kitchen. "Even now the purified ashes of the horse tail and phallus are ready to be moved to the penates and—"

"What are you talking about?" the Virgo Maxima interrupted with a near growl. Her face, scored with deep wrinkles, was dark with disgust.

When I turned to the pontiff, his wide face was red with exasperation. My heart sunk. "What... what are *you* talking about?"

The Pontifex slapped me hard across the face. "Impertinent foul thing," he muttered.

I grabbed my cheek in surprise and confusion. What was happening?

It was not unusual for the pontiff to lay a hand on me. He was the only man who had the authority to touch us without having to die for it—but only in the service of disciplining us. He could—and did— beat us regularly. For our own good, of course.

"You will come with me now," he demanded and out of habit I followed behind him and the Maxima, feeling like a chastened child instead of the grown woman and respected priestess that I was. I hated that they still had the power to elicit that reaction.

They led me to the courtyard between the House of Vestals and the priest's own "Public House." A crowd had gathered. The priest of Jupiter and the priest of Mars refused to meet my eyes, their faces contorted with disgust.

The pontiff unrolled a scroll the priest of Jupiter handed him. He waited for the crowd to quiet before speaking.

In a stentorian voice, he thundered, "In consultation with the Sibylline Books and by certification by the Senate of Rome, we now understand why the deathless gods of Rome abandoned us at Cannae. They withdrew their protection in disapproval over terrible impiety. The signs are clear. A Vestal virgin has broken her vow of chastity and has befouled the peace of the gods, drawing the ire of the gods. The gods will not restore their protection until Rome is cleansed of this abomination. We formally charge you, Opimia Pansa, daughter of Senator Lucius Opimius Pansa, with crimen incenstum."

I stared wide-eyed at the priests and the Virgo Maxima. This *wasn't* about using my own blood on the altar? But the idea that they would accuse me of breaking my vow of chastity was so preposterous, so outrageous, I had to force myself not to laugh. "But I have not broken my vows," I finally managed, trying to match the Pontifex's volume. He'd set up this little theater to witness my fall, but I would not comply without a fight. "I am a virgin still, untouched by man!"

"The portents and the Sibylline Books say otherwise. You, as the youngest and most intractable of the priestesses, have clearly made the gods turn away from us by your foul and impious behavior. The rage of the gods and their abandonment of Rome will prevail unless we are purified and cleansed of your outrage. Only then will the gods restore their protection and help us smite our enemy."

I had no words. How could this be happening?

The priest turned to the swelling, murmuring crowd. "By the sacred strictures from the Sibylline Books and the ancient tradition of expiation, the accused Vestal will be whipped and then buried alive for her crime—"

"Wait, you cannot do this without a trial!" I exclaimed. "I demand the opportunity to prove my innocence, which is my right!"

Did they really think I would not defend myself? That I would submit to their inhumation of me without a fight?

Their expressions of surprise told me, unbelievably, that they did.

"There is no time. We must be cleansed," the priest of Jupiter yelled. "It is what we must do to be saved from Hannibal. We *must* restore the peace and confidence of the gods before Rome is destroyed."

"Justice is also a requirement for the peace of the gods," I yelled back. "By law, I must be given the opportunity to prove my innocence." Many in the crowd nodded their heads, "The goddess of justice, Justitia, is watching and we must not insult her!"

More murmurs of agreement. *"A trial. Yes. We must follow tradition."* The priest of Jupiter turned to the Pontifex Maximus and they argued in short, hissing whispers.

The pontiff turned away from the red-faced priest of Jupiter. "While we must act quickly to restore the peace of the gods, we will honor tradition and legal protocol and judge the Vestal at trial. However, because of the direness of our situation, we must move immediately. The trial begins at sunrise tomorrow."

"You cannot mean this," I cried out. "Surely the Senate will not—"

"This is a *religious* court," the pontiff shouted. "And in moments of religious emergency, we call a trial as necessary. We begin in the morning."

Enthusiastic applause moved over the crowd, but in a flash turned ugly. Chants vibrated with the threat of violence. As if the pontiff's win gave them permission to release their hatred and fear all at once.

"Purify us now!"

"We must be cleansed!"

"Bring back the peace of the gods!"

"The Vestal must die!"

This was happening too fast. "A trial at sunrise does not give me enough time to build a defense," I said as the pontiff signaled to the guards that they were finished. "And I need an advocate who will represent me."

"As you are barred from your official duties while charged, you may spend the rest of the day seeking representation," the pontiff said, abruptly turning his back to me and marching away.

"Wait, you have not even told me which man is accused!"

The pontiff, the Maxima, and the priest of Jupiter pretended they had not heard me as they disappeared into the atrium of the priest's public house. Why? How could they accuse me of breaking my vows when they could not find even one man who could reasonably be a suspect? I had been so careful!

An old pang of worry for Attius took my breath, until I remembered he was gone. And that I never broke my vow of chastity with him or any man. I imagined doing so of course, many times, but never did. I refused to even hug him after he underwent his manhood ceremony!

Guards shepherded the crowd away from the sacred precinct and toward the center of the Forum. The crowd moved reluctantly but not before spitting more insults in my direction:

"Whore."

"Wicked."

"Defiled."

Frozen with disbelief, I stood rooted, unable to move, unable to understand what was happening. A primitive part of me thought, *"Run,"* just as I had secretly urged the October Horse before the warrior raised his spear. But I spotted the guards who had been newly appointed to watch my every move. I was trapped. An old fear clutched my heart and squeezed. I did not break my vows, yet a part of me wondered perhaps if I was guilty anyway. Of something as yet unspecified. That was the power of being told all my life that my body contained the honor of Rome. And since Rome was near to falling, it had to mean I had failed in some way.

There was a time I believed a Vestal virgin's outrage could cause the gods to smite Rome. But this? Fifty thousand of our best men— including Attius—dead in one day? No. Even if I had broken my vows, that level of destruction was too awful, too wildly out of proportion, even for the angriest of gods.

Breathe. Think. What must I do first?

Get an advocate. Yes, someone strong who could defend me against these false accusations.

Calling Ketet, I rushed to my consulting room where we composed requests for help from leading advocates. I started with my senator father, even though I knew, deep within, he would ignore me. I had been schooled from my earliest days to never do anything to compromise the dignitas of Senator Lucius Opimius Pansa. What could be more distasteful and undignified than having your own daughter accused of enraging the gods with the vilest of crimes?

Someone will help me, I told myself. There were always people ready to undertake unpopular cases for coin. But by the end of the day, my worst fears were confirmed. Every advocate in Rome refused or ignored my request. Either the pontiff had threatened everyone, or no one was willing to associate themselves with the taint and horror of a fallen Vestal. Probably a bit of both.

Another realization made my stomach squeeze: the truth rarely mattered when a woman was accused of sexual depravity. Men saw the accusation itself as "proof." After all, I would not have been accused if it were not true, yes?

When darkness came and I found myself abandoned by all who could help me, I rushed to the Temple of Vesta to stand before the goddess' sacred fire, hoping it would clear my head and slow my racing heart. As I hurried up the marble steps, I was awed and surprised, as I always was, by the sheer force, the fierce heat, and the crackling roar of so much fire power contained in such a pretty little temple, with its graceful circular shape, painted columns, and decorative bronze trellises. Thankfully, it was Floronia's turn at the overnight watch so I was spared the ugly, murderous looks of the elder priestesses who believed I had sullied their pristine reputations. Floronia took one look at my face and guessed at what had happened. "No one will represent you?"

I nodded, despair clogging my throat.

"Have they at least announced the name of the man they are accusing of debauching you?"

"There is no such man," I said dryly.

"Of course, of course," she mumbled.

Something about the way she refused to meet my eyes… "Floronia, you believe me innocent, yes? For I am!"

"Of course, I believe you," she said, thrusting a long iron poker into the fire. Flames burst and crackled. Plumes of fragrant smoke danced through the ocular opening at the top of the painted domed roof. Still, she refused to meet my eyes.

My heart sunk. The insidious power of the accusation had already wormed into my friend's mind. She was likely wondering if she had ever really known me. What hope did I have against people who were predisposed to hate me?

Earlier, I had planned to press the Maxima for a name, because after all, I could not debauch myself, but she refused to see me. Perhaps they were keeping the name from me to throw me off-balance. Or to prevent me from combining resources to help prove our innocence. But then again, they were prepared to bury me alive this very morning without naming anyone.

That they would blame *me* for the tragedy at Cannae was beyond comprehension. That they imagined I would touch any man but Attius was even more inconceivable. Even for him, I never yielded.

But how did one prove a thing *did not* happen?

And yet. And yet. From the day we were selected as young girls we were told that, as priestesses of Vesta, our bodies were vessels for the honor of Rome. That we were physical manifestations of the purity the gods demanded we uphold to keep us safe. And since Rome was not safe from Hannibal, it could only mean our holy purity had been polluted. To them, the logic was impeccable.

Yet Vesta knew it was not true. Closing my eyes, I held my hands out to the massive blaze and breathed in the deep woods scent of the spikenard powder I'd tossed in as a gift to her. "Help me, O Goddess," I whispered. A gust of wind bent the flames away from me and my heart dropped. Had the goddess turned her back on me too? Had she finally seen my secret doubts and was punishing me for them?

Then I remembered how often I saw priests and haruspices argue over interpretations of omens. What if the flames moving away from me were not a bad omen but a sign of something else?

The flames leaned toward the back of the temple—where the Palladium lived. And where the "miracle" sieve was housed. In my overwhelm and fear, I had almost forgotten about Tuccia's miracle. Hadn't she been falsely accused as well?

My heart swelled with hope. I could prove my innocence before the trial even began. I rushed to the back of the temple and headed straight to the cabinet of miracles. Carefully, I slid out the sieve with its near-invisible glass and tucked it beneath my mantle.

"What are you doing?" Floronia asked and I startled, almost dropping the precious artifact.

"The goddess pointed me this way," I said. "I will demand the court let me use Tuccia's sieve to prove my innocence."

Floronia blinked. "So why take it now?"

Did she not know about the fakery? Maybe only the Maxima knew.

"If you call for the right to prove your innocence with Tuccia's sieve," she pointed out, "it must be witnessed that it is her ancient sieve obtained from the Temple for it to be understood as above reproach. Do you understand?"

She did know, then. But why was she being so cagey?

"I must have it in hand before I call for the chance to prove my innocence…"

"If you have it in hand, they will know what you are planning and will insist you use a sieve of their choosing. Not this one."

She was right, but in my panic, I could not think clearly. My fingers curled around the sieve's green-tinged metal handles. I could not put it back—this was my only hope!

"Trust in the goddess," Floronia said. "She will see you through this."

If the goddess was truly protecting me, I wouldn't be accused of breaking my vows. Because she'd know that I hadn't!

"You must act strategically," Floronia said in a calm, measured undertone.

Nodding and with shaking fingers, I reluctantly returned the sieve to its box. "It must be this sieve, though. It can be no other," I said, closing the cabinet door.

Floronia nodded and yet the tight way she held her lips, left me wondering if we were being spied on. Yet we were in the safest place in all of Rome, the goddess' own sacred temple...

"This sieve must be used only as a last resort, for the powers that be may disallow it for any number of reasons," she whispered. "Do you understand?"

Was she warning me that the Maxima might deliberately prevent me from using this? To ensure I failed and was subsequently executed? But this would make her look bad, would it not? Surely, she would help me clear my name.

Then I remembered how she refused to see me when I wanted her advice on securing an advocate. Of how she had always hated me. Hated that I was so young and undisciplined when I was selected. Hated my impertinence, my endless questions. She'd felt cheated when I was selected so many years ago. She'd wanted an older, more compliant girl from an old Roman family. She was on the pontiff's side on this. "I will turn to it only as a last resort," I whispered back.

Lingering at the sacred fire, my mind drifted to my closest friend, Prisca. How I missed her. She would help me think more clearly. But she was about to birth a babe any day now. Worse, once I learned that her husband had been one of the few survivors from Cannae, I avoided her out of sheer jealous rage and exhaustion. How could I look upon her husband without raking my face in frustration that he lived while Attius died?

How ironic that all those years ago it was Prisca—not me—who *wanted* to be chosen as a Vestal virgin that terrible Selection Day.

***

Fourteen Years Before

I was six, newly in Rome, and being trussed up like a roasted pigeon in a fire-red tunica and a new pair of bright saffron shoes. The dress was scratchy, but the shoes were a marvel with their scalloped edges and leather so soft and supple they felt like the inside of a petal. Mater tightened a strangely knotted belt around my waist and I immediately tried to wriggle out of it.

"Opimia, leave it," mater snapped. "It's the kind of belt brides wear on their wedding day."

"Am I getting married?" I asked, confused. When neither my nurse, Melantho, or mater responded, I added, "Am I marrying Attius?"

"No, nothing like that," Melantho said.

"Your pater is going to walk you to the Forum," mater announced as he entered the room.

I ran excitedly to pater but he too took a step back away from me. Standing tall in his striped senatorial toga and red shoes, my father frowned down at me. "Good girls do not run. You must act like a lady. Especially today, do you understand?"

Staring at my beautiful new yellow shoes, I vowed to sleep with them under my pillow.

"Opimia, pay attention," mater snapped. "You must act with great dignity to reflect well on your pater."

Right. Preserving the dignity and reputation of my father had been drilled into me since birth. I nodded.

The Forum was packed with people chattering excitedly. Melantho led me to a roped-off section in the Comitium, the open-air public meeting space facing the Senate house. Above us in the Rostra, the bronze beaks of defeated enemy ships cut into the sky. Rows of benches sat unoccupied below the symbols of our military power.

Fresh flower garlands hung from the tops of columns, scenting the air with cloying sweetness. People waved immense palm fronds, their dry clattering creating a strange percussion. Bakers hawked special "virgin" treats—small round biscuits dusted in flour for the white dresses Vestals wore. Laughter and excited murmuring echoed all around us. The air buzzed with energy, and I bounced on my toes when my nurse ushered me into the roped off area. She was not allowed in.

It's an animal pen, I thought giggling, but just for us girls! We were all dressed alike in red and with our hair parted in the ceremonial six braids of Roman brides. When I spotted a girl about my size and age, I ran up to her. "Hi, do you want to play Atalanta and the bear?" I asked. With Attius, we usually played Hippolemes to my Atalanta, but playing mama bear and her foundling seemed more appropriate. The girl blinked at me. "No, let's play Vesta."

"How do you do that?" I asked.

"Let's gather wood and light a fire," she answered. "My name is Prisca. What's yours?"

When I told her, she shook her head. "Mia sounds better. That's what I shall call you." I felt instant kinship with her.

We raced back and forth chattering while we gathered huge armfuls of pretend wood that we swore came from an angry giant's forest. We ran fast to escape its giant hairy fingers as it tried to grab us, laughing and screeching the whole way. We threw our pretend wood into a pretend pile that was so high, it almost reached Mount Olympus. Then, grabbing Jupiter's lightning bolts, we threw our fire-power into the pretend wood pile, and screamed, "Whoosh!" at the resulting pretend firestorm.

"Quiet," hissed an old woman with scowl lines so deep they looked carved into tree bark. She wore all white and her hair was covered in a white cloth, bordered by a twined band of red.

"Who is that?" I whispered. "She looks like a witch."

Prisca's eyes grew big. "That is the Maxima, the Virgo Maxima."

"The Greatest Virgin?" I asked. "What does that mean?"

"It means she's the one in charge of all the Vestal virgin priest-esses." Prisca leaned in toward me. "My mater has been making extra offerings to Vesta so that she will choose me."

"You want to get chosen?"

"Yes," she said, her eyes wide as if she'd never considered not being happy about the prospect. "Don't you?"

I shook my head.

"Oh, don't let the Maxima know that!" she whispered leaning into me with an expression that seemed to convey both horror and delight at the same time. We both turned to look at the old priestess and noted that she was staring at us with narrowed eyes. Had she heard me? Did she know I preferred Diana, the huntress of the wood? The gods were jealous—maybe that made their servants jealous too.

"Is the Maxima leaving?" I whispered. "Is that why they need a new one?"

Prisca shook her head. "An old virgin has died."

"Older than her?" I asked.

My new friend giggled. "Sshhhh! I don't know. But my mater says the sacred laws say that there needs to be six Vestal virgins at all times to keep the gods happy. And right now there are only five. And if we don't get a sixth one soon, terrible, awful things will befall us."

"What terrible, awful things?"

Prisca shrugged.

"How does the choosing happen?" I asked. "Does the goddess' hand come out of the temple's sacred fire to tap us on the shoulder?" I asked.

Prisca giggled. "Now that would be exciting! My mater told me the goddess chooses by lots."

"What does that mean?"

The girl raised and lowered her shoulders again. "I dunno."

An older girl overheard our exchange and leaned in. "The Pontifex Maximus has a stick for each of us. He throws them into a sacred container and then picks one up without looking. If he picks yours then you are the next Vestal."

"But wait," I said. "I thought the goddess selected us."

"Well, she's the one that guides the Pontifex's hand to the one she wants, isn't she?" She said this with the disdain of one who thought everyone around her was unbearably stupid.

"Not everyone can be a Vestal you know," she continued. "You have to be special." She held up her fingers to count off what she knew. "Both your parents have to be alive because that means the gods favor them, they have to be patrician and must still be on their first and only marriage, the girl has to be between six and ten, the girl must be a virgin and… and," she paused over four fingers. "And you have to be blemish free."

When we looked at her blankly, not understanding what "blemish-free" or "virgin" meant, she said, "You can't have any scars or strange markings and must be untouched. You have to be pretty!"

"What if you don't want to be selected?" I asked.

This time both Prisca and the older girl stared at me in bewilderment. "It is a great honor to be selected by the goddess to serve her," the older girl said. "You can't say no because that might anger her and the other Olympians."

My face must have shown dismay. "Don't worry," the older girl said. "My mater told me that Vesta prefers girls who are on the older side because they are better behaved. She said the last three Vestals chosen were all my age—nearly ten!"

I breathed a sigh of relief.

"Oh, I almost forgot," the older girl said. "If the goddess selects you, you have to serve for thirty years."

Stealing a glance at the Maxima, I whispered to Prisca, "She looks like she has served for one million thirty years!"

Prisca and I laughed, covering our mouths.

"She has already surpassed her requirements," the older girl said. "But she is choosing to stay."

"Why are they dressed liked that?" I asked, pointing to men in costumes—dark brown tunics with strange overshirts designed with diamond and key shapes. Conical shaped war helmets were pushed up onto their foreheads and they leaned on large oblong shields painted in vivid reds and overlaid with gilded star bursts. The girl turned and said, "Oh, those are the Sabines. They must always witness the selection."

"Why?" Prisca and I asked at the same time. The old men, with their arms crossed, looked menacingly at all of us girls in the pen.

The girl gave us another look that screamed, how did we live when we were so stupid?

"We reenact the rape of the Sabines," the girl named Claudia said in a tone as if she were reciting an ancient tale. "The priest and the father must pretend-fight over the girl. The father represents the Sabines of old and the priest is Rome. Our priest must win. He takes her just like our ancestors took the Sabine women from their families. It is the rite of Captio, do you understand?"

Prisca and I looked at each other and then back at her. No we did not understand. "What do you mean, 'took?'" I asked.

"And what does rape mean," Prisca demanded at the same time.

The girl flushed and gestured with her hand, lowering it rapidly, telling us to speak more quietly. "Being taken is when a man takes a woman against her will," she hissed. "Our ancestors took the women of the Sabine tribes against their will and that is the only reason we are here today. So, to honor our ancestors, we recreate this history with every new Vestal."

Prisca and I turned back to the line of Sabine men in their traditional dress, staring at every girl and evaluating each of us in an ominous manner. Our fathers were supposed to be like them? Then why were they here? Nothing made sense. The air suddenly seemed filled with a sense of restrained violence that we did not understand or like. Prisca grabbed my hand and we scuttled away from the older girl.

A hush fell over the crowd. The area around our enclosure cleared out. A parade of mothers and attendants entered the pen. Each woman carried a veil of brilliant orange-red along with a crown of laurel intertwined with rose buds and wildflowers.

I looked for Mater but only spied Melantho approaching. "Come, child," she said. "Let's put this on."

"Where's Mater?" I asked, noticing that Prisca's mother had cupped my new friend's chin and kissed her on both cheeks.

"She is not feeling well," my nurse said. "Do not worry. I am here. I will walk you to your father."

She placed the veil over my head and secured the crown with ivory pins that scratched my scalp. The world was transformed. The gauzy veil hazed everything in a red-orange light, which seemed magical. I blew on my veil to make it dance.

"Behave," my nurse whispered. "This is an important ceremony. Do not embarrass your father, do you hear me?"

Prisca and I stared at each other through the orange film and grinned, already imagining how we might use the veils in pretend fire-fights.

Melantho tugged my arm and we began the procession of mothers and attendants toward our fathers. Prisca's father and my father stood next to each other. It was likely due to our similarity in ages, but to me it seemed like a divine nod of approval of my new friendship.

Pater grabbed my small hand in his large one. A flash of pride washed over me as I looked up at my tall, handsome father, one of the big men of Rome. I tried to move my fingers to incite a game of finger-war but he gave my hand a firm tug and a quick but very strong squeeze to keep still.

Right. Preserve my father's dignitas.

A short, round man wearing a large white conical hat approached. Pater squeezed my hand before I could shout, "We know him!" or worse, "That's the frog priest!" The Pontifex Maximus, the head priest of Rome, was resplendent in a brilliant white toga. The jowls of his face seemed both soft yet pressed hard into a rigid expression of per-petual anger. He held a bronze bowl filled with pungent incense. The smoke curled around the strange hat. How did it stay on his head?

Suddenly, the line of fathers—all dressed in togas and daughters all dressed as brides in red dresses, yellow shoes, and orange veils crowned by flowers—moved forward. The large crowd hushed as my pater and I shuffled through the procession. We passed by the line of angry looking Sabines. When I looked back at Prisca behind us, pater pulled me forward with a swift and painful jerk of the arm.

Our fathers somberly took their seats on the benches in the center of the courtyard facing the priest and the College of Priests behind him. Then, as if by some invisible signal, we were each hoisted onto our pater's lap. This was nice, I remember thinking. Pater usually did not allow this, especially when he was wrapped in his finest toga. I patted the pleats of the wool fabric and was about to remark on its softness when pater squeezed my thigh.

"Stop swinging your leg," he commanded.

Remembering that Prisca and her father were to my right, I tried to signal her but saw that her face had gone pale and that her father was whispering reassuring words into her ear. A strange stab of jealousy shot through me as I watched his big hand rub her arm in a soothing gesture.

My pater's hands gripped the sides of my face and jerked my attention forward.

"Focus," he hissed.

The pontiff sang strange-sounding hymns and the large body of priests surrounding him sang back in a call and response. It seemed to go on forever. Hymns turned into prayers, turned into lectures and I grew restless. I turned to try and catch Prisca's attention when two things happened at once: my nose filled with the scent of wood smoke and sweet incense mingled with the reek of fresh sweat soaking through wool, and the world grew dark as a massive form blocked the sun.

"Vesta has chosen!" the head priest yelled and grabbed my arm. "And by the sacred Rites of Captio, I name the child, Opimia Pansa, daughter of Senator Lucius Opimius Pansa, the chosen one by the goddess to serve Rome as our exalted virgin priestess!"

The pontiff pulled me hard toward him, but pater's arms tightened around my waist. Shocked by the sudden violence, I twisted and turned and kicked, trying to wrap my legs and arms around my father. Pater would stop this man. He was bigger and stronger. The crowds exploded with joy. Shouts of, *"She has chosen! We are safe once again!"* rang throughout the Forum.

The now red-faced priest gave a mighty tug, and pater's hands slipped to my ankles and I thrashed and whipped like a maddened snake.

"Tata," I cried as I tried to dive back into his arms. Unbelievably, the priest gave another massive tug and pater was left standing there with his arms wide, hands open, his eyes strangely sad, as I flew through the air toward the priest.

Gripping me under my arms, the priest held me up and roared into the sudden silence. "Even as the best law has been so do I take thee, Beloved One, to be a Vestal priestess, to perform the Sacred Rites, which is meant for the priestess of Vesta to perform for the Roman people and citizens and to keep the Pax Deorum for all of Rome," he roared in an exceptionally strong voice.

He whipped me around so all could see me. As if in a dream I caught Prisca's horrified expression. The crowd erupted with joy. Chants of *"It is done! The gods rejoice! He fought well! The Sabines are ours. They are six, they are six, and now we are safe!"* rolled up and down the massive crush of people. Great skins of wine were being passed around to even more excited yelps of joy. Flower petals rained down around us in an explosion of color and sweet scent. From the corner of my eye I saw the strangely-dressed Sabine men mimicking defeat and despair. One man threw down his helmet.

Although I'd been momentarily stilled by the spectacle, I resumed bucking and kicking in the priest's arms to no avail. "Enough child," he hissed. "Stop screaming! You have acted your part well, but now you must stop."

Acted?

He and the other priests surrounded me and shuttled me into a small building, and I was blinded by the sudden darkness. In a small room, the priest tossed me away from him and I scrabbled onto the rough, tiled floor, determined to run and find my pater. And then if not him, maybe my new friend Prisca. She would hide me!

"All yours," the frog-priest called out. An old crone's face emerged from the shadows as my eyes adjusted. The woman from the pen. She grabbed me by two of my six braids—what had happened to my pretty orange veil?—and yanked me up hard. The pain was excruciating. She brought my face close to hers.

"Stop. Screaming. Now." She turned a furious face toward the Pontifex. "This one is too young and wild," she complained to the head priest. "The Claudia girl is nearly ten. We talked about this!"

The Pontifex narrowed his eyes at her. "The goddess must have appreciated this senator's daughter more," he said with a twisted smile. "His gold shined the brightest," he added as he slammed the door behind him, leaving me with the witch of my nightmares.

***

Chapter Six

Once back in the dark and silent House of Vestals—without the sieve—I paced in my private consulting room. Everyone slept but I could not relax. How could I? The trial was in a matter of hours. I stopped cold when I heard voices in the atrium. At this hour? Now what? My heart sunk even lower.

To my surprise, Ketet entered the room. "Apologies for the interruption," she said, "but you have a visitor."

I saw no warning in her expression, yet we both knew no one visited us at this hour unless there was some sort of emergency. Ketet gave me a soothing smile as my old friend glided into my room.

"Prisca?" I whispered, staring in confusion as Ketet closed the door behind her. Had my friend sensed my panic? Was she here to tell me her husband would defend me in court after all? Prisca removed her cowled cloak to reveal herself in the low light of the hanging oil lamps. "What are you doing here?" I asked, unable to read her expression. She looked blank and tired. "Did you come to tell me... will Sulpicius represent me in court tomorrow?" Then I remembered tomorrow was here... it was only a matter of hours before sunrise. Maybe he had been reluctant but she'd finally talked him into it. For a moment, my heart soared with hope.

Prisca gave a quick shake of the head. No, Sulpicius wasn't going to help. My heart sunk into my belly. When she refused to meet my eyes, I wondered if she doubted me too. The judgment of a woman

I'd known since childhood, whom I loved and respected deeply, would crush me. But if she doubted me, she wouldn't be here, yes?

"Why are you here?" I stammered. "Isn't it dangerous for you to be out this late?"

"I snuck out," she said. "But do not worry, I was accompanied by a guard."

Good. The streets of Rome were increasingly dangerous as people starved. Hannibal had control of the surrounding farmlands to feed his own men and we'd had no deliveries of grain, produce, or animals since Cannae.

Prisca moved toward me, her large baby belly leading the way and I marveled at the strangeness of her advanced pregnancy. Of how she managed to look like herself except for the immense protrusion at her front. Then, the familiar pang of regret—of knowing that I would never have a child—enveloped me like a heavy shadow.

"You are well?" I asked, recalling the depth of the lethargy and melancholy that overtook her in the early days of her pregnancy. Prisca did not dislike the man she was forced to marry, but neither did she love him.

"I am nothing more than a broodmare," she had cried, when she'd realized she was carrying his child.

I cleared my throat. "And the babe?"

She put a hand on her belly and nodded.

Once again tamping down the rage that her husband lived while Attius and so many other good Romans died, I forced myself to ask. "And Sulpicius? He fares well?"

"He is fine," she said. Not looking at me she added, "He is sorry he cannot assist you." Prisca cleared her throat. "He... um, he also despairs over the accusations against his general and, therefore, his own dignity and reputation."

Her husband was one of the survivors in the cavalry attending Varro, the general who should have known better than to challenge Hannibal in pitched battle in a field of his choosing. The Carthaginian general had already destroyed several of our legions. But Varro wanted glory and so ignored the pleas of the more prudent general, Paullus, who advocated waiting until we controlled the battleground. That the impulsive Varro survived and not the more cautious general seemed like a cruel joke. Attius served with Paullus, and I consoled myself with the knowledge that his general never abandoned the field and died alongside his men while Varro and his cavalry, including Prisca's husband, ran for their lives. And now Varro claimed that he was *not* the one who called for battle, and that it was the prudent Paullus who had. That people believed the lies sickened me. But no one in Rome wanted to admit the horrifying truth—that the wrong general died and all our lives were left in the hands of an impulsive, glory-seeking coward.

A flare of rage filled me at how many people believed the lie of who was actually responsible for the tragedy at Cannae. Especially when the truth was so easily verifiable. Varro demanded the legions fight that day, and he ignored Paullus' counsel to wait. It was his fault! But instead of focusing on that truth, people blamed me.

"While Sulpicius should not be held personally responsible," I managed carefully, trying not to grit my teeth, "it *was* his general who called for battle at Cannae."

Prisca shook her head and flicked her fingers. "None of that matters anymore."

Again, I swallowed my grief and dismay. It mattered because Attius was gone! And so many other good men. But she knew nothing of Attius, so I kept my tongue. To my surprise, Prisca suddenly thrust a small leather bag toward me. "I'm here because I need you to take this."

"What is it?"

"Your means of escape. But you must act now."

My mouth dropped. She expected me to run? Impossible! All of Rome was watching me. They would hunt me down and slaughter me in the streets! Besides, only the guilty ran. And I was innocent.

Prisca looked at me with concern, her arm still extended, holding out the small sack.

"I cannot take this," I said. "It's too late for that."

Prisca shoved the pouch—heavy and jingling with coins—into my hands.

"It is never too late. Go back to the Sibyl at Cumae. They would not dare hunt you there if you take shelter with the Holy Lady. She would give you sanctuary." Shaking my head, I pointed out that it takes days to get to Cumae. "They would catch me on the road."

She looked at her hands. "I should have come to you sooner. I should have!"

"Why would you," I soothed. "How could you possibly know this was going to happen?"

Her face flushed.

My chest constricted. She knew I was going to be accused? No, no, impossible.

"It was something I overheard," she said. "I told myself it couldn't be real, that I must have heard incorrectly."

"What did you hear?"

"Varro's men discussed creating a 'situation' to unite the people and distract them from the horrors of Cannae."

Varro's men—*didn't that include her husband?* "What do you mean by a 'situation?'"

Prisca gasped, as if she couldn't take a deep breath with the baby pushing against her lungs. I took her hand and led her to the couch and bade her sit.

"What words did you overhear?" I tried again.

70

"Your name. And the name of the other younger priestess, 'Flora.'"

"Floronia?"

"Yes. And sacred fire. Vows. Expiation. Trial. Time. I could not make out specifics but—" She swallowed. "But I think your arrest and the scandal are part of a larger plan."

I wanted to scream or burst out laughing. This, at least, made some sense. A heaviness came over me though. If Varro's men planned this, then I was doomed. "I don't understand. To create this kind of scandal on purpose, while all of Rome is teetering on the brink of destruction and panic. It makes no sense."

"It makes perfect sense," Prisca said. "It serves as a distraction from the people's endless grief and panic."

"By making them even more panicked?" I cried, shaking my head. "What is the use of that?"

"It buys them time," Prisca explained. "To get the people preoccupied with spiritual affairs, while we negotiate with foreign generals for help…" Prisca slapped a hand to her mouth as if she had said too much.

"Foreign armies?" I had not heard any talk of such a thing, not even in the fiercest debates in the Senate. Going outside our borders for help was deeply un-Roman. Most of the Senate would be fiercely against such a thing, especially if it meant the possibility of being beholden to or controlled by a foreign power. Wasn't that the very reason we were fighting Hannibal in the first place—to avoid that fate?

If Prisca had heard correctly, her husband was involved with a group that could reasonably be accused of treason.

"Who is your husband's faction trying to engage?"

"The Phrygians and Galatians," she whispered back. "They want us to build a temple here to their goddess Cybele as part of the terms of their support. And there is the issue of needing time to bring over additional forces and resources, as well as the cult statue of Cybele. An

71

all-consuming distraction while terms and transports are arranged will keep the people from giving up in despair."

"Then why are they moving so quickly? My trial is in the *morning*. They've given me no time to prepare. And they still have not announced who my so-called debaucher is. None of this makes sense."

Prisca took a deep breath. "If a Vestal is charged and... punished..."

I noticed how she couldn't bring herself to say *buried alive*.

"...A lot of rituals and cleansings consume the people for weeks," she pointed out. "If not months. Especially since a new Vestal will need to be selected. You know how people become consumed with these things."

I stared dumbly. "There is something else too, isn't there?"

She nodded. "They are rushing because the Dictator, Fabius Maximus Verrucosus, has left for Greece to consult with the Oracle of Delphi on how to defeat Hannibal. He is vehemently against asking for outside help, but now that he is away, they must act before word can reach him. By keeping Rome preoccupied with scandal, they can better control the Dictator's supporters who remain here—those who are against aligning with non-Romans. Don't you see—the timing is deliberate. They get rid of the offending Vestal and then suddenly we have outside help miraculously available to dispose of our enemy and the mood moves from despair to hope. It will appear divinely sent."

The cynicism and manipulation of sacred beliefs was stunning. Yet I could see why they chose me. I was the youngest Vestal and many claimed, the friendliest. Some called me The Smiling One, because I like to engage with children and the elderly. How easy it would be to turn that epithet into lasciviousness.

"But there is still the issue of a man not yet being accused," I added. "Are they so sure they will have the mob's support that they can con-

veniently forget there's a supposed man involved? And once they accuse someone, are they really prepared to condemn an innocent man
to death?"

Clearly, they had no problem condemning me to death. But a male
citizen—someone who could fight back in court? That would give
them pause.

Prisca sighed and rubbed her forehead. "There are factions pushing
for different candidates to accuse. There is in-fighting over which political enemy should be targeted."

"Allow me to guess," I muttered. "The candidates are enemies of
Varro and supporters of Paullus, yes?" If they were going to rewrite
the story of which general was responsible for Cannae, then of course
they would target someone who would argue for the truth.

I knew at least one man they would target. Lepidus, general
Paullus' nephew, who continued loudly pushing back against the lie
that it was his uncle, and not Varro, who gave the directive to fight
that day. I'd asked him for help with representing me, but he had refused me as well. But according to Prisca, they were considering other
targets too. The wondering kept me off-balance.

My stomach clenched with dismay and disbelief. "But to create an
artificial scandal for distraction is anathema. It would insult the gods
more than anything I could ever be accused of."

Prisca rubbed her eyes. "They are beyond worrying about what the
gods might think, especially as we are on the brink of destruction." She
pointed to the small bag still in my hand. It was heavy with coins.
"Look, if I'm wrong, at worst you ease my mind. If I am right, you
will be safe in a holy site, under the care of the Sibyl."

Exasperation tightened my throat. "Prisca, don't you see that it is
too late? I cannot run now. They will hunt me down like a dog." And

then, without meaning to, I blurted out the question that was breaking my heart. "Why… why didn't you come to me earlier? When you first suspected what they were planning. I might have run then!"

Prisca cupped her belly. "I thought what I overheard were the ramblings of panicked men. I never thought for a moment that they would actually do this. I am sorry I didn't act sooner, but please, do something now. Go to the shrine of the Sibyl in the Albans if you don't want to go to Cumae," she said. "That is much closer is it not? And being protected by the Holy Lady will buy you time to prove your innocence."

Could I really do this? "But how?" I asked, my mind reeling. "I cannot leave Ketet behind. They would punish her as well."

"She can go with you. There is safety in numbers."

"I cannot just make for the open road. Every gate in and out of the city is guarded."

"We have thought of that."

We?

"My freedwoman has agreed to hide you. You need only go to the woman's house on the Aventine. I will spread rumors that you have left the city. Once they send men out on the roads searching for you, you and your lady can sneak out as slaves."

I shook my head trying not to laugh. It was the most ridiculous plan I ever heard. And yet, I knew the power of rumor. If gossips chattered that I was seen escaping on the Via Apia at the same time others claimed they saw me on the Via Sacra, and others claimed they spied me sneaking out on the new Flaminium Road, the panicked Senate would be forced to send contingents of soldiers over every major road to check. Meanwhile, I would be hiding in plain sight in the Aventine.

"But Ketet," I said again.

"I will give her sanctuary in my home in the meantime," Prisca responded. "Nobody will recognize her without her attendant's robes and Vestal slave collar and I will claim that I have hired her to nurse me after birth. When their attention is elsewhere, we will bundle you both off to the Sibyl. Then, when everything is calm, and the ruse is exposed and you are cleared, you can return."

Hope swelled in my chest despite the ludicrousness of the situation. All this *during* a feared invasion by Hannibal's army? Impossible. Still, I was moved at how she was trying to help. "You would do this for me? Even if it means possible ruin for your husband if he is identified as one of the plotters?"

Prisca's eyes filled and her face softened as she stared at me. "Of course I would. You are my oldest and dearest friend. I only wish I had taken their plans more seriously when I first heard them."

I could not fault her for not believing what she heard. Learning that you were married to a coward *and* an idiot would make anyone deny reality.

"Who is this woman who has agreed to hide me? Does she understand the danger involved?"

"She doesn't know your identity. She has provided secret sanctuary for wives in my circle who have been abused to the point of near-death. She will likely think you are one of those women."

My stomach dropped as she refused to meet my eyes. Prisca had never come to me about violence in her household. Had she wanted to spare me the ugly truth? Or was she ashamed? I thought of the many times, before she'd married, that I'd lamented being of no real help to women who were being abused by husbands, fathers, or brothers. How I was schooled only to advise being more compliant and making a greater sacrifice to Vesta for peace in the home.

My own best friend couldn't come to me for help.

So she found her own solution, her own getaway to hide when she needed to. Despite my own shame, a swell of pride brought tears to my eyes. Prisca had always been clever and resourceful.

"The address for my freedwoman is inside. You must act quickly though. The fourth hour of the night is the best time to move for that is when the watchmen change shifts. And that is soon approaching. You must dress as a slave so that if you are questioned, you can say that you are running an errand for your master, for why else would you be out at such an hour. Have Ketet also change her clothing and send her to my home right away as well."

My mind reeled between hope and panic. When I looked into Prisca's face, a jolt of fear reminded me how risky this was for her too. "Why are you doing this, Prisca?"

Her eyes welled. "Because I love you. And something inside—" She made a fist and gently pressed it between her breasts. "Something inside tells me I will not survive this," she added, motioning to her belly. "And I want to do all I can for those I love now."

My head snapped up. "Do not say such a thing," I chastised, quickly drawing the symbol for healing in the air over her. "All new mothers worry about this. You and your baby will be fine."

"May it be so," she whispered but I could tell she was not convinced. Did she have a premonition or was she reflecting the entire city's mood?

"I will make a special sacrifice to Vesta every night until your baby is born," I promised. "You both will survive. I know it."

"Thank you," she said while we both pretended not to be keenly aware of how many women died in childbirth, especially first-time mothers. Disturbingly, the incidence of mother and baby deaths dramatically increased after Cannae, as if the reverberations of mass trauma on the battlefield wafted like an evil mist into the hearts of grieving and broken Roman women, robbing them and their fatherless babies of their futures too.

"I must go now," Prisca said and we clutched at each other in a long hug, her baby pressing hard into my torso.

"You are my longest and dearest friend," I whispered. "And I intend to keep it that way. Promise you will send for me when the birth pains come, no matter where I am."

She nodded. "The fourth hour approaches. You must act now," she said and disappeared into the dark hall as silently as she appeared.

A flood of energy coursed through me and my heart pounded in my ears. Could I do this? Did I want to do this? Despite my innocence, there was a part of me that wanted to acquiesce to the inevitable, to let them kill me so I joined Attius in the Elysium Fields. But then I remembered that they would punish Ketet as well if I were found guilty. They'd accuse her of being my accomplice and blame her for not stopping me from breaking my vows. I would not allow that to happen.

I rushed to my room, then to Ketet's anteroom. Empty. Male voices exploded outside and I jumped. My heart sunk. Had Prisca been caught?

The gods couldn't be this cruel... to show me a way out and then snatch it from me in moments, could they?

"What is happening?" I demanded as I stepped out into the public courtyard to the sight of three guards surrounding Ketet. Gods, she looked so small among their muscles and weapons.

"Step away from her," I commanded in my priestess voice, but they ignored me.

"Unhand, my lady," I demanded as I realized one of the guard's beefy hands was squeezing her above the elbow.

The leader of the trio stared at me with disdain. "Do not bother us, slave. This one has been caught trying to leave the compound."

Slave? He didn't know who I was? In my haste I had rushed out with my head uncovered, my long, thick curls floating around me like a nimbus. I'd long suspected people never saw us as individuals but as an anonymous group of interchangeable women in white. People saw what they expect to see.

"That is not true," Ketet said. "I... I just wanted a breath of fresh air." She flicked a gaze at me and then at the gate behind us, where Prisca and her guard likely barely escaped. Ketet must have created this distraction to help them.

"Send these slaves back inside," their captain said, emerging from the dark, his red cloak the color of dried blood in the light of his men's flickering torch. "They are doing no harm. It is the Vestal we are watching for. And for any one of her lovers who may come and try to rescue her. Not these two."

A part of me grew indignant that they did not recognize me and I was about to inform them of their grave mistake when Ketet shook her head slightly at me. The soldier released her and she stumbled into me.

"Say nothing," she murmured.

We moved back as one inside the House, slamming the heavy wooden door behind us. The soldiers' hobnailed boots clinked against the marble walkway as they jogged back to their positions.

"When the shift change comes, do not leave your post," the officer in charge called. "We are doubling up until the trial is underway. No one, not even a slave with food or medicine for the priestesses may enter or leave this compound. Understood?"

"Yes, sir!" they cried in unison.

Realization hit hard. It was too late. Prisca had been too late. The city was swarming with guards and bystanders ready to pounce on me should I try anything. I did not know whether to laugh or cry.

Why, why hadn't Prisca come to me earlier?

"It is a good thing they did not recognize you," Ketet whispered as we scuttled back to our chambers. "If they had, they would have claimed you were trying to escape and made things even worse for you."

She was right. Ketet led me to my sleeping couch. "You must try and get some rest before the trial, Mia. You must be able to think clearly."

Then she added, "Your friend told me to come to her house right away, this very night. I did not understand why she would say this to me. I am no midwife!"

Since Prisca's plan for escape had disappeared before my eyes, I decided not to try and explain what she meant. What would have been the point?

Even after Ketet snuffed the oil lamp beside my bed, my mind would not quiet. Despite everything, I was still touched Prisca had tried to help me. Still, something niggled at the back of my mind. Something Prisca had said years ago. Something I could use to defend myself. But what?

***

Four Years Before

As my friendship with Prisca grew, she often invited me to stay at her home overnight, which the Maxima allowed because hers was a good patrician family. And because she liked having me out of her way. During those rare times we had no rites to perform, I was allowed overnight—as long as I was at the temple, dressed correctly, at sunrise.

One night, when we had just turned sixteen, we lay giggling and whispering in her draped cubiculum, a small oil lamp throwing light against the dark red walls. "I found something naughty in my pater's tablinium," she whispered with a light nervous laugh. "Want to see?"

"What is it?"

"You must promise not to get mad and not to tell anyone!"

"Of course, I promise."

Prisca placed the bronze lamp between us and pulled out a scroll from a trunk at the foot of her bed.

She tittered nervously as she unrolled it. "Look at this," she whispered. Colored paintings of human bodies came into view and it took me a moment to understand what I was seeing—a naked man and woman entwined.

I gasped. "What... what is this?"

"Drawings... of the ways, you know, men and women... get together."

"We shouldn't be looking at this," I muttered, unable to turn away.

"But aren't you curious?" Prisca whispered.

Of course, I was curious! But the very idea of a Vestal virgin being curious about such things seemed wrong. Shameful.

The first images showed a couple kissing then moved to naked bodies. The drawings were finely wrought and it was clear a lot of money had been spent on their colorful creation. I didn't know where to look so my eyes roved over every part of the image—the woman's nipples, his shoulders, her hips, and goddess above, the young man's erect phallus.

I must have made some sort of surprised noise for Prisca said, "I have only ever seen these things carved on signs or as lamps. I never knew how it worked on a real man's body."

"Me either." The sight was both terrifying and exciting. So many scenes of couplings emerged, heat crawled up my neck and flooded my cheeks. "Look at this one!" Prisca whispered.

It showed a naked woman leaning back while a man kneeled before her spread legs.

"What is he doing?" I asked.

"He's giving her Venus' kiss," Prisca said as if I should know what that meant.

"I don't understand."

"He is kissing her there," she said.

"Why?"

The next drawing was of the roles reversed, the woman taking the young man's phallus into her mouth.

"What in Pluto's pouches. How…"

"I know!" Prisca whisper-giggled.

With every image I imagined Attius, whom I had continued to regularly chastely see in secret at the sacred grove, with his long-limbed beauty. I was both strangely repelled and fascinated. I knew I shouldn't be looking at the drawings and wondering about Attius, but I could not help it. What would his phallus look like? What would his warm body pressed against mine feel like? And yet I knew I was not allowed to wonder about these things. I was at war with my body and, so far, had been successful in suppressing every new or strange thought or sensation that might be considered impure. The drawings were knocking down my defenses like a horse tamping down a mound of hay.

"We shouldn't be doing this," I said as guilt washed over me. "Roll it back up. Put it away."

"No," Prisca said. "There is more to see." As she unrolled one side of the scroll even further, I caught sight of a woman on all fours and a man behind her.

"I should not be doing this," I repeated.

"Too late," Prisca giggled. "Pandora opened the box already."

Despite knowing that me—of all people—should demurely turn away, I continued exploring the images with Prisca. They were simply too fascinating, too strange, too outrageous to turn from.

"There is some writing here," she pointed out. She read a poem about the perfect girl. "Young and hairless and smooth and warm with a delicious 'moist pearl.'"

"What's a moist pearl?" I asked.

Prisca shrugged but something about her pinking cheeks hinted that she was merely pretending not to know. My own "not knowing" was embarrassing but necessary. To survive—and to make sure Rome continued surviving—I had pushed away all thought and awareness of physical sensations and desires. It was necessary for the safety of Rome. Not to mention avoiding the possibility of being buried alive for any related transgression.

She changed the subject. "My friend, Septima, has already kissed a boy."

"What did she say it was like?"

Prisca shrugged. "She didn't say much about it. We could find out for ourselves," she said giving me a furtive playful smile.

I scoffed. "You could, but I'm forbidden."

"We could be each other's first kiss! To see what all the fuss is about. That way when we kiss a boy, we know what to do?"

"I'm never going to kiss a boy," I reminded her.

"Right. Sorry. I keep forgetting. But are you not curious? The rules say you are forbidden from kissing a man. Since I am not a man, we are breaking no rule, yes?"

My heart started to thump hard and fast. "I suppose that is true."

"It is true," Prisca said, her eyes wide with excitement. "Look!" She unraveled more of the scroll to show women with women and men with men. Again, I felt the breath knocked out of me. I knew so little of the world! One drawing had a woman giving a Venus kiss to another while the next one showed a man with an erect phallus poking between another man's posterior.

"So I think it would be okay to practice kissing," Prisca continued. "As I am a girl and not a boy."

Feeling heat climb up my neck, I swallowed. "I don't know…"

"No one would ever know," she said.

This was true.

Prisca leaned toward me and paused. "Turn your head a little this way," she instructed. "So we don't hit noses."

I did as she suggested and closed my eyes. Her lips tentatively brushed mine then pulled away. She did it again, this time pressing a little harder. Her lips were soft and warm and I felt a honeyed loosening deep in my belly.

She pulled away. "That was nice," she said. "Now let's try opening our mouths a little."

I followed her lead, surprised every time at the taste of her, of the feel of her warm breath. "You like it?" she whispered.

"I think so," I whispered back.

"I like it," she said.

Prisca had been right—we had thrown open Pandora's Box and there was no closing it again. The permutations of the nude bodies on the infamous scroll flashed through my mind continuously—in the flames of the temple fire, in the water basin before I rinsed my hands, on the crusty bread before I took a bite. And then there were the physical recollections—the softness of Prisca's lips, the warmth of her skin, the feel of her tongue. My chest thrummed with fascination and excitement but also fear—what had I done? Would I be judged as impious? Would I be buried alive for a kiss?

Sometimes I would lose myself—pestle limp in my hand when I was meant to be grinding sacred salt for the mola cakes—imagining what Attius' mouth might feel like, what scent lingered on his skin, and then wished yet again that I was back in Prisca's small room with her so I could study the lurid and forbidden images more carefully.

Weeks later, we were back in her cubiculum, whispering in the dark, waiting to make sure her parents and the servants were well asleep before she pulled out the forbidden scroll. When we determined it was safe, we lay on our stomachs on her soft sleeping couch. Silken pillows in bright colors cocooned us.

Her little oil lamp—in the shape of a nymph swimming with a dolphin—threw a small circle of flickering light. She brought it as close as possible without setting the papyrus aflame.

"I want to show you something," Prisca said, unrolling the long scroll to a specific point.

"Is this something new?" I whispered, my heart pounding with fear and excitement.

She shook her head, rolling and unrolling the scroll until she settled on one panel, triumphantly. She pointed to the image of the two naked women entwined. My gaze took in the entirety of the image in pieces—a small round breast, a waist expanding into curving hips, a woman with her legs held wide. Again, I felt the shock of discovery. I knew I shouldn't be looking. At the same time, I wanted to look more, especially at the painted illustrations of the young men so I could try to understand the mystery of their phalli.

While we Vestals were forbidden from being touched by men, we could never escape their sex. Penises were everywhere in Rome, especially as symbols of hope and goodwill. There were penis statues in public gardens to rub for good fortune, penis shaped oil lamps, and winged penis wind chimes. Carved penises pointed the way to popular whorehouses, just as often as they directed people to popular bakeries or tavernas. At crossroads, there were helms with carved small erect penises, and of course, many of the paintings and statues of the gods as well as heroes showed them in the nude. At weddings, people often threw fascina—tiny erect penis charms made of clay or wood for good luck and fertility—at the bride during the wedding procession to her new home. There seemed no end to the ways in which the male member could be captured. We were never to see one in the flesh, of course, which made them all the more fascinating to me.

I moved Prisca's hand to unscroll further—I thought I'd spied drawings of young men—when she rolled it back and said, "No, this is what I wanted you to see."

"But we saw that last time," I said.

"I know," she said, excitedly, her face flushed in the soft light. "What I am trying to tell you is that I know what this is like."

I stared, confused. She turned on her side, rested her head on her arm and grinned.

"What do you mean?"

She pointed to the picture. "This. I have done this."

A crater opened into the center of my world. "Wh-what?"

She smiled sheepishly and shrugged as if she had not just admitted to the most shocking revelation imaginable. I could not comprehend that level of physical intimacy, the raw unselfconscious sensuality the images hinted at.

"Yes. With Aula. You know her?"

I nodded. They were often together when I ran into them at the Forum or at the flower market. "You are... lovers?" My insides churned with the sense of being left behind. Everyone around me was speeding toward their adult lives while I would forever remain separate, untouched, unknowing. A flare of something else rose too... jealousy?

"It is still fairly new to me," she said, dropping her gaze and coloring a little.

"And... and I found myself wishing it were you."

A roaring swelled in my ears.

She looked up at me. "Oh no, now I've ruined it haven't I?"

I blinked. "Ruined what?"

"Our friendship."

I shook my head. "Prisca, my beloved Prisca, you are my best friend. Nothing could ruin that. But you must know… that world is forbidden to me!"

Prisca raised an eyebrow. "Is it truly?"

"How could it not? I am not allowed to love anyone lest I endanger Rome."

"That is not true."

I blinked at her. "Of course it is true. It has been beaten into me since the moment of my selection."

"The rules of your priesthood say only you may not love a man, you may not be touched by a man. It says nothing about women."

I shook my head stubbornly. "I am forbidden from such things. The consequences for all of Rome are too high!"

"That is not true," Prisca repeated. "You are not allowed to love or touch a man. There are no rules against loving a woman."

Was this true?

In that moment, a great understanding flooded through me—I loved Attius, I always would, but he was forbidden to me for another twenty years. All our talk of running away and creating the life we'd dreamed about as children—living free in the country—were unachievable fantasies. I needed to face that reality. He would tire of waiting for me, marry, have children, and forget all about me.

Yet in the midst of that cold reality, the possibility of experiencing love in a different form was being offered to me in that very moment. It was almost revelatory. I had so effectively blocked all dreams of love and touch, when she grabbed my hand, it felt like a small lightning bolt crackling up my arm.

Instinctively, my hand tightened around hers. Her thumb caressed my knuckles. "But… I am not allowed," I whispered.

Prisca shook her head. "We are not meant to live without love. Or without loving touch." Her fingers trailed the underside of my wrist and I shivered.

"But… the laws say—"

"According to their definitions, you are no longer a virgin when you are taken by a man," she repeated. "When a man enters you. That is it."

My expression must have remained unconvinced because Prisca shook her head. "You must know there is no physical way to tell if a woman is a virgin," she insisted. "That's why there is the ritual at the Temple of Juno. As for the fabled blood upon the first time, all it does is prove the man was not gentle. Even a woman who is not a virgin will bleed if she is handled too roughly!"

"How do you know all this?"

"Remember I have four older sisters," she said smiling. "They like to talk." After a moment, she added, "I would not have taken any risks if I thought I might suffer later. Remember, I too will have to pass the Temple of Juno test to prove my virginity before I marry."

"Right." Every girl of the noble classes knew and expected to comply with this ancient requirement.

"One of my sister's best friends loved a girl before her test and she passed, proving her virginity. And so it is the gods themselves who do not consider being loved by a woman as a loss of virginity. Even Juno acknowledges this!"

I stared at her in wonder, trying to take this all in.

"If someone in the future required you to perform the rite of virginity in the Temple of Juno," Prisca insisted, "you would pass, just as I will pass before my own wedding."

A silence stretched as I tried to make sense of her words.

"Mia," Prisca said quietly. "Are you not aware of the relationship between the Maxima and Fabia?"

I stared at her blankly as I recalled how they often shared a room and exchanged intimate smiles. "You mean... they are...?"

Prisca grinned.

"Goddess," I cried. It was so obvious now. How had I not seen it? And those two had always been considered pinnacle examples of pious virgins!

Prisca laughed gently at the expression on my face. I thought of Floronia and how she suddenly preferred going to the Furria spring instead of the Egeria because it was closer to the home of the widow she had befriended. Was Floronia in love with her? Were they together in this way?

Prisca gave my hand another squeeze. "You may be a priestess, but you are human. And no human is meant to live without love or affection. Or touch."

As Prisca warmed my hand, I tried to remember the last time anyone had touched me. It was lovely when Ketet braided my hair of course. And when the baths attendant scraped me with a strigil before a caldarium. But this was different. An entire new world was opening up and I didn't know how to take it in.

The hunger for touch and affection was so intense and confusing I grew almost dizzy.

"Did you like our kiss?" Prisca asked shyly, looking down at our hands.

Slowly, I nodded.

Prisca leaned into me and paused, staring into my eyes as if asking permission. I didn't wait to give her an answer. I moved toward her and pressed my mouth on hers.

Her lips were soft and tasted of the mint citron tea she'd sipped. My awareness of the world shrunk to our mouths, the smell of her skin, the brush of her hair, the warmth of her hand as she cupped my neck.

She pulled away, her cheeks pink, and murmured, "That was nice."

I nodded, unable to speak. And then backed away as if scorched.

"We can go as slowly as you need," she said, as if gentling a startled cat.

During the following weeks, I took her at her word, feeling like a skittish kitten, one moment approaching near, the next running for my life. When I finally surrendered to loving her completely, the experience—the touching, stroking, kissing—was revelatory. I had been denied touch and love for so long, when I finally experienced the full expression of it, I wept like a child.

Occasionally I surreptitiously made offerings to Venus in thanks for bringing love into my life in such an unexpected way. Whenever I stared into the face of the smiling Venus statuette in our garden niche, I had the distinct impression she was greatly amused by it all—as if she appreciated the joke. She brought me physical love while skirting the rules of men. The goddess of love did not care whom we loved as long as we loved. For that, I was grateful.

My affair with Prisca did not last long. She soon reunited with the first girl she loved, which she later admitted to me was her true love. I was not hurt, for I had grown increasingly guilty about imagining Attius during our infrequent trysts. In some ways, it was safer to shove my experiences back into Pandora's Box and slam it shut for good. Or until I no longer served Vesta.

***

I sat up with a loud gasp. The niggling thought in the back of my mind suddenly became clear. Prisca, dear Prisca, had come to the rescue again. I knew exactly how I would defend myself in court.

Chapter Seven

As pre-dawn light purpled the sky, Romans had already gathered at the outdoor court in the square between the temples of Saturn and Concordia. The Forum echoed with the squeaks and groans of hastily assembled wooden risers as the crowds scrambled for view in the open-air court. People chirped and murmured like morning birds. An air of unreality surrounded me, and I could not tell whether it was the lack of sleep or the impossibility of my situation that made it seem so.

Ketet spent extra time dressing me and making sure my Vestal robes were impeccable. I must not give them any excuse—no stain or wrinkle or smudge—they could use to claim I was as shoddy with my appearance as I was with following the rules of my order.

"May Isis, Vesta, and the Great Mother protect you," Ketet said, squeezing my hand. I squeezed back. In a moment of panic, I said, "Please try to sneak into the temple to get the sieve for me. Yes? I should have taken it last night! I should've!"

Ketet sighed. "You know I cannot go into the temple without you," she whispered. "Especially now. If I am caught, they will know why and you will lose your chance."

At my expression, she added, "Floronia was correct. We must be strategic. If you pulled it out now and attempted to use it, there is a good chance that the pontiff and his minions would insist you use a different sieve. You must try to get *them* to suggest using Tuccia's sieve—or at the very least, be seen approving its use in public. Only then will it work in your favor."

I took a deep shaky breath, hating how vulnerable I felt without the sieve in hand. But she was right. There was no way for me to know if the pontiff knew it had been doctored. And, I reminded myself, thanks to Prisca, I had a different strategy to try first.

When I approached the lictor ready to escort me to the court, he refused to meet my eye, as if doing so might contaminate him. Or, as with Medusa, turn him to stone.

"Follow," he ordered.

Despite the early hour, the Forum was mobbed beyond anything I had ever seen, even during the near riots of confusion after Cannae. A wall of sound came at me.

"There she is! Whore of Rome! She must pay!"

They had spotted me, the Romans who slept outside, determined to get a view of the person they'd been told was responsible for the deaths of their sons, husbands, brothers, and fathers at Cannae. They mobbed the square, hung off pediments, and screamed from rooftops.

Raging, contorted faces swam in and out of my awareness. Pounding fists. Stomping. Garbled shouts. The acrid smell of unwashed, sweating bodies. When an arm reached between the guards to rip off my white head covering, I winced. Thankfully, a guard slapped it away.

There was no doubt that the mob would rip me into pieces if they could.

The mob surrounded us, howling and spitting at me. Most were in mourning black. Some had anointed their heads and cheeks with ash as a sign of active grief.

A memory flooded my awareness. I was very young with wild unbound hair, running barefoot through the woods near our country farm. I "hunted" Attius as he was Aktion to my Diana. "I shall kill you now!" I whooped when I found him and drew my arrow.

"But why?" he had cried and the question stopped me cold.

Forgetting what characters we were acting out, I shouted, "Because... because I *can!*"

Attius had laughed and I aimed my blunt-tipped arrow straight at his head. He ducked, still laughing, and the arrow flew into the brush.

Attius, they're going to kill me because they can. Why, why didn't I run away with you when you asked?

Once at the Comitium, time folded in on itself. It was here that I had happily joined the pen of girls on the Vestal Selection Day when I was six. And it was here where the same men who once consecrated me as "chosen" wanted me to die a slow, agonizing death.

Once I stepped into the interior of the outdoor courtroom, the shouts and groans grew even louder. There in the center was the Pontifex Maximus ready to decide my fate. His round head was once again topped by the pontifical conical hat of his office. Swathed in ceremonial white, he still managed to look like a toad. An albino toad. His brilliant carnelian ring sparkled in the sun.

All of the most important men of Rome were there as well, of course, including the consul, Tiberius Simpronius Gracchus, and Rome's newest acting emergency dictator, Marcus Junius Pera, who was taking over for Fabius while he traveled to Greece to meet with the Delphic Oracle. Gracchus boomed a laugh and slapped Pera on the back as if they were in on a great joke. Pera laughed too, though his smile faded when he caught sight of me.

A quick scan told me General Varro was not here. Coward. He bore responsibility for the massacre. He was the general in charge that day. He was the one who called for pitched battle, despite being advised not to. But no, the real reason the gods withdrew their favor at Cannae was because I supposedly broke my vow of chastity. What a relief it must be to escape accountability, to have me absorb the endless hate and opprobrium that rightly belong to him.

The Collegium of Priests, all thirty of them—representing the oldest and most powerful gods of Rome—stared as I passed. None of my sister Vestal priestesses were present. It was not unexpected, but it still hurt. The Virgo Maxima had forbidden Floronia from showing support, even after her shift at the fire was finished. At the very least, by oaths of loyalty, the Maxima should be by my side until a verdict was reached, but the very idea that she would back me in any way was laughable.

On a tier above the priests milled the senators, magistrates, and patricians of Rome, the balding, perfumed men who ruled all. In the open-air court, several tables had been set up. The prosecutor, the man who will argue for my death, was the pontiff's brother-in-law, Gaius Manlius. He took his seat at the prosecutor's table with a slow, almost languid elegance. He had the air of a man who rarely lost. No wonder no advocate dared help me.

My defense table was empty, a nice little piece of theater likely arranged by the pontiff himself. The lack of an advocate implied guilt, for if I were innocent, surely *someone* would have stepped up to defend me, no? Everyone knew I was the daughter of a senator. That my own father did not stand for me either was proof enough of my guilt for most.

With my head held high, I walked right past the chair of the accused—where I had been instructed to sit—and sat where my advocate should have been. A great murmur of confusion swelled through the crowd. The wooden risers creaked as people shifted nervously. Even the dictator stilled. All around me the mob swirled with whispers and questions.

"No woman may sit there!" shouted a senator finally. "Where is your advocate?"

"I have none," I announced, standing. "I shall defend myself." I made sure my expression remained impassive for it was important not to appear too angry or too threatening. I had to play it just right—too much confidence and I would be too "haughty" and they would want to take me down a peg or two. Too incensed and their fear of my anger would incite even more violent threats.

At my words, the entire Forum erupted as one. *"Sacrilege! Women are forbidden from speaking in a court of law! Is there no end to her outrage!"*

The complaints amplified and echoed ominously in the open courtyard.

"Quiet," the pontiff roared, standing up and holding his arms out in a dramatic gesture. His face was red and puffy. Despite the cool October morning, beads of sweat appeared on the rolls of his neck. In the sudden silence, a man shouted, "No one will defend her because she is guilty!"

Laughter mixed with hisses of hate.

Again, the pontiff signaled for silence and exchanged a look with the consul and dictator. "It is true the law forbids women from speaking in court," he began. As if the words had to be dragged through clenched teeth, he added, "Unless she is a Vestal virgin. Vestal priestesses have the right to testify in a court of law."

The crowd erupted and I released a long, shaky breath, taking my seat. My small moment of triumph was quickly drowned out by the resuming taunts, though:

"She is defiled! We must be cleansed!"

"She is why we suffer!"

"Guilty! Guilty! Guilty!"

A short trumpet blast called the trial to order and I swallowed hard, ignoring how my heart raced with the sound. An image of the October Horse flashed through my mind, and how I'd begged the beast to run before the race started. My whole body ached to run away and keep running.

The man in charge of the proceedings, the court chairman, stepped into the center. He was old and craggy, with threads of white throughout his black beard. He wore the authority of his office with great dignity. He was like the patriarchs of old, reassuring on one hand, but terrifying on the other, for if he turned his judgment against me, my life was over. After assuring the court that he had made the proper obeisance to the gods, he lifted a heavy bronze staff and banged it twice on a marble plinth to call the trial to begin.

Manlius the prosecutor stood and tipped his head at the blue-robed chairman. He boomed out the charges against me:

"The Vestal virgin Opimia Pansa is accused of 'Crimen Incestum,' of breaking her sacred commandment of chastity and losing her virginity to a man. She has outraged the gods of Rome and caused them to turn from us. In rupturing the Pax Deorum, the peace of the gods, she has incited the Ira Deorum, the wrath of the gods. She is the reason why the gods abandoned us at Cannae. Because of her impurity and impiety, all of Rome suffers with the incomprehensible loss of Rome's brightest and strongest young men."

The crowd roared, a terrifying mix of gutting pain mixed with vengeful bloodlust.

"Worse," he yelled. "Her very presence is anathema to the gods. The gods *require* her removal. Only then will they be satisfied. Only then will they help us survive the scourge of Hannibal. We must cleanse Rome of her stain!"

An even greater roar shook the wooden rafters and I forced myself to breathe. Like a good actor, Manlius waited for the noise to wane before holding his arms out and booming, "The gods are growing impatient. They demand we restore the purity of our most sacred servants of Vesta! Immediately! The danger is nigh. We must have a cleansing. Restoring Rome's virtue and safety is a matter of life and death!"

"We have suffered enough! The Vestal must die! Hannibal is at the gates!"

"The gods speak to us through signs and wonders, through prodigia that cannot be faked," Manlius continued. "The proof of this woman's guilt has been writ upon the skies, in the waters, and on the earth again and again." The prosecutor paused and read from a scroll he had begun to unroll.

"Two weeks before the tragedy at Cannae, the statue of Juno Suspita at Lavinia cried blood."

People groaned. Despite knowing I was not responsible, I still suppressed a shudder. A statue crying blood was always a horrible portent.

"Soon after, in Apulium, a calf with two heads was born. Rocks rained from the sky on the Alban Mount. And, most telling of all, a young maiden in her garden in this very city was hit by lightning, which scorched her clothing, leaving her dead in such a shameful position, it was without doubt an expression of exactly what the gods were angry about!"

The mob stomped and roared. It sounded like Jupiter himself was kicking the edge of the sky in disgust.

"The prodigia all point to one incontestable truth: a Vestal virgin has been unchaste," he thundered. "And the prodigia never lie! This, the youngest and most defiant of all the priestesses, was the only one in a position to defile herself in this way."

"Die! Die! Take her now! Now, now!"

"Remember, it is this priestess who is known as The Smiling One, the one who uses her pretty face and seductive smiles to lure men into impure and lustful thoughts. It is this priestess who flaunts her feminine attributes every time she sashays through the streets. She displays her vulgarity without shame."

To my horror, Manlius mimicked a bouncing chest as he parodied the walk of a mincing, silly woman. Derisive laughter and hoots of disdain roiled throughout the courtyard. This despite the fact that I bound my breasts even more tightly than normal this morning, lest my body incite lustful attention. *I did everything you asked*, I wanted to scream.

"We must cleanse ourselves of the pollution of her dishonor," Manlius continued. "Only then will the gods restore victory to Rome. The College of Pontiffs has no recourse but to condemn this unclean woman to the death she deserves so we might finally repair the Pax Deorum, the peace of the gods. And convince the gods to keep us safe from imminent destruction!"

People jumped to their feet and stomped. Their roars bounced off the marble temples around us, swelling with so much outrage, the reverberations hung in the air like a miasma of rotting meat.

Despite the early morning chill, sweat gathered under my arms and made my scalp itch beneath my white head covering. When the noise settled, the court chairman turned to me.

"Statement of the defense, please."

I stood and gathered all the breath and strength I had to throw my priestess voice to every corner of the courtyard:

"On the charge of breaking my sacred vow of chastity, I am innocent."

A great cry rumbled through the Forum. *"Liar! Liar! Whore!"*

"I have never lain with a man," I proclaimed after the noise settled. "I have kept my vows to the letter and have served Rome faithfully for sixteen years. That so many of our beloved Roman warriors and leaders died in Cannae has nothing to do with me, but with the miscalculations of those who marched our legions directly into yet another of Hannibal's traps—"

A wall of sound crashed over me. Everyone was on their feet, stomping and screaming. *"Outrageous! Who does she think she is? How dare she!"*

My heart sped at the intensity of the mob's reaction. I had expected some resistance to placing the blame where it belonged—on the decisions of the general in charge—but not this. I reminded myself to be careful. This crowd was primed to hate me. And they would not abide by any insult to the only general left alive to protect us.

The chairman put his arms out for quiet. When the screams continued, he pounded his bronze staff on the marble, the enormous clang echoing again and again through the open courtyard until order resumed. The chairman gestured for me to continue.

"I can prove my innocence this very night," I proclaimed. The senators stilled. The pontiff exchanged a concerned look with the priest of Jupiter. "As everyone knows, only the gods—only Juno—can verify true virginity as there is no other test or means to determine purity. I call for this court to allow me to undertake the ancient rite of the Test of Virginity in the Temple of Juno tonight as practiced by our sanctified ancestors in Lavinium. For what better proof is there than a message directly from the goddess?"

The pontiff's jowly chin dropped. He had not expected this. Good. My heart lifted with hope. The priests could not deny the validity of this ancient rite. Silently, I thanked Prisca for insisting all those years ago that I would pass this test—as all the other young women who have loved women had.

This could all be over by morning. All I needed was one temple snake to consume my offering and I would walk out a free and exonerated woman.

To my dismay, the pontiff and several of the elder priests stood and shouted, "Absolutely not!"

Others took up a chant around them. *"No, no, no! There is no time! Hannibal is at the gates!"*

The yelling mob felt as if it were closing in on me. Senators and priests alike spit fury through open mouths on anger-flushed faces. How could they deny me this? It was a holy rite!

The chairman pounded his staff for order. With his arms, he signaled everyone back to their seats. The pontiff remained standing. The chairman signaled for him to speak with a nod. "The sacred snakes of Juno dream with the gods during the cooler months," he said. "It would be nefas to disturb them before the spring. The accused is trying to buy time, which Rome does not have," he shouted. "We must act now to keep Hannibal from invading!"

I swallowed hard. He *knew* Hannibal's forces were hundreds of miles away. He was needlessly stoking terror. Was he part of the faction soliciting help from foreign governments? Had he agreed to this distraction? I bit back the impulse to accuse him and the Collegium of collaborating with traitors to create chaos, but I stopped myself only because I had no proof. And I didn't want Prisca to suffer for telling me of their plans.

"We must repair the peace of the gods *immediately*. Therefore, the request is denied."

A great swell of clapping ensued and the chants began again. *"Kill her now! The virgin must die! Purify us now!"*

"Our ancestors relied upon the power of this ancient tradition," I shouted over the noise. The mob quieted some. "Now is not the time to anger Juno! Denying the goddess' final word on the matter is more nefas than awakening her snakes—"

The pontiff jumped up and cut me off, yelling, "The Pontifex Maximus rules over all religious questions. The decision has been made. The request is denied."

The priest of Rome claimed his word trumped Juno's ancient rites? And no one challenged him on it? The hubris alone should've brought down the wrath of all the gods in defense of the great goddess!

The mob clapped but I also heard murmurs of dismay. Clearly, some agreed with me that undergoing the trial of virginity would be wise. But, as if sensing the slightest softening toward me, a senator reminded them of their terror by howling a new chant: *"Hannibal is at the gates! We must act now! Hannibal is at the gates! We must act now!"*

The mob adopted it in a frenzy and their cries echoed off the marble walls around us. My insides squeezed. I had been so sure they would not deny Juno during these trying times. After all, if this circus was meant to buy time and distract the people from their fear while they negotiated with allies, they could extend the pomp around the test and create an even greater diversion than this trial. But they were like a pack of wild dogs catching the scent of an injured doe. Their blood lust, combined with the need to blame someone for their pain, was too potent for the mob. They wanted resolution now.

The court chairman, unsurprisingly, agreed with the pontiff. The man held his arms out, looking like a great blue heron and called, "The court and the College of Priests unanimously deny this request. The trial must resume."

My lungs grew tight as if I were already suffocating in the underground chamber where they planned on entombing me alive. The chairman banged his staff onto the marble plinth and the crowd quieted.

Breathe, breathe. If all else failed, I would demand to prove my innocence with the miracle of Tuccia's sieve. But I had to have it in hand. *Wait. Just wait.*

Manlius smirked in my direction and called, "As the defendant has nothing more to say, we will proceed with my case."

I must have missed the prompt to continue my defense. As the mob laughed and whistled, someone threw a rotting pomegranate at me. It splattered at my feet, exploding with juice and staining my white hem red. Hissing whispers claimed it was a sign from the gods of my guilt. My stomach twisted. Even knowing the truth, a rush of uncertainty made me pause. From the moment of my birth, I'd been told the gods spoke through symbols and dreams and portents. Even though I never broke my vow with a man, the blood-like splatter left me wondering if they knew something about me I did not. Old shame wound its way up my spine and flamed in my face.

Stay calm. Remember what Larce said. The gods are not swayed by the tantrums of little girls—nor do they speak through pomegranate juice.

Chapter Eight

"For my first witness, I call the Pontifex Maximus of Rome, Cantilius Cornelius Lentulus," announced the prosecutor.

Everything in me dropped. It was outrageous that the most powerful priest in Rome was allowed to be—all at once—my accuser, a witness against me, *and* my judge. But the rules for religious courts were not as clear as they were for magisterial courts. I stared in dismay as he lumbered down the wooden steps toward the witness chair.

The pontiff made a show of arranging his pristine toga around himself with exaggerated dignity. He raised his chin—if one could call the mass of flesh there a chin—and nodded. I suppressed a shiver remembering the first time I met the man who controlled my fate for nearly my whole life.

***

Sixteen Years Before

Soon after we arrived in Rome, pater took me on an excursion to the Forum. It was my first outing into pater's world and it was thrilling. Senators and powerful men hailed him by name in the streets and I puffed my chest out with pride. Some even clapped for him! We marched past a circular temple where great gusts of fragrant smoke billowed out of the oculus of a domed building. A shining bronze trellis circled the marbled exterior, surrounded by columns painted a warm, beautiful red.

"What's that?" I asked.

"The Temple of Vesta," pater said tersely. I knew who Vesta was, of course. However, I didn't pay much attention to her. What was there to like in a goddess who did nothing but sit by a hearth fire? The goddess of the hunt was my favorite. Melantho, walking behind us, paused by the temple to bow and mutter a quick prayer.

We approached a small house across the courtyard from the round temple. Pater leaned down with a severe expression. "You must be on your best behavior—"

"I promise a million times I will—"

Pater shook me quiet. "Do not speak unless asked a question. Do you hear me? You must not anger or irritate this man, because if you do, it is like angering or irritating the gods."

A shot of dread tore through me. "Is he a god?" I whispered, feeling as if my feet were dancing on hot stone.

"Be still. He is not a god, but he is the head priest of Rome, which makes him closest to the gods among men. He is very powerful."

Could he throw lightning bolts? Could he crack the sky open with thunder? The sound of a servant sweeping with a twig-broom behind me moved in rhythm with my racing heart. To my shock, when the man emerged, he was short and round with a balding head and wide jowls.

I had expected him to look tall and majestic, like a statue of Jupiter. His full face and downturned mouth reminded me of the toads I chased at the farm, and I was about to inform him of this fascinating fact when Melantho pulled my hair ever so slightly, her signal for me to stay quiet. She knew me well.

"Is this her?" the man said after greeting pater.

I often thought about how my life would've been different had I not tried so hard to be good for pater that day. If I'd screeched or run or talked over the man—I might have been spared everything that led to my false accusation. But I was desperate to impress my often-distant father, so I tried to be the good little girl he wanted.

Pater turned to me and took my hand with an encouraging smile. "Opimia, say hello to the Pontifex Maximus, the head priest of Rome."

"Hello," I said, scanning his bulbous face with fascination.

The priest frowned. What had I done wrong?

Later, Melantho would reprimand me for holding his gaze. Good girls did not look directly at men if they were not family.

"She seems… spirited," the head priest said, frowning down at me and crossing his short arms over a silken dark green tunic. That he had not put on his toga to greet my father was an insult, though I did not know it at the time.

"What does he mea—ouch!"

Pater squeezed my hand hard and I closed my mouth.

"But she is also smart," pater said quickly. "And under the close eye of the Maxima, she will do fine."

The Maxima meant a woman who was the greatest, but the greatest at what? Knowing me well, Melantho surreptitiously pulled my hair again before I could ask.

"Hmmmm," the priest said. He signaled me to twirl for him a few times.

When I finished, he held my chin up and moved my face right to left.

"Open your mouth."

He peered inside. "Teeth good, though small. No blemishes. Pretty enough. No strange marks on her body?

"No," pater said.

"And a virgin?"

"She is six," pater said, insulted. "Of course!" He must have sensed I was going to ask what being a virgin meant because he gave my hand another firm squeeze for silence.

"And your wife, is she healthy?"

"Yes," pater said.

"And neither of you has been married before?"

"No."

We must have passed some test because the priest told pater to join him in his tablinium.

"We must stay here," Melantho said when I trailed after pater. My nurse dragged me toward the sweeping girl and asked about the location of the latrine. The girl pointed and Melantho pulled me with her.

"I don't need to go," I whined, locking my knees. "I want to stay out here!"

Melantho looked distressed, as if she needed the latrine immediately. The broom girl waved Melantho on. "I'll watch her," she said. Melantho huffed a thanks and scurried in the direction of the small kitchen, where a pipe from the main water line diverted flowing water to wash away both waste and food scraps.

As soon as my nurse disappeared, I turned to the girl. "Do you want to race?" I pointed my chin to the column at the edge of the courtyard, hiked my tunica, and crouched into racing stance, waiting for her to put down her broom.

She had longer legs, yes, but I was sure I could win. I had only ever raced Attius and I wanted to test myself. To my disappointment, the servant shook her head and resumed sweeping as if I'd never spoken. I sighed loudly and kicked at the nicked stones of a fading geometric mosaic in the center of the courtyard. A short brick wall surrounded a flowerbed near the door where my father had disappeared, and I climbed atop it, fighting imaginary hydras on one side and lions on the other. Like Diana, I shot arrow after arrow until the monsters died in agony.

The sound of arguing popped me out of my game. It came from the room the men had disappeared into. I jumped down and inched closer.

"But that is an outrageous amount," pater said.

"It is yours to decide," the priest said. "But if you want the goddess to bless your family in this way, that is the 'offering' I require."

They argued back and forth with numbers for some time. Eventually, it went quiet.

"Fine," pater said. "I will deliver it in full by the ides."

At the time, I thought nothing of it. Pater was "doing business" with the head priest of Rome. He did business with a lot of people.

***

Manlius the prosecutor turned to the crowd and then to the rows of priests and boomed into the courtyard. "I outlined the long list of prodigia showing the accused's guilt."

Hisses of hate swirled like snakes around the wooden rafters.

"Please, Dominus, as Rome's highest priest, explain why this is enough to proclaim this priestess guilty."

Although I had rarely questioned signs from the gods as interpreted by our priests, this time, I could barely hold back a snort of disgust. It was clear they were creating a narrative that somehow "proved" my guilt but something else continued to bother me. They had yet to accuse a man. Why had the crowd not demanded the head of my so-called debaucher?

But I had to tread carefully. If I challenged them on this, they could accuse me of being over-eager to defend my so-called lover. Or claim that there was more than one man. Even a hint of that would sink me deeper into their trap. So I waited. The pontiff's jowls expanded as he sucked in air, preparing to pontificate. "Not every strange occurrence is considered prodigia. There is an official process legitimizing it."

"Please describe the process." The prosecutor pretended to not know the process well, of course. He wanted the mob to hear every detail of every sign to prove their "interpretations" were true messages from the gods. And if I dared challenge them, they would accuse me of impiety.

"Priests within Rome and our allied territories send word of strange occurrences which have the potential to be messages from the gods," said the pontiff. "We, the priests, examine the details and check the sacred Sibylline Books for their significance. If we find meaning in the Books, we inform the Senate which then votes on their legitimacy and the necessary corrective action. Once certified, the prodigia is recorded in the Annales Maximi, the official record of all religious phenomena."

"In other words, prodigia cannot be faked," Manlius intoned. "Several layers of protective checks ensure they are actual messages from the gods rather than random events."

"Correct."

A respectful murmur moved through the crowd.

"And so, these interpretations are protected from being abused by the wills of individual men," continued the prosecutor. Turning to the chairman and the masses behind us all, he added, "Please explain the most powerful of the prodigia proving one of our Vestal virgins has broken her vow," the prosecutor said.

I jotted a note in my wax tablet: *If prodigia claim "a" Vestal has fallen, how did they determine which one was at fault?*

Still, I kept my tongue, waiting to see if they would reveal themselves by which man they accused. If I were found guilty, he would die too. Prisca had indicated there was infighting among factions. Perhaps they'd hoped in the chaos and outrage of the accusation yesterday morning, I would have been hauled off to the Evil Field and buried alive without having to "bother" naming a man whose innocent death would likely disturb them more than the elimination of a mere Vestal.

"The most damning of the prodigia happened three days before the disaster at Cannae," the pontiff continued. "A young girl was riding in her garden when lightning struck and killed her and her horse."

An uncomfortable murmur flowed through the crowd. Lightning strikes were rare and alarming and were always a direct communication from Jupiter.

"The young girl named Helvia died, as I said, but it was her position in death that was the clear message," the pontiff continued.

"Go on," Manlius said, arranging the lines in his face to just the right level of fear and concern.

"The girl Helvia was found with her shoes and all her jewelry scattered around her. Her tongue was out lewdly and, well, her dress had been pulled up to her waist and her legs splayed, showing her private parts. The message from the gods couldn't be clearer."

"And the message was?"

"Our youngest Vestal virgin priestess has broken her vow of sexual purity and the gods are incensed by her shamefulness. They let us know by the violent and indecent way the young girl's body was laid out. For not purging ourselves of the vile Vestal immediately, the gods punished us with the terrible loss of life at Cannae."

A great murmuring swelled around us. Manlius shook his head with theatrical horror. He signaled to the row of pontifical judges. "The priests called upon the scene drew out in detail the precise arrangement of the body, it's shameless position, so that it could be explored against the wisdom of the Sibylline Books," he said, passing small pieces of papyrus copied from the original drawing to the priests.

With a flourish, he presented a copy of the drawing to the court chairman.

The chairman's face scrunched in disgust.

My stomach roiled. They took the unfortunate death of a child and turned it into a sexualized drawing. A bunch of dirty old men discussing how much of an exposed vulva meant I was a whore.

"As everyone knows," the prosecutor boomed, "a lightning strike is always, always, sent directly by Jupiter as an expression of his wrath. We did not act quickly enough to cleanse Rome of the Vestal's disgusting impurity, and so the gods expressed their rage by abandoning our soldiers to the slaughter."

A great swell of outrage and grief bounced and echoed from off the marble buildings. The mob accepted every single word as truth.

Goddess help me, I prayed, but had I ever felt her presence? No one was coming to help me, not even the goddess whom I had served for fourteen years. *Stay calm, stay calm. Breathe.* I had to think strategically. Until Tuccia's sieve was in my possession, I dared not make my plans known lest they foist an ordinary sieve on me and I guaranteed my own death in the most humiliating way possible. There were no second chances—the miracle had to be convincing enough to sway not just the priests, but the mob.

When it was my turn to question the priest, I stood and gave the man in charge of my fate a respectful bow. "Esteemed Dominus," I began and the pontiff's left eyebrow arched. He seemed amused that I actually sounded deferential.

"Our most powerful priest should not be questioned by a woman," someone screamed.

"It is an outrage! It's unnatural!"

The chairman raised his arms, his toga draping dramatically like unfurling wings, and shouted, "We have already determined that the law allows this. Quiet so that we may proceed."

It took some time for the grumbling to die down. Only then did I take a deep breath and project my voice as loudly as possible. "Dominus, how much did my father pay you to pick me as the sixth Vestal priestess on that autumn day in the year of our consuls Pomponius Matho and Papirus Maso?"

There was a moment of shocked silence as the pontiff narrowed his eyes. Senators in striped togas jumped from their seats. "Outrage!" they screamed. "She insults our most sacred priest and our sacred traditions, even her own *father!*"

The crowds howled.

"How much more will the gods stand? Condemn her now. Condemn her now. Unnatural, evil woman!"

The bronze staff once again reverberated against the marble. "Order! There will be order in this court!"

I stared defiantly at the head priest of Rome. Clearly no one had ever called him on his corruption. It was shocking no one ever asked how the priest—who received a small stipend from the state—could have amassed such a fortune, with a mansion on the Palatine Hill. He "lived" in his simple public house in the Forum only when he needed to have people see him act like a humble servant of Rome. The rest of the time he lived it up like a potentate from Persia on the Palatine.

The mob's cries grew deafening. Some of the older women wailed and keened, bemoaning the way I insulted both the priest and the gods.

"How will the gods punish us now? She must be stopped!"

It was a risk to speak aloud the truth of how the powerful operated in Rome—that only coin bought loyalty and power. Bribes and exchanges happened in whispers in private studies and chambers all up and down the corridors of the rich and powerful. Meanwhile the priests told the masses that they had to sacrifice more and more of their own wealth to the temples in the hopes that the gods might reward them with gold too. And if nothing ever changed, the only answer was to tell them their sacrifices weren't sufficient and they needed to try again.

The court chairman held his staff out, demanding silence. He nodded to the pontiff.

"*All* fathers of serious applicants make offerings to the gods via the priests," the Pontifex Maximus said with bored insouciance. "You were not chosen because of the amount your father contributed *as was his duty*. Indeed, why the gods selected you to serve Vesta continues to be a mystery. We never fully understand the minds of the gods after all."

People sniggered at the insult. I was taken off-guard over how expertly he twisted a bribe meant to increase his personal wealth into something ordinary and expected, like an offering. No, something *virtuous*.

Desperate, I jumped on what he said. "When you question why the goddess Vesta selected me, are you not suggesting, Dominus, you believe the goddess Vesta made an *error* in selecting me? That you know better? Surely the gods are insulted by such monumental hubris."

A wall of sound broke over me, shaking the ground and bouncing off the marble façade of the temples nearby.

"*How dare she?*"

"*The gods will never protect us now!*"

"*Take her now! Take her away!*"

The speed and level of outrage took me aback. I had to be careful. Speak too directly and they would accuse me of being too angry and unnatural. Hoping the chairman would bang his staff to quell the crowd, I noticed he was looking at the pontiff, as if waiting for guidance. The pontiff was too busy exchanging smirks with Manlius, the prosecutor. They knew how to let this moment play out in a way that benefited them. By the time the paroxysms of hate and fear calmed, the mob would be convinced I was the one who questioned the goddess' judgment and not the most powerful priest of Rome upon whom they depended.

My only hope was to introduce doubt until such time as I could get Tuccia's sieve in hand. "Let us return to the issue of prodigia," I said. "Is there not the risk of misreading the prodigia in favor of what one wants and desires?"

Murmurs roiled around me.

"Is she questioning the sanctity of the high priest?"

"Again? Who does she think she is?"

The pontiff smiled indulgently. "As I explained earlier, we protect ourselves from misreading the messages from the gods by having several layers of experts analyze their meaning. With guidance from the sacred Sibylline Books, along with expert interpretation from men who spend their lives serving the gods, and final approval by the learned men of the Senate, we ensure the gods' will is interpreted correctly."

Sporadic clapping echoed around the outdoor chamber.

"And if you're wrong?"

The pontiff's eyes narrowed. "What do you mean 'if we are wrong?"

"Surely, there have been instances when the messages from the gods have been misinterpreted. For example, general Varro claims the omens for engaging Hannibal in pitched battle at Cannae were good. Yet the outcome was catastrophic."

"It was Paullus who called for battle," a lone voice shouted. "It was his augurs they ignored!"

Choruses of assent rippled up and down the stands. No matter how many times I heard the lie, I was shocked anew at how easily people accepted it. Even when the truth was plain before them, they believed the lie if it promised them someone to blame and a future of safety. The records clearly showed that Varro was in charge that terrible day, not Paullus. But a lie convincingly told without cease was a lie that became fixed as truth in the minds of those who needed it to be true.

Some of the senators stood, yelling and waving their arms. Having a woman—even a priestess—question the wisdom of the surviving general was outrageously bad form. And since Varro was shamelessly lying about who called for pitched battle at Cannae—blaming Paullus—he was exactly the type of man who would attempt to twist auguries to match his personal desires. Once again, the fault was in the hands of the men who made the choice to do battle, not me. But how could I get people to see it?

"My point is, *men* not gods do the interpreting and men are easily influenced by their personal desires," I added.

The prosecutor jumped up. "Chairman, please, she is making speeches, not asking questions!"

"Do you have a question, priestess?" the Chairman asked.

I cleared my throat. "Have the augurs who claimed the gods approved of General Varro's determination to march into battle been questioned about their conclusions?"

"Paullus called for battle! It was Paullus!"

The pontiff narrowed his eyes at me. "The general's augurs too were slaughtered that day, so no, they have not. And if they had survived, it would have been an insult to the general and to the gods to question them."

No one found it odd the battle augurs also died? Or that he was saying "the general's augurs" rather than naming Varro so he could have plausible deniability about his support of the big lie?

"Dominus," I pointed out. "The priests are typically the first ones removed from danger before battle. Do you not find it odd—or convenient—that they too were massacred?"

The crowd seemed unsettled by my questions. The pontiff took advantage quickly. He jumped to his feet and turned to the mob, jowly cheeks aflame, and gestured toward me with a sweeping arm.

"Do you see the depth of her impiety?" he yelled. "She angers the gods even now!"

As expected, roars of outrage shook the rafters. Their hatred meant now was not the time to demand I prove my innocence with Tuccia's sieve. I had only one chance to get it right and the mob needed to be on my side when I tried, or I would be denied. But they seemed almost drunk with hate, and I had no idea how to shift that.

Guide me, O Goddess. Show me when to act.

The goddess of demure obedience answered my plea with silence. Or perhaps the mob baying for my blood drowned her out.

Chapter Nine

When it was the prosecutor's turn again, Manlius gave me a small smirk before he thundered, "I call to the witness chair the Virgo Maxima, the head priestess of Vesta and Sacrosanct leader of the Vestal virgins, Gegania Macerina." Of course, the second "witness" had to be the woman who hated me from the moment she spotted me on the day of my selection. She should be protecting me, not tossing me with relish into the slavering maws of hungry wolves!

When she was escorted into the court arena, I was not the only one who gasped in surprise. Who was this woman taking such slow feeble steps? Who was this fragile wraith bent over as if grieving? The Maxima I knew had a grip of iron and a death glare that made inanimate objects combust. She could walk six miles at a pace that would make a soldier blush.

The mob stared at the old priestess with reverence as if she were an ancient, wise woman. "This brilliant, kind woman has served Rome for more than forty years," the prosecutor began. "She gladly chose to stay past her thirty-year requirement to lead our Vestals in the purification and protection of Rome during troubled times and has stood stalwart in the face of threats by Gauls and Carthaginians alike." He turned to me and pointed. "But this young woman nearly broke our most revered lady with her countless outrages." Hisses and moans erupted. "Tell us, Maxima," Manlius boomed, "about the character of the accused."

The old priestess leaned forward, a sudden gleam in her eye, as if she had forgotten her frail act. "She was stubborn, difficult, and disobedient. There was no rule we imposed that she did not question or challenge. I kept her away from public duties—for two years—until I could be sure her behavior wouldn't outrage the gods."

The Maxima refused to look in my direction during her testimony. Even now, after all these years, her scowl of disapproval had the power to make me feel like an errant child. But I could not afford to let her intimidate me.

The prosecutor's voice rose in pitch, signaling to the crowd he was about to make an important point. The mob leaned toward him as one. "So, you are telling us you kept this priestess away from public Vestal rites for *two years*?"

"Correct," the Maxima said, putting on a face of such sweet but loving regret and disappointment. I had to curb the impulse to snort. "Indeed," she continued, "in all my decades of service, I have never come across such a rebellious child. And obedience, above all, is what's required for a servant of the goddess of the hearth."

Whispers of "marked from the beginning" flowed up and down the rows of spectators once again. A blast of cool October air whipped through the open arena, setting togas flapping and people murmuring ominously. Why did no one notice that, in the same way the pontiff had earlier, she was coming dangerously close to questioning the judgment of Vesta in choosing me to serve her. But when I accused the pontiff of such an outrage, the crowd turned on me. I hated weighing everything I said and did against how the mob may react, but I would be stupid to incite them further. So I said nothing.

The prosecutor's booming voice continued. "Your usual forms of discipline were inadequate in dealing with this defiant priestess?"

Manlius asked, putting his hand to his heart, signaling his "distress" at how she suffered with me.

"I object!" I said, standing and facing the Chairman.

"To what?" asked the prosecutor. "You must be more specific." His *I'm speaking to an idiot* tone made the audience laugh in derision at me. Again, I was reminded of my vulnerability without adequate representation.

"The forms of discipline the Maxima employed when I was a mere child have no bearing on this trial!"

"Of course they do," the Maxima said before the advocate could speak. "It proves you have a history of disobedience and defiance. And that only someone with that history would have dared break her vows in such a disgusting way."

The mob hissed and roiled, throwing insults aimed in my direction.

"My behavior as a child has no relevance to the crime being prosecuted," I proclaimed over them.

Before the chairman could respond, Manlius jumped in. "The relevance is this," he boomed. "Her wild nature proves she was the only one of the pious sisters who could have—or would have—dared be so reckless with her chastity and enrage the gods in this terrible way!"

People on the risers stomped their feet and the sound echoed like thunder throughout the entire courtyard.

"The only thing it proves is the Maxima was not capable of managing a strong-willed child," I countered.

Predictably, the mob roared in defense of the Maxima.

The chairman nodded at the prosecutor. "I will allow the questioning," he announced. "You may continue."

Reluctantly, I sat. The Maxima smirked, but in a blink she had her face readjusted into the soft lines of a pious servant of the state, forever pained by my behavior. And so began the litany of my outrages:

The time I threw a particularly difficult piece of Greek translation down the latrine. "Sacred texts, no less," the Maxima exclaimed, as fearful murmurs mounted throughout the courtyard. *Liar*, I thought. I'd been made to throw away a mistake-riddled translation of an ancient play I was using to perfect my lettering.

The time I fell asleep by the sacred fire. I was barely ten years old, too young to watch the fire on my own. An elder Vestal kept the true watch. But judging from the crowd's frightened reaction, she'd hit her mark.

The time they had to throw away batches of the sacred salt cakes I'd prepared because I'd used regular flour instead of the ashes of sacrificed baby cows as tradition dictated. In my childish mind, I'd thought that if we didn't use their ashes, the calves wouldn't be sacrificed and burned in the future.

The time I...

As the litany continued, I wondered what questions—if any—I could ask the Maxima that would not make me look too aggressive or churlish. Did I dare expose the evil of her vindictive punishments? Would they see the depth of her ugliness? Or would they blame me for not being the sweet little girl they were promised?

***

Fourteen Years Before

I was barely eight years old when the Maxima came for me in the deepest, darkest part of the night. Her frightening face floated over mine like a wax death mask.

"Get up," she commanded. "Now." She stomped out of my room.

It took a moment for my breathing to restart. I sat up, wondering what it meant that she had been dressed in black. Vestals always wore white, didn't we? Had it been a bad dream? Another small light bobbed into the room. Floronia.

"Come," she said. "I am here to help you dress."

"But why?" I mumbled. "What is happening?"

"I do not know," she whispered. "But we must obey."

Right. Obey the Maxima to avoid her rage, just as we must obey the gods to avoid theirs. **But what** had I done now? Floronia seemed alarmed, which frightened me even more. She wriggled me out of my sleeping tunica and shoved my small head through the opening of a child-sized black dress. She was wearing black too.

"Who died?" I asked. Black meant mourning, though I never saw a Vestal in anything but white.

"Nobody that I know of," she said. Then whispering, she added, "Stop asking me questions, I do not know what is happening. I've not participated in anything like this before."

After shoving my feet into strange, dark slippers much too large for me, Floronia ushered me out to the atrium where the Maxima and the other priestesses—all with the hair loose and wearing black—waited. They seemed to me like a wall of witches.

"Come," the Maxima said after inspecting me coldly.

"Where are we going?" I asked. "What is happening?"

"I do not explain myself to you," the Maxima snapped. "Do not speak again."

We lined up in procession and silently moved into the dark night as unease skittered down my spine. I looked back at our circular temple as we left the compound. The copper trellis decorating the outer walls glimmered and danced with reflections of the giant fire inside. I thought I spotted the priestess Horatia staring out at us through the open temple doors, but I may have only imagined it.

119

Away from the temple, the darkness descended like a smothering blanket. There was no moon. The watchmen's lights had been snuffed. With our black clothing, we melted into the gloom. Only the little flame from the Maxima's bronze lamp broke through the inky blackness of night.

As soon as we turned another corner, we stopped while Floronia unwrapped something from her wrist. Her hands were shaking. It looked like a black veil. She rolled it up and wound it around my head, covering my eyes.

I must have made a noise and tried to wriggle away, for I felt the Maxima come in close and shake me. "You. Will. Be. Silent."

Blinded, my breath sounded like a monster panting, our footsteps like the dragging sounds of revenants, the dead who walked. Even as Floronia guided me by the shoulders, I put my arms out trying to feel where I was. "Hands down!" hissed the Maxima.

I strained for any sound that might tell me where we were going or what was happening, but to my dismay, there was only silence. Normally, the streets of Rome clamored with noise, even at night. Usually farmers and vendors with squeaky axels trundled on the uneven cobblestones as they made deliveries for the next day's market. The clip-clop of hooves from donkeys or oxen normally lulled me to sleep. Where were the taverns still selling wine, the drunkards singing through the streets? The parties of men surrounded by torches held by bodyguards as they left their favorite tavernas?

I was sure the Maxima had somehow magicked Rome quiet. Disoriented, I began to whimper. The Maxima grabbed my upper arm and shook me. "Quiet! Do you want to attract the shades of the vengeful dead?"

No, I most certainly did not, so I clenched my teeth, trying to stifle my gasping breaths. In my child's mind, we seemed to walk for an entire lifetime, which only added to the terror.

Finally, we entered a chamber of weeping stone walls, the cold wetness discovered when I accidentally brushed a craggy corner. The air was fetid, reeking of festering sores, stale human waste, and the dank despair of the abandoned. In my imagination, I was certain we were walking into the sulfurous caverns of Pluto's realm where she would abandon me. This sense only grew when we descended into a chamber whose darkness was so absolute, I could feel the weight of it, even though I was still blinded. Inexorably, she led me down what seemed like endless stone stairs.

Strange moans and cries echoed weakly from somewhere below. The souls of the dead! There could be no other explanation but that we were descending—step by evil step—into the underworld. I locked my knees and refused to move further. Someone pushed me from behind and I was forced to continue.

Finally, we stopped descending. The gasps and murmurs from the other Vestals were too much. I tore off my blindfold. We were in a stone room where the walls wept. The underworld! I knew it. The Maxima would surely feed me to Cerberus, the lord of the dead's three-headed hound. Or maybe she would try to drown me in the river Styx. I turned to run but where had we come in? The Maxima shoved me forward and I found myself alone as the other priestesses encircled me.

When they began to sway and sing, all the small hairs on my arms and neck stood on end. With their unbound hair and black mourning dresses, they looked like the hungry witches rumored to haunt crossroads where those who failed to sacrifice to Mercury were devoured alive. The metallic tang of blood filled my mouth—I must have bitten my cheek.

The words to the hymn they chanted broke through my frozen horror:

121

"…thou coverest Pluto's shades and chaos immeasurable…Bestow on me, O revered Goddess, your will to submission…I pray that with the favor of your majesty…for obedience to serve as my guiding light as thou demands…"

It was a song to Prosperina, Pluto's wife and queen who ruled beside him in the underworld half the year. Had I done something to anger her too? When the song ended, I turned in a circle trying to understand what was happening. The other Vestal's looked stone-faced, but Floronia was wide-eyed and seemed both confused and angry.

The Maxima grabbed my upper arm and yanked me toward a dark mound that reeked of misery and death. I planted my feet, but the old woman was stronger than she appeared and she dragged me to stand before a mound of some sort. I choked on the smell of decay and rot. At first, I could not make sense of what I was seeing.

The Maxima held the small lamp out with a fully extended arm. "Look upon the price of disobedience," she hissed. The light flickered upon the edges of an old dirty couch.

Initially, I thought it was a large doll. The image sharpened in pieces—scraps of dusty white cloth, leather, and frayed, red ribbon. Something ivory. No, not ivory, a foot bone. I whipped my head away and the Maxima grabbed my chin and pulled me toward the other end. Hair. Still braided. Over a skull, mouth open as if in an endless scream.

"A Vestal who disobeys—a Vestal who is unchaste or lets the sacred fire go out—must die according to the sacred laws," the head priestess intoned. "This Unclean One was buried alive for impiety. Such was the price for her disobedience. Do you understand?"

I nodded, unable to make a sound. I'd never seen a dead body before. Sure, I'd seen memento mori paintings, but this was different. This one had once lived. A Vestal virgin!

The Maxima shook me. "Say it. My purpose is to obey."

Despite my terror, there was still a part of me that wanted to fight back, to yell, "No, my job is to disobey you." But I was only eight and I wanted this nightmare to end.

"My purpose is to obey," I said in a dull voice, repeating everything she bade me.

"My purpose is to remain pure"

"My purpose is to serve Vesta."

"My purpose is to obey."

"My purpose is to obey."

The Maxima pointed at the carcass. "She who was once one of us broke these promises and she was buried alive for it."

The old priestess grabbed my hand and placed it over the dusty skull. I swallowed a gasp and tried vainly to pull my small hand out of hers. She jerked me hard and pressed my palm over the horrendous empty nose and gaping mouth. It was strangely dry and hard and completely horrifying.

"Promise it," she growled.

I could not speak. She pressed my hand down harder on the skull. Would the dead Vestal's shade haunt me for this desecration of her body?

"I... I... promise... to... obey," I finally managed between sobs.

"She who died for her disobedience will remind you how to behave. Do you understand?"

"Yes, Maxima," I muttered through chattering teeth.

I have no memory of climbing out of the chamber. Nor of walking through the empty streets in silence—blindfolded once again—back to the Aesdis Vesti. Once in my sleeping room, I must have been given a draught of medicine that made me feel like I was falling, falling, falling forever into blackness. When I woke, I was so disoriented I thought perhaps I had dreamed the terrible descent into Pluto's realm.

Floronia confirmed it had been no dream. Sweet, gentle Floronia expressed her outrage to me, but only whispers when we were alone lest the Maxima hear and punish her as well.

***

The Maxima's plan twelve years ago was to frighten me into being a good little virgin. It worked. Outwardly, at least. After that horrible night, I had learned to act more docile and compliant, but on the inside, I seethed. My rebellion, if one could call it that, went underground. Literally. I dug in the dirt for small critters and placed them where they would most surprise and shock the Maxima. One morning, she awoke to find a coiled, gray snake on the pillow beside her. I had heard her screams from the baths on the other side of the large house and grinned to myself.

Worms had often mysteriously showed up in her shoes. Or her hair comb. When I overheard that she had consulted with the Pontifex Maximus to determine what the sudden appearance of dirt-serpents "meant," I expanded my repertoire to include spiders. She woke up the entire household with her shrieks of horror when a particularly hairy one crawled over her open mouth one night. In my defense, I'd thought the spider was dead when I placed it on her pillow.

It was only years later that I learned where she had taken me that terrible night—to the pit in the center of the Forum, the Tullianum, the underground stone cavity where we held convicted traitors or foreign enemies until the day of their execution.

And the body she had claimed was a Vestal? Likely a prop from the theater, made to look like a dead priestess. Even the Maxima would not be so bold as to touch the impure dead, no matter how angry she was at me. Her mastery of the power of religious theater remained unmatched. The terror of it still haunted my dreams.

Debating whether I should bring up the "punishment of the cave" as an illustration of the rageful madness that sometimes overtook the Maxima, I decided it was too risky. A frightened people will always side with the powerful, if they believe the powerful will protect them in some way. Even when they actively hurt them. The promise of safety and protection was more potent than the strongest poppy tincture. If I dashed their hope, they would turn on me like maenads on Orpheus.

A sudden change in the energy of the crowd pulled me to attention.

"We have clearly established that this priestess has always been the only one who could have broken her vows," the prosecutor boomed then paused theatrically. He gestured toward me and then toward the Maxima and shouted, "And soon we will have the name of the man who befouled this priestess so that we may be cleansed of his pollution as well…"

The crowd erupted in howls and hisses, followed by: *"Kill him too! Name him now! Kill him too!"*

My heart pounded in my ears. As if by habit, my mind went to Attius, until I remembered he died at Cannae too. And I had not broken my vow with him.

I am innocent. And so is any man they accuse.

"Has her lover been legally accused?" Manlius asked the Maxima. At the word "lover," the crowd erupted again. Manlius quietly smirked then reassembled his features into the staid, stern, concerned visage of a good and pious Roman citizen.

The court chairman banged his staff against the marble plinth, but the sound was drowned out by the chorus of chanting.

Tell us! Tell us! Who is the man?!

Even the people covered in ash for mourning seemed enlivened by the drama of the moment. Despite their grief, the chaos, and the danger, this was grand entertainment, outrageous theater, a distraction from endless grief and terror.

The Maxima preened with importance. "We are following legal protocols," she said. "And are holding the accused priestess' slave in the pontiff's public house where she will be tortured for the lover's name—"

"No!" I yelled, shooting up. "You cannot!"

In a Roman court, a slave's testimony was only admissible if it had been obtained under torture. It was a deterrent to ensure angry slaves didn't make false accusations against their masters, but it also meant a slave's testimony was legal only when it had been wrought by brutal mistreatment. Many died in the process.

"I own no slave," I yelled over the Maxima. "My lady is a freedwoman!"

The Maxima turned to me with a sneer. "Of course you own a slave," she cried. "You bought her when you turned twelve, as custom dictated."

"I secretly manumitted her immediately after," I yelled. "The person you think is my slave is my freedwoman, Tarpeia Ketet Opimia." I turned to the chairman. "It is against the law to torture a free Roman."

Bellows of confusion and anger ricocheted off the nearby pediments. The chairman held up his arms for silence and turned to me.

"You say she is your freedwoman and not a slave?"

"Yes, and I have the manumission papers to prove it. I call for a court recess so I may present her legal papers."

The Maxima's face was red with fury. Not knowing this key fact about the lady of one of her priestesses embarrassed her. The chairman conferred with the Pontifex Maximus. The pontiff's jowls quivered as he hissed into the chairman's ear. Most of the audience stood, craning their necks. The sounds of their shuffling feet echoed off the marble facades of the temples surrounding us. The sky was covered in ribbons of thin, gray clouds.

The court chairman walked away from the pontiff who looked as if he wanted to murder him. "Under the rule of law, we cannot torture a free person for testimony," the chairman finally announced. "We must examine the papers before we can proceed. Court is adjourned until the claim can be verified."

***

Ten Years Before

As soon as I turned twelve, the Maxima announced I would be purchasing my own slave, per tradition. But being twelve meant everything she wanted me to do required a loud and dramatic rejection.

The Maxima planned on taking me to the slave market after a trader sent word that he had a "special shipment of suitable virgins for the House of Vestals." I did not care. I crossed my arms and refused to obey at our break-the-fast meal that morning.

"I am not getting one," I said.

The Maxima slammed her hand down on the wooden table, making our ceramic cups rattle. "Why do you insist on making everything so difficult?" she yelled. "Most girls your age would be thrilled and honored to be granted their own private slave. But no, not you. I will no longer be shamed by your lack of compliance with our norms. Do you understand me? You will be getting a slave today."

"You can't make me," I mumbled, a sentiment that earned me ten lashes because, of course, she could. And did.

We set off for the slave market near the Juturna Spring behind the temple of Castor and Pollux. Like the divine twins, it was divided in two: one side was grimy and overcrowded, while the other was reserved for the most expensive, beautiful, and educated slaves.

The Maxima never looked in the direction of the low-status market, but I couldn't help staring. Most of the chained captives looked starved and miserable, even those who appeared strong. Their empty staring eyes hinted of unimaginable pain, loss, and misery. They knew what came next—being worked to death by millers, stonemasons, miners, and farmers. Some would be purchased by fullers who would make them spend their days stomping togas in vats of urine to bleach them white. These men and women would die from burns in their lungs as they breathed in toxic fumes hour after hour or from ulcers on their feet which were never given the chance to heal. The suffering in their glances made my stomach hurt.

It suddenly occurred to me to wonder if Larce had been free. He must have been a freedman, I concluded, as I had a vague memory of him wearing the green felt cap of freedom at certain festivities, especially at the Saturnalia feast. There had been so much laughter and joy at the farm during those winter celebrations. A pang of longing for my old life swept through me. Even after six years, it had the power to twist my heart and take my breath.

The Maxima escorted me and the other gray lady, Fabia, past the breastfeeding section, where patrician ladies purchased lactating women for the babies they were about to birth. I wondered if it was at this market that my parents bought Melantho for me. These women were cleaner and appeared to be well fed, presumably to keep their milk flowing. Some of the women had babies on their laps. As I watched, one woman pulled out a heavy breast—blue veins showing through her pale, northern Greek skin—and began milking herself into a cup to demonstrate her fecundity. One young pregnant woman—girl really—and her mother, presumably, watched this display with mingled fascination and disgust. The Maxima, with eyes on the back of her head, hissed at me to stop staring.

We continued on to the "fancier" side of the slave market, which faced merchant tables strewn with bronze statuettes, elegant colored glassware, strange spices and incense in delicately carved wooden boxes, as well as emeralds, pearls, and rare, white-threaded onyx stones.

The platform on the cruder side of the market was wooden and bare, but the one on the finer side was laid with carpets and was divided on each end with poles holding up brilliantly dyed cloth panels for privacy.

"Ah, priestesses," the slave trader said, clapping his hands and rubbing them together. "Come, come, we must make your selection before the crowds arrive."

The Maxima gave him the slightest of acknowledgements and sniffed ever so slightly in disapproval. The slaver led us to the panels draped in orange and red cloth, double layered so no one could see inside. He signaled to someone and suddenly, five girls shuffled toward us in a line.

"These are the special virgins I told you about. They are lovely and will go fast when the men arrive, so it is good you have the first pick."

"You have verified they are virgins?" the Maxima asked. "The gods demand this be so."

The slaver nodded enthusiastically. "Of course, of course. A priestess of Juno performed the proper rites last night for confirmation."

The Maxima nodded. The unctuous slaver reeked of perfumed oil. He added with an overbright smile, "They all speak Greek, as it is the universal language of the east, and some even know rudimentary Latin."

Two of the five girls were not much older than me. One was younger. Only one held her head up and looked me in the eye. I walked over to her.

"Where are you from?" I asked in Greek, looking up into her eyes as she was a couple of finger lengths taller than me.

The girl opened her mouth to answer but the slaver spoke over her. "From Egypt, she is," he said loudly. "Her name is Ketet. A descendant of one of the royal lines."

The girl clenched her teeth as if biting her tongue to keep from expressing scorn at the man's outrageous lie. Her eyes were dark—almost black—like her hair, and they shone with intelligence and strength of will.

"How did you come to be enslaved?" I asked Ketet. Many slaves were born into it, I knew, but not all. This one, I was sure, had only known freedom. What were the turns of fate that led her to be presented to me like a heifer?

Egypt was big and powerful and run by the Greek descendants of Alexander the Great's brother, Ptolemy. Ketet, with her long shiny black hair, dark brown eyes and creamy russet skin, looked more classically Egyptian than Greek. The slaver had clearly been lying about her being descended from the Greek Ptolemies. Maybe he meant one of the long-lost pharaohs of other eras. Rome had a good trading relationship with Egypt, I knew, so how did a free Egyptian come to be here in chains? When I asked Ketet this, her eyes flashed.

The seller jumped in. "Oh, you must not bother your virtuous ears with their stories," he began, but I put a hand up to silence him. From the corner of my eye, I saw the Maxima and Fabia exchange a look. It seemed a mix of humor and irritation at my aping of her commanding gestures—and that the man so quickly obeyed, given I was still a child.

"Answer please," I said to the girl.

"My seaside village bordered Libya," Ketet said. "Libyans invaded. Those of us who were lucky were killed. The rest of us were sold and brought to Rome."

That Egyptian forces did not come to their defense during the invasion almost made her lose her faith in the gods, she later admitted.

The slaver shifted from foot to foot, trying to find a way, no doubt, to redeem his story of royal connection to the House of Ptolemy.

The Maxima sniffed at Ketet's borderline rude tone, but I liked this confident girl. "I do not like the Egyptian," the Maxima said, grabbing my arm and steering me to one girl who trembled and kept her gaze on her bare feet. "Pick one who looks more like you."

"I like Ketet," I said, pulling out of her grip. "I choose her."

"Wait, wait, wait," blubbered the slaver. "You haven't spoken with the others. Either one of these two in particular," he added pointing to the Greek girl and the one standing next to her, "are quite docile and will behave nicely!"

"Yes," agreed the Maxima. "This one looks to give us trouble," she added, staring at Ketet with narrowed eyes.

Which was precisely why I wanted her, of course. "This one," I repeated.

"No, Opimia," said Fabia, through gritted teeth. "We've been over this. You are to select the most obedient of the girls. This one is the least."

I quirked my head slightly to the side and blinked at the two older Vestals. "I was told I was to select my own handmaiden, using my own money, and that this tradition goes all the way back to Rhea Silvia, the first Vestal priestess and virgin mother of Romulus and Remus. And I have made my choice."

Both older priestesses reddened and prepared to argue with me, but the rules were clear. I selected my slave and I used my own money to pay for her. They could do nothing.

"How much?" I asked, and the haggling began.

When the coin and the papers were exchanged, both older priestesses turned on their heel and stomped back toward the House of Vesta. It was a testament to their irritation that they would leave me alone in the Forum but, of course, I now had a handmaiden as an attendant.

Still, what I overheard next left me swallowing spit. Fabia turned to the Maxima and triumphantly whispered, "Victory is still ours in the end." After all, I now had a slave, which was what she wanted.

Well, letting the Maxima "win" was unacceptable! I turned to Ketet, drew her to a private corner and whispered, "If I were to give you your freedom right now, what would you do?"

She blinked wet lashes several times, her chest expanding, as if the very idea of being free again filled her heart. "I would be extremely grateful." But then her expression changed and her eyes grew wide. "Wait. Does that mean you would abandon me to these terrible streets?"

Groups of men of all ages had already assembled before the draped tents, murmuring excitedly. I thought of the shy, trembling girls left behind and my heart sunk for them. Some of the better dressed men looked like they might be bored husbands seeking a distraction, while the ones with bored expressions likely came from prostitution houses ready to bid high for virgins to resell at premium rates.

Ketet shuddered and her breathing became ragged. She moved closer to me. "I saw the terrible things men did to the women of my village, including my mother and grandmother. I could not... do not make me..."

"But you could go home," I said as if setting her free fixed everything.

Ketet made a funny sound in her throat. "I have no home or family left. My village is gone. My little sister died on our caravan across the desert. I know nothing about this city and have no money."

The beautiful Egyptian girl looked hard at me then. "If you plan on freeing me only to abandon me to the streets of this foreign land—"

"I would not leave you to the streets!"

"Then why do you speak of freeing me?"

I opened my mouth, suddenly realizing how foolish it sounded to admit that I was doing so only to defy the Maxima. "You do not want freedom?"

"Of course, I want freedom," she snapped. "But of what use is freedom if I am turned into prey to be devoured by Roman jackals in the streets. Anubis, save me!"

A wave of embarrassment washed over me. What was I thinking? Freedom was not a game. I had held out the lure of freedom for my own selfish and admittedly immature reasons without thinking of what it meant to her.

I cleared my throat, aware that it seemed terrible form to offer freedom one moment and then snatch it back on a whim. "I can grant your freedom and keep you safe and pay you to work for me as my handmaiden," I offered. "Would you be willing to do that, knowing you must live as a virgin and serve me for the duration of my obligation as priestess?"

"Which is?"

"Another twenty-four years."

She closed her eyes and released a shallow breath through lips turning up in the corners. She murmured rapidly in her native Egyptian, repeating what sounded like the word "Ee-Set" over and over again. Later she would explain that was how her people called upon the goddess we knew as Isis.

"I will serve you."

I smiled. "Follow me to the clerk's office at the Basilica, and I will file your manumission papers."

I didn't tell any of the other Vestal virgins I'd set Ketet free for fear they would make fun of my decision. They would call me stupid, silly, intemperate, unwise, and foolish—which would all have been true. I also knew they would worry their own slaves would ask for their freedom and if they didn't get it, they would be fussy and disobedient. Worse, I knew they would treat Ketet horribly and make her life miserable. I warned her of all this and asked her to keep her manumission a secret. She did not mind, for she knew she was free and that I would pay her fairly. And that her status—or what people believe is her status—kept her safe from violation.

***

I would not allow Ketet to be tortured and killed for their personal and political distractions. I would not.

Chapter Ten

As soon as the chairman called for a short recess, I raced to find Ketet. The Maxima said she was being held at the pontiff's public house next to our House of Vestals. Male torturers would not have been allowed to step inside our sacred dwelling, so they must have lured her out in some way. Three very large men—slaves who typically guarded the pontiff's larger properties on the Palatine—loomed outside the atrium of the small house. My heart sunk.

Forcing myself to slow, I approached them with my chin high. "Step. Aside," I commanded. They exchanged glances but did not move. "I am going into that room and if you try to stop me and touch me, I will have you arrested and whipped for violating the sanctity of my body. Do you understand?"

One of the big men, as hairy as Hercules, shifted from side to side. "You are not sanctified. You are on trial!"

"Until the religious court rules otherwise, I still serve the goddess Vesta as her priestess. And as such, the rules of my sanctity still apply. Now let me by."

The men looked at each other, shrugged and stepped aside.

Ketet sat alone at an oversized wooden table in a small dark room. My throat tightened at how small and vulnerable she looked, her face puffy and tear-stained. Thank the goddess I saw no blood or bruising anywhere. The torture had not begun. Her claim of being free confused her interrogators. They awaited word from the pontiff on how to proceed.

"Ketet, you are my freedwoman and it is against the law for them to hold you as if you were enslaved," I said, using my most official voice. "You will come with me."

A frowning slave uncrossed his arms. "This slave's name is Tarpeia, not Ketet, and I am not to release her without the pontiff's approval," he said.

I whirled on him. "You were told to hold the *slave* Tarpeia, but this is my freedwoman, Ketet Opimia. You have the wrong person."

I turned back to Ketet, grabbed her hand and dragged her out of the house and into the private breezeway connecting the pontiff's house to ours. The men argued in hushed tones, but none dared to stop me. They too knew the price for touching me. Outside the compound, chants and screams for my blood continued like an endless chorus of Furies I could not outrun.

Once inside my consulting room, I locked the door and pulled Ketet into my arms. She shook with terror.

"They didn't hurt you, did they?" The torture of female slaves often included rape and after the traumas she'd witnessed as a child, I knew she feared this form of violence most of all.

Ketet shook her head and I almost wept with relief. "They refused to let me retrieve my manumission papers, but they were scared to touch me until the pontiff told them what to do. They sent a note during the court…"

"Thank the goddess," I murmured and Ketet let go, weeping so hard her whole body trembled. We rocked together until the worst passed.

"I'm sorry, I'm sorry," she said when she gained control. "I was so frightened."

Wiping away her tears with my sleeve, I said, "Ketet, it is not safe for you here. You must leave. Now."

She blinked. "I am not leaving you to this nightmare. They told me I was to be tortured for a name. That must mean they have decided on a target."

We both knew—as I was innocent—the man they would name was likely a personal or political enemy of the pontiff or the consul. We already knew Paullus' nephew Lepidus was vulnerable—and had sent him a warning to be careful—but we could not come up with any additional targets.

In the meantime, Lepidus had written back, claiming he had nothing to fear for surely the pontiff would not dare impugn the character of a man related to Rome's greatest hero. I almost laughed at the man's hubris but then realized he likely knew the pontiff's spies read everything coming in and out of the House of Vestals. It had been a warning message to the pontiff, not me.

Lepidus was the obvious choice to accuse but were there others in the Senate whom they wanted to punish for refusing to consider foreign assistance? Perhaps some of their enemies were on the ship headed to the Delphic Oracle with Fabius. Perhaps they hadn't counted on their absence and they'd been arguing about whether they could condemn a man to death in absentia.

But where was the theater in that? If all this was meant to distract, they needed someone here in order to feed the mob's need for blood and vengeance. There was no satisfaction or catharsis unless they watched a vile debaucher being flogged to death and flung from the Tarpeian Rock.

"Ketet, there is a very good possibility they will claim your manumission papers are false and torture you anyway," I said, holding her by the shoulders and forcing myself to focus on the immediacy of Ketet's vulnerability. "You must leave."

Ketet paled. "I do not want to leave you. Besides, where would I go?"

"Follow me," I said. Inside my cubiculum, I led her to the heavy, locked chest under the bed. Together we dragged it beside the couch. The thick iron chain rolled to the tiled floor with a cold thud when I unlocked it.

"What are you doing?" Ketet asked. Her hands, I noticed, had not stopped shaking.

The chest opened with a rusty creak. "Take your savings," I commanded, knowing she'd been frugal with the regular payments I made to her for service to me. Since that needed to be secret too, I kept her money hidden in a compartment next to my own. Vestals typically stored their money in state vaults, but I had always preferred keeping the money paid to me under lock and key in my room. It seemed to me a Vestal's sleeping room was likely the safest place in all of Rome.

I grabbed several of my own bags full of silver denarii and gold aurei coins and added it to her own savings. "Take it and leave. You are a free person and have the right to do so."

While Ketet—still in shock—stared at her own money and the coins I'd pushed onto her, I quickly rifled through my papers to find her proof of manumission and shoved it into her hands as well.

Ketet looked at me with wide, uncomprehending eyes. "What are you saying? Where would I go?"

"Go to Prisca's house on the Palatine," I said. "Do not wear anything that identifies you with this House. Slip into one of the plain tunicas worn by the laundress. Prisca is expecting you. Explain to her household that you are the nurse she has hired to help with the birth. Once things settle, you can go wherever you want, even back to the Sibyl's compound in Cumae, if you like."

Ketet had felt safe in the small community devoted to the goddess. She brightened at the idea. Then her expression fell. "I cannot leave you."

"You must," I said in a low tone. "I will not have them hurt you. You will be safer in the mountains of Cumae."

"Come with me. Let us go together," Ketet pleaded, grabbing my shoulder. "In the chaos, they may not even notice! I can dress you as a slave. No one would recognize you outside of your raiment and without your head covered—"

My chest squeezed as I thought, *yes, yes, let me change right now and I will go with you!* But too many eyes were on her. On both of us. If they found us trying to sneak out, they'd kill her too. Besides, I would look guilty and that I could not abide.

My mind swam with all the times Attius begged me to run away with him before he signed his life away to the legions. If I'd been strong enough to act then, he would be alive today and we might be living quiet lives on a small plot of land like we always dreamed.

Stop, think, think. There had to be another way—one that didn't risk the lives of those I loved. The sieve. Now was the time to demand the miracle. Before they named a man, because it would be hard to come back from that. Especially if he were a known enemy of Varro.

"Go," I said and kissed her cheek, hoping my placid expression hid my turmoil and fear. "There are too many people watching us. For your own safety, change your garments and your hair and go to Prisca's. Do you understand?"

Her eyes filled, but she nodded.

"May the goddess keep you safe," I whispered.

Ketet pulled me in hard for one last embrace. "I will see you soon," she said and I nodded. We both needed to believe that.

Get to the temple. Grab the sieve. But the mob was still baying outside. They might try to stop me from entering the sacred space. Could

I create a distraction? But how? As my mind spun, I wondered if I should send another message to Lepidus, Paullus' nephew. Surely, he was aware by now how close he was to being murdered for political expediency. In my panic, I wanted to rage at him. *Why didn't you take my warnings seriously?*

***

Six Weeks Before

As we began to understand the depth and scale of our loss in Cannae, the city ricocheted between outright denial and hopeless grief and despair. Like most in Rome, I refused to believe the stories that continued to swirl—that all of our eight legions were destroyed, that the slaughter was so vast, even Hannibal was said to have been taken aback by the sight. I could not—would not—believe that Attius' was dead. I counseled supplicants to wait for official word. Any day now, the senators who had marched out to join our forces—and there were eighty of them—would triumphantly return and announce our victory.

Still, the stories kept coming. They claimed many of our men died of asphyxiation under the crush of bodies. Those who were felled while still alive on the bottom layers dug holes in the ground so they could suffocate themselves in the dirt.

No, no, no, I did not want to believe these horrible rumors. I could not bear the idea of Attius suffering in such a horrible way. Until the day came when we could no longer lie to ourselves and one of the few surviving magistrates re-entered the city to make an official report: 50,000 Roman dead, 4,000 taken prisoner. Among the dead was general Paullus, Attius' general. And the litany continued: All eighty senators killed along with two consuls from the previous year, twenty-nine military tribunes, and an additional 10,000 of non-combatants who served in the Roman camps.

I was sitting in the upstairs listening chamber of the Senate House as the haggard, stoop-shouldered man confirmed the tragic details. The massacre had been total. General Varro, who was in charge that day, had insisted on entering into pitched battle, despite Paullus' pleas to wait. Forced to obey the ruling general, Paullus had led his legions into the center. Hannibal's pinching maneuver turned into a murderous rout. Paullus and his men were trapped in the center and slaughtered like livestock while our flanks were defeated by fresh Libyan cavalry troops. I began to rock, covering my mouth, squeezing my eyes shut as if I could physically ward off the news.

Attius served in the center with Paullus.

No, no, no. It could not be true. The chamber erupted in shouts and cries of distress. So unusual was the sound of grief emanating from the Senate House, there was no way of suppressing the news. Within moments, it seemed, all of Rome knew the truth. The city exploded with howls of anguish. I joined the cacophony as I wailed my distress. I wanted to run, to scream, to tear at my hair, to set fire to the city, to spit in the face of the gods whom we'd given everything in exchange for the safety of our loved ones and yet they had still failed us.

Failed me.

Failed Attius.

Floronia found me hours later, curled up in a ball in a corner of the listening room. "Mia, what are you doing?" she called. "The Maxima is searching for you. We must make an appearance at the Temple. Now!" She took one look at my face and stilled. "Mia? What is the matter. I don't understand."

How could I explain? Attius was my secret. The heart of my childhood joys and the source of all my fantasies of an alternate life. He of all people should've had the chance to fulfill his dreams of a farming life in the country—with a lovely young wife, children, and a kennel full of hunting pups, like his own dog, which he had named Ulysses but I had renamed "Useless" for the pup's incorrigible nature. We would never laugh together over that again. He was gone. It was as if all the light in the world had been snuffed out.

"Tell the Maxima, I am ill," I said through a raw, jagged throat. "That I cannot attend. Perform your rites without me."

Those first few days after hearing the news were a blur. Somewhere along the way, by some act of deeply ingrained training and instinct, I slipped on the mask of impassiveness and returned to my duties. In the chaos of those days after Cannae, not even the Maxima noticed my gray affect. We were all in deep shock as we grappled with the meaning of such an unimaginable loss.

The city echoed with the keening of women and children as they grieved for lost fathers, husbands, brothers, and sons. Yet I could not grieve publicly for Attius. I could not even say his name.

I was in such a fog of grief and shock that when I received word that Varro and several hundred of his men survived, including Prisca's husband, I could find no joy or relief. They'd escaped on horses while tens of thousands were slaughtered around them. The Senate, gutted by a third, tried to quell the increasing panic. They locked all the city gates. No one was allowed to leave the city. We no longer had a functioning army to protect us, and Hannibal could attack any day.

The Senate charged battalions of enslaved men and stone masons to shore up the city's ancient walls and recruited veterans, slaves, and even teen boys to assemble a new legion. While no one was allowed out, refugees from the farms and cities in Hannibal's path swarmed in. They arrived in droves, bearing carts of grain and produce, as well as livestock. The city rang with the bellows of frightened cattle and the keening of terrified and grieving people.

In the midst of mass grief and terror over Hannibal's impending attack, the Senate created new laws: Women could not grieve in public after thirty days. Women were not allowed to wear black or wail in public after the designated grieving period. Women were not allowed to wear more than one-half ounce of gold in public, nor don multi-colored garments, especially anything trimmed in purple. Reasons for these new rules were never articulated though given the self-satisfied grimaces of certain old-fashioned senators, it appeared they were deeply offended by women's show of emotion in public and by any display of independent wealth not managed by men. Taxes and fines were levied for any woman who broke these rules and many a widow's wealth was siphoned off to pay for the reconstruction of our legions.

Once again, we Vestals were employed to calm the people and help them grieve in the "proper way," which gave everything an air of un-reality, as I continued acting as if I had not been personally gutted. Only Attius' dog seemed to sense my pain and Zena thankfully let him sleep with me most nights.

Meanwhile, the Maxima doubled down on the importance of pro-jecting an air of calm confidence and dignity. No matter what kind of pain we felt or witnessed, our impassive expressions were to prevail. My face hardened into stone.

As I suppressed my grief for Attius, a different emotion burbled to the surface—rage—which was harder to contain. When the rumors were confirmed that Varro and his cavalry had escaped the massacre, my fury became incandescent.

How dare Varro sacrifice good men like Attius in pursuit of his own misguided glory.

How dare he survive.

How dare he.

Varro and his men snuck back into Rome by night. The crowds, I was sure, would have torn them apart had they come by day. So it was a shock to learn Varro had begun rewriting the story of the defeat to deflect blame. Paullus had called for battle, not him, he claimed. Paullus had been the reckless hothead, not him. Perhaps if our senses had not been so dulled by grief and anguish, more people would've pushed back and told the truth—Cannae was Varro's and his alone. To my dismay, the masses embraced his lies because facing the alternative was too frightening: we were in the hands of an impetuous man who, by law, was now the sole military leader of Rome.

The wrong general survived.

Meanwhile, from morning until night, we purified the grieving and consoled the lost. Weeks after the battle, Numidian envoys presented the Senate with a formal request for Rome's surrender. Hannibal had always shown mercy to those cities that surrendered to him. We also knew what happened to those cities that didn't—our skies were still thick with the smoke drifting in from the regions Hannibal had burned to the ground.

A large faction cried out, "Accept the terms, accept the terms!" With a defeated army still in disarray outside of Rome, we had no protection. We either surrendered or prepared to be burned alive within the city walls.

The Senate sent Hannibal back a one-word reply: No.

Added to the grief was now a terrible fear of being massacred in our beds. How quickly would he come for us? Why had our senators not tried to buy time by negotiating?

The days of grief and terror blurred together. A ray of hope emerged when rumors spread that some warriors had, in fact, survived Cannae. Witnesses claimed thousands had limped away from the battlefield to the city of Canusium. Hearts soared everywhere—including mine. Maybe Attius still lived!

Like everyone else, I increased my sacrifices and prayers in the hopes it was true. Despite the announcements to stay home, women and families crowded the eastern gates in the hopes of spotting a re-turning warrior they once thought dead. Occasionally, stragglers came through and those names were posted in the Forum. I checked every day. No Attius.

My hopes were dashed again when senators insisted all of Paullus' legions had been destroyed. Still, witnesses claimed to have seen sur-vivors, in the cities closest to the battlefield, Canusium and Venusia. When I learned most of the survivors had served on the flanks or were non-combatant camp followers, I grieved anew.

The Senate finally acknowledged that some of our legionnaires had indeed survived—as many as ten thousand. But they would never again be allowed to set foot in Rome. They were condemned as cow-ards for leaving their swords on the field.

Again, the mob nearly rioted. The Senate was being unreasonable. If they were injured in battle, they hadn't run! They weren't cowards. Why didn't we use the survivors who could still fight after recovery to reassemble our legions? Senators closed their ears and their hearts against the pleading of the people and no one could explain why.

Later, I would understand that the Senate, as deeply superstitious as the rest of Rome, had deemed survivors as forever tainted. Real he-roes died fighting. Survivors might spread the rot of bad luck and cause us all to die. All survivors who had not made it back to Rome were dubbed, "Ghosts of Cannae" and forbidden re-entry.

My insides turned to stone as I was told again and again that none from Paullus' center survived. I went through the motions of consol-ing others. Many new widows committed suicide, leaving children abandoned to the streets. We Vestals set up and managed emergency temporary orphanages until family members could be found—or if there were none, adoptions could be arranged.

Meanwhile, the Senate quietly stripped Varro of his powers and declared Fabius the "Cunctator"—the man whose prudent strategy had been abandoned at Cannae—as dictator of Rome once again. Then, to my utter astonishment, Fabius announced he was arranging an expedition to Greece to consult with the Oracle of Delphi for guidance on defeating Hannibal. It seemed inconceivable to me that our leaders would risk their lives to cross the sea during wartime. That they would leave the city they were charged with protecting! Why didn't they visit the Sibyl of Cumae, the prophetess of our own lands? Why seek a foreign priestess?

In the midst of the chaos, Varro's campaign to tarnish Paullus' name and reputation intensified. Every time I overheard someone blame Paullus for the devastation at Cannae, I corrected them. It was ill-omened to speak lies of the dead, I told them. And I would not accept being told up was down, white was black, and truth was false even as our leaders spat falsehoods with impunity.

The goddess of lies and deceit, Fraus, I told them, must never be given more credence than the goddess of truth, Veritas. Still, Varro's lies took hold and spread.

Word must have reached Paullus' nephew, Mamercus Aemilius Lepidus, about my refusal to besmirch his uncle's name. He sought an audience with me, but I was too busy and declined. He must have complained to the Maxima and she insisted I meet with him.

She had never insisted I meet with anyone before, so I knew I had to comply. But in my extreme caution—which had become second nature by that point—I insisted we meet in a public place, in full view, and attended by two women.

Lepidus met me in the small seating area on the front lawn of the Temple of Vesta. Since we were in the heart of the Forum, we were in full view of all who happened by. Ketet and one of the house servants stood guard beside me.

Lepidus had been injured at Trasimene and was still recovering, which was why, he was quick to explain, he had not been at Cannae on that terrible day. It was the first thing he said as he lowered himself down onto a marble bench. He mentioned this multiple times. Clearly, he was torturing himself with guilt for not fighting beside his uncle. The young man's sword arm was missing three fingers and he walked with what looked like a painful limp, his left leg being unable to bend fully.

With my hands clasped demurely, I lowered my gaze before speaking, exaggerating the theater of my piety in this public space as people stared curiously. "I grieve with you the loss of your uncle and so many of his loyal men. How may I help you during these trying times?"

"You are aware that the former consul-general is blaming my uncle for the tragedy in Cannae, yes?"

"Yes."

"And you are aware he is blatantly lying? It was Varro who insisted they engage Hannibal that day."

"I am aware."

He sighed. "There are those in the Senate who are warning me off from publicly disputing his lies and defending my uncle. I seek support from the religious community in telling the truth."

"You have my support, but I am curious. Why come to me? Have you spoken with the Pontifex or the Collegium of Priests—"

Lepidus gave a rude snort. "They have dismissed me at every turn, including the Vestalis Maxima. They claim the people need to be kept calm and believe that the gods saved the 'better' general and to do otherwise risks mass panic."

"If you have already appealed to my superiors, why come to me?" I asked.

"Because I have heard you defend my uncle." Lepidus gritted his teeth and pushed himself up to standing. His agitation made his limp even more pronounced as he paced. "Terrentius Varro is a plebeian," he nearly shouted. "The son of a lowly butcher! That he dares to besmirch the honor of the Aemilius family, one of the oldest patrician families in Rome, is beyond insult!"

"I agree," I said soothingly. "However, I must ask again—what do you suppose I can do?"

"Convince your sister priestesses to speak on my uncle's behalf on this matter. Beseech the head priestess of Vesta on my behalf. A unified statement would be ideal—"

I shook my head and he stopped. "I'm afraid we answer to the Pontifex Maximus and he has pointedly not condemned Varro's version of the events of that terrible day. And then there is the not inconsiderable issue of hundreds of surviving cavalry officers who are also desperate to save their names and reputations." *Including Prisca's husband*, I reminded myself.

Lepidus made a sound of disgust in his throat. "Nevertheless, they should not do it by dishonoring the true hero! The man who refused to leave his men when given the chance!" Lepidus' face flushed an almost purple red. "Not at the cost of my family's name and reputation. We are patricians!"

I agreed with him. That was the hardest part. It gave me small comfort to know that Attius had not been abandoned by his general. But if the Pontifex Maximus and the majority of the surviving Senate agreed to "keep the peace" by not pushing back on Varro's version of events, there was little I could do.

"I promise to continue speaking the truth when the false story is spoken in my presence and to continue defending your family name," I managed. I could hear the weakness of it and it embarrassed me.

Lepidus nodded but by the slump of his shoulders, I could tell I'd disappointed him. He'd wanted a firmer promise. Perhaps he even hoped I would publicly stand against the pontiff and the Maxima.

How could I explain that even speaking the truth privately was dangerous—that if I dared publicly contradict my religious elders, I would be declaring war on those who controlled my fate. Steeped in my own private grief, I could not muster the will to fight.

As Lepidus left our meeting, I warned him to be careful. If he continued angering Varro's supporters in the Senate, he might find himself targeted in some way. It was a wonder that I sensed his vulnerability, but had no inkling of my own. "Hire a scribe to write down a true accounting of your uncle's heroism at Cannae," I suggested. "Having a written record of events will protect your family's name and legacy in the long run. The truth must be preserved."

***

With Ketet on her way safely to Prisca's home, it was imperative I made it to the temple for Tuccia's sieve but the mob, in its frenzy of rage, had grown and blocked the front steps. I considered sneaking around the back and entering through the storage area but if I were caught, I had no doubt they would tear me apart like crazed maenads.

Guards barked commands to clear the area so there was still hope. If they successfully herded everyone back to the open-air court, I could slip inside undetected. Pacing through the halls, I tried to gain control of my breathing. As I made another pass through the atrium, I felt someone emerge from the shadows behind me. Assuming it was one of the servants, I said nothing.

"Oh, I am wounded by your lack of regard," came an oily male voice.

No man other than the pontiff was allowed in the House of Vestals. I whirled around, surprised. My insides dropped as if I'd jumped off a great height. "Cantilius. You know you are not allowed to enter these sacred halls." I wanted to scream, *Go away, I need to think.*

He snorted and waved a hand. "My uncle allows it."

As the pontiff's secretary and nephew, Cantilius acted as if he had the same rights as the head priest of Rome. He did not, yet the pontiff never interceded on our behalf. Despite the fact that Floronia and I had both—verbally and in writing—complained about his sudden appearances in our halls, and the lecherous looks he seemed to reserve only for the two youngest Vestals, nothing had ever been done. We were told that he was harmless and that we should ignore him.

I continued walking and he extended his stride to match mine. My back prickled with distaste. Cantilius, like his uncle, was stout with a round face and dark, curly fur covering his arms, peeking up from his shoulders in the back of his tunic.

"This is not a good day for you, is it my dear?" he said as a roar echoed toward us like a bad dream. I made a quick turn into the darkened hallway near the Maxima's tablinium. I was not sure she was in her office, but even Cantilius quaked in her presence. It might be enough to shake him off.

"You need to leave," I said. "I am headed to the Maxima's office. She is waiting for me."

"I 'need' not do anything I do not want to do," he said, inspecting me from head to foot—lingering on my chest—and I increased my pace.

"You should not be walking around unattended," he warned in a mocking way. "Now that you have been sullied, someone might see it as their right to take what has already been given away."

Is he threatening me?

The man always managed to say things in ways that made him seem innocent when challenged. After all, with Ketet gone, what he said was technically true. I was alone, which was always dangerous for women, even us priestesses. But not in this house. A flare of rage burst in my chest, but I tamped it down and walked with even more purpose toward the Maxima's tablinium.

Even so, I could feel his lascivious gaze travel all over me as he caught up. He made a disgusting sound in his throat. But he had to know that touching even an accused Vestal meant death for him.

"You should leave," I said coldly. "Lest someone accuse you of impiety. I assume you do not desire to be whipped to death and thrown from the Tarpeian Rock." Again, he snorted. "I am untouchable. My uncle will never allow anything to happen to me."

He moved closer and, thankfully, that was the moment I turned the corner leading to the Maxima's office. "I apologize for my tardiness, Maxima," I called loudly. "I will be right there!"

That froze him. He had never been lecherous to me or Floronia in front of the powerful old lady and he was not about to begin now. He melted away behind me, returning, I presumed, to whatever slimehole he'd crawled out of. I entered the room adjoining the Maxima's study—a small scroll room—slammed the door and called out a greeting as if I really were with the head Vestal.

But I was alone. And in the dark. When I did not hear footsteps approaching, I released a slow breath. No woman, not even the most sacred priestess, was safe from men like Cantilius, who presumed they had the right to comment on our bodies and make sexual insinuations. And if we called him out for his behavior, he would claim innocence and accuse us of being too sensitive.

In the silence, my eyes slowly adjusted to the darkened small room which smelled of decaying writing skins and ancient papyri. Why, I wondered, did the gods take a good man like Attius, and leave men like Cantilius? The man slimed everything he touched, including a young Attius, for which I would never forgive him. It was because of Cantilius that Attius joined the legions. If he had joined the cavalry as was his right as an equite, he might have survived, like Prisca's husband. But he was desperate to get far from Cantilius.

***

Four Years Before

The day I learned that Cantilius would play an outsized role in Attius' life was the day I understood what true powerlessness meant.

As we'd grown older, our ability to make it to the wood at the same time became increasingly rare, so when it happened, it felt like a gift from the gods. That day, I found Attius sitting at the base of a tree dozing, his dog was curled up by his side, muzzle fluttering as he snored. Upon sensing me, the dog thwapped his tail but he was clearly too comfortable to move and did not raise his head.

"Lazy bag of bones," I whispered, grinning at him. "You truly are Useless." After my intimacies with Prisca, Attius' physicality was a constant fascination. His dark curls—glimmering with strands of bronze in the dappled sunlight—reached to his shoulders. His lips were slightly parted and his hands were loose in his lap. I drank him in. An overwhelming sense of "wanting" filled my senses. I wanted to press my nose to his neck and smell his skin. I ached to trace a fingertip against the sharp line of his lips separating the pink flesh. I wanted to grab his curls. I wanted to bite and taste him. I wanted every part of him. But that was all that I would ever have—the wanting.

He opened his eyes and we both jumped. "You scared me," we said at the same time.

Attius swallowed and cleared his throat. "Sorry." He rubbed his eyes like a child and for a moment he was both the young boy I first met in the country and the about-to-be-a-man Attius at once. "I have some good news," he said. "I have chosen a mentor."

My chest constricted. *No, no, too many changes.* Getting a mentor meant he would be tied politically to a man who would eventually become his patron, cementing his ties to Rome, and a future that required he marry and have a family. "I thought you weren't going to get one because you didn't want any part of the Cursus Honorum," I said. The Cursus Honorum was the ladder of political service and advancement all Roman men traversed if they wanted a political career. "I thought you were going to go to Greece to study philosophy."

Attius sighed. "Thanks to Hannibal's invasion, I cannot leave Rome. And I must serve in the military. According to my pater, only by entering the Cursus Honorum will I get aligned with a family with ties to an elite officer rather than one from the lower ranks."

Goddess, I didn't want to think about him fighting Hannibal! But it was inevitable, wasn't it? All Roman men would eventually be required to do so. And if his new patron ensured him greater safety in the inner circles of high-ranking officers, then that was a good thing.

Still, my skin crawled, as if I sensed the ugliness of what was to come. In the moment, I ascribed it to jealousy. I didn't want to share Attius with anyone. Especially a suave older man who might steal his affections. It was well-known that these mentoring relationships— where an older man guided the education and career of a young teen— often became sexual. In those cases, the youth was referred to as the eronomos (beloved) and the older man as the erastes (the lover). These arrangements were a rite of passage in the upper classes and ambitious youths often competed fiercely for the men who would give their families the best political advantage.

"I didn't know you were in search of a mentor," I said, twisting my hands. Again I reminded him that he always said he never wanted a political career, so why do it?

153

Attius sighed. "Because my father commands it."

I wanted to insist that he disobey his father, but I knew it would be foolish. He could not. The pater familias had full rights over the lives of everyone in his household and by law, Attius had to comply by the dictates of his father. Still, a flash of fear over losing him swept through me. While it was against Roman law for men to have sex with other men, it was not against the law for an older man to have sex with a youth who had yet to grow his beard or go through a formal "manhood" ceremony. Some youths fell deeply in love with their mentors. Over the years I had counseled many mothers of sons who were in great distress after being sexually rejected by their mentors once they'd grown to manhood.

Despair and jealousy warred in my belly, and I shifted on the stump I'd folded myself onto. "Who is this man?" I finally managed.

"A powerful patrician," he said. "My father is very happy because it is such a great honor, but I am not so sure."

"What is his name?"

"Lucius Cantilius."

My stomach clenched.

"What is that face?" he asked, his brow furrowing.

"Nothing. It is merely… well, I know him."

"And?"

How could I explain his odiousness?

"He is the Pontifex Maximus' nephew," I said. "And he serves him as secretary." I didn't add that Cantilius acted as if his connection to the most powerful priest in Rome gave him special rights, including entering our House of Vestals at will. Even when we complained about his sudden appearances, the pontiff did not discipline him, calling him harmless. Only Cantilius' fear of the Maxima's rage kept him in check.

"What are you not telling me?" he asked. When I didn't answer, he added, "Is Lucius Cantilius unkind to you?"

"No. Are… are you alright with the nature the relationship may take?" I asked looking down, feeling my face flush. It was borderline impious for me to ask such a personal question, but I had to know. The idea of him being touched by the odious man made my skin crawl.

"We have spoken about my desire to keep matters… political only. He took no offense at my words and swore he would never take someone who is unwilling." He too flushed and did not meet my eyes.

"Ah," I said but my uneasiness increased. How well I knew Cantilius' penchant for ignoring rules and standards.

Sensing my concern, Attius added, "Lucius said several times I might change my mind once we begin working together."

Lucius. Already. "And that troubles you?"

"No, no," he said. "After all, it is possible. I am told that once taken under an older man's wing, feelings change. I have more than one friend who has fallen in love with his mentor."

No, no, you can't fall in love with anyone else, I screamed inside my head. And especially not with someone as vile as Cantilius.

"There is more news," he said. "Part of the arrangement involves me being betrothed to Cantilius' youngest sister. Her dowry will allow me to enter the patrician class."

The air went out of my chest. I knew Attius would marry someday, of course I did. But it always seemed an idea to consider "someday." A huge welling of envy—*why couldn't it be me?*—and rage—*how dare you leave me to live your life?*—made my vision go blurry and I swallowed hard.

"Congratulations," I managed. "Do you… do you like this girl?"

He shrugged and squinted into the distance. "She is only eleven so it will be at least five years before we marry."

"Sixteen is still too young," I blurted.

He nodded absently.

"Do you like this girl?" I tried again.

He shrugged, looking at his fingers as he picked apart a fallen leaf. "She is very quiet. She seems timid."

"She is likely awestruck to be arranged to one such as you." A strange tightness closed my throat and I could say no more. I wanted to brush a curl off his neck. I wanted to touch his skin. I wanted and I knew I should not want, which only made me want with a deeper, piercing ache.

"It's you who I want to be with," he said softly. "If it were up to me, we would run away together this very moment and live in the country where no one could find us. Orion and Diana forever running freely through our woods."

"We would hunt together and grow our own food," I said, warming to the familiar fantasy we repeated every time we were together in the grove.

"And have chickens and cows and make our own wine," he added.

"And have kennels full of Useless' puppies," I said, scratching the dog behind his ears.

We stared at the ground in silence. "Let's do it, let's run away," he said quickly. "I hate Rome. I don't want this life. We should be in the country together and not apart in this crowded, ugly city. I don't want to be tied to a man and a family that lords their status over mine…," he trailed off.

Goddess but he looked so beautiful and vulnerable. The pull of him was so strong, I had to avert my gaze. "I wish I could run," I said.

"You can," he said. "We could disappear. Maybe we could go north to Feoria, where the land is supposed to be rich. Nobody would think to look for us there."

I shook my head.

"But why? You are not happy in this life, are you?"

"No I am not."

"This could be our only chance," he said. "Once I am tied to my mentor's family, disappearing will be that much more difficult."

"I wish I could. I want to," I said. "But I cannot risk it." The relentless indoctrination by the Maxima and the Pontifex Maximus about the consequences of my misbehavior had sunk deep into my bones.

I had taken a risk with my intimacies with Prisca, but only after being convinced that I broke no rules and even the older Vestals enjoyed such arrangements. But running away? Loving him physically? That was unthinkable, no matter how much I dreamed of such a thing.

"I have been considering this for some time and I've analyzed every possible problem we could face and how to get around them all," Attius said, speaking quickly and leaning forward. "We start with dressing you as a tradeswoman or taverna owner. No one will recognize you out of your Vestal whites. We will go north instead of south as everyone will assume we would go back to Capua—"

"You don't understand," I interrupted. "I want to. More than anything. But if I break my vows, if I don't serve the entire thirty years, the gods will punish Rome with some calamity. I... I could not bear being responsible for inflicting pain and sorrow on the innocent. I cannot knowingly cause suffering."

He ran his fingers through the top of his curls in exasperation. "Oh Mia. It's not true. None of it is true."

"What do you mean?"

"Everything! All of this," he said, touching the white fabric of my headdress. "How could Rome's safety be dependent on what one girl does?"

157

Larce's old words—the gods are not swayed by the tantrums of little girls—echoed in my head. While that may have been true for ordinary girls or women, I had been told every single day, for more than a decade, that the gods cared very much about the status of my purity. So much so that they would smite us all if I dared disobey. While there was still a part of me that pushed back against such a notion, the fear that it could be true kept me from daring to take any action.

After a long silence, Attius said, "I have been studying the works of Epicurus. Do you know who he is?"

My eyes widened and I nodded. I had heard of the philosopher but we were forbidden to read any of his writings. The Maxima railed against Epicurus' assertion that the only path to peace was to avoid pain; that the key to happiness was to focus on the pleasures of life—in moderation. She always missed the moderation part. She heard the word "pleasure" and dismissed it all as wanton, weak, un-Roman, and dangerous, especially for us virgins.

"Well, he writes about a paradox that reminds me of some of the conversations we've had about the gods."

Curious, I leaned forward, urging him to continue.

"It's called the 'Epicurean Paradox' and it goes something like this: Is God willing to prevent evil, but not able? Then he is not omnipotent. Is he able, but not willing? Then he is malevolent. Is he both able and willing? Then whence come evil? Is he neither able nor willing? Then why call him God?"

Attius looked at me expectantly. Clearly, these questions had captured his imagination, but I could barely breathe. Could he not see how dangerous they were? He could be prosecuted for sacrilege! "You must never say these things, especially around Cantilius," I cautioned. "Remember, he is related to the Pontifex. If you anger him, he could accuse you of impiety." Which meant a death sentence.

He blew out air. "My point is that if you slow down and really think through what we are force-fed about the gods—especially you—we might be able to see the fallacies more clearly."

"I do nothing but 'think' through these questions—by my very actions, every day," I replied with growing irritation. "I cannot afford to play semantical games on these matters. Don't you see? If there is a chance that any of it is true, then I am obligated to do what I can to protect others!"

He tore his fingers more violently through the top of his hair again, making his curls stand even higher. It was ridiculous and adorable. "To order your life around something that *may* be true… it is impossible…" He stopped. Sighed. Closed his eyes. "If the gods were real, they would most assuredly hate me because I can't seem to extricate myself from a life I do not want."

"You could deny your father and not enter the Cursus Honorus," I pointed out. "You could deny the betrothal." And run from Cantilius.

He shook his head. "My pater is depending on this alliance. The weight of my family's future is on my shoulders."

As branches and leaves rustled above us and birds called to each other in our small wood, we stared morosely at the ground.

"I dream of you sometimes," Attius whispered after a long silence.

"What do you dream?"

A flush spread up his neck. "That we are together in the woods. Where no one can find us."

"How I wish," I murmured.

My fingers slowly pulled apart a leaf. To my surprise, he draped his hand over mine. His fingers were long and graceful, like a kithara player's. The soft touch was so unexpected, so surprising, I gasped and froze.

When his thumb rubbed the tops of my knuckles, he said, "See? Nothing happens. Jupiter has not sent a lightning bolt to destroy us because we have touched."

The warmth of his hand on mine was a revelation.

"May I kiss you?" he whispered. "I dream of kissing you."

I knew I should say no. That the right thing was to get up and walk away. But a storm of defiance swelled in my chest. So, with my gaze still on his hand, I nodded. Slowly, so slowly, he moved closer and lifted my chin. I closed my eyes. His lips lightly brushed mine. It felt nice at first—soft and sweet—and I felt a familiar honeyed loosening in my belly, just as I had felt when Prisca kissed me that first time. He did it again, pressing harder against me, lingering, and suddenly all of my senses seemed to overload at once—the smell of his sun-warmed skin, the sight of his lashes over his cheeks, his hair curling at the nape of his neck, the soft press of his lips and a soft, wet tongue touching my bottom lip. I opened my mouth a little and he made a little sound deep in his throat. Then there was the warmth and feel of his tongue—his tongue!—in my mouth.

I shivered and pulled away.

His face was flushed and I imagined mine was too. I wanted to hold him tight to me, I wanted to run away, I wanted to scream, I wanted to put my hands on his warm skin, I wanted his hand, his whole body between my legs… Goddess! What had I done?

I scrambled up and stared at him wide-eyed. He looked up confused and hurt and the moment hung between us like a long-drawn out discordant musical note. I was frozen between wanting to soothe the hurt on his face away with kisses and race to the temple for purification lest my actions bring down the wrath of the gods. The spell was broken when he stood and reached out for me. "I cannot," I whispered. "Terrible things may happen…"

"They won't," he said. "It's not true."

"I'm sorry," I said. And ran, panicked.

Was I still pure? I had not lain with a man, I reminded myself. Kissing a boy was not the same thing. Thoughts were not actions. I could not allow myself the luxury of thinking otherwise. But the danger was real—I wanted more. I wanted him. Did the gods know my heart? Would they punish me for my desires for Attius, even as they ignored the love I had shared with Prisca? Everything seemed jumbled and overwhelming. The only recourse, it seemed to me, was to repurify myself and avoid Attius, to avoid temptation. I ran as if my veil was on fire.

Months later, when I saw Attius accompanying Cantilius, I was shocked at the change in him. I'd been sent to the pontiff's tablinium to research an old ruling on a change to a religious rite when I heard Cantilius' voice. I was about to jump up and shut the door, but then I heard Attius respond. Hoping to catch a glimpse of him, I kept my head down as their steps approached. A shadow fell over the table and I looked up pretending to be startled.

"Ah, the youngest of our virgins," Cantilius said in his usual oily way.

"Good afternoon," I managed.

"What are you doing in my uncle's tablinium?" he asked.

That he would question me when I was a consecrated priestess and he was nothing more than an underling! I swallowed the irritation back as always. "The Maxima sent me to research a ruling," I said. Despite myself, my eyes flicked toward Attius and although I knew I must pretend to have never met him, my lips quirked in a flash of a smile in greeting.

"Ah, yes, 'The Smiling Virgin,'" Cantilius said. "Doing so at handsome boys could get you in trouble, my dear."

"I wasn't smiling," I said.

161

"This is my protégé, Attius Tullius Corionalus. His father hails from Capua, probably near your family's winery estate, yes?"

"That name is indeed familiar," I noted.

"Surely, you must have met," Cantilius said.

"It is possible," I said nonchalantly. "But if we had, we would have been very young—well before I joined the order of Vesta."

"I remember meeting your parents, but not you, priestess," Attius said in a dull voice. His tone was so deadened and unhappy, I couldn't help but look more closely at him. He looked wan and seemed somehow... defeated.

"Please excuse my protégé's truculent attitude," Cantilius said, waving his hand dismissively. "He is acting quite spoiled today."

A flash of something—hate? disgust?—moved over Attius' face. When Cantilius looked at him, though, Attius' expression was blank if not slightly bored.

"I am giving my young man here a tour of the pontiff's offices," he said. "It is rare for a youngling of his background to get so close to the seats of power." One of the pontiff's junior priests walked by and Cantilius perked up. "Wait here," he commanded Attius, as he scuttled away. "Junius," he called. "Let us discuss what you owe me after last week's chariot races..."

They turned a corner and I looked at Attius. "You seem... unhappy," I whispered as he moved in closer.

"That's because I am," he whispered back. "I hate Lucius Cantilius. And I am unable to do anything about it."

I didn't want to ask. I did not want to know. But nor could I sit silent in the face of Attius' suffering. "Does he... hurt you?" I whispered.

Attius nodded once, not looking at me. It was as I had feared. Cantilius was forcing Attius into being his eronomos—raping him—and he could do nothing about it. I sensed his anger and shame, and I knew anything I might say would make him feel even more powerless and trapped. The romanticized version of these relationships painted a picture of mutual attachment. Older men always claimed the youth had all the power because the young man selected the mentor and set the physical boundaries. But in reality, only one side had the ability to make or break a young man's political future. Which meant only one side had all the power. And Cantilius was most certainly the type of man who would abuse any scrap of power he amassed.

"Could you not complain to…"

"To whom?" he asked desperately, still whispering. "My father is thrilled we have allied to his powerful family. To any of my friend's mentors? They would decline to do anything lest they embarrass a man from such a powerful and connected patrician family. I am trapped."

"I read about a legal case once where a man was sued for taking a young man against his will. The accuser won."

"You don't understand," Attius said. "He is too powerful. Everyone would take his word over mine and call me ungrateful. I would succeed only in injuring my family's status and angering all of the other powerful patricians in his circle. And I would forever be marked as a traitor or as an effete for daring to complain."

"But surely he would stop if he knew how unhappy you wer—"

He laughed bitterly. "He takes pleasure in causing pain and unhappiness," he said. "I do not know how to explain. He is doing what he does because I asked him not to." He blushed and looked down again. "I… I know he prefers women. He has filled his household with slave girls to satisfy his needs."

This made no sense to me. "Then why do this to you?"

"Because he can. Because it humiliates me. Because he likes having that kind of power over me. And now he's told my father to delay my manhood ceremony."

"What? Why would he do that?" I asked.

Attius' face worked as he mastered his rage. "Because it is my only way out. Once I don the toga of manhood, he cannot touch me. It's against the law for a man to take another man."

I knew the rules—men could take boys, girls, women, and slaves with impunity, but the law forbade grown men from loving another grown man of the same or higher status as that supposedly compromised the dignitas of both. As a youth, Attius had no means to stop Cantilius. As a man, he had the law behind him. So delaying his manhood ceremony was especially cruel.

"He can't do this," I cried. "Only your father can decide when you are fit for the manhood ceremony."

"Cantilius has convinced my father to delay it because of the threat of Hannibal. Pater doesn't want me to go to war yet. And since my beard has not come in, I cannot push the point."

Attius rubbed his cheeks angrily. I had noticed some boy's beards came in early and how proud they were to be named men after their first shave. It had never occurred to me how awful it was for the young men who by nature had smooth cheeks long past the time their friends could shave and were called men. "He knows exactly what I was trying to avoid and now laughs at me for it."

"Gods!"

Cantilius' unctuous voice echoed in the hall and we both froze. "I would hate to add interest to what you already owe me," he called out in a threatening sing-song tone to the departing priest. Attius stepped out of the room and leaned against the wall as if bored and I turned toward the wall of scrolls. "What are you doing out here, boy?" Cantilius sneered. "You should be enjoying the view."

Not understanding his meaning, I turned to see him leering at me. His gaze traveled from my head down to my toes and back up again.

It was a slow, disrespectful gaze that lingered on my chest for an uncomfortably long time. He met my eyes with a wolfish grin as I instinctively pulled a leather scroll case over me like a shield. Attius' fists tightened and his jaw flexed. Before he could step forward, I said, "I must return to my work. May Vesta bless you," turning my back to them, silently praying Attius would not react to the man's boorishness. I prayed too for Diana to help Attius escape his trap. I should have been more careful about what I asked of the goddess.

Many moons later, my heart leaped to see Attius enter the Egerian grove via his secret path. He smiled when he saw me approaching and the dappled sun dancing over his skin made him so beautiful, I had to look away.

"Where is Useless?" I asked. I missed the dog.

Attius huffed. "Cantilius hates him and insists I leave him home. Listen. I've made a decision. I found a way to break from Cantilius."

"How?"

"I am joining the legions."

My lungs squeezed. "What? I don't understand…"

"With Hannibal in the north and our armies still fighting in Spain, I will likely be conscripted soon anyway. The Senate is desperate to arm up."

"You will join the cavalry?" As an eques, this was his right. And his alliance with Cantilius was meant to funnel him into the higher echelons of service.

He shook his head. "As a legionnaire. An infantry-man."

"What? Why would you do such a thing?" Legionnaires were usually from the plebian or working class. Why would he want to make himself more vulnerable on the ground?

"If I stay or follow through as an equite, Cantilius will send me to one of his corrupt cronies and I'd be even more beholden to him and gods only know what kind of man he'd send me to. But if I sign up as a fighter in the legions, I am my own man. And who could argue against my love of Rome and my patriotism?"

"But don't you need your father's permission?" The delay in his manhood ceremony I thought was to keep him away from battle and in Rome a bit longer. Attius grinned excitedly and paced under the tree. "The Senate changed the rules to encourage recruits. If you volunteer to fight before they conscript you, father's approval or not, you are considered a man as decreed by the state. Instead of handing over my bulla to my father, I will surrender it to my military commander, and be designated a man," he said, fingering the small leather pouch that marked him as a boy who needed special protection from evil.

"So you are tricking your family to get away from your mentor," I finally managed.

"Yes. It will be worth it. And I am not formally breaking our connection. But as a man, Cantilius won't be able to touch me," he said. "And I will have some power."

My hands twisted and I stared at him. This was the moment I knew would come one day—when I'd lose him. I had not imagined, however, it would be so soon. Or it would be in a way that could mean his death.

"What will this mean to your betrothal arrangement?"

"I do not care," he said shrugging. "I hope Cantilius ends it. I would rather not be tied to that family for the rest of my life anyway."

"When are you planning to do this?"

"Tomorrow. I'm assuming my training will begin here, but I may be sent south to train in one of the outposts. I've heard recruits are needed there to keep our Latin and Etruscan partners in check. We do not want them rebelling and going over to Hannibal as have so many of our northern allies."

My stomach clenched.

Attius' smile faded as he looked at me. "What is that face? I thought you would be happy I found a way to free myself from Cantilius the Slimy."

"I am happy you have found a way to escape him. I am not happy you may lose your life in war. Nor am I happy about you demeaning your family's status by signing up as a standard soldier."

He looked down, took my hand in both of his, and brought it up to kiss. "I'll serve my time and come back to you when you are free and we will marry and build our lives in the country like we were supposed to."

How much I wanted that! But I still had many years to serve. And he had his whole life before him.

"Attius, you know you must marry and start a family long before I am free," I finally managed.

"But I am breaking tradition, don't you see? I found a way around their rules. And because I will be but a lowly soldier, no family of status will want me marrying their daughter, including Cantilius' family. I have worked it all out. I will either convince you to run away with me after I return from war, or I will wait for you."

My throat grew tight as I looked up into his shining eyes. I wanted to tell him he was being silly, that he needed to forget about me, to live his life, fall in love, marry and have children, and live on a farm as we'd always dreamed. I could not form the words. Instead, I touched the curls reaching his shoulders. "They will cut all this off, won't they?"

"I do not care."

"I do," I murmured. I grabbed a handful of his hair and roughly brought his mouth down to mine. My hunger for him was so intense I would have lain with him right there in the sacred grove if I could have. Within moments we were both panting as we pressed hard against each other.

Attius stilled and pulled back, his eyes wide. I heard it too—Ketet's warning whistle. Someone was nearing the spring.

"You will come see me before you leave for training? Promise me."

He smiled. "Tomorrow. Here. At the same time."

He kissed me below my ear and whispered, "I love you," and was gone.

***

Chapter Eleven

Coiled and silent in the dark room to avoid Cantilius, I shook my head at the intrusion of painful memories. How I wanted to punish that snake for what he did to Attius. If not for Attius' desperate need to get away from his abuses, he might have served alongside some of the men in Varro's cavalry. He might have even survived, like Prisca's husband.

Focus. I had to take action and get that sieve. The mob seemed quieter. Perhaps the guards had succeeded in moving the masses back to the courtroom, preparing for the court to resume. Which meant I likely did not have a lot of time. Making sure the hall was clear of Cantilius, I moved quickly to the kitchen where I grabbed a small burlap bag on Zena's table. My plan was to slide the ancient relic into the sack and keep it hidden under my palla until just the right moment.

The surprise of my actions would, I hoped, keep the pontiff and the other priests off balance long enough that they would be forced to accept my performance of the "miracle"—the mob loved a whiff of the supernatural—and would be moved by proof of it. I could be on my way to the Tiber before they realized I had Tuccia's sieve. Even if they suspected what I was up to, they would not dare take the sieve away from me in front of so many witnesses. The risk was too great. They might expose themselves for all to see just how cynical and unfaithful they were. It would ruin their performance of piety.

As I neared the temple steps, I was suddenly surrounded by lictors.

"We are to escort you to the court now," one of them said. "The Court Chairman has confirmed the manumission of your freedwoman as filed in the government records office and demands the trial's resumption immediately."

"I need something in the Temple. It will only be a moment. You will wait here," I commanded, walking around him. Two other lictors blocked my way.

"What is in that bag?" the head lictor said suspiciously. To my utter amazement, he ripped it from my hand, managing to do so without touching me. "No weapons are allowed in the court."

"There is nothing in there," I cried.

"What are you going to get in the temple then?" the other one asked.

"None of your business," I snapped back. When I saw them exchange meaningful looks, I realized, unbelievably, that they thought I was going into the Sacred Temple of Vesta to make off with a weapon! I would laugh if only I could breathe. "Vestals are forbidden from spilling or even touching blood and the Temple of Vesta has nothing that can be used to hurt anyone," I said, trying to keep my voice steady.

The crowd watching us grew restless. Many seemed alarmed. Great. Now rumors would spread that I had threatened violence. All the more reason to hate me. Yet I had to get that sieve! "This is ridiculous. Give me back the bag and leave me to my business in the Temple. It will only take a moment!"

A roar echoed from the court indicating the mob's growing restlessness. The head lictor shook his head. "Our orders are clear. We are to escort you to the court. Immediately."

My heart pounded in my ears as I considered my options. I could grab the bag and run up the steps to the temple—where they cannot follow me—but this will likely alarm the crowd watching us. And the guards would demand to know the contents and then everyone would know my plan. Especially the pontiff. He would know what I wanted to do and would stop me.

"Fine," I said through gritted teeth. Though not ideal, I could still demand the right to perform the miracle without the sieve in hand. *Dear Goddess, make it so.* I opened and closed my hands to relieve the tension of not having the sieve in my possession. *Stay calm. Breathe.*

The howls of hate increased as I took my seat. The crowd had been primed. They had not gotten blood from Ketet—nor a man's name— and they were thirsting for a catharsis of some kind.

"Name him now."

"Name him now. Remove them both!"

"There is no time. Cleanse us now!"

The court chairman banged his staff and demanded order. The chords in his neck bulged but because the crowd was so loud, I could not hear his words. His face reddened and he slammed his staff of office even harder on the plinth.

It took many, many tries to quiet the crowd. "We must obtain the name of the defiler *legally*," the chairman roared and the crowd finally quieted. "There is a *legal* process we must follow. By rule of law, we could not torture the accused's freedwoman and so must legally obtain the name of the accused in other ways. Do not forget—Justitia, the goddess of justice is watching our every move. We dare not anger her too! When we have legally obtained a name, we will announce it!"

Now they cared about justice? They were prepared to send me to my death without a trial!

What did it mean that they were not naming a man yet? Grabbing Ketet for torture indicated they were ready to accuse someone. Had the delay caused more infighting? How could I use this?

The mob continued to murmur for the head of the man with whom I broke my vows, but the threat of angering yet another god brought them to heel. The chairman's words left me wondering if they were torturing another slave for a name. Their accusation had to seem indisputable. And what could be more compelling than to display the broken, tortured dead body of a slave who finally "surrendered" a name with his or her last breath?

"I request to speak," I called, standing tall. But the chairman didn't hear me as people began yelling at my sudden movement.

Again, I called to the chairman. "I have the means to prove my innocence," I yelled, but people booed and stomped and it was clear he hadn't heard me or understood.

"I can prove my innocence this very moment with spiritual proof," I yelled even louder but the chairman's attention was diverted by the prosecutor, who signaled him. Using his practiced stentorian bellow, Manlius overwhelmed my calls with this: "Until the accused debaucher is identified and summoned, I have yet more evidence to prove she is the cause of the ire of the gods."

The crowd moaned and stomped.

"*Tell us! What depths of evil has she summoned?*"

"*The virgin must die! Remove her now!*"

Once again it was clear to me that the mob was enjoying this. The display of frenzied emotion—one minute crying for blood, another overflowing with righteous indignation—seemed like a dangerous fire that could burst out of its grate and devour us all. The roar of their shouts rolled over the open-air courtroom like a sudden burst of grumbling heat lightning, drowning out my appeals to use the sieve. I waved to get the chairman's attention. "Wait, I demand the right to prove my innocence—"

The red-faced chairman whirled on me. "It is still the prosecutor's turn to show his evidence," he screamed at me, exasperated. "You will have a turn to defend yourself. And it is not yet that time."

"But I have a spiritu—"

"Silence!" he thundered. "If you continue to break protocol, I will have you removed. Do you understand? Now sit down!"

He chastised me as if I were a child and the humiliation sent a hot warmth up my neck to my cheeks. The mob loved it and began a new chant.

"Sit down. Shut up! Save us from her impiety! Sit down. Shut up! Save us from her evil!"

"I insist on proving my innocence in the way of our ancestors—"

"You already tried that," the pontiff roared, likely thinking I was making another appeal to prove my innocence with the snakes at the Temple of Juno. "And it was denied."

"No, this is diff—"

"Lictors, remove her from the court!" the chairman yelled.

The mob roared with excitement as people pushed and climbed over each to witness my humiliation. I sat. "I withdraw my comment," I called out desperately. "Until it be my appointed time to speak."

The chairman stared at me with narrowed eyes. The crowd hooted at my capitulation as I forced myself to bend my neck slightly in acquiescence even though I wanted to take his staff and ram it through the underside of his chin.

"Good," he muttered. "Prosecutor, you may proceed," he called, sweeping his arm toward Manlius in an exaggerated way. I forced myself to breathe slowly, raising my chin, despite the continued hoots of derision thrown my way.

"Thank you," Manlius said as he gave the chairman a slight bow. "For my final witness I call to the chair, Aulus Postumius Albinus, former esteemed consul and Flamen Maritialis, priest of Mars, He Who Serves the God of War."

There was respectful applause but, to my surprise, a fairly large smattering of hissing and grumbling.

"He is the one who has angered Mars," someone shouted from the edges of the courtroom. "Not some priestess!"

Others joined in. "*Yes, yes. The priest of the war god is at fault. His arrogance forced Mars to leave the fields at Cannae!*"

My chest swelled with hope but then I deflated just as suddenly when I saw the majority of the crowd turn on those who sought to hold the priest of war accountable.

"*Liar. You fool. Now is not the time to insult the servant of the unpredictable and rageful god of war!*"

Like a shoal of silver fish moving as one, the mob immediately turned back to their hatred of me.

The priest of Mars stood and moved through the Collegium of Priests to make his way to the center of the court like a wolf calmly trotting toward his prey. My stomach lurched at his appearance, for he carried power well. As former consul and general in the first wars with Carthage, he exuded an air of confidence and command. One could imagine Albinus shouting orders to the army in a victorious rout, a feat he accomplished against our enemy in his last military command nearly two decades ago. The last time we'd enjoyed a decisive victory over Carthage. But that was before Hannibal marched his elephants and armies over the Alps.

As Albinus made his way to the center of the court, people reached out to touch him. One man rubbed the priest's toga as he passed and then touched his forehead and his chest. He breathed deeper and stood straighter, as if some of the former general's power had somehow strengthened him. It took everything I had not to roll my eyes.

Albinus walked as if he were marching in a military parade—straight-backed, eyes forward. He wore the leather cap of his office pushed off his forehead like a general surveying the field. His somber craggy face and his jutting beard exuded command.

Manilus began as soon as the priest took his seat. "Tell us, esteemed general, consul and priest—why you assert that this Vestal, of all our Sacred Servants, could be the only one responsible for angering the gods in this way."

The priest straightened his shoulders. "Her crime goes beyond the breaking of her vows," he said and the entire courtroom leaned forward like hungry beasts at feeding time—all to hear the juicy details of my horribleness.

"Before Cannae, the Collegium of the priests of Rome, had—after following the correct spiritual protocols, including consulting the Sibylline Books—determined to revive an ancient rite to mollify and appease the gods," he said. "Especially Mars, the god of war. Her insolence deprived the god of the sacrifice he demanded and we all suffered for it! And will continue to suffer for it until she is removed and we are purified of her stain."

The crowd went wild. *"Remove her now! The Vestal must die!"*

"That is not true, I object," I yelled, but the chairman waved a hand in my direction, shushing me. I seethed at the insult. I stood and spoke anyway. "The rite he demanded be changed is older than Rome itself. I did nothing more than ask questions—"

"You introduced doubt into the proceedings," Albinus yelled back, his face engorging with rage. "The god of war was clear. You inserted yourself into the business of men and ruined it all!"

The mob roared. This I had not expected. I had not realized just how much the priest of Mars hated me. He was deliberately NOT describing the rite he wanted to change, likely because it would disgust the mob the same way it had disgusted me.

Do I expose him or will he somehow turn it around on me?

The priest of Mars now stood, theatrically extending his right arm—the folds of his toga wavering on his scarred yet still strong forearm—and pointed a finger at me.

"The god of war wanted us to perform one of our most ancient primitive rites in the way it was done in the days of Romulus and Remus. The god of war was incensed with Fabius' womanly delays in not attacking Hannibal. We were turning into women. He demanded Roman men act like men and handle the invader the Roman way— through blood and annihilation. But once again, this one inserted her female perspective into conversations she had no business in and muddied the waters. The god Mars was angry and we lost. Because of HER!"

The courtroom erupted with wails of disgust and outrage. Once again, I was dismayed that they could accuse me of having that much power. I was a junior priestess of Vesta. How was the annihilation of our armies my fault? The unfairness—the bewilderment that they believed that I was both worthless and sullied and yet, at the same time, powerful enough to sway the god of war, left me speechless.

"It is not true," I called out. But my voice was drowned out in the melee. As the accumulated rage over the tragedy broke over me like a great wave, I wondered whether I was on trial for breaking my vow of chastity, or for daring to speak on the "matters of men."

***

Eighteen Months Earlier

A year before Cannae, we Vestal virgins created and assembled twenty-seven effigies—life-sized straw men—and placed them in special Argei shrines throughout the city for an ancient spring rite of cleansing. Throughout Rome, the effigies absorbed all the sins, misdeeds, and pollution of the people in that region or district. A month later, on the ides of May, we traveled to all of the shrines in a solemn procession and collected every polluted "being." We then took them to the oldest bridge in Rome and ceremoniously tossed each one to their ritual deaths into the Tiber below. Thus all of Rome was cleansed of our communal sins.

The Argei was so archaic, not even our oldest books could explain its origin outside of pointing out that in the early days of Rome, we threw twenty-seven living men to their deaths from the high bridge in a ritualized communal cleansing. One day, Jupiter's own son—Hercules—appeared to our forefathers and forbid us from sacrificing living men. He instructed us to create life-sized effigies instead, assuring us our group sins would continue to be expiated without having to perform human sacrifice.

After the disaster at Trasimene, the Argei seemed more important than ever. Clearly, the gods demanded a cleansing and the Maxima had gone on daily rants about the importance of us Vestals not making a single mistake when it was time to parade the polluted effigies through the city then throw them to their symbolic deaths. We were two weeks out from collecting and disposing of all twenty-seven effigies when I stumbled upon a meeting in the private garden of the pontiff's public house. The entire Collegium—all of the head priests of Rome, including the Maxima—were present. Some sat on benches, others leaned against red-painted columns. These meetings were usually held in secret and I was surprised to stumble onto it. The Maxima would later accuse me of spying, but I was doing no such thing. The Vestal Fabia had sent me to deliver a note to the Maxima, which I held in my hand.

In the shade of a warping trellis of newly budding roses, I paused in surprise, still in the shadows when the priest of Mars exclaimed, "We must do something. While Fabius' impressive promises of future sacrifices to the gods are important, they have no power in the moment. The people need something now to calm their fears and give them hope and confidence."

After that second major defeat, the dictator Fabius had promised the gods extensive gifts—including sacrifices of all of the surplus animals after the harvest season, outrageous amounts of grain, new festivals in their honor, and even a new temple. The people were awed and appeased by such a powerful show of piety from our emergency leader.

"The people need something now," Albinus, the priest of the god of war insisted. "We need a powerful way to expiate their pain and jolt the people out of their debilitating grief. And returning to our archaic practices with the Argei, I believe, will accomplish it."

I froze. Had I heard correctly?

"I support the measure," said the priest of Quirinus. Quirinus was one of Rome's oldest and most revered gods.

Was the priest of Mars casually suggesting we sacrifice twenty-seven living men to appease the gods?

"You cannot be serious," the priest of Vulcanus said, as if echoing my own shock. "Human sacrifice is forbidden! Hercules himself instructed us to abandon the practice!"

"It is not human sacrifice when it involves enemies of war," the priest of Mars insisted. "The great heroes of our past regularly sacrificed war prisoners to honor the fallen and win the favor of the gods. What do you think Hannibal is doing with our captured warriors? We must reclaim our honor by showing the gods we quaver before nobody."

My heart hammered in my ears. They were actually considering throwing more than two-dozen living men to their deaths. Holding my breath, I leaned in further.

"Need I point out we do not have in our possession twenty-seven prisoners of war to use in this way and…" began a younger priest.

"We will use immigrants, non-Romans. Criminals. Even slaves if we have to," the priest of Mars snapped.

"But will the people accept them as representing expiation of all the sins of their specific districts?" asked the priest of Ceres. "Will they feel cleansed?"

The war-god priest gave him a disdainful look. "This city swarms with foreigners and outsiders. We will find plenty within each district. Outsiders are the ideal bearers of the community's sins. It will be a great catharsis for all Romans."

"There will be resistance to this," warned another elder priest, though I could not tell who had spoken.

"We shall tell the senators we've all had the same dream and the Sibyl of Cumae was also touched by this knowing," the Maxima said. "I agree we need to do something extraordinary to shock the people out of their hopelessness and misery."

I had begun to accept that the desires of the most powerful sometimes influenced our religious decisions, but I had always assumed consulting the gods or the sacred books happened first, not the other way around. And that the dreams of our priests and priestesses actually meant something. But to hear our most powerful religious leaders casually speak of killing twenty-seven men as a strategy to manage community despair and to cite dreams that never occurred was disorienting. I must have gasped or made a noise.

"Who is there?" cried the pontiff. "Who dares enter my home to spy?"

I stepped out of the shadows. "It… it is I," I said, my voice embarrassingly unsteady. "I wasn't spying. Fabia sent me to deliver this to the Maxima." I held up the sealed scroll.

Her eyes narrowed at me. "How much did you hear?"

For a brief moment, I considered lying, but I could not contain myself. "You cannot possibly be considering throwing twenty-seven living men to their deaths," I sputtered. "It is forbidden! The son of God himself came to us and told us we must not!"

Several priests stared at me with mouths slightly open, as if one of their hunting dogs had suddenly started speaking.

"Captured enemies of the state don't count as 'people' as they are not Roman," snapped the Maxima. "Neither do criminals, immigrants, or foreigners. Difficult times require dramatic sacrifices."

"But the dictator's extraordinary vows should carry—"

"Why are we allowing this female to have an opinion on this matter?" the priest of Mars asked, cutting me off. He waved a battle-scarred hand in my direction as if shooing away an insect. Turning to the other priests, the priest of the god of war continued. "Now, if it was good enough for our ancient warrior ancestors, it is good enough for us."

"But Hercules came to Rome to tell us to stop the practice," I insisted, "Shouldn't we at least consider consulting the Sibylline Books before we do something that might outrage the gods?"

The Maxima stood, her face a knot of red fury. "Hercules told us to stop throwing ROMANS to their deaths. He never said anything about enemies, foreigners, or outsiders."

"But—" I tried.

"We have arrested Numidians and Iberians living in Rome," the priest of Jupiter pointed out as if I weren't there. "They are likely spying for their Carthaginian masters. Their sacrifice would be powerful indeed!"

The Maxima was suddenly next to me. "You are not part of this conversation," she nearly spat. "Give me that and leave," she said, snatching Fabia's now crumpled note from my hand.

The priest of Volturnus stared at me, considering. "Perhaps it is a sign from the gods that she interrupted this discussion at precisely this moment," he said, gesturing in my direction. "Perhaps this is their way of warning us to be cautious. After all, if we do this, it could backfire. Any further tragedies or setbacks will be blamed on us and could cause more destabilization."

The pontiff and the priest of Mars exchanged looks. Volturnus was an ancient primeval god of fecundity and the Tiber. To have his priest oppose their plans was a serious problem, for they dare not enrage the god of our nourishing waters.

The Maxima whirled on him, her face reddening with rage. "The gods have never spoken through this obstinate and undisciplined child!"

Child? I was in my second decade of service to the order!

The priest of Volturnus' jaw clenched and his eyes narrowed. "Oh and I suppose the gods only bless you in this way?" By his disdain it was clear he did not like the Maxima. I never imagined I might feel protective of her but it suddenly became clear why she always seemed so prickly and angry. It was she against this wall of smirking, dismissive men.

The garden erupted into shouts and arguments. By the sound of it, the group was split evenly—half favored the sacrifice of living humans (as long as they weren't Roman citizens) and the other half was dead set against it.

The pontiff must have signaled to one of his guards to remove me, for I suddenly found myself facing a lictor's chest. The man held up his fasces across his breastbone and raised his chin to the path behind me, signaling me to leave, which I did out of habit.

The arguing went on for days. Eventually they brought in a Haruspex to break the tie. The Haruspex arrived at the pontiff's house carrying a snow-white, late-spring lamb.

Unsurprisingly, I was barred from attending.

I had watched a Haruspex divination a few years earlier. The Etruscan Haruspex had been a long-haired and long-bearded priest hailing from Volterra, one of the leading cities of the ancient Etruscan league—all of whom were now Roman. That Voltarren Haruspex also arrived with his own pristine white lamb.

With a number of spine-tingling, atonal intonations over the bleating beast, the strange priest got to work. After cutting the small beast's throat and catching first blood, he opened the lamb from chest to groin and carefully pawed through the still pulsating innards in search of the liver. With a thick, sucking sound, he pulled the shining organ out of the small body, his hands slick with blood and viscera. He held it up to the sky as if allowing the gods to inspect it first, then placed it on a metal tray and began poking and pushing the organ with his bloodied fingers, arranging it into various positions as he worked. All the while, his face was scrunched in concentration, and he made strangled little noises of surprise or affirmation. When he finished, the Haruspex claimed the sacrifice indicated the answer to the question posed to the diviner had been a clear, "No."

I presumed the answer to whether we should throw twenty-seven living men to their deaths at the Argei was also no because we did not change the rite. At the appointed date two weeks later, we threw straw effigies—and not living men—off the bridge to their symbolic deaths in the Tiber.

**

I hadn't realized how much the priest of Mars blamed and resented me for interfering with his plans on reviving the original Argei sacrifices and thus winning the favor of the gods. Ultimately, it was the Haruspex who nixed Albinus' plan, but somehow, the priest of the god of war held me personally responsible for thwarting his plans for drowning men in the Tiber. In court, he sat on the edge of his seat as if astride a stallion and based on his look of triumph as he stared at me across the court, he was relishing the opportunity to sacrifice me to distract from *his* gods' failures.

If any religious leader should be blamed, it should be him since he served the god of war. War was the business of men—started by men, run by men, and carried out by men. Yet somehow they'd convinced themselves and everyone around them that a priestess of the silent goddess who sat by the fire was more responsible for inciting the wrath of the gods than the priest who served the god of war himself. A strange, panicky impulse to laugh crawled up my chest—a recognition that this circus would be funny if only it weren't my life on the line. But, as always, I tamped it down for sometimes a laughing woman created more terror than a raging one.

Chapter Twelve

Albinus smirked as the mob chanted for my head again. He had the arrogant dismissive look of a general at the height of his powers. When he aimed his craggy stare at me, it was as if he were counting the dead bodies of a battle he had already won.

Manlius the prosecutor allowed the outraged murmuring of the crowd to reach a crescendo before speaking again. "And how," he thundered, "was this outrageous interference by a junior priestess disciplined? Surely, she was punished for her shameful hubris, no?"

"No," Albinus shouted to the moans and boos of the increasingly agitated crowd. "In fact, she was *rewarded*. In the midst of Rome's darkest period, two months before the disaster at Cannae, this rebellious Vestal, took a holiday—*a holiday*—to Cumae!"

My jaw fell open as the thunder of stomping feet and screams of indignation erupted. "Not true," I shouted, bolting up again. "The Maxima ordered me out of the city to appease *you* and mollify your infantile anger!" But no one heard me. It was like a nightmare where I screamed and shouted for help but no sound emerged from my mouth.

"A *holiday?*" Manlius howled over the crowd with mock outrage. "How was this allowed?"

The priest of Mars lifted his shoulders and jutted his lower lip with the practiced exaggeration and helpless expression of a poor, overwhelmed man in the face of a scheming woman. A wave of exhaustion and despair weakened my knees and I fell back into my seat.

It amazed me how easily people swallowed the most ridiculous lie as truth. No matter what I said now—no matter how many times I tried to explain what *really* happened—the people would believe the priest over me. For no better reason than his story was the one they heard first. And that it was outrageous. So outrageous it made the people's blood boil. And they secretly loved the surge of passion that came with outrage.

Reality was nowhere near as interesting.

***

One Year Earlier

The day after the Argei rite went as tradition dictated—without murdering twenty-seven men—the Maxima called me into her tablinium.

"Pack up your things," the Maxima said as I entered her study. "You are going on a trip."

"What?" I cried, startled. We Vestals didn't go on "trips." We had to stay in Rome!

"You leave right away," she said from behind her desk in her gloomy and ancient tablinium.

"I don't understand. Where are you sending me?"

She put her stylus down, crossed her arms, and stared up at me. "You are going to the Sibyl at Cumae."

I shook my head. "Impossible."

The Maxima rubbed the deep groove between her brows and closed her eyes in irritation. "Arrangements have already been made. Your lady is packing your things as we speak."

"But...why?"

"Because you have angered the priests of Jupiter and Mars and I need to throw them a bone."

Taken aback by her bluntness, I finally managed, "You well know it is especially important for us to be visible at the rites and by the fire to reassure the people."

"It is," she said. "But as I am sending you to the Sibyl, the people will be reassured by the religious significance. And we will satisfy the priest's need for vengeance."

But to travel during wartime? Wasn't that dangerous?

"You will be protected," the Maxima continued. "Besides, Cumae is on the western coast and Hannibal is still in the eastern midlands."

I had never heard of a Vestal virgin priestess being sent to the Sibyl for any purpose. "Am I to pose a question to the Sibyl?"

"You can pose any question you like to her. I just need you out of Rome for a time." At my shocked silence, she added. "Despite what you think, this is for the best."

"How can it be for the best? The Fortuna Primagenia is only three days away. I look forward to it every year. I do not want to miss it."

At the Primagenia, we Vestals led a long procession of young mothers with babes in arms and young women who hoped to be mothers to the Sanctuary of Fortuna Primagenia, the primordial goddess of the "First Bearer," right outside the city. It had special poignancy for me as I watched women my age or even younger nurse infants and soothe toddlers. I watched their faces break open with love when their babies smiled up at them. It was as close as I would ever get to experiencing what was forbidden to me.

The Maxima waved my argument away. So I changed tactics. "I believe it's important for me to participate in the Primagenia this year more than ever to help the newly widowed mothers and their fatherless children deal with their loss."

The Maxima stared. "You will not be joining the procession this year. Floronia will lead it. And that is final."

I secretly worried the Maxima was sending me to die or disappear at the hands of the most terrifying prophetess in Italia. She could claim the gods "took me" and finally have another selection ceremony and get a more compliant acolyte. I pushed those fears away, though, and reminded myself that the loss of a Vestal priestess during the war with Hannibal would be catastrophic for the emotional well-being of Romans. Sending me away to a spiritual site would at least smooth the ruffled feathers of angry priests while reassuring the people that their priestesses would be strengthening the bonds with the Sibyl, who represented the land's most ancient and primeval gods.

The priest of Mars wasn't just angry at me, though. He fumed over our army's inability to purge Hannibal from our territories. After the tragedy at Lake Trasimene, the ruling general, Fabius, refused to engage in pitched battle with the North African invader. Instead, he dodged and weaved and nipped at the edges of Hannibal's army and attacked his supply lines in the hopes of starving him out.

But to a large group of traditionalists, including the priest of Mars, this tactic was unmanly and dishonorable. It insulted Rome's dignitas. True Romans engaged in battles, not avoidance strategies. He and others began calling the general, Cuncator, The Delayor.

"We look like timid women," he complained to the Senate. "We appear weak. We must reclaim Roman virtus!"

Still the general had the support of the majority until one fateful day. Led by bad information, Hannibal found himself trapped by the general's legions in a narrow defile just south of the mountain of Ager Falernus in central Campania. They had no escape.

We needed only to attack and destroy Hannibal's ensnared forces and the war would have been over. But because of the late hour of the day, the general thought it prudent to wait until morning. Unfortunately, Hannibal outwitted him with an ingenious trick.

Hannibal ordered two thousand cattle brought to the edge of one of the mountains. He ordered his men to tie bundles of kindling to every horn. When night fell, they lit the kindling and sent the panicked animals thundering down the mountainside toward the Roman camp.

In the darkness, it looked like thousands of men carrying torches were on the attack. Fearing the worst, the general pulled his forces guarding the pass to help fight the swarm. By the time he realized the ruse, Hannibal had silently marched his forces out from under his nose.

The general then lost the confidence of all the people, not just the priest of Mars. He laid down his dictatorship and two co-consuls were elected—generals Gaius Terrentius Varro and Lucius Aemilius Paullus. Varro was a rash man who advocated fighting Hannibal directly. Paullus was more circumspect and had promised to continue the successful strategy of caution and harassment. I had been greatly reassured to learn Attius' cohort had been folded into Paullus' legion. The general's prudence and patience would keep him safe.

Albinus' frustration over what he saw as a "feminized" approach to dealing with Hannibal and my daring to have an opinion on "men's matters" boiled over and his solution was to get rid of me. I had no doubt he wanted me killed, but even he knew that it would be seen as a terrible omen. Sending me out of the city was at least one thing he could control. My temporary exile to Cumae was a punishment. Another way of cleansing Rome from my polluted nature. It felt as if they were sending me to the Gorgon to be devoured.

With Ketet and an accompanying guard on horseback, we traveled on a rickety, awninged carriage pulled by two mares. Having never seen the sea, the coastal road leading to Cumae was a wonder. One moment we were on a craggy hill, the next we turned a corner onto a breathtaking vista of wide-open ocean. Even the horses slowed as if in awe at the glittering expanse. The sea was inky dark on the horizon, gradually lightening to glittering sapphire and melting into a nearly transparent aquamarine—as if lit by an unknown sun—where the water caressed the shore.

Ketet too seemed enchanted. "It reminds me of home," she said. "We called our turquoise waters Isis' Tears of Joy for their beauty and healing power," Ketet continued. "But when we lost men to the darker waters, we knew they were her salty Tears of Rage as well. I once dreamed of serving as a priestess of Isis-on-the-Sea."

"You would have made a wonderful priestess," I said.

She turned to me. "I am serving her still," she said, her large brown eyes shining. "Isis manifested her grace through you, which is why I was protected from a crueler fate. And so I serve her when I serve you."

"Isis is not like Vesta, though, is she?"

Ketet shook her head. "Much more powerful. Wielder of magic, goddess of night, mother, and protector of children."

"She sounds a bit like Diana, the goddess of the hunt and wild woods."

"The goddess appears to us in many different forms," she noted. I needed to remember that, especially when I grew angry at Vesta's passivity. She was aunt to Diana, I would tell myself. Still, the sense I'd been "given" to the wrong goddess—that it was punishment for all my known and unknown transgressions—haunted me. Ketet smiled and added, "Our gods are many in One and One in thousands."

It took three days to arrive at the community serving the Sibyl near her cave. At the foot of her mountain, was a small and bustling village. On the valley below was a constellation of rich cultivated fields—orchards of olive and fruit trees, square fields thick with emerging barley and spelt sheafs, and dark rows and rows of grapevines on the slopes. A cow bellowed into the silence and a goat answered back. I had such a longing for Attius and Larce and the simple life we dreamed of, I almost staggered. Seeing the look of longing on my face, our guide— a sun-darkened, bent-over woman with a wide, sweet smile—leaned toward me and conspiratorially whispered, "When your obligations to the goddess are complete, you are welcome to join us here."

I nodded, my throat tight. Ten more years.

Ten more long years.

After days of waiting and being ignored by the Sibyl, I approached the priest who guarded the pathway up to the Sibyl's cave. "When will I see the Prophetess?" I asked.

He raised his eyebrows. "When she feels like it," he snapped. "After communing in the cave she is often exhausted. She will summon you when she is ready."

And so we waited.

Ketet and I spent time walking the jagged rocky cliffs and staring out at the ocean. Occasionally we broke bread with some of the women who lived on the compound. One afternoon, a young mother, with a toddler on her hip, brought us warm honey bread and we invited her to sit with us in the shaded corner of the courtyard.

"How did you come to live up here in the Sibyl's compound?" I asked. It still surprised me how many people bustled around us.

"You do not know about us in Rome?" she asked, surprised.

"No," I said as Ketet poured her some fresh citron water. At least, I hadn't known.

"Ah, perhaps it is best. Many of us do not fit anywhere in Rome's world. My husband and I are both freedmen, and when the man who manumitted us died, his greedy children claimed the papers were false, and tried to enslave us again."

The woman patted her baby's head of dark curls and said, "We did not know how to fight them and I was pregnant with this one. If we didn't win our case, he would have been born a slave and be the property of the family, which we could not risk..."

"How did you know to come here?" I asked.

The two-year-old on the mother's lap gave Ketet a shy grin from across the table. "We come from Nuceria which is not so far from here," she continued. "We had long heard about a community far from any big city-center that was peaceful and devoted to the goddess. We had nowhere else to go and left in a hurry when we realized we had no chance to fight such a powerful family. At the very least, we hoped the priestess would give us sanctuary until the baby came."

She kissed the gurgling boy's head again while he swiped at his mother's ceramic cup, which she kept moving away just in time. My chest ached staring at this happy, chubby-cheeked cupid, imagining a baby with Attius' black curls and laughing eyes. Not for me. Not with me.

Attius had been gone almost two years after joining the legions, training at outposts to our south. That he had not been deployed at Lake Trasimene was something I thanked the gods for every day. I had not known, at the time, that his unit had joined Paullus' legions and that they were already following Hannibal into the trap that would end in Cannae.

Not knowing what the life of a legionnaire was like, I tortured myself by imagining him falling in love with a beautiful local girl. Together they would live out the fantasy life we had so often imagined for ourselves—a simple life in the country, caring for vines and animals just as Larce had. I pushed away the familiar ache of feeling left behind while others lived rich, complex lives.

As a week went by and we were still not summoned, I grew increasingly anxious. Later, I would understand that inside the Sibyl's cavern, vapors changed the perception of time. The Sibyl, out of courtesy, liked to wait three days after serving in the cave before meeting with anyone lest she speak in the god's dream language to those in the nondreaming world and potentially anger the gods.

Finally, we received word we were to dine with her. The Sibyl's house was not in the community but attached to an ancient moss-covered boulder near the sacred cave. It looked out of time, as if it might have been the home of Circe or Penelope of Ithaka or the First Peoples of the Stones. The long uphill trek emphasized its isolation and sense of otherness.

The sun hovered over the horizon as we approached. Workers lit torches around the courtyard. A servant led us to the table where we spied a small woman with long graying hair worn loose down her back. Her otherworldly air left no question as to who she was.

I bowed and greeted her formally, presenting my gifts from Rome—wine and silver and fine fabrics. The older woman examined me from head to toe and looked into my eyes for longer than was comfortable. In my priestly robes and with my hair covered, I felt both overdressed and slightly ridiculous before her simple yet elegant appearance. After a weighty silence, she welcomed us and bade us sit. The Sibyl insisted we call her by her name—Amalthaea. Knowing that was the name of the priestess who sold the original Sibylline Books to King Tarquinus in ancient times, I assumed it wasn't her real name.

As the silence stretched, a servant passed Ketet a terracotta jug and Ketet bent over me to pour what smelled like a brewed mixture of flower petals, grasses, and mint.

"Your Lady's name?" Amalthaea asked, signaling Ketet with her head.

"This is Tarpeia," I said.

The priestess brushed the air irritably with her hand. "Not her Roman name. Her true name."

"Ketet, Domina."

To my surprise, she addressed her directly. "Ketet, my dear, there is no need to continue the pretense of your enslavement here. You are a freedwoman and I invite you to join us for this meal."

Ketet's eyes went wide and panicked. Mine must have been as well. How did she know this? Ketet stared at me, frozen, unsure of what to do. Did the Sibyl's spiritual gifts as an oracle extend to secret knowledge of even something like this?

I cleared my throat and in a quiet voice said, "We are most intrigued you are aware of Ketet's true status," I finally said. "We operate under the pretense she is still enslaved so she may stay safe and continue to live with me in the House of Vestals."

She squinted at Ketet. "Oh dear, I have frightened you. Your brow is quite disturbed."

"But how did you know when…when even the Virgo Maxima is not aware of this?" I asked.

The woman leaned forward and smiled conspiratorially. "I do my research."

I blinked, not knowing what to say. This was not information gifted to her from the gods?

"I have people loyal to me inside the records offices," she said. "It is amazing what is filed away, unknown to the rest of the world." She turned to Ketet and swept her arm toward the empty chair. "Please sit, sit. You are a free woman and my guest here."

Ketet shakily took a seat.

"Who else knows her true status?" I asked. My heart continued pounding and I knew Ketet was frightened too. Goddess knew how the Maxima would take out her rage on the both of us if she knew she had been misled all these years.

"Do not worry. Your secret is safe. As are all the delicious secrets I learn about the powerful in Rome," she added with a delighted cackle.

When I did not smile or laugh, she looked from Ketet to me and sighed.

"Let me reassure you both. Nobody will know about this for as long as you want to keep it hidden. My spies are extremely loyal."

"Spies?" I squeaked.

"Yes, spies," she said with a surprisingly loud, bark-like laugh. "When the powerful leaders of Rome and the surrounding city-states come to me for prophecy, it is important I know who they are and what they are truly seeking as opposed to what they say they are seeking. So I have very well-paid spies inside the records rooms of most of the area's surrounding cities."

Amalthaea raised her ceramic cup to us and said, "I admire your resourcefulness and commitment to maintaining secrecy. I am most curious as to the reasons for this...er, arrangement."

My face flushed as I remembered the original reason I'd manumitted Ketet—in childish defiance against the Maxima. It seemed so petty now, but the consequences of that impulsive act had humbled me. Ketet was free and I would do whatever I could to ensure she remained both free and safe. "It was a secret that bound us," I said, lamely.

The Sibyl turned to Ketet. "And yet you continue to serve while pretending to be enslaved. Why?"

Ketet raised her chin. "Where else would I go? What else would I do? My entire village was destroyed. My family attacked and murdered. If Domina had not selected me, I would have been sold as a sex slave. As long as people think I am her property, my status is quite high and I am protected from abuse."

She turned to me. "Are you paying her as you would pay a freedwoman for her service?"

"Of course!"

The Sibyl raised an eyebrow at me and turned back to Ketet. "We have many women living here who have escaped terrible circumstances," she said. "They are free here to choose how they want to live. Some who have been abused choose to live separately in the women's section, while others have relationships and even have families. If you find yourself in crisis, you are welcome here."

Was she…was she trying to lure my lady away from me to her compound? How dare she! A surge of possessiveness straightened my spine.

The prophetess turned to me and smirked. "Do you only speak the language of freedom or you do actually support it in practice?"

I turned to Ketet, my heart pounding. Could the prophetess see something I could not? Was I keeping her with me against her will?

Ketet looked from me back to the Sibyl. "Priestess Mia is my family now," she said. "She is a sister to me, a true friend, and the means by which I honor my goddess, Isis."

"A friendship based on lies. Can you be friends with someone pretending to own you?"

"Yes," said Ketet. "When the truth is lived in private. When the lie provides sanctuary and safety for one without protection, family, or people in a strange land. And when one takes great joy in fooling others who cannot see what is directly in front of them."

The Sibyl must not have expected the latter part of Ketet's answer, because she gave a barking laugh and raised her cup to Ketet. Meanwhile, I was unsettled by the strange turn in conversation. Of the sense she judged me and saw right through to my essential wrongness and shamefulness.

After a meal of grilled octopus along with crusty breads, fresh olives, porous cheeses, and salted lettuce leaves—mostly eaten in unnerving silence—the Sibyl came alive again once the table had been cleared.

"You may pose your questions, now," the Sibyl said, looking hard at me. "You look like you swallowed a toad, you are working so hard to keep them back in your throat."

Ketet uncharacteristically laughed, which she pretended was a cough.

"Sibyl, with great respect," I began. "I ask for your guidance in protecting a childhood friend who is serving in the legions."

She blinked as if she had not expected that question. "Guidance? What are you really asking?"

"For any special spells, prayers, or rites that I could invoke to protect him..." I trailed off, my face warming. Could she tell how I felt about Attius?

"Interesting," she said. "Why do you ask this of me? I am not a magician, nor a dispenser of spells."

"Yes, I know, but I thought—"

She waved a hand in irritation. "I do not involve myself with men who gather to kill each other. Your friend's survival is the purvey of the god of war, and I stay away from his foolishness."

My heart pounded in my ears at her insult. Now was not the time to enrage Mars! I had angered him—or at least his head priest in Rome—well enough for now. So stunned was I by her unexpected dismissal, I could only stammer, "But…but when you commune with the gods—"

"I do not 'commune' with the gods, as you put it," she said, her eyes blazing. "I connect with the Great Mother, She Who Provides Life."

"But Apollo is the god of oracles," I blurted, confused. "It is through him that you receive your prophecies and he is brother to Mars—"

"And that is why your Senate is discussing sending a team to the Greek Oracle at Delphi for insight on how to defeat Hannibal."

They were? I had not heard talk of sending a team to Delphi. But then again, the Sibyl had her spies, so she probably knew more than I did. "It makes no sense to seek counsel with a foreign prophetess for the protection of Rome," I said. "They should counsel with you, the Lady of our own Homeland."

She smirked. "Now you are coming to the heart of it. Why would they prefer the Oracle in Greece over one of us Sibyls?"

Was this a rhetorical question? "I do not know," I said after a long silence. "We hold the Sibylline Books in the highest of religious esteem. Why would they entertain traveling to Greece over seeing you?"

She made a great rude sound in her throat, turned her head to the side, and unceremoniously spat into the ground. "Because we Sibyls have refused to do what the Pythia at Delphi did generations ago to survive—claim it is a boy-god and not the Great Mother who speaks through the mists in the Cave of All."

I blinked, still not understanding.

The Sibyl leaned back and stared at us with narrowed eyes.

"The Pythia of Delphi pretends it is Apollo and not the Great Mother, who speaks to her to please the men in power and keep the gold coming," she said. "Here in Cumae, we do not pretend a mercurial boy-god who can't keep his hand off his cock has more wisdom than She Who Bears Life, The Devourer, The Timeless One Who Feeds Life from Her Breast. Cumae means 'Mother' in the Old Language and that is whom we worship here. So your Romans prefer traveling to Delphi to consult with Apollo because they put their faith in him over the Mother."

I swallowed hard and my heart raced. Was she deriding Apollo? Was I endangering Attius with this strange turn of conversation? "But surely," I began, "we dare not question or challenge Apollo—"

The Sibyl slammed her palm on the wooden table. "We must! Because they are silencing the Great Goddess. They take over her shrines and caves and pretend life didn't begin with her. Then they claim their male gods as the true creators and bearers of life, even as they rampage in war and spread death." She shook her head as if she were in real pain.

I looked over at Ketet and her eyes were large and shining. She leaned forward. "Isis was once the Great Mother of All, even above Amun Ra. But now they say the Mother played no part in creating life, that Amun did so by pleasuring himself!"

"What?" I stared at Ketet confused. I had not heard of this story. "Life was started how?"

"By Amun Ra, who pleasured himself," she repeated. "He released his seed into the Waters of Nun and created all life from his effluence."

"Without a mother?" I asked. That made no sense.

Ketet nodded.

"Isis is the one who hunted down all the pieces of her murdered husband and resurrected him?" I asked, vaguely remembering the story.

"Yes," Ketet said.

"Bringing someone back from the dead is no small thing," I said.

"Neither is giving life," the Sibyl said. "Men fear and hate the Mother because she gave them life and they remember their helplessness and vulnerability. They vowed never to feel that way again so they force their women to be small and helpless instead." She turned to me and added with venom, "Like you."

It was as if she had punched me in the chest. I could not draw a breath to respond.

The Sibyl raised an eyebrow and smirked. "Tell me, priestess of Vesta. What does Vesta teach women except to sit demurely by the fire, never speaking or acting, until she eventually disappears unnoticed into the flames."

My heart pounded in my ears as I looked around, half expecting a demon or hellhound to tear us apart for her words against Vesta.

"Priestess, the quiet dignity of Vesta should not be insulted," I said in almost a whisper. To my dismay, she laughed.

Without thinking, I took too large a gulp of the grassy drink to cover my anxious confusion. When I put the cup down, a loud and unexpected burp escaped from my throat, low and rude. Immediately I covered my mouth and looked down, "Please forgive me," I said, imagining how horrified the Maxima would be at my vulgarity.

"Forgive you for what? Living in a body that makes noise, in a body that bleeds every month, in a body that sweats, eats, and shits?" The Sibyl raised an eyebrow. "I foretell this," the Sibyl continued, pointing a finger at me and Ketet. "One day, the erasure will be complete. There will be no goddess, only a male god. No priestesses, only priests."

"Impossible," Ketet and I said at the same time. The Sibyl was surely mad.

The Sibyl smirked at us as if she knew what we were thinking. "It is a slow process, this killing of the goddess. So slow you do not notice.

But we Sibyls, we see all of time at once." She made a dreamy circular shape in the air.

Had years of inhaling sacred cave vapors addled her brain?

"With all due respect," I said. "How can you talk of a disappearing goddess, when a powerful priestess of Vesta sits before you?"

The Sibyl leaned back, turned her head and glared at me from the side. "You believe yourself powerful, do you?"

"I am certainly more powerful than most women in Rome! I am not under any man's hand, unlike all other women who are controlled by fathers, husbands, uncles, or brothers. I earn a considerable living for my services and I control my own finances. I can invest in property, which other women cannot. I can testify in court and I can witness a patrician's will and—"

"And you call this power?"

"What would you call it?" I snapped.

"Crumbs. In exchange for these pittances, in exchange for sacrificing thirty years of your life, you are held personally responsible for the honor and safety of Rome. One step out of line—you love a man or the fire goes out—and you are blamed for the endless suffering of countless innocents. That is not power. That is pre-arranged blame."

"But—"

"All of the priestesses of Vesta report to the Pontifex Maximus, yes?"

"Yes."

"A man who dictates and controls your every behavior," she continued. "Tell me, does the priest of Jupiter Optimus Maximus 'report' to the Pontifex Maximus? What about the priest of Vulturnos?"

"Well, no." The very idea was laughable.

"So you see, you and even your Maxima are not as powerful as you think, for you are continually silenced, controlled and threatened with impending disaster should you not be perfectly pious and chaste. I presume the pontiff and the other priestlings have no such controls over their private actions."

I wanted to argue but suddenly had no words. She was not wrong, yet I did not want to view it that way. Goose flesh rose on my arms, despite the warmth of the evening.

"Are there other priestesses of Rome like you," the Sibyl asked, downing the last of her drink.

"Well, yes. There are six Vestals, after all."

"No, I mean priestesses who wield power in their own temples, in their own rights. Or have they all been replaced by men?"

"We have many priestesses of Isis and Hathor in Egypt," Ketet said.

The Sibyl nodded but continued giving me a hard stare. I felt like a fly speared to the table by a stylus. "I ask again," the Sibyl said. "Are there other priestesses in Rome or are you the last of the women so imbued?"

"We have the priestess of Ceres," I argued.

"Does the priestess of Ceres have a seat at the Collegium of Priests?"

I shook my head, thinking hard as my mind whirred trying to prove her wrong. "We have a priestess of Diana," I said emphatically.

The Sibyl leaned forward. "She too does not have a seat at the Collegium."

My throat grew tight and I felt a strange defensiveness. I wanted to—no needed to—prove her wrong. "We have the Sardecos Liberli, the priestess of the gods of fertility, Liber and Liberia."

The Sibyl again raised an eyebrow. "Once she was very powerful. Now her post is open only to an old woman who is relegated to selling honey cakes at the festival of the Liberalia. And she reports to the priest of Liber."

This was technically true. My face flushed. "The priestess of the Bona Dea, then, the Good Mother!"

The Sibyl nodded. "Again, she used to be very powerful. Today in Rome these priestesses are known more as mere herbal healers, are they not?"

I nodded.

"And who presides over the rites of the Bona Dea?"

I paused. "The wife of the consul or the praetor. The rite is held in her home."

"Right. So the person leading the ancient rites of the Mother changes depending on which man is consul or praetor that year. They lead the rites of the Mater only to enhance the status and power of their husbands." In the silence that followed she added, "Only the Virgo Maxima has a seat at the table of the ruling priests. And she must give up every aspect of being a woman for the privilege of having a voice. If she continues past her thirty-year tenure, she must continue to be a virgin. And, like her priestesses, if she lets the fire go out or loves a man, she will be ruthlessly buried alive. The silencing of the Mother and her priestesses has been slow but inexorable."

"This is outrageous," Ketet said with a burst of feeling, her face bright with outrage. "How do we stop it? I do not want to live in a world where Isis is belittled, dismissed, or killed!"

"I do not have an answer for how to stop this desecration. I do not fully understand it—nor why the Mother allows it. And so I say unto you, when the men finally declare her dead or irrelevant, when they confine her to being an empty vessel—either a virgin, mother, or whore—know that they lie, that she lives still, and you must keep her alive in your hearts. Here we love and honor the Mother in the old ways. If that does not suit you, you may leave."

She must have seen in our faces that we would not—could not—leave. With an impish smile, the Sibyl pushed against the table, her ornately carved stool scraping hard on the tiled floor. As she stood, shadowed by the mountain behind her and the stars glittering above, I felt her power and swallowed, keenly aware that she had brushed away my request for protection for Attius.

As if sensing my distress, the Sibyl loomed over us. "Now. Listen closely. Both of you will come to me for a ceremony of communion in the Cave of All in two days. You may ask the Mother then for her help. You will fast until sunrise of the second day and enter the Cave of the goddess."

"We would be honored," I said quickly and Ketet murmured the same.

The Sibyl nodded, belched loudly, and grinned at us before turning away. She waved goodbye and headed back to her cave house. She must have felt our stares because she looked over her shoulder at us. With a devilish childlike grin, she stuck out her backside and released a series of rude noises. Her cackling laugh echoed all around us as she disappeared into her home without saying another word. Ketet and I giggled like small children as we slid down the pebble strewn mountain road—accompanied by a somber torchbearer—all the way back to the compound.

After days of fasting and purifying dips in the hot springs, Ketet and I set off upon the craggy path to the Sibyl's cave at sunrise. We paused as we climbed, awed by the beauty of the vista. A band of orange light pulsed on the horizon, melting upward into layers of pink and lavender. Thin purple clouds hung motionless over blue tipped mountain ridges. It was eerily quiet, as it often was at that hour, as if the whole world held its breath to celebrate the arrival of rosy-fingered dawn.

The air smelled of the sea—briny and strong—cut by the clean sharpness of pines and junipers and wild olive trees. The path to the cave's entrance had been smoothed by the tread of countless pilgrims and supplicants. To the right of the cave opening, carved into the rock were ancient columns and a pediment in the Etruscan tradition, painted with bright reds, blues, and yellows. The mountain wind whipped Ketet's hair out of her braids, and sent my head covering flapping like the wings of a wild bird.

A young woman welcomed us as she added wood to the fire in the cauldron that had been banked overnight. It flared and the acolyte sprinkled a mound of myrrh powder, scenting the air and reminding me of our daily practice at the Temple of Vesta.

"Take your head covering off. Unbraid your hair and remove your sandals," the woman commanded. "Remove any belts or rings. You shall not enter the holy space with any knots or ties in place."

"I am never to be seen with my head uncovered," I began.

"I will not look upon your face," she said.

We complied.

Once my hair was released and all vestiges of my priesthood were removed, the Sibyl's assistant moved a smoking briquette from the fire into a small bronze bowl and danced the smoke over us in a purifying manner. This rite I knew and I closed my eyes and breathed deep of the cleansing smoke.

As the first rays of sunlight caressed the tops of the craggy mountains, the young woman said, "Now drink this."

We each sipped from a shallow bowl. The thick drink tasted of grape must and something else that left a loamy, acrid aftertaste. We took turns until it was gone. The sacred drink warmed our empty bellies.

"The Sibyl awaits you," the young woman said with a sweeping arm gesture toward the opening of the dark cavern. She held her hands out to the fire and began singing an old hymn of safekeeping for those undertaking the Great Journey.

I grabbed Ketet's hand. The walk toward the cave opening seemed to shrink and expand before us, as did the sense of time. We could have been walking for moments or years. We paused on the threshold, feeling the cool, moist air of the darkness within. "I do not think I can do this," Ketet whispered. She sounded very far away.

I understood Ketet's trepidation. It was well known that not everyone survived their journey into the Sibyl's cave. I could not let go of the idea that the priest of Mars, along with the Maxima, intended for me to die inside the cave. After all, that would solve all their problems—the Maxima would be rid of me while gaining acclaim for having the wisdom to send me to such a holy place. She could claim the gods of the underworld took me, and she and the Pontifex could claim it as a prodigy of hope, perhaps even as an appeasement that might change the tenor of the war with Hannibal.

If that were the case, Ketet should not have to die too. I wanted to tell her this was my journey. She should not have to suffer what the gods intended for me. She was truly free—which meant she could choose not to go into the cave. But my tongue felt swollen and the words would not come. When I tried to extricate my fingers from hers to tell her to leave, to save herself, she gripped me harder.

As if reading my mind, she said, "It is my journey too and the Sibyl invited us both." Ketet raised her chin. "The Sibyl speaks for Isis. I will not turn my back on my goddess now."

Shaking with dread, we squeezed hands and stepped into the darkness at the same time. The air was cool and damp and smelled of wet earth and something else I did not recognize. "Do not look back," I whispered, remembering the story of Orpheus. But my words came out garbled, and I grew confused—it was only on his way out of Pluto's realm that Orpheus was supposed to not turn. We were going in. Ketet whispered something about the Duat, the name her faith used for the underworld and fell back into the language of her child-hood, murmuring prayers in her native Egyptian. Somewhere along the way, we had released hands.

Time expanded and contracted with every step. The light of a small cauldron attracted us like moths—we followed it, afraid to lose sight of it lest we become lost in the cavernous labyrinth. Ketet fell to her knees before the light. With arms up she sang a hymn in her Old Tongue, staring up at something. I focused on what at first seemed a drawing in the cave. It gradually filled out into full dimension, a figure of a woman so ancient we trembled before it. A stone carving of an immensely pregnant woman—large breasts, enormous belly, swollen vulva.

The Great Mother.

I also fell to my knees, speechless before it, the sense of time before time never ending emanated from its serene, faceless form. This was the primal place of all. The womb of the world.

A woman's voice called to us, bid us come to her. A great swell of love propelled us up and around a rocky corner into another cavern. We coughed at the sudden burst of vapor that reeked of sulfur and something else—something the Sibyl poured from her hands into the fire, her head thrown back, her long gray hair swinging, her face twisted in what could be either despair or ecstasy. The old woman's coppery skin turned reddish orange in the light. Her ancient song of welcome sent chills down to my toes and a great desire washed over me to be held within the Great Mother's arms, to be loved, touched, wanted, protected.

"Do not stop," the Sibyl urged. "Come to the fire and take in the essence of the goddess." There was a fissure in the earth behind the Sibyl, which belched a misty vapor every few heartbeats.

Strangely, the Sibyl began to laugh and it echoed alarmingly throughout the multiple cavernous entrances around us. She mimed inhaling deep over the dried flowers she had crumbled into the flames and the vapor that rose beneath it. "Breathe in the stink of life and death which lives within the womb of the Great Mother," she said. "Do you feel her heartbeat in her cleft?" She pointed to the fissure in the earth.

Yes, yes, I felt it! My breathing, my own heart, thrummed in time with it.

"Breathe deeply for this is the essence of life, both beautiful and devastating, sweet and revolting, desirable and disgusting."

She was right. The combination of vapors and plants she had crumbled over the fissure gave off a scent hovering in that strange place between disgust and desire. Like a dog, I wanted to roll in the scent to understand it, to steep myself in it, and lose myself in the mingled ecstasy and revulsion until it made sense, until I could become it and also free of it, until I could understand it and control it, though I knew I never would or could.

"We live in the stench of blood and shit and decay. Sweet milk, sour sweat, the goddess embodied. In bodied. In. A. Body," the Sibyl chanted. She turned to me, her eyes wide, her pupils shining darkly. "This is man's fear, the stink and decay of life itself, and so they purify, purify, purify you until you are not but a sanitized shell, a depository for their seed, a vehicle of their honor."

Before I could speak, she added, "No no no no no no," closing her eyes and shaking her head so hard her gray, stringy locks whirled around her. "Mother. The Eternal One. Made of soil and mountains and oceans. Needs no purification."

A small and ancient looking stick with shells on its end was suddenly in the Sibyl's hand and she shook it rhythmically, singing words I could not make out. Ketet began to weep. She threw her arms out and twirled. "Isis comes. The sistrum brings the goddess. The roar of Sekhmet devours and protects us."

The world was blinking in and out of awareness and I thought I might get sick, but the Sibyl was suddenly in my ear. "Dance!" she commanded. "Move your body as it was meant to move."

Suddenly I was a child again in the woods, running and stalking a wild beast with Attius. "Shhhhh," I told him. "You must be silent to hunt!" I exaggerated my silent stalking to show him how it was done. He raced past me and I flew after him. "No fair," I screamed. "Wait for me, Attius!"

I chased and chased but I never caught him. When I found myself lost in the dark, I remembered to ask the goddess to keep him safe, but I received nothing, no sound, no feeling, no promise. I wondered, later, after we received the news about Cannae, if his disappearance into the dark cave had been the goddess' way of preparing me for his death.

Panting, I rested my hands on my knees until I stopped feeling my heartbeat at the back of my head. The music of the Sibyl's shells and her chanting sounded very far away. I was in a different cavern. Alone. It was cold and dark. Where had Ketet gone? I turned in circles, trying to find the Sibyl's light. A presence. Someone called to me. Was I to meet the goddess face to face?

I fell to my knees and bowed my head.

"What happened to my wildcat kit?" a voice whispered.

My head snapped up. That voice—familiar and strange, both a man's and a woman's. I knew it and did not know it. I spun around, trying to find the source.

"Know your sovereignty," the voice said, echoing with the sound of the woods as if emanating from within a forest—the rustling and scratching of a large bear against a tree, the chittering of squirrels, the screeching of an eagle on a dive, the thunder of hooves of startled deer, the caw of an angry crow.

Diana? Had the huntress come for me? At last?

"Please save Orion for me," I begged. "He is marching with the legions." I'd meant Attius. Why had I said Orion? Why had I made such a mistake—it was only later that I remembered that Diana herself killed her lover, shooting Orion by accident. Had I called upon Attius' doom by reminding her that love is not meant for her or for her daughters?

The silence filled me with dread. I fell to my knees. "Goddess, what must I do to save him, to save Rome?"

Laughter echoed all around me, as if I'd asked a stupid question.

Suddenly Larce's voice was in my ear, "The gods are not swayed by the tantrums of little girls."

Larce was here! I jumped up and was running in the sun among the neat rows between our grapevines. Insects droned around me, the summer heat burned the back of my neck, my bare toes sunk into the loamy ground, thick with the scent of the earth after a warm rain. "Where are you?" I called. I wanted to jump onto his back and let him carry me as he often did when he made his rounds at the farm. But I could not find him, not amongst the vines or the barley fields, the pastures of even the pig pens. Did his absence mean he was dead? Was that what the goddess was trying to tell me?

"Am I to join you in the underworld today?" I asked the beloved old farmer. "Have you come to help me cross?"

"Not yet."

"But I want to be with you. Can't I be with you again?" My entire body ached with intense desire to go back to those childhood days of playing in the woods with Attius, of the strange yet calming conversations I always had with Larce as we tended the land together.

But in a blink, the light and land were gone and I was back inside the Mother's dark and dank cave. The sense of abandonment drove me to throw my arms out in front of me and collapse further into the ground.

"Listen carefully," Larce's voice called out of the dark. The tenor of his voice faded as if he were walking away from me. "It is not your fault. Do you understand? You never had that kind of power…"

As one does in a dream, his words made complete sense when they were uttered but moments later seemed impenetrable. "Please stay. Tell me what you mean," I cried, sensing that his words were the key to understanding something essential I could not name nor define. "Stay, stay, stay, stay with me," I begged as his voice melted away until all that was left was the silence of death.

I keened for him, for Attius, for the lost life I was supposed to have until my throat was raw and the world turned black.

The Sibyl's acolyte shook me awake. My eyes were pasted shut and when I tried to open them the flare of her torch made me recoil. I covered my head with my hands and curled into a fetal position on the cold, stone ground.

"Your time with the goddess is finished," she said gently. "Remember the gift she has given you and take it out into the world."

As memory of my encounter with Larce flooded my mind, I marveled at the acolyte's words. The goddess had brought him to me? I began to cry in gratitude. "Thank you, Mother," I whispered.

"Come now," the young acolyte said. "You must re-enter the world of the living."

"I don't want to leave," I murmured.

"The price for merging with the Mother is death," she said. "And the Sibyl tells me it is not your time. You must come."

I remembered hearing that some people who sought to meet the Mother goddess in the Sibyl's cave never made it out, that the goddess absorbed them into her womb-mountain. It sounded lovely.

"Let me stay with her here," I murmured. "Leave me be." Maybe the Maxima's plan to kill me here was a good thing. I could join Larce in the Elysium fields where the sun shined always and whose warmth felt like a caress and a blessing. I would wait for Attius there…

I fell back into heavy darkness but was soon jolted awake by the sound of insistent drumming. It sent my heart into my mouth. The acolyte banged a stretched skin drum beside my ears, chanting a song of rebirth.

I struggled to sit up. "Stop, stop!" Every strike of the drum reverberated in my bones and made my teeth ache.

The young priestess slowed her drumbeat until it stopped completely. "I have called you back," she said triumphantly. "The goddess has spoken. It is not yet time for you to disappear into her. Come, I will guide you out."

I was suddenly out of the Sibyl's cave, blinking and gasping at the sudden surge of light and heat. "Drink this," the young priestess said, handing me a large ceramic cup filled with honey water, which I downed in two large gulps. I held it out for more. My mouth felt like it had been filled with ash.

"Where is Ketet?"

"She has already been escorted back to the compound."

A different young girl emerged and took my elbow. "Come," she said sweetly. "I will take you back."

"Cover my head," I murmured. "I am never to appear in public with my head uncovered."

"Those are the rules of men," the young woman grumbled. But I refused to move until she handed me a piece of fabric that I could draw over my head like a cowl. Only then would I rejoin the village.

Before following my guide, I turned to the woman. "I wish to thank the Sibyl."

"Your donation is thanks enough," she said. "The Sibyl left a message for you, though. As you are in no state to remember it, I have written it down for you."

She handed me a bit of papyrus, used and reused, scraped clean countless times it seemed. The words danced and disappeared before my eyes as I swayed. "What does it say?"

She cleared her throat and squinted at the scrap. "It says, 'No the goddess' sovereignty.'"

"That's what the goddess told me," I said. The thrill of recognition filled me with excitement and I wanted to jump up and down like a child. "That I should know her sovereignty!" That the Sibyl heard the same message and captured it for me made my heart soar. "I do know the goddess' sovereignty."

The young woman frowned and shook her head. "Not *Know. No.*"

"What?"

She read it back to me, emphasizing the word, "No," and put the scrap of papyrus in my hand. It was jagged and scratched my palm.

"I don't understand," I said. "It makes no sense."

She smiled, "It is written in the precise manner the Sibyl delivered it. There is no error."

"But what does it mean?" I cried. "To know and accept her sovereignty is one thing, but is she telling me to deny her sovereignty?" A strange sense of betrayal clutched in my belly. Did I misunderstand the words inside the cave? Why would the prophetess write the very thing—the disempowering of the goddess—that she railed against at her own table and inside her cave?

"The Sibyl's message is often unclear at first. Its true meaning will be revealed. It is up to you to find its truth."

She closed my fist over the small scrap of paper.

I did not remember the trip down the mountain and awoke hours later groggy and confused. Within days of the rite in the cavern, the Sibyl ordered our return to Rome. We weren't given the opportunity to see her again, despite my requests for clarification of her message from the cave. Nor were we able to thank her for the journey. It all felt strange and unfinished, but I had no choice.

My cave experiences haunted me throughout the long journey back to Rome and continued to haunt me even now. I railed silently against the Sibyl and her message to me that I should deny the goddess' sovereignty. It was cruel to make me understand the power of the Great Mother and then, in the same breath, tell me it was useless. I felt betrayed by both my experience in the cave and the Sibyl's words. Why would she mislead me in that way?

***

Inside the court, the priest of Mars smiled as the mob continued raging over my impudence at "taking a holiday" during such perilous times. A great and heavy sense of despair pressed upon my shoulders. Their hatred, combined with the deep disappointment of the Sibyl's strange message—*No the goddess' sovereignty*—left me feeling utterly and completely alone. A feeling that only grew as the nightmarish specter of twisted faces and spitting mouths moved in and out of my awareness.

Chapter Thirteen

In the tumult that threatened to turn into a riot, I wondered if they would allow me to call the Sibyl to testify on my behalf. She would verify—by the papers she received—that I was sent by order of the Pontifex Maximus and not as a pleasure-seeking traveler. But she was in Cumae, days away. And I did not trust that she would help me, especially after the betrayal of her message. A familiar bewildered rage roiled in my chest. Was this what she foretold? That I would be falsely accused and killed and the goddess would not save me? That she would say 'No' to my own personal sovereignty? But why?

Panic rose at the realization that even if the Sibyl testified on my behalf, no one would believe her. They would turn it around and claim that her refusal to honor Apollo at Cumae—instead of the Mother—was the true crime. After all the powerful Delphic Oracle bent a knee to the god of light and prophecy.

I looked up to see the priest of Mars smirking and expanding his chest as if breathing in a treasured scent. His eyes followed the path of one of his junior priests as the young man pushed through the crowd and finally broke through into the courtroom's center. The Mars priest cut his eyes back at me triumphantly and I suddenly could not breathe.

"What is the meaning of this?" the Chairman called at the inter-ruption and the mob's roar quieted like a beast raising its snout after catching a whiff of something even more interesting than the prey before it.

The priest making his way to the Chairman wore a pointed leather hat, his junior status announced to everyone by the fact that it was topped by a leather nob rather than the wooden spike—carved from a sacred olive tree—that his seniors wore. The priest silently waved a folded piece of papyrus at the Chairman and cried, "I have information pertinent to this case, your Eminence."

The Chairman looked at the pontiff who gave him a slight nod. After unfolding it, the Chairman stared, blinking at the ragged piece of papyrus in his hand. Dread spread to all my limbs.

The Chairman turned to the crowd and bellowed, "Via the testimony of a true slave, obtained legally through torture, we have the name of the man accused of outraging the sanctity of this Vestal! The accused has been charged and his trial will commence after this one. Based on that evidence, we can vote on a verdict against this priestess immediately."

A deafening roar of excitement broke over the entire arena stretching, I imagined, to fill the Forum, the walls of Rome, the whole world.

"No," I called, standing. "I am untouched. And I can prove it!"

The sieve. I had to act now. But no one heard me over the screaming, stamping mob.

Name him now! Name him now!

"The goddess herself will prove my innocence with Tuccia's miracle," I shouted.

The Chairman appeared not to have heard me, but the pontiff must have because he startled. He whispered something into an attendant's ear and the man rushed off.

No, no, no. Was he going to gain possession of it so I could not?

Again, I called out my demand but the Chairman either didn't hear or had been instructed to ignore me. Just as the hysterical roars momentarily subsided, he shouted out, "Mamercus Aemilius Lepidus stands accused of outraging the gods by debauching the Vestal Opimia Pansa."

"That is a lie!" I cried. An incandescent rage carried my voice over the chaos, even though the name was not a surprise. I told Lepidus to be careful! I warned him to hire a scribe to write down the true events at Cannae and to record the nature of our meeting. Now we would both die.

"We have witnesses who saw them together as they arranged a tryst and have proof in the form of a letter sent by the Vestal herself to her lover," the Chairman announced.

"Not true," I called, but no one paid attention to me. Yes, we met, but in public, and the letter I sent only gave instructions for hiring a scribe to record his uncle's histories. And later for help in representing me. How easily they twisted everything!

The Chairman pounded his staff. "Order, order," he roared. "In addition," the Chairman thundered into the frenzy, "we also have a confession this man seduced another Vestal virgin as well!"

The Forum seemed to quake with shock. My heart jammed in my throat. What was he talking about?

"Our defiler has admitted to not only seducing the Vestal priestess Opimia Pansa," the Chairman shouted, "but the Vestal priestess Floronia Aquila as well!"

The mob erupted with even more frenzied cries of surprise and outrage.

Manlius the prosecutor stood and played to the crowd, "Finally, we have what we need to cleanse Rome of the pollution that has caused the wrath of the gods! The gods demand the deaths of two impure, disgusting Vestals—and their debaucher—to cleanse Rome of their impiety! Only then will the gods help us overcome and remove the invader."

"Bring out the other whore! The virgins must die! Kill them now!"

Crowds flooded into the court center, ready to tear me apart. "Order, order," the Chairman yelled, banging his staff on the plinth so hard it's a wonder the marble didn't split. A look of panic crossed his face as he was jostled by a swarm of people flooding into the court.

I was so stunned by the accusations against Floronia I did not at first recognize the danger of the out-of-control mob. I was frozen with confusion and wondered why they would do this to her. She was innocent!

The Chairman's now panicked screams for order snapped me to attention. *The mob will tear me apart with their bare hands!*

"Guards! Lictors! Clear the court. Clear the court!" the chairman yelled.

Lictors and guards flooded in like choreographed dancers, keeping the people from swarming us all, including the College of Priests and the senators on the highest risers. The guards surrounding me took the brunt of the attack—the spitting, the yelling, the throwing of rocks and rotted fruit. Time seemed to slow. All I wanted to do was run to protect Floronia. How could this be happening? What did it mean?

Behind me the Chairman yelled, "Court is adjourned until order is restored and can be maintained. Disperse now! Anyone caught inciting violence will be arrested and forbidden from attending the rest of this court's proceedings. Clear the court! Clear the Forum NOW! Guards! *Guards!*"

The ring of guards surrounding me resisted blows and rocks with their shields as they walked me back—in testudo formation—to the House of Vestals. I saw nothing but the blur of bodies, the shouts of rage, the screams of panic as people were trampled.

217

Once back into the House, I ran for Floronia. Sweet Floronia, they couldn't do this to her! Why were they doing this? Suddenly it became more important to save her than myself. I raced to her private rooms. She wasn't there, or even in her sleeping cubiculum. I found her in the bathing room sitting on a bench, with her hair damp and dressed in a bathing robe. Her lady consoled her as she wept. Her lady gave me a stricken look and I ran to Floronia's other side.

"What is happening?" I cried. "Why are they accusing you?"

Floronia seemed incapable of speech through her chattering teeth. I looked at her lady, who now had both arms around her as she tried to stop Floronia's spasmodic shivers.

"Floronia, please let me help you."

"You can't help me," she managed. Her lady wrapped another towel around her shoulders like a blanket as she rocked her. Floronia stared off in a glassy-eyed trance. "I am defiled. I must be punished."

I looked at her lady for help. She mouthed, "Attacked. Raped." She pointed with her chin to a blood-stained Vestal dress on the stone floor.

Rage almost swallowed me whole as I turned back to my sister priestess. Suddenly, I saw the black eye. The bruises on her arms. The swollen lip. "Who did this to you, Floronia?"

"Ca-Cantilius. He found me alone. Told me I was going to be accused next so he might as well make it real before I die."

"Wh-what?" I asked, horrified. Lucius Cantilius. The pontiff's nephew and secretary. Attius' abuser. Even a snake like him wouldn't dare attack a Vestal virgin! Would he? With a shudder I remembered his veiled threat: "Now that you have been sullied, someone might see it as their right to take what has already been given away." As vile as his words were, I never imagined he was serious. And to attack Floronia, the sweetest, kindest one of us all—it was beyond comprehension.

Floronia shuddered. Her lady answered for her. "He told her the pontiff will always protect him. That he is untouchable." She swallowed hard and lowered her gaze. "I should be punished too for not being by your side, my lady. That bastard."

I tried to make sense of what they were telling me. Cantilius had raped Floronia? My entire body trembled with rage.

Floronia's lady turned to me. "He warned he would get what he wanted from you too now that you will also have to die. Be careful, lady."

My back muscles spasmed in disgust. Never before had I wanted to physically harm another human being. But I would have gladly cut his throat, one deep, clear gash like the knife-wielder at a bull sacrifice.

"You must name him publicly! He must be punished for this outrage. How dare he!"

I thought of all the times he gazed lasciviously at my body, of the way he took too much space when he was near Floronia or me, of how he had trapped and abused Attius. I sat on the other side of Floronia and she leaned into me and began crying again. Her lady stood. "I will get her a warm drink."

"Add a tincture of poppy from the medicine chest," I called as she hurried out. "It wasn't your fault," I murmured to Floronia as I rocked with her. "You did nothing wrong."

In between sobs, she added, "He waited until everyone was out of the House. Oh goddess, I am defiled. I am so ashamed. Goddess, forgive me."

"You are not defiled," I said. "The defiler is the one who attacked. The shame is his, not yours." She shook her head and I wondered why the tea was taking so long.

"It is not your fault," I repeated and imagined hanging the carcass of a gutted Cantilius from a hook in the butcher's stall. He deserved nothing less.

"Of course, it is my fault," she muttered. "It must be my fault *otherwise it wouldn't have happened!* Goddess forgive me, Goddess forgive me…"

My heart clenched. That circular reasoning again. If the gods allowed it, then she deserved it. "Floronia, it is not your fault," I repeated lamely. Self-blame and self-recrimination only deepened the pain but she could not seem to stop. It was the only way to get some sort of answer to the question, *"Why?"*

When she began to sob again, I rocked her and whispered, "Sssshhhh, you are safe now."

When the door opened, I muttered, "Thank Vesta—" thinking it was her lady with the calming drink. But it was the Maxima instead. Amazingly, she was carrying a tray with the tea and a small bowl containing something that flickered silver in the light from the hanging oil lamps. My arms tightened around Floronia reflexively. Never in my entire life of service with the Maxima had I ever seen her do a kindness of this sort—serving one of her junior priestesses—in such a manner. For a moment, I think, for once, she will act with compassion and kindness to one of us. But her face was twisted with anger as usual.

"Cantilius has outraged her—"

She turned to me with a furious scowl. "You are never to say his name aloud. I curse it. I have ensured the pontiff will punish him. He is being exiled to Greece…"

"Exile is his 'punishment?'" I asked incredulously. "He should be whipped to death as the law requires!"

"It is the most we can expect from the pontiff. He is protecting his family."

"No," I exclaimed. "Floronia needs to tell the truth about that piece of sewer scum. He should be punished according to the sacred laws."

"Leave us now, Opimia."

"No."

"That is an order."

My body stiffened, ready to defy her but Floronia whispered, "It is fine, Mia. I need to pray with her."

Something did not feel right but I didn't know what or what I could do about it. "Come, sweet child," the Maxima whispered on the other side of Floronia as she urged my friend to sip the warming tea.

What was this honeyed mothering tone? What was happening?

"Let us speak to Vesta together," she whispered in a soothing voice and Floronia was so grateful she almost nestled into the old woman's neck like a sleepy child.

"Go," the Maxima signaled to me. Unsure of what else to do, I obeyed, almost running down Floronia's lady as I left.

A great swell of noise from outside rattled my nerves. The mob was still rampaging. Unchecked, they would burn us all down without hesitation. The pontiff and the Collegium hoped to incite the mob against me—it would be fitting if they were devoured and destroyed by it too.

I paced in my consulting room, missing Ketet, hoping she was safe, and trying to make sense of what happened to Floronia. Somehow, I had to find a way to keep her from being punished for a crime perpetrated against her, not *by* her. But I also knew we Vestals were different. Our purity was sacrosanct. They will not care *how* her virtue was taken from her, only that it was. And they will claim it was somehow her fault and she had to die for it.

I had a sudden vision of holding Floronia's hand as we were abandoned together underground in the dark, our breaths stolen, our hearts broken, until the world blinked out.

"By the sound of it, it appears the mob is still out of control." I jumped at the sound of the Maxima's voice behind me. It was only when she bent over my small table, that I noticed that she had brought in yet another tray.

"You brought me tea?" I asked dumbfounded. After all her accusations and lies in court? What was she up to?

"Sit," she commanded. She handed me the rough clay cup of tea and signaled me to drink.

My shaking hands curved around the ceramic cup. "Why are you here?" I asked.

The Maxima pulled out a small bit of papyrus and looked around. "Where is your inkwell? I need you to sign this." She spotted it in the corner and brought it over to me along with my stylus.

I was so dismayed by the Maxima's seeming kindness, I could only continue staring at her.

"Drink. And then sign," she said, frowning furiously and I thought, *Ah, this is the face I know.*

"What am I signing?"

"Your confession."

"What?"

"It is over, Opimia. You know there is no use fighting anymore. And now with Floronia…well, you must see there is no other option."

I snatched the piece of papyrus and read it quickly:

I, Opimia, daughter of Senator Lucius Opimius Pansa and priestess of Vesta, admit to breaking my vows with Mamercus Aemilius Lepidus and beg the gods to accept my death as proper purification so that Rome may be protected and our enemies may be turned away and banished from Rome for all time. I beg that

my removal will satisfy the gods and Restore
their Peace and Protection.

"I am not signing this," I said, my resolve hardening, slamming the cup onto the table. "I have never touched the man and he has never touched me. This is an outrage! He is innocent. Why are you willing to sacrifice me—as well as an innocent man—in this way?"

The words "accept my death as proper purification" suddenly hit me. I looked at the tray—at the tea I had put down, at the knife in the bowl. "You...you want me to sign this and kill myself?"

"It is for the best for all of—"

Oh Goddess, Floronia! I lept up and careened out of the room, pushing past the Maxima, bouncing off the door post. Goddess! Was I too late? I rushed into the tub room, empty. Slipping on the wet stone, I flew to Floronia's cubiculum. Not there either. I burst into her private consulting room and there she was, in her lady's arms. Two empty cups. Both faces slack, eyes open and unblinking. Her lady joined her? Images jumped at me so fast, I could not make sense of them. Floronia's open, filmed eyes. The smell of urine from their emptied bodies. Floronia's arm flopped into the small bowl the Maxima had given her after using the knife to cut from the inside of her elbow all the way to her wrist, her blood nearly overflowing. She used both methods to ensure her death came swiftly.

"No. No. Floronia, oh no," I whispered. "This must be a nightmare."

"How you die is the only thing over which you have control," the Maxima said from behind me. "Die with dignity or be buried alive. Floronia made the smart choice."

Despite gasping for air, I was unable to tear my gaze away from the sight of Floronia and her lady's bodies, immovable and empty of the spark of life. How could this have happened? Why did this happen? Why Floronia? Why me?

The Maxima took me by the arm and led me out of the room. My utter and complete aloneness overwhelmed me. Attius was dead, Prisca's life was beyond my reach, Ketet was gone, and now Floronia…

It took a moment for me to realize I'd been led back into my consulting room.

"Sign the note and then drink," the Maxima said coldly. Where was the honeyed warmth she'd given to Floronia?

My eyes focused and I looked at her scored face and into her hard eyes. "Why should I make this easy for you when you know I am not guilty of what they accuse me of? When they are also killing an innocent man."

"Death is the price of sanctity. Of safety. Of security. We must do what is required for the greater good."

"It is only the price because you *say* it is and because you need it to be."

She gave me a look as if to ask, "And…?"

"You know I am innocent, don't you? You know I have only physically loved a woman. Yet you lead me up like a cow to the sacrificial altar nevertheless."

"Innocent?" she barked. "You have *never* been innocent." She shoved the poisoned cup up to my face. "You were always the disobedient, wild one."

When I refused to grab it, the creases in her face grew darker and deeper. "Your defiance, your lack of obedience is your crime. You must die for your endless daily outrages. That one should die so others may live is the way of the world. That is what sacrifice *means*."

"So it is better to sacrifice me and Floronia, to whip an innocent man to death, than it is to hold accountable the power-hungry generals, not to mention the disgusting Cantilius, who brought us to this point?"

Her face grew even harder and colder. "In a word, *yes*."

I stared at her open-mouthed. "Close your mouth," she spit. "Evil spirits will enter, you fool. Although I don't know why I bother, they were always inside you."

Ignoring her barb, I finally, eked out, "But why?"

"Because Varro and men like him—even Cantilius—are more important than you. Rome needs them. We do not need you. *You* are replaceable. It is that simple."

When I didn't say anything more, she held the now cool tea out to me again. "Drink."

I shook my head.

"You would rather suffocate underground?"

"No, I would rather be exonerated for I have done nothing wrong. I will go out there and demand to prove my innocence with Tuccia's sieve."

The Maxima reared back. "I will not allow it."

"You cannot stop me."

"I will denounce it as fake," she said.

Pausing at the door, I turned to glare at her. "You would not dare impugn Tuccia's miracle because then you would have to admit you were complicit, that you knew how she falsely performed it. You too would be reviled for lying to all of Rome."

The old woman blinked rapidly, the scores on her face growing pale like the skin of a weathered apple.

I stared defiantly at her. "I will use the sieve to exonerate myself and will tell the court that Lepidus is innocent and that Cantilius attacked Floronia. He should be punished for his outrages." That he would also finally pay for how he abused Attius—and gods know how many others—as well seemed goddess-sent. "You can be on the side of justice too, if only you will act."

"I want him punished but we have no power here. And his connection to the pontiff makes him untouchable."

"You have power that you refuse to use," I cried. "We need only adjust Floronia's note to state the truth. Or simply tell them Cantilius attacked her. You have the authority and gravitas to be believed. Then she will at least be avenged and justice will be served."

She shook her head. "Too late. Any doctoring of the note would have it dismissed. He would still walk."

It was all I could do not to throttle her. "Speak for her then. Speak for *us* as you were always meant to."

She looked over my shoulder as if calculating her options, then hardened her expression. "No. This has gone too far. Rome needs the cleansing that your death will provide. The people are at a breaking point."

"The cleansing can come from the miracle. Don't you see how much more powerful it will be? The alternative is that you will forever be known as the leader of two fallen Vestals. With Floronia gone, once Cantilius is punished and I use the sieve, the focus will be on how the goddess interceded on the behalf of one of *your* priestesses. A miracle is a source of hope and that's what people need now. That and the fact that the pontiff's stature will be diminished because of the shame to his family—that can all serve in your favor."

I saw the idea take hold in her mind—she would be redeemed along with me. She would be the leader of a priestly order blessed by the gods with a miracle. And by removing Cantilius, she would strike a blow to the family of the Pontifex Maximus. Making herself more powerful appealed to her. She nodded. "I will have Floronia's suicide note redone."

Without looking at me again she hurried out of the room. "I will retrieve the sieve now," I called out. "But this will only work if you back me," I reminded her. The Maxima said nothing and a flicker of fear tightened my stomach. Would she undermine me? But I had no choice—I had to act. Now. Only with the altered sieve in my hand did I dare make my request to bring water from the Tiber.

The guards had cleared the Temple courtyard, which enabled me to race up the steps to the interior of the Temple without interference. The crackle of Vesta's fire—and her intense heat—pounced toward me like a growling beast. Claudia, the Vestal virgin on duty, sat up in surprise at my sudden appearance. "What are you doing? What is happening?" she asked, clearly alarmed. "You can't come in here."

"I am still the goddess' sanctified priestess," I said, pushing past her and the immense sacred fire to the inner sanctum where the ancient relics were kept beside the palladium.

"Stop—this is an outrage!" She reached for me but I was younger and faster. I dove for the drawer and spotted the glimmer that told me the sieve was untouched. Finally, Cantilius would pay for his crime and I would clear my name and escape suffocating to death underground.

Claudia huffed hard beside me. "What are you planning to do with that?"

"What do you think? I am going to prove my innocence. The Maxima has agreed now is the time."

"Liar," she called out. "Gegania wouldn't change the plans without telling me."

Change? Does that mean all the Vestals conspired with her to have me "removed?" They all agreed to keep the secret of the sieve from me?

"Step away from me, Claudia," I said.

"You cannot do this!" she spit as I gingerly pulled the ancient relic from its box. Unbelievably, she grabbed the green tinted edge of it and tried to wrestle it out of my hand.

"You idiot, leave it," I yelled. "This is delicate—you must not handle it so roughly!"

The old woman was stronger and stringier than I anticipated and we struggled for a few grunting moments until—with an exasperated vicious tug—I finally ripped it from her hands. Her sudden release sent my arm flying behind me. Time slowed as the sieve crashed into the marble wall with a horrible, soul-crushing clang.

A bone-tingling vibration shot up my elbow. Before my eyes, the thin fragile glass coating the sieve shattered and cascaded to the ground in a series of horrifying tinkling, glimmering flashes of light.

Claudia slapped me hard and I stumbled, crunching on the slivers.

The old Vestal yelled, "Now look at what you've done! No other Vestal will be able to use this like Tuccia did!"

Bursts of orange and yellow light from the sacred flames danced in the tiny pieces of shattered glass. This was it. This was my only way out. My lungs seized so that I could not take in air. The miracle, my only means of convincing men that I spoke the truth, was gone.

An old terror of the Maxima seized me. She would be furious to learn that the miracle sieve had been destroyed. And she would blame me for it. But perhaps not if I got to her first and explained. Perhaps we could come up with an alternate plan together. Yes. Maybe even devise a new miracle that would enhance her status and ensured people believed us. She had the means and the ability to help me. We could create something together.

As I flew down the temple steps, reverberating shouts from deep inside the Forum reminded me I did not have a lot of time—I had to get to the Maxima, to convince her to continue supporting me even though the sieve was gone.

I was nearly out when the same five guards who had escorted me from the rioting court earlier stood shoulder-to-shoulder in front of the door to our House, arms crossed. *Not again.* "Move aside, you dolts," I roared. They took a step back from me in surprise and I stalked past them, fists bunched. Almost at the door.

"Priestess Opimia Pansa, the Court Chairman and the Pontifex Maximus require your presence at the court. You must come with us now," one of them said to my back.

I kept walking. Their hobnailed boots scratched the marble pathway as they scrambled around to block me. Again.

"Get. Out. Of. My. Way," I said through gritted teeth. "I must speak with the Maxima."

"She is already being escorted to the court," one of them said, pointing with his head behind him.

My stomach dropped as I saw two guards with the Maxima, leading her toward the court arena. No, no. I had to talk to her. We had to come up with an alternative plan. "Call them back. It is imperative I speak to the head priestess this very moment."

The soldiers exchanged looks of terror. The Maxima, apparently, cowed even armed warriors. They refused to budge. "I must meet privately with the head priestess," I insisted again. "You are to get her for me. Immediately."

"We have been given our orders," said the senior lictor. "You may speak with her in court if you must."

Shouts of shock and dismay coming from the center of the forum likely meant Floronia's death had been announced. The Maxima disappeared from view into the maw of the restless mob and my moment was gone.

Chapter Fourteen

The courtroom quieted as I took my place at the defendant's table once again.

"Good of you to join us," the prosecutor said with a smirk.

Confounded and deflated, I stayed silent. I could barely hear anything over the buzzing in my ears. People praised Floronia for doing the right thing by removing herself as the stain of Rome. So many people stared at me with disgust that the hair on the back of my neck prickled. I imagined them asking why I couldn't be more like Floronia and make things easier for them by removing myself. Why I always had to fight.

I scribbled a note explaining to the Maxima what happened to the sieve and how we must devise a different miracle to convince the court. A flash of white told me she had stationed herself just to the right of the Collegium. She had been waiting for me to spot her. She pointedly stared at my empty hands and raised her eyebrows.

I shook my head. "Gone," I mouthed silently. "Broken."

Her eyes flashed with rage and I felt like a small child again, desperate to explain myself. It was an accident—it was because of Claudia. I straightened my back and raised my chin to shake off those old feelings. We needed to come up with a different miracle and it had to come from her. It was the only way the court would even consider it.

The messenger handed her my note. The wrinkles on her face deepened and her lips disappeared as she read. She pointedly looked away from me and ripped the note into tiny pieces and let them flutter to the ground, where they were immediately stomped on by the countless individuals crowding the arena. My stomach sank.

"Aemilius Lepidus will also pay," the prosecutor shouted and I realized they still intended to flog to death an innocent man, simply because he insisted on telling the truth about who was responsible for Cannae. Now was the Maxima's chance to tell the truth. Cantilius should not be able to walk away from his crime. He had to be punished. Didn't she want revenge?

She gave a slight nod in the prosecutor's direction and I knew it was over. She had made her calculation. Without the ability to create a miracle through the sieve, she chose the easier path. To let the trial resume as it was—to have me be condemned and allow an innocent man to be flogged to death, while Cantilius walked free.

I could not let that happen. "You have the wrong man," I yelled, springing up. "Mamercus Aemilius Lepidus is innocent."

The crowds rippled in unison toward me. Some hooted in derision, as if to say, "Of course she would say that." The prosecutor exchanged a quick look with the pontiff but I did not give him time to respond. "Lepidus is innocent. And I am ready to divulge the name of the man who defiled the priestess Floronia."

A great swell of gasps and murmurs flew around the packed forum like a hard gust of wind and the energy heightened and sharpened, as the people hungrily anticipated even more drama. My heart pounded in my ears and I could barely get air into my lungs, but I had to avenge Floronia and Attius, and every person he ever forced himself onto.

"Lucius Cantilius, Secretary to the Pontifex Maximus, is the man who outraged Floronia."

The pontiff and all his attendants stood as one, howling in disbelief. "*She lies! The whore! Liar!*"

Throwing my priestess voice, I spoke over them. "The priestess Floronia, with her last words, named Lucius Cantilius as her attacker and defiler. As the secretary to the pontiff, it was known that he had unprecedented access to the House of Vestals and was never disciplined for abusing that right."

"She lies," the Pontifex Maximus roared as his neck swelled alarmingly.

I projected my voice even louder. "As witness to Floronia's last words, the Virgo Maxima can attest to this fact." I turned to her and the crowd quieted a bit. "The gods of the underworld do not take kindly to having a dying person's words stolen from them, so I am confident she will speak the truth."

There. I trapped her. The old woman's eyes grew big as she stared from me to the pontiff. She must speak the truth now, especially as I invoked the dark gods of vengeance if she didn't. Whispers of Cantilius' family name and connection to the pontiff sped around us and a grumbling outrage began. A dangerous swell of hate turned toward the pontiff.

The Court Chairman slammed his staff on the marble for quiet. He pointed to the Maxima and bid her stand. Slowly, he asked, "Did the Vestal Floronia, with her last words, name Lucius Cantilius as her debaucher?"

All heads turned to her and it was as if the world held its breath. I glanced at the pontiff's red, outraged face. He had lost control of the proceedings.

The Maxima straightened her spine as her eyes flicked to the pontiff. Something about his impotent rage must have given her the courage to speak up. She stared directly into the Chairman's eyes. "Yes, Floronia named Lucius Cantilius as her defiler." And then she landed the blow I never saw coming. "And the priestess Opimia has confessed his name as her defiler as well."

There was an explosion of noise that shook the rafters. My throat closed so hard I was unable to take a breath and grew dizzy. She had outplayed me. Whatever denials I attempted now would be brushed away. She had the authoritas to be believed. I knew she never cared for me but to lie like this, to condemn me to death in this way…

"Arrest Cantilius!" someone yelled.

"Arrest him! Arrest him! Remove their stain! Cleanse us now!"

The pontiff's face was twisted in shock and outrage that his own Maxima dared name a member of his family as the true criminal. My mind broke in two—one part rejoicing that Cantilius would be punished for his crimes, the other filling with dread. The Maxima had sacrificed me as surely as a priest leading a cow to the altar. She was removing me and hurting the pontiff in one fell swoop. And there was nothing I could do to counter it. My denials would be ignored and laughed at.

Priests and senators mobbed the pontiff. They seemed to be arguing heatedly. The top of the frog priest's white conical hat bobbed in the center of the melee. The Chairman pounded his staff on the marble. The high priest of Jupiter broke from the small circle of agitated priests and stepped forward as if to speak.

I had to be heard first. I shouted, "I am innocent. I am still untouched!" But I was drowned out in the wave of noise clamoring for my blood, for redemption, for hope spiking like a fever that the "reason" for their pain and suffering would finally be removed. The truth was irrelevant.

The war priest's deep voice cut through the clamor and the crowd turned as one to him, like a stampeding herd of oxen spotting an open field. "The Pontifex Maximus recuses himself from this pronouncement," he thundered. "I, Caseo Quinctius Claudus, priest of Jupiter

Maximus Capitolinus, am announcing the final ruling by this religious court: The Vestals Floronia and Opimia are guilty of incestum, of breaking their sacred vows of chastity and thus outraging the gods, who abandoned us on the fields of Cannae. Both named Lucius Cantilius as their seducer."

"I named no one, I am innocent" I screamed, but it was like I was in a nightmare and no one heard or acknowledged me.

"The only means of bringing back the favor of the gods is to cleanse ourselves of their vile defilements with punishments as dictated by law and the Sibylline Books!"

The Chairman struck his staff when the roar of approval drowned out the priest's words. When the mob quieted, he nodded to the priest of Jupiter to continue. "The Vestal Floronia has committed suicide," he announced.

Screams of dismay and relief vibrated around us.

"The charges against Mamercus Aemilius Lepidus are retracted and he will be set free. A contingent of guards has already been sent to the home of Lucius Cantilius for his arrest."

"Kill them now. Cleanse us! The gods demand it!"

"In accordance with sacred law," he continued. "Lucius Cantilius will be whipped until he is dead and thrown from the Tarpeian Rock while the Vestal Opimia Pansa will be scoured and interred alive in the infernal chamber within the Campus Sceleratus, the Evil Field. Only then will we appease the rage of the gods as is written in the Sibylline Books and was practiced by our noble ancestors when Rome was beloved by the gods!" Roaring. Stamping feet. The crowds pushed inward. Individual faces—contorted with rage, twisted with hate, crazed with indignation—lunged toward me. I hadn't noticed the guards encircle me but I was glad they had as the entire arena exploded in a catharsis of grief and rage.

"Punish the whore. Kill her now. Purify us of her stain!"

The pontiff pushed his way into the circle around me, face red and twisted. He grabbed and squeezed my arm with such force I felt it all the way up my neck. He dragged me toward the basilica. Protected by lictors and guards, we moved as one, hunched over, our steps small and shuffling, like children miming the old and infirm. Then the coolness of sudden shadow as we entered a breezeway in the basilica. The press continued, the air filled with the coarse animal stink of sweating, overwrought, unwashed bodies. The pontiff kicked a door open and threw me inside an empty, cavernous room, slamming the door behind him. Screams of panic as people were crushed against the walls outside. The howls of pain as guards broke bones pushing back with their shields and slammed heads with the flat sides of their gladii.

The darkness only enhanced my terror. When my eyes adjusted, the twisted, enraged face of the pontiff looming over me became terrifyingly clear. There was no doubt he wanted to kill me himself that very moment.

"How dare you attack my family?" he said through gritted teeth.

Lunging at me, he ripped at the thick red ribbons holding my white headdress in place, sending pins skittering on the floor and my white headdress flying from my head like a dying bird. My scalp stung from the scrapes of the ivory pins.

"Stop," I cried. "What are you doing?"

"What I must—what I have a right to do now," he said as he kicked my head coverings in disgust. My heart stuttered. I took a step back in horror. Surely, he could not mean...

He seemed to understand my look of fear and spat. "Not that, you bitch. I wouldn't let my cock within ten feet of your disgusting impurity. Everything you touch is defiled and destroyed. Take your braids out," he commanded. "You may not retain anything of your life as a

235

servant of Vesta, for you are officially declared heinous and sacrile-
gious, an insult to the gods of Rome and too impure to wear any of
the sacred robes of the Order."

But…I was innocent. Why couldn't I get anyone to see the truth?
The terrifying sense of running for my life but being unable to move
made my bones feel they had been encased in iron.

"Where is the Maxima?" I demanded. "I must speak with the Maxima." It was not too late for her to retract her words. For all of this to
stop.

Still out of habit, I obeyed and with shaking fingers, began undoing the sacred six braids. Nervously, I scratched my scalp as I always
did when my hair was freed. How often I'd wished to stop braiding
my hair so tightly to my head, to shake my head free of the deep scores
into my scalp from the hairstyle I'd worn for more than a decade. But
not like this.

The pontiff paced, muttering, "If it wouldn't upset the people I
would choke the life out of you right now, but no, they need the
pomp, they need to see the rite and the ritual carried through before
they feel purified. Cantilius always had to test the limits and this is
what he gets." He groaned, his voice sparking with anger. "My sister
will never speak to me again!"

I was going to die and he was worried about his sister being angry
with him? "He didn't merely test the limits," I said angrily. "He *raped*
Floronia. And she was not the only victim."

He stared at me. "How dare you make such an accusation—"

"He told Floronia I was next. And he raped the last boy he men-
tored—"

"Liar. Whore—"

"I am not lying. Why do you think the young man he was mentoring—Attius Tullius Coriolanus—signed up for the legions when
he could have gone into the cavalry? He had no other way of escaping

236

the man's humiliations and now he is dead. And you pretended not to know."

"I did not know—"

I snorted with disgust, a sound which seemed to shock him. "You had to know," I said. "The stink of his abuses followed him wherever he went. This is all *your* fault, for if you had disciplined him when he came into the House of Vestals, none of this would have happened. Your weakness caused this!"

Not realizing a man of his heft could move so quickly, I was not prepared for the stinging slap. I clutched my cheek but continued glaring at him. He raised his arm to strike me again and I recoiled. He did not hit but kept his arm up as if in warning.

"You lie. All women lie about these things. Oh, I am going to enjoy flogging you. Your cries will soothe me to sleep for the rest of my life."

"I am going to be whipped?" I asked stupidly as my entire body grew cold. How had I forgotten this was part of the punishment? I had always been so focused on the horror of being buried alive, I paid little attention to what happened before. "Oh, Goddess, help me," I whispered. Why, why hadn't I taken the poison the minute the Maxima had offered it to me? Why hadn't I seen that she would betray me? I looked wildly around as if I could escape but I was trapped. Too many guards, too many screaming people, despite the soldier's commands to disperse.

A young man carrying a folded bundle slid into the room, slamming the door behind him. The flash of light, color, and noise from the briefly opened door added to the sense of being trapped in a nightmare. The young man leaned into the priest's ear to whisper, but I heard every word: "Cantilius has been arrested and is being prepared to be whipped, Dominus."

The priest growled and snatched the bundle from the young man. "I will not do it. I cannot do it. I will not witness it either. Tell the priest of Jupiter he must discharge the punishment."

The man nodded and ran out. Another flash of light and sound before the door slammed. The howls and roars echoed around us and I wondered if these were the last sounds gladiators heard before they died.

The pontiff hurled the bundle at me, revealing a plain square tunica—like the one state servants wore—which I caught with one hand.

"Remove the shoes and change from your Vestal dress," the pontiff barked pointing with his chin to the dress in my hand. "All your things will have to be burned to be rid of your disgusting impurity."

When I hesitated, he rolled his eyes and turned his back. I wriggled out of my heavy white palla and dress and slipped into the tunica. Why, *why*, hadn't I run away with Attius when he begged me to, why? If we had, he would still be alive and I would not be being prepared like a sacrificial lamb for the mob to devour. Why hadn't I gone with Ketet when she'd said we should try? Why hadn't I listened to Prisca and at least tried to make for the house on the Aventine and the woman who would hide me until I could escape? Anything would be better than this!

My hands shook as I untied the delicate strips binding my white lambskin shoes to my ankles and kicked them off. Dread spread to all my limbs, like a sleeping demon had bound me in ropes.

A different young man—one of the religious slaves assigned to serve the Collegium—entered the room like a silent shadow. The pontiff called to him. "Tie her up and escort her to the square. She is to witness the cost of her crimes."

"No. Please, let me speak to the Maxima. Bring her to me!"

The pontiff ignored me as he and the young man quietly argued. "But she is untouchable," the young man whined.

"Not any longer," the pontiff said.

The young man pushed back. "Not true, Dominus. The rules clearly state that any man who touches her outside of the ruling pontiff in this process must be put to death. That is why she must walk into the chamber unassisted when it is time to bury her—you yourself taught me that."

They are talking about me as if I'm not here.

The pontiff's face grew almost purple, his neck expanding like the true reptile he was. "Fine." As he was the only one legally allowed to touch me, he grabbed the ropes from the pale-faced young man and roughly tied my wrists together. All the while grumbling under his breath that the little people took this crap altogether too seriously.

Again, I had the strange impulse to laugh. His disdain, his cynicism, his hypocrisy was almost too much to bear.

"Give me your belt," he barked at the man. He tied the slave's rope belt around the binding between my hands and extended it out to him like a leash. "Now. Do as I say. Lead her out like the impure beast she is. She must witness every lash. She must pay for every lie."

And so I was dragged out by a rope into the bright light, squinting. Barefoot, I stumbled as the man's tether pulled my arms in spasmodic jerks. Nobody paid attention to us. I must have appeared to them like a wild-haired slave trussed up and trotted out to witness what might happen to me "if I didn't behave."

The man pulled me to the other side of the basilica toward a crowded square. We climbed a riser meant for officials. The crowd surrounded a center ring, and the air was filled with anticipatory violence, as if a gladiatorial match was about to begin.

But they weren't here to watch trained gladiators perform their choreographed combats. They were here to watch a man be whipped to death.

Unbelievably, no one glanced my way. I had steeled myself to be rushed upon, spit upon, and torn apart but people's gazes floated right past me. It took me a moment to understand—they did not recognize me. They did not see me at all—they'd never seen me. I was one of the interchangeable Vestals in white. An anonymous woman held responsible for the crimes and wrongdoings of men. Out of the costume of my sacredness, I was invisible. The understanding made me want to run. *Go! Run. They will just think I'm a disobedient slave escaping a harsh master.*

My muscles tensed and my heart sped up as I looked for an opening. It would be easy enough to disappear in the crowd. Everyone's attention was on the upcoming flogging, on the spectacle of bloodletting. Necks craned and people angled for the best viewing sight. While they were oohing and ahing over the shininess of the oiled whip, I could run. I could make it to the Aventine, to Prisca's freedwoman's house. As if reading my thoughts, the young man pulled my leash taut and wrapped it around his wrists and palms as if I were a mad dog slavering to break free.

I had the sudden urge to bark and launch myself at him. The shock of my actions might cause him to release his hold. But a surge of wriggling bodies craning forward pulled me off balance. Lucius Cantilius was being marched out.

They'd stripped him naked for added humiliation. People hooted and laughed. His pale hairy body looked soft and weak and as harmless as an exposed worm in a rainstorm. But he wasn't a worm. He'd attacked Floronia. And Attius.

A guard lifted his bound hands over his head and attached his wrists to a post. Cantilius sobbed and was unable to clear the mucus that dripped from his nose. The priest of Jupiter cracked his whip into the air as if testing it, and with every flick, the crowd grew even more excited. Over the chaos, Cantilius screamed, "I am innocent! The girl lied. All women lie! I never raped anyone!"

People laughed at his distress and at how the pitch of his voice rose higher and higher in terror, his small round body twisting in desperation. The crowd grew even denser. It seemed like hundreds—no, thousands—had gathered to watch the show. Children were hoisted on shoulders. Young men shimmied up columns. A boy clutched at the thick branches of a date palm tree, his bare feet gripping the trunk like a monkey's.

The crowd hushed. "For the crime of incestum," announced the priest, "for violating the sanctity of the holy order of Vesta, for defiling not one but two priestesses, Lucius Cantilius is bound by the laws of this land to be whipped until death and his unclean body thrown from the Tarpeian Rock. Rome requires this cleansing to be made safe from the Monster of Carthage and to restore the peace of the gods."

The crowd roared.

A large man appeared at Cantilius' side and placed a hand on his rounded back. Cantilius twitched away and the people laughed. The man mimed caressing his back and gasping over the sweet, softness like an actor on stage. The crowd loved it. The priest of Mars furiously yelled at the man and signaled the guards to remove him. The man bowed as he was being escorted away and the people clapped and hooted as if they were at the theater.

I looked around, bewildered and aghast. This was a joke to them? More and more I felt as if I were in a nightmare where nothing made sense. All the while, my heart raced, my mind screaming over and over again: *I am innocent. This cannot be happening. I am innocent!*

Quintus Claudius, the priest of Jupiter, approached him and the crowd drew in a breath as one in anticipation. The priest raised his weapon, contorted his body like a discus thrower, and slammed the whip down on Cantilius' flesh with a horrifying wet thwack. Cantilius screamed. My entire body winced. People cheered. Again and again the priest raised the whip and violently slashed the man's back.

"I don't want to see anymore, I don't want to see anymore," I begged but the pontiff's assistant ignored me. More likely, he couldn't hear me. Closing my eyes did not help, as it did nothing to shield me from Cantilius' cries as his skin ripped open, of the unholy snapping sound of the lash on wet, bloodied flesh, and of the ecstatic roars of the cheering crowds.

It took a long time for Cantilius to die. His flesh was flayed until the grayish nubs of his spine and the flat white blades of his shoulders emerged from his body like islands from a disappearing tide. And yet he continued breathing, even though long unconscious by then. But even when blood and gore emerged from his throat and it was clear he was gone, the crowd demanded more.

Eventually, the priest of Jupiter tired and stopped flogging the dead body. He turned to the masses and held up his arms like a winning gladiator, drinking in the howls of praise and approval. Cantilius' body was dragged through the streets on the way to the Tarpeian Rock, where it would be thrown down the rocky cliffs. The crowd followed the body like ants trailing dribbled honey. The pontiff's man pulled my leash hard and led me back to the basilica. Only this time, instead of the pontiff in the room, it was the Maxima waiting for me.

The Maxima untied my hands while the guard scuttled away from me to bar the door. "It is not too late," I insisted. "Tell them the truth. Tell them you know I am innocent and that you made a mistake—"

"I made no mistake," she said harshly.

"You didn't have to lie—"

"Yes, I had to." She released my hands and I backed away, rubbing my wrists where the rope chafed.

"Why?"

"You don't see it, do you?" she asked, narrowing her eyes. "Men need a miracle to believe a woman innocent, but they will always believe her guilty even without proof. Without the sieve, they would just claim I was lying on your behalf. I must protect my authority."

It took me a moment to take in what she was saying. "So you lied, you condemned me, to save yourself?"

"They will only believe one of us, and it needs to be me."

Her face grew dark. "Do not look at me like that. At least Cantilius paid for his outrage against Floronia. You should be glad about that."

My mouth opened and closed like a landed fish as I struggled to find the words. "This cannot be happening," I finally eked out. "You want me to be happy that Cantilius got what he deserved—but at the expense of my own life? You know that I am innocent!"

"I know no such thing," the Maxima said with chilling indifference.

"Did you bring the poison from earlier?" I asked. "Or even the dagger? ...I don't think I can go through with this." Flashes of the sound of the whip hitting bloodied flesh, of the screams of pain filled my head and I barely contained a whimper.

"Too late for that," the Maxima said coldly. "Now go empty yourself." She pointed with her chin to the chamber pot in the shadows.

"W-what?"

"You don't want to embarrass yourself in front of everyone do you? Empty yourself."

"You think I might *embarrass* myself while I am getting whipped?" I asked, fighting the urge to laugh like a madwoman. "*That* is what you are worried about? Please, let me have the poison now."

The Maxima sighed. "I did not bring poison. We must see this through. The people need to witness you being whipped and brought to the chamber. They need to see you climb down into it. They need

243

to see the chamber sealed, and they need to see the priests shovel dirt over it. Only then will they be assured that the world is safe and ordered again. That the gods will return to protecting us from enemies and evil."

This was worse than any nightmare I could have conjured. "But...but you know I am innocent. I have never lain with a man!"

"We are long past innocence or guilt, Opimia. The truth no longer matters."

Did it ever?

"But it's impious to condemn an innocent woman to her death! You know I am a virgin still. The gods know the truth!"

To my horror, the old woman laughed—an ugly, snorting, grating sound. "What the gods demand is *obedience!* And that you lacked from the beginning." With a darting glance at the guard she came closer and lowered her voice. "However, I will help you. Here, let me escort you to the chamber pot and I will explain."

Despite rage at her betrayal, my heart soared with hope. She was the leader of the Vestal priesthood. She would find some way to get me out of this. She was the only one who could!

In the dark corner, the Maxima leaned into me. "I do not have poison, but I have something that will make the pain, the er... experience, bearable," she whispered. "So that you do not embarrass our Order. You must be as dignified as possible. Now. Empty yourself and I will give you the tincture."

That was her gift? Something to help me act a bit more lady-like so I didn't embarrass *her?* It was clear she was not going to renounce her testimony. Not free me. Not fight for me.

"Give me enough to die, please," I begged. Terror gripped me so hard, I knew I would do anything, take anything, to avoid the public whipping to come. The shame of my weakness was strong—but not strong enough to keep me from begging.

She shook her head. "The people of Rome *need* this. This will help us heal so we can concentrate on protecting the city and rebuilding our strength."

Prisca's words came back to me—of how she warned me that Varro's men wanted Rome consumed by scandal while they worked out secret deals with foreign powers. If the yelling outside was any indication, this "scandal" had indeed unified and distracted all of Rome. Goddess, why hadn't I run when I had the chance?

"Are the Phrygians coming?" I asked the Maxima. "And the Galatians? To help us fight? Are they bringing the statue of Cybele? If they are on their way, I don't need to die, right?" I was babbling but I could not stop.

The Maxima blinked. "What are you talking about? You are making no sense. Now go."

As if sleepwalking, I did what she asked of me and as I returned to her, she held out the small glass vial. "This concoction will not make you sleep," she explained. "However, it will make you feel as if you are not in your body so you may bear the pain with dignity."

I remembered how often I was told to protect the dignitas of my father as a young child, and then later, how important it was to project solemn dignity in public as a priestess of Vesta. The Maxima cared nothing for my upcoming agony, only that I didn't shame her with my physical reactions, that I didn't piss myself and wail and therefore reflect poorly on *her*. It had nothing to do with easing the horror of what was about to happen to me.

As always, my first impulse was to defy the Maxima and refuse the mixture on principle, but she'd said it would take the edge off the experience. I would be a fool to not accept the only kindness she had ever shown me. I slurped down the bitter liquid and continued long after it was empty in the hopes of sucking down every atomos of whatever she had concocted for me.

When I thrust the vial back to her, she nodded and said, "Good girl." Snorting, I suppressed a laugh. It took this moment—before torture and my death—for her to give me a warm word. And only after she falsely condemned me. I was finally serving a purpose for her.

The potion burned my throat and I remembered how often the priests of Beasts drugged the ornery bulls and resistant animals before leading them to the sacrificial altar.

An echo of a roar from a distance left me wondering if that meant Cantilius' broken body had finally been thrown off the Tarpeian Rock. That meant they were heading back to witness my whipping.

The room wavered. Garbled words floated my way. Leaning against a post, I turned to the Maxima to ask her to repeat herself, but she was not there. When had she left? The sense of something horrible about to happen to me gripped my gut. What was it? It was something dreadful. Yet I could not remember.

A guard spoke harshly. Had he been there the whole time?

"It is time," he repeated, pulling on the leash attached to my bound wrists. When had my wrists been retied? I stumbled after him and he growled, "It is your turn now."

For what? I wondered. The concoction the Maxima gave me made me feel as if I were in a dream and idly, I wondered if she had given me too much.

I stumbled barefoot beside the man pulling me by a rope leash out of the dark building into the searing light. Terror gripped my belly once again as contorted faces, filled with hate, lunged at me. Screams of, *"Whore! Defiler!"* echoed in my ears. Why would they say such things? Hadn't I given up everything for them?

Suddenly a man was tying my wrists—again without managing to touch me—to a rusted iron ring on a post. Out of habit I murmured thank you when he was done. Then I remembered why I was there and my politeness seemed ridiculous. I began to laugh then. The mob backed away in horror and their fear of my laughter made me hoot even harder.

"She has gone mad! Punish the demon-whore!"

"Whore! Whore! Cleanse us of her Stain! The Vestal Must Die!"

The pontiff called for order as he practiced the snap of the large leather whip. Someone ripped my tunica to expose my back. Thankfully, the rough fabric did not fall to the ground. The position of my shoulders kept it from exposing my breasts and I gave a small thanks, despite the ridiculousness of trying to preserve my modesty in the moment, but the thought shattered with the first lash.

The pain was hot and searing and indescribable. A great roar burst from the crowd as another one came, followed by another and yet another. Each lash felt like a bolt of lightning coursing through my flesh and it threw my mind to strange places.

A jolt of fire and I was dangling from my old nurse's grip as she shook me, telling me that thunder meant Jupiter was angry with me for disobeying. Another bolt and I was being ripped from my father's lap on Selection Day. Another and I watched myself run from Attius in the grove on the day he came to me as a man.

The pain soon blotted out all thought, all memory, all hope, and the world went black. I swam into awareness when I realized the searing jolts had stopped, though the pain on my back was sizzling fire. Someone released my hands from the iron ring to the sounds of a celebrating mob.

I found myself in a dark room again. Someone untied my wrists and my torn tunica dropped to my feet. Pain thrummed and sparked and sizzled through every inch of my back. A strange sound vibrated in my ears and I realized my teeth were chattering as deep shivers wracked through me.

"What is wrong with her?" a female voice asked. "Why is she not crying in pain?"

"She is in shock," said the Maxima.

The Gray Ladies surrounded me. Someone smoothed cooling unguent over my lashes. At this I howled and whimpered, trying to breathe through the pain like a birthing mother.

"Slather an extra layer so the fabric doesn't stick to the broken skin," one of them said, and I found myself thinking, *How considerate!*

Like a living doll, I was manipulated—one arm at a time—into a long, plain tunica. The fabric was worn and soft and thankfully did not press or stick upon my lashes. They left me barefoot but wet down my curls to put it into a loose braid. Kindly, someone gently placed my single long braid over one shoulder so as to avoid it brushing against the open wounds on my back.

Someone led me to a chair where I was guided to sit as a wave of exhaustion hit. Recognition came slowly. The chair was on a bier, surrounded by flowers, most of them dead or dying. The smell was putrid. A funeral bier. On it, I would be carried to the Campus Sceleratus, the Evil Field near the Colline Gate, where I would be required to climb down unassisted into the chamber of fallen vestals and be buried alive.

I stayed on the edge of the seat to avoid anything touching my seared and lanced back. Memories of parades of the dead flashed through my mind. The shrouded bodies of powerful men propped onto throne-like chairs and carried through the streets before being finally burned in funeral pyres outside the city. Only those bodies were venerated. Mine would be paraded through a sea of hate and vitriol so I could absorb even more of the people's pain and hatred. My head was still wooly with the Maxima's potion so I did not understand when someone draped a veil over my head. Despite excruciating pain when I moved my arm, I tried to yank it off.

"Leave it," one of the Gray Ladies said.

Right. It was not a veil, but a death shroud. I had to look like a cadaver. The now familiar sense of unreality took hold as I stared through the wavy lines of the unevenly woven fabric.

"On three." Burly men I had never seen before lifted my chair and secured it with pegs and rope to the funeral bier. They shoved even more flowers around the chair as if I were truly dead and they needed to mask the smell of rot. Dying flowers over the ones about to die.

Someone wept nearby. Who cared enough about me to have such a reaction? Then I understood. They were not lamenting for me. They finally—finally—had someone to blame, someone who was paying for all their loss, pain, and agony. It was a cathartic release. They were weeping *in relief.*

As the litter bearers carried me out of the Forum and settled into a steady pace, I fell into a half-dreaming state. Attius was suddenly walking beside me. Sweet, beautiful Attius. "I took revenge on Cantilius for you," I told him. Long-haired Attius, the one before he enlisted, smiled up at me and my heart melted for all that was lost. I was so angry at him for signing up as a legionnaire, I never allowed myself to feel the full depth of how much his absence meant to me. "I'm sorry you died," I managed and he disappeared.

I should have made love to him, I thought. Then at least this would make sense.

A heavily pregnant woman crossed my vision. *Prisca, you are here!* A wave of gratitude washed over me as I realized the risk she had taken to be by my side. *Oh, my friend. I should have listened to you. Why didn't I listen to you?*

But it was not Prisca, of course, for when my vision cleared, I saw the face of a grieving stranger, dressed in dark mourning clothes, lamenting the loss of her baby's father on the fields of Cannae. Blaming me for her pain.

On the street past the incense market, the familiar scent of bathing oils took me back to the room with a crying Floronia. "It is not your fault," I said aloud, taking her hand in mine.

She shook her head, denying the truth.

"It is not your fault," I insisted. "Cantilius hurt you. The fault is *his.*"

I blinked and she was transformed, unmoving, eyes open, a hollow shell, freed from the agony of self-blame and self-disgust.

A litter bearer stumbled and I gripped the sides of the chair as the others grunted and staggered at the interruption of their pace. I became aware of priests dressed in black escorting me on both sides of the litter. Had they been there the whole time? The procession of black-clad priests sent me back in time to the Tullianum the night the Maxima dragged me there to scare me into "acting right" and being the gentle, demure, obedient virgin they demanded. For a moment I was eight years old again and in terror of the Maxima's awesome power in bringing me into Pluto's realm.

The winding streets, filled with Romans, were strangely silent. Where in the Forum people screamed and yelled and threw insults at me, now they seemed cowed, perhaps even guilty as they watched me being carried over the cobbled streets to my death. As we neared the chamber by the Colline Gate, the crowd expanded but, strangely, grew even quieter. The silence added to the dream-like feel, especially after all the insults and yelling at the Forum.

We must have arrived at the Evil Field because my carriage bed swayed as the bearers shifted the litter poles off their shoulders and placed me on the ground. They took great care not to send me tumbling into the dirt. But not for my sake. They were protecting the priests' dignitas. It was *their* reputations at stake. The rite had to be perfect so they could look good.

The dreamy sense of unreality took over again as I watched an endless parade of phantom animals march past me, compliant and unaware of their coming slaughter. We sacrificed so many animals in our desperation over Hannibal to no avail. Our streets ran with blood. The shades of all the countless animals we sacrificed year after year—chickens, puppies, rams, bulls, cows with gilded horns, bulls wearing elaborate flower chains—all marched placidly to their deaths at the hands of people who they believed protected them.

Then the gleaming shade of the sweating, magnificent October Horse trotted past. With eyes rolling in terror, it turned its massive head my way and whisper-hissed, "Run!" Then disappeared.

What did all those animals do to anger the gods I wondered, confused for a moment at the image of the river of blood flowing down the cobblestone streets from our endless sacrifices. And then I remembered that we sacrificed them to bargain with the gods. We'll give you this gorgeous specimen, and in return, you will protect us. Right? *Right?*

Larce was suddenly lifting me up to pluck the sweetest of the new grapes on a brilliant fall day. "Remember, the gods are not swayed by the tantrums of little girls," he said. What had I done to get in trouble that day? I could not remember but breathed deep of the smell of moist earth and sweet stickiness of heavy grapes about to be harvested.

A new thought. If the gods weren't swayed by the tantrums of little girls, they likely also didn't care about the behaviors of grown women. There was something important about that thought but it disappeared when the pontiff bent to my ear and hissed, "Quiet!" I had not realized I'd spoken.

Right. Be quiet. Be good. I had to be a good girl right up until the moment they killed me for being bad.

Dizziness swarmed through me and I gripped the chair tighter trying to grasp the notion hovering just on the edge of my awareness.

The gauze shroud covering my face fluttered when I exhaled. Suddenly I was six with my father and making the orange veil of my Vestal selection outfit dance with my breath. From a pretty veil to an ugly death shroud in no time at all.

A baby cried into the heavy silence. It was quickly shushed.

Someone brought a baby to watch me die?

"It is time," the pontiff said.

We were at the Field of Evil. The large mound of dirt meant the chamber was to my left.

I knew what was expected of me—I was to rise and silently walk to the underground chamber, and climb down the ancient steps unassisted, as so many vilified and soiled Vestal virgins had done since Rome's beginning. I was a living dead woman made to march into my own death chamber. And I felt dead too—heavy, cold, paralyzed.

"Get up," a priest whispered in my ear in a harsh tone. "Do your duty!"

No man could assist me because touching me would require his death. Even a defiled Vestal priestess, it seemed, could not be touched by any man without consequences. Again I looked at the mound of dirt they planned on piling on top of the sealed chamber once I made my descent.

The priests told themselves that they could not be blamed for killing a sacred priestess because they had so thoughtfully outfitted my chamber with a couch and a table with a lit oil lamp, bread, and wine. They claimed this gave the goddess time to appear and rescue me, if I were actually innocent. Only a miracle wrought by the goddess could save me.

The goddess never saved any of her priestesses throughout Rome's history. They never mentioned that. Why did it always take a miracle for a woman to be believed?

No the goddess' sovereignty. The Sibyl's inexplicable message echoed in my ears and an even greater heaviness overtook my limbs. Perhaps I was a corpse after all.

"This is an outrage," the pontiff said through gritted teeth. He pointed a finger at the Maxima and hissed, "Make her obey. It is time for her to walk into the chamber!" A look of panic flashed across the old priestess' face as we both realized at the same moment there was no dignified way to "make me" do anything in this most theatrical moment. There never had been, despite all their canings and beatings. I never was and would never be the obedient girl they had always wanted.

When the Maxima did not move, the pontiff turned his enraged toad-face back to me. "Get. Up. The rite cannot be completed until you climb down there."

The Maxima grabbed my arm and shook me and I cried out at the pain of fabric scraping my lashes. "Do as you are told, girl," she commanded.

When I refused to move, murmurs of alarm grew all around me. *"What is happening? A bad omen!"*

An old man yelled, "Are the gods angry at her impudence?"

One of the younger priests bent to my ear. "You must finish the rite," he whined. *"Please."*

The more death-like my pose, the more agitated the energy around me grew. Interesting. Murmurs swelled and swirled all around me: "Why isn't she moving? Is she dead already? Are we cursed? What does it mean?"

Panicked murmurs and cries roiled up and down the masses. But what could anyone do? The pontiff could order a man to lift me and force me down the chamber, but no man would dare, as it would mean certain dishonor and death for him. Only the pontiff may legally touch me but he will not attempt to wrestle me off this bier and into the chamber because of what it would cost him: his dignity. He must have sensed, rightly so, that if he tried to manhandle me, I would fight. And potentially bring him down into the dark chamber with me. They would lock us both in there.

Coward.

The priests began arguing amongst themselves. The pontiff told the Maxima and the other Gray Ladies to drag me into the chamber, but they recoiled. They would not risk their dignity or the chance of being pulled down either.

The pontiff ordered a soldier to throw me down into the chamber. The young soldier blanched. He turned and ran, getting lost in the crowd. The man's sudden movements alarmed the mob. The murmurs of fear grew louder. Wails erupted as old women keened.

A realization seized me. They were scared because I broke the agreement binding us all. That if I behaved in a certain way, the gods would be satisfied and they would be safe. I was ruining the illusion of control.

We are trying to control the uncontrollable. I thought of the augurs who told Varro the gods approved of engaging Hannibal in pitched battle at Cannae. And of the terrible massacre that followed. Of the priests in the garden discussing throwing twenty-seven living men to their deaths at the Argei because Rome needed a "dramatic show" of expiation. Of the year our crops failed despite the perfect sacrifices of pregnant cows throughout the city. Of me using my own blood on the altar to avert the despair of the already-grieving masses during the rite of the October Horse.

All performed in a desperate bid to control the uncontrollable. And it never worked. Never. It was never my fault.

It was not my fault tens of thousands of men died at Cannae, just as it was not Floronia's fault Cantilius raped her. Blame helped us manage the agony of loss and grief; it helped us make sense of a world where bad people like Cantilius hurt good people like Floronia and Attius. Where tens of thousands of young men died before fully tasting life. Blame was an attempt to make sense of the insensible.

I thought again of the Sibyl's strange message: *No the goddess' sovereignty.*

The idea that had been hovering at the edges of my awareness suddenly sharpened into clarity and I gasped with surprise. The Sibyl wasn't being mysterious or obtuse when she wrote "No" instead of "Know." She was showing me the nature of the goddess' power, where her sovereignty lived: in the word, "No."

"No" was power.

A burst of energy thrilled through me and my hands twitched in my lap. "No," I said loudly, startling everyone around me.

No, I will not be sacrificed so you can feel better about the future.

"Get up, you whore," the pontiff said desperately over the growing cacophony.

"No," I repeated, as the power of the goddess' sovereignty filled me with strength. "*No!*"

And then I laughed loudly and freely like the Sibyl, because I finally, finally understood. I marveled at how one small word had the power to send the entirety of Rome into a wailing panic.

"No," I repeated.

Chapter Fifteen

Despite the continuing burning pain of my lashes, I straightened my back, keenly aware of the chaos I'd created, of the panicked buzzing of fearful questions about what my actions "meant." My resolve—and my face—hardened into marble. The squabbling priests, the pale wide-eyed virgins, the reddened face of the furious Pontifex Maximus—I watched them from a very long distance. Their tiny efforts to control me, control life, were almost laughable.

Someone must have called for soldiers and guards from the training fields. The rhythmic pounding of their hobnailed boots echoed in a terrible rhythm. Then came the hoarse demands. "Clear the streets! Go home! The augurs have announced that the gods want the rite completed in the morning. This was the gods' will!"

So that was how they were going to play it. Of course, it was the god's will. Otherwise, it wouldn't have happened, right?

Reluctantly, the mob complied, but only after violent prodding with shields and raised swords. By the time the streets had been emptied, an ominous purple dusk, trailed by a cape of black, descended over the land. A hiss and a flare of light meant someone nearby had lit a torch. As the last stragglers were ushered off, the pontiff repeated the official message. "All is well and in hand. We will complete the rite in the way the gods require in the morning."

Pay no attention to the woman refusing to comply.

Still on my death bier, I was carried back to the House of Vesta, though this time, with a lot less solemn and tender care. The litter bearers wanted to get away from me as fast as they could. My "sister" Vestals escorted me into the house and into my chamber where they left me without saying a word. Everyone seemed angry and confused and a little frightened of me. The latter was oddly satisfying. When I pulled off my shroud, they turned away from my gaze as if I were Medusa and scurried off to whisper amongst themselves.

Their panicked whispers floated to me. "The pontiff and the College of Priests, along with key senators, are consulting the Sibylline Books at the Temple of Jupiter Maximus this very moment!"

"Everyone is scared."

"What possessed her?"

Good. I rattled them. Still, I was surprised no one expressed grief for Floronia. My sweet friend. Had they decided that she was guilty too? That she did not deserve their grief or compassion because of her "crime" of being attacked?

An old tray of barley water and bread was on a small table in my cubiculum and I lunged for the jug, drinking it down greedily. I tore chunks of bread and ate like the starving children we sometimes saw in the Subura.

I unwound the single braid they'd twisted my hair into before the procession to release the tension in my head and to make sure the heavy braid didn't brush my still burning back.

Revived, I dove into my chest and pulled out my remaining savings—gold, silver, and bronze coins in several soft leather bags. I poured them all into one satchel and stared at the considerable wealth I'd collected over the years. When I added the coins from Prisca's bag, it was an impressive pile. I did not know what I was going to do with all my earnings—only that I did not want the Maxima or the state to claim it, on principle.

Maybe I would give it to Zena the cook. She had always been kind to me and Attius' dog. And if they found some other way to kill me, the money would help her take care of him. Yes, I would give it all to Zena when she returned in the morning. I sinched the bag of money and tied the rope around my hips to remind me to keep it from the Maxima.

Or you could run, a small voice whispered in my ear. *Now, while everyone cowered and trembled at their private shrines.*

But an overwhelming exhaustion swept over me. The pain of my lashings came in waves so fierce I grew dizzy when they crested before subsiding, only to begin again. And no doubt, the Pontifex Maximus will have every available man at every opening in and out of both this House and the Forum itself to keep me from running.

I imagined Larce whispering into my ear, "Focus on controlling only what is yours to control." And right now all I could control was where my money went. As another wave of overwhelming pain and fatigue crashed over me, I gingerly stretched out to rest on my front side when a small piece of papyrus fluttered to the floor.

The stiff paper crackled as I unfolded it. Written in neat lampblack were the words:

Prisca Liberta Tira
Fifth House on the Street of the Faun,
Aventine

It must have fallen from Prisca's bag. Well, it was too late now. I did not want Prisca or her freedwoman to suffer, so with my last gasp of energy, I placed the crinkled piece of papyrus to the flickering flame of my bronze lamp. The papyrus caught and I held onto it until the heat reached my fingertips. When there was nothing left but ash, I sunk into heavy black nothingness.

Something tickled my nose, then my throat. A strange, yet familiar tune pulled me up from the depths of the sea and I resisted it.

Let me sleep. Leave me be.

Suddenly I wheezed and coughed as a familiar dry dust covered my tongue.

What in Pluto's world?

My eyes felt sealed shut and I struggled to open them. When I did, it was to stare into the nightmarish face of the Maxima. She sprinkled something over me. I batted her away as she murmured the hymn of appeasement before sacrifices. She tossed another handful at my eyes and I closed them just in time. Coughing, I recognized the smell and taste of salt and ash and ground barley as the Maxima crumbled a sacred salt cake over me. The salt cakes we used to sanctify beasts before they were sacrificed at state ceremonies.

"Have you gone mad?" I hissed as I scrambled away from her, the lashes on my back sending searing jolts of pain through me.

The old woman continued mumbling the prayer of ascension, where we beseeched the gods to accept both the animal and the burnt offerings of the sacrificed beast.

"What are you doing?" I demanded but she refused to answer. My muddy mind slogged through what happened next in a state ritual sacrifice—after breaking the mola salsa cake over the sacrificial victim, the cultrarius, the knife wielding priest, cut the throat of the animal and collected first blood. I looked around as she performed the circular procession around me, three times, but there was no man holding a ceremonial knife. Was I dreaming?

She's not allowed to touch blood, I reminded myself. *She would not dare cut me.*

The Maxima's eyes—blazing and wild—alarmed me. Hate emanated off her like heat from a clay oven. There was another smell. Rancid, stale olive oil. Was that what she was pouring from a bowl?

259

"What are you doing?"

She did not answer except to grin at me. Perhaps it was a grimace, I could not tell. In that moment, she looked like a Graeae, one of the three ancient sea hags who shared a single eye and tooth between them. The Maxima straightened after wiping her hands on my blanket. Still, the crumbs from the salt cake stuck to her oiled skin.

"Have you gone mad?" I asked, scrambling onto my knees on the small couch, the movement making me hiss in pain as my lashes stretched.

"The priests and senators are still in the Temple of Jupiter Maximus arguing about what to do with you. I, however, already know. And only I can do what they are too weak and scared to do."

"It is forbidden for a Vestal to touch blood," I reminded her in a soothing voice. "You cannot kill me for you will be tainted too."

She blinked in surprise. "I'm not going to cut your throat, you fool. That would be *nefas*. Besides if I were going to murder you by blood, I would've done it already. No, the goddess requires a different purification."

My eyes darted from her to the entryway, which she blocked. Should I run, pushing her out of the way? She was an old lady after all. But where would I go?

The old woman held out a ceramic cup, the same one she'd given Floronia. "Drink. The gods like their sacrificial offerings placid and calm."

"What is in there?" I asked, slowly edging to the end of my sleeping couch.

She shoved it closer to my face with irritation. "Poppy mixture! The goddess does not want to see or hear you screaming in agony. It would insult her. And your pig squeals might call rescuers too early. So drink!"

Right. We often drugged sacrificial animals—especially the larger ones like bulls—before leading them to the altar. One leg down. Slowly I moved the other, my muscles tensed and ready to run. Again, the Maxima shoved the drink at me and I shook my head.

"No."

As if still in a dream, I imagined hearing the Sibyl's amused laughter in my ear. *You understand now, yes? No is the language of sovereignty.*

The Maxima's face twisted into a mask of rage. "You have defied me for the last time." I moved back from her, though I struggled to keep from swaying. Pain and exhaustion made me dizzy, adding to the sense of unreality.

"You must pay for your defiance—"

"It is YOU who have defied the gods by lying about me."

"How dare—"

"You claimed I was unchaste with Cantilius when you knew it wasn't true. And now, you enrage the gods by defying their will."

"What are you talking about?"

"You yourself burned into me that we determine the will of the gods by what they allow. Because I am here, it means the goddess herself saved me from death today," I claimed with as much authority as I could manage. "You defy her by trying to kill me."

Her eyes ignited with fury. I had touched a nerve. *Did a part of her fear this may be true?*

"The goddess wants this. She wants to be purified of you. I should have killed you in your sleep when you were a child."

There was a strange thrill of horror when something you'd long suspected is revealed as true. I suppressed a shiver.

"Funny how the goddess' wants and your desires always inexplicably align," I managed.

The rage that flickered in her eyes terrified me as a child. But now I was a grown woman and could defend myself from her tyranny.

261

"*Drink*," the Maxima insisted through gritted teeth, shoving the cup toward me again.

"No." Two steps sideways and I was very nearly to the door. But she moved quickly for such an old woman and blocked me.

"You must drink the poppy," she said. "The worst thing that can happen now is for someone to mistakenly rescue you before it is done. Now swallow."

A quick glance out revealed a dark and empty hall. She was by herself. Did the others know she was here and what she was doing? With a sudden movement I knocked the cup out of her hand. I hadn't noticed what she had been holding in the other: a small ancient bowl bearing the still smoking embers of our sacred fire.

"Fine. Die screaming." She held up the small fire bowl and threw it into the pool of oil. Time slowed. Then came the sound of breaking crockery. The heat from a sudden flare. Light that blinded us as fire swallowed my bed.

"The Fire of Vesta purifies us," she shouted. I lunged for the doorway. The old woman grabbed handfuls of my hair at the scalp and jerked me back.

"You must die," she hissed as I writhed against her hold. "The men are too weak and frightened to do what must be done. Only embers from the sacred fire can cleanse us of your filth now."

The wall hanging in my small room flared. In desperation I nearly dragged her with me out the door, but the old lady had a grip of iron on my scalp and had planted her feet. Again and again, I hit at her skeletal fingers but she did not let go.

I heard the words "Proserpina" and "demons" and "torture" and realized she was reciting a curse over me. Thick black smoke erupted as my whole room ignited. I managed to get my head into the hallway where I tried to gulp fresh air, struggling against her grip.

"Must die. Must cleanse. I am the instrument," the old crone muttered as she tried to throw me by my hair into the conflagration. Couldn't she see her own hem had begun to smoke? With a roar, I wrenched around and slammed both hands down on her wrist. She cried out in pain and I ran.

The mad priestess was on the ground bellowing behind me, crawling out of the inferno like a demon from Pluto's caverns. Fabia sprinted out of her room, eyes wide looking past me at the billowing smoke and at the screaming Maxima.

"What has happened?" she shouted, blocking me.

I froze. She raised a hand as if to slap me. "Speak, slave!" I was in a servant's tunica, barefoot, and wide-eyed, with my hair in untamed curls. She did not recognize me because her eyes were locked onto the screaming demon in the hall.

"Fire, Domina," I squeaked, disguising my voice. "I am to tell the guards!"

"Go, idiot!" She turned from me and ran toward the sound of the old lady's roaring and coughing. The other Vestals flowed out of their rooms and followed Fabia to rescue the Maxima. They too only seemed to see a panicked slave and looked right through me. They knew she was in my room. Did they assume I was still in there?

I made it outside. Screams echoed eerily. A guard ran toward me. Household slaves and servants rushed out of the house. "Where is the fire?" the guard yelled. "I must set up the sand and water chains!"

I pointed and ran, hearing Useless barking like mad. Was he locked in the kitchen? If the fire spread, he would die too. I couldn't leave him.

Rescuers from outside our compound rushed in. "Where is it?" a man screamed into my face. "Where is the source?"

"In the Vestals sleeping rooms," I finally managed, once again disguising my voice. Inspired, I added, "The accused virgin burst into flames and was taken by the goddess of fire! It was a miracle! The Virgo Maxima witnessed it!"

Some of the running slaves and passers-by heard me. Murmurs of awe spread almost as fast as the fire. *Miracle. The Maxima saw it!*

If they only ever believed a woman when a miracle took place, I would give them one.

Something pulled at my tunica. Useless! Someone must have released him and he was trying to drag me away from the fire. "Let's go," I cried and we took off running into the dark recesses between buildings.

Even if the Maxima called for me to be chased, talk of a miracle would confuse everyone, buying me precious moments. A great swath of people rushed toward the house, chattering excitedly about a miracle. A real miracle in their own lifetimes! The excitement was palpable.

People *wanted* to believe the divine acted in our lives. Needed it. If the Maxima lived, she would be forced either to admit she'd tried to kill me or claim the "miracle" was real. She might even convince herself—in her enraged madness—that I was indeed consumed in flames sent by the goddess.

More people flowed out of the pontiff's compound toward the fire, many of them guards carrying buckets of sand or water. If just one sharp-eyed guard recognized me. Or if the pontiff himself saw me…I shuddered. But no, they'd said all the priests were consulting the Sibylline Books in the Temple of Jupiter.

Fortunately, no one glanced my way and I joined the flow of frightened servants and slaves exiting the compound as well. I was just another barefoot, frightened slave moving toward safety. As soon as I could break away without detection, I scuttled quickly into the dark recesses of the Forum, trying to catch my breath, trying not to cough lest I gave up my location. Useless whined and pawed me and I fell upon him. "Good boy, good boy," I repeated over and over again.

Running deeper into the dark maze of the Forum I noticed something bouncing against my thigh. The money satchel. I had tied it to
my belt to remind me to give it to Zena. If anyone saw me with such
a thick money bag, they would assume I stole it off a rich person. And
arrest me as a thief. A piece of cloth fluttered on the ground, which I
quickly swept up and tied around the satchel. It would keep it out of
sight and muffle the tell-tale sounds of coins clinking.

My arms were too pale, too noticeable. I rubbed against the walls
of the alley, cringing inwardly, but knowing that I had to look like I
belonged to the streets. I smudged some of the dirt and ash on my
tunic, onto my face, onto the tops of my bare feet. With unbound hair
and soiled clothing, I hoped I could pass for a particularly unkempt
slave or vagabond.

No one would imagine that a refined Vestal could look like this.
Or even allowed herself to be seen in this state. Still, my heart pounded
at the base of my neck with terror at every sound, sending lightning
bolts of pain through my still weeping lashes.

Although I did not know all the alleyways and cut-throughs, we
scurried silently in the dark toward the Argelitum, Useless panting beside me. The drunken thieves who may have otherwise accosted me
took one look at the big dog and kept moving. More and more people
were awakened by the clamor of the fire and raced to the Forum. A
begrimed drunk man, who had clearly not seen Useless, grabbed my
arm and tried to drag me into an alleyway. Useless leapt upon him,
jaws snapping, and the man reeled back, horrified. His screams attracted notice so I projected my priestess voice into the throng and
called, "A miracle! Did you hear about the virgin miracle?"

"Miracle? What miracle?" voices clamored. "Tell us!"

And so I spread the story of the Vestal who was taken by the flames
of the goddess of fire in the House of Vestals. Energized by the possibility of witnessing a true act of the gods, most people sprinted toward

the scene. Even the drunkard who accosted me lurched in that direction, but not before Useless took a sizeable a chomp of his backside.

"Good boy," I murmured and he smiled up at me, tongue lolling.

Once past the publicus road, I made my way to the Aventine. After finding the fifth house—a grubby ground floor apartment—on the Street of the Faun, I knocked on the faded but sturdy planks of the freedwoman's door, hoping I had the right place. Hoping I wouldn't be turned away.

A voice called out warily, "Who is disturbing my privacy at this hour?"

"Prisca Tira? Your patroness, Prisca Sulpicious, has sent me." I whispered this into the tiny space between the door and the door jamb, praying no one overheard.

There was silence on the other side and my heart pounded for what seemed like a million beats. The surge of frantic energy that had kept me running began to recede and a wave of pain and fatigue almost buckled my knees. I steadied myself by leaning my forehead against the door.

Finally, iron fittings scraped against locks and the warped door creaked slightly open. Half a woman's face peered out at me.

"Your patroness promised you will help me," I said in a whisper.

She inspected me slowly from head to foot and back again. Finally, she nodded warily. "The dog stays outside."

I gave Useless the "wait" command and slipped inside. We stood awkwardly in the still-dark room as the woman slammed and relocked the door.

Something tickled my foot and I jumped. It was only a cat winding around my ankles.

"She likes you, that's something at least," she mumbled to herself. Staring into my face, she asked, "Who are you?"

Had she not recognized me?

Cautiously, I asked, "Who were you expecting?"

Had Prisca's freedwoman been told she might be asked to harbor an accused Vestal? Would she turn me over to the priests?

The woman shrugged. "I received instructions I was to help whoever showed up at my door bearing the name of my patroness."

I grew dizzy with relief.

"What is your name?" she asked. "And what do you need?"

"I need to get to Cumae," I said and patted my satchel of coins. "I can pay for transport."

The woman raised her eyebrows. "You dare go south in these times?"

"I will take the coastal roads which are safer," I said with confidence, silently hoping it was true.

"I will help arrange it. But I must know your name."

"It is Mi—" I caught myself. "Call me Diana," I managed. "My name is Diana. Like the huntress."

Epilogue

Six Months Later
Attius

Begrimed, exhausted and thirsty, two legionnaires trudged slowly up
the dusty mountain road leading to a tiny village near the Sibyl's cave
in Cumae. One soldier gave the other a small shoulder nudge, his signal to step to the right to avoid a divot in the road. The blind soldier—
who lost his sight after an infected head wound spread to his eyes—
grunted in thanks. They resumed their slow, rhythmic march, one step
after another, in the months-long silent, painful journey to the only
place they knew to go after learning they'd been banned from Rome.

"Your sister knows you are coming, yes?" Attius asked. Again.

Marcus chuckled. "Yes, I told you. She is expecting us."

Attius glanced at Marcus, catching his friend's quirked lips. It
amazed Attius that Marcus still had the ability to smile, let alone
laugh. Perhaps his injuries at Cannae saved him. Even before the in-
fection had set in, his friend's eyes had been swollen shut. He hadn't
seen the hellscape that greeted Attius when he'd regained conscious-
ness on the field.

The horror of it replayed continually in Attius' mind like a hateful
song he couldn't expunge. He'd become aware of the strange silence
first. No metal clashing, no horses screaming, only the pitiful groans

and cries of the dying all around him. He'd come to in that strange twilight time when the enemy had withdrawn before returning to finish off those who still lived and recover their own dead.

Attius had crawled out from under a horrific pile of twisted, dead, and dying bodies. The only reason his breath hadn't been stolen, he realized, was because of the odd way a couple of men had fallen onto their upright shields. It had given him enough room to breathe. And survive. When he'd finally stood—covered in blood and gore, sweat and mud—he was convinced he'd emerged into the darkest realms of Pluto. Never before had he seen so many dead and destroyed bodies. Severed limbs and heads. Men with their inner organs spilling out like burst pods. The ground slick with blood and the liquefied waste of the dying and the dead.

The cries of those leaking out their lives broke his heart as they called out weakly for their loved ones—the younger ones for their mothers, the older ones for their wives and children. Despite the fierce blow to the head, as Attius got his bearings, he called out for Marcus, hoping he too had survived. Attius' voice had been hoarse and ragged, barely recognizable even to himself. Amazingly, he heard his friend respond. To get to Marcus, Attius came across a young Roman whose thighs were slashed and flayed to the bone, tendons cut. Dying, he locked eyes with Attius. The kid extended his throat, begging to be put out of his misery. Attius found a discarded gladius and approached him. The look of pain and gratitude he gave Attius as he cut his throat still haunted his dreams.

He didn't remember much after pulling Marcus free. Marcus swore he carried him for the whole twenty-mile walk—following the line of staggering survivors—to Venusia for help. Attius had vague impressions of kind women who took them in and attended to their wounds, who fed them and soothed them with cool cloths night after night when the fevers and nightmares struck.

When Attius learned they'd been called cowards and tainted just for surviving, that they'd been accused of running and were therefore banned from ever returning to Rome, he'd felt it like a sword thrust to his chest. Getting back to Rome and seeing Mia had been the only thing that had kept him going. The unfairness of it galled him to the bone. They had not been cowards. They'd stayed and fought. How could Rome turn their backs on them like that?

He had also heard they called them, the "Ghosts of Cannae" now. Their living, breathing bodies a reminder of Rome's failure and so they had to be shunned into insubstantiality.

Neither man had expected to survive the battle that destroyed their general and tens of thousands of their comrades in arms. They had no explanations for why they still lived. Marcus claimed that it was the gods who saved them, but that only enraged Attius. Couldn't he see that raised the question—why didn't they save the others then? The gods had nothing to do with it. It was pure random chaos. And when he'd heard on their travels that Rome had blamed the two youngest Vestal virgins for their destruction at Cannae and that they'd put the priestesses to death, he wished that he'd died where he'd fought.

He lived only to get his friend to safety.

"You should stay with me and my sister," Marcus said. "You might as well rest until you decide what to do next."

"I will think about it," Attius lied. He fully expected to fall on his sword once he knew Marcus was settled. His only other option was to rejoin the remnants of the scattered Ghosts of Cannae who had formed a new legion in Sicily. But he was likely to be rejected for his limp after having his thigh muscle slashed. And why would he want to continue fighting for Rome when Rome turned its back on him? When Rome sacrificed Mia and another Vestal in a ridiculous religious frenzy? He could not think what to do beyond putting one foot in front of the other to get his friend to his family.

"According to Marcia, anyone who manages to make it to their compound has been led there by the goddess and so must be welcomed and accepted," Marcus said.

"Bullshit," Attius scoffed. He didn't want to be anywhere near a place devoted to the gods. Any god who stood by and did nothing about the carnage at Cannae was more demon than god and he didn't believe in those either. And any goddess who did nothing to help Mia and her friend while they scapegoated and killed them in such a cruel way wasn't worth an ounce of his piss let alone his gratitude. "Liars and charlatans," he muttered. "All of them."

Marcus chuckled. "If you did not believe in the gods, you would not rage at them with such vehemence."

What else could he do with all his grief and fury? He had no power to hold accountable the assholes who foolishly marched them into Hannibal's trap at Cannae or the zealots who blamed Mia for their own stupidity. It was bad enough when Attius learned that he and the other survivors of Cannae were being called cowards and were banned from Rome. But hearing about Mia's death gutted him.

They'd killed her. They'd whipped her and then buried her alive. Just as they'd lied and called him coward, they'd lied and called her whore. But he knew, more than anyone, that Mia would never have risked such a thing. How many times had she told him that if there were even the slightest chance that her behavior might cause suffering, she would not do it? She had even refused to touch him after he'd been officially named a man.

But none of that mattered to the powerful in Rome. And now they dared use her death to explain why Hannibal had not attacked Rome after Cannae. The removal of the offending virgins, Rome claimed, restored the "peace of the gods." And that was why the enemy had not attacked.

Anyone with any military sense would know Hannibal didn't attack Rome because he didn't want to lay siege on a walled city with winter right around the corner. Especially since he had no siege engines. But sure, the killing of two Vestal priestesses was the real reason the general did not pounce on Rome after Cannae.

Irritated, Attius didn't see the rock he was steering his friend into. Marcus stumbled forward. Attius caught him.

"You little shit," Marcus said. "You did that on purpose!"

"Absolutely not," Attius replied "The gods must have done it."

"Asshole," Marcus said grinning.

Diana

Diana and Ketet mopped up their mashed fava bean stew with hunks of crusty, dark bread. They gathered at the communal breaking fast table—a warping mass of old wood planks in the shade of sycamores and pines. Diana's back stiffened as she overheard the old kitchen lady pontificate on her favorite topic: the scandal of the Vestal priestesses in Rome who broke their vows of chastity.

Ketet gave her a barely perceptible shake of the head to remind her of their agreed-upon strategy of survival in the Sibyl's compound: *Ignore it. Ignore it all.* If Rome discovered her true identity, the Senate would command the entire community be burned to the ground, Sibyl or no Sibyl. She must not react or tell her truth.

That was easier said than done, though. With a sigh, Diana took a sip of barley water. Even out here in the secluded mountains of Cumae, it seemed she couldn't escape talk of her former life.

"It's because Rome killed them two whores who was virgins," the old woman continued, wiping her hands on her apron. "Once they done got rid of them, the gods were happy. That's what did it. 'Tis the only possible reason Rome still stands."

We were never whores, Diana wanted to scream, but of course she did not. She was amazed no one mentioned the story of the "burning virgin." They spoke only of the one who killed herself and the one who died in the traditional underground burial chamber. She herself had spread the rumor of the virgin who was consumed by the goddess' fire, yet the Senate recorded into the annals that she had descended into the chamber, as was "proper." She shouldn't have been surprised. Whatever the powerful in Rome claimed to be true—and wrote down as true—became "fact." And with enough repetition, lies always seemed more true than the truth.

An old warrior named Titus Pullo limped into the conversational fray. "Caudex!" he cried at the old woman, while Ketet and Diana tried not to laugh. It was his favorite insult—*you stump!*—delivered while raising his own handless wrist in the air for emphasis. He'd lost his appendage in the first war against Carthage more than two decades before.

"The gods had nothing to do with it," he said with his usual growl. "Neither did no virgins."

When the old woman looked askance at him, he puffed out his chest, ready to impart warrior-wisdom. "Hannibal don't have a proper army," he pontificated. "They're mercenaries—paid foreigners—and gold is the only tongue they speak." He spit on the ground. "Not like us Romans, who fight for honor and country! His barbarian mercenaries woulda rebelled if Hannibal made them march on Rome. So he took 'em to Capua where they could loot and pillage and get fat off the city's gold through the winter."

With his uninjured hand the old man pointed to his shaggy, white-haired head. "It was strategic, you see. The gods and some stupid whores had nothing to do with it."

Every time the subject of Rome's continued existence came up, Diana had to fight the impulse to defend herself and tell the truth. But she had to stay anonymous to ensure the safety of the entire community. In her former life, she had to be the perfect virgin to protect Rome. Now she had to be perfectly anonymous to protect her new community. Still, her old self sometimes spilled out. "The gods are not moved by the tantrums of little girls or the sex lives of young women," she mumbled to herself.

"What?" the old woman called.

"Nothing," Diana answered with a sweet smile.

Diana stood, grabbed Ketet's cup and plate, and returned both to the old woman, who dumped them in a bucket. When she rejoined her, Ketet whispered, "I will never get used to you serving me."

Diana grinned. She made a point of waiting upon her friend whenever possible as a reminder that they were both free from their old identities. It tickled her that people assumed their roles had been reversed in their prior lives—because of the scars on her back, everyone assumed Diana was a slave and because of Ketet's quiet dignity, many assumed she was once a priestess of Isis in her native land. Nobody ever asked outright, of course, because everyone there was escaping something.

Still, sometimes people looked into Diana's face, and asked, "Have we met before?"

She always told them, no, that she simply had "one of those faces" everyone thought they knew. Plus, she always wore her thick curly hair free, knowing that no one had ever seen the Vestal who had visited the summer before without her head covering. Diana's wild unbound curls drew the eye away from her face. That, combined with the fact that everyone "knew" that the unlucky Vestal priestess who had visited them had been burned alive and taken by the goddess of fire helped her remain anonymous.

People saw what they wanted to see.

Only one other person beside Ketet knew the truth. Months after Diana made it to the compound, they had run into the Sibyl as she presided over a community-wide celebration of the Great Mother. The old woman had looked from her to Ketet and back again for many agonizingly long moments, then burst out in uproarious laughter.

When she calmed and wiped her tears, she put a finger to her lips, winked and walked away, still chuckling. Nobody noticed or paid much attention. Everyone knew the Sibyl often had strange outbursts that made no sense after all. That was her way. Their secret was safe with her.

Diana and Ketet grabbed their basket and headed to the herb gardens. Diana whistled for her dog Useless to follow along. The dog would nap in the sun while they gathered and sorted stalks for drying. It was tedious work, but also meditative and it reminded Diana of one of the few tasks she actually enjoyed in her former life, grinding sacred salt and sifting flour for baking ritual salt cakes.

Their baskets were in mid-swing when a woman with a toddler on her hip called out. "Diana, wait!"

Both women turned to the young mother, eyebrows raised.

"My brother Marcus is arriving today," the young woman named Marcia announced.

"Is he?" Diana said, smiling. "How wonderful!" Few people dared travel now that Hannibal occupied Capua, a mere day's march away.

"I…well, I was hoping to make a special meal to celebrate," Marcia said.

Diana held her arms out to the chubby two-year-old and the child dove into them. Diana grinned, kissing the child's fat, soft, milky-smelling cheek.

The one-handed veteran Titus, hobbling out behind them, overheard. "He one of them Ghosts of Cannae?"

Marcia's face scrunched and she wheeled on the old man. "Tell me, please, how someone who was injured and blinded *on the field*, can be accused of running? Of being a coward?"

Titus held up both arms, waving his stump. "Steady now. I know what it's like to be tossed aside when you can't fight no more," he said.

"Where is he coming from?" Diana asked.

"Venusia. But they've mostly only traveled by night to avoid Hannibal's scouts. He sent word months ago and I had not heard anything and feared the worst."

"How do you know he will arrive today?" Ketet asked.

"One of the hunters saw them at dawn and told me. They showed them a safer, more hidden route, which should bring them in soon. And in celebration," Marcia said turning to Diana, "I was hoping to cook Marcus' favorite stew and well…I need some hares."

"Ah," Diana smiled, understanding. "The hunters this morning didn't return with any?"

She shook her head. "They were after bigger game. They did come back with some birds though, I think. You don't mind checking the traps?"

Diana smiled. "Not at all."

"Wonderful!" the woman beamed. She grabbed the child from Diana and waved. "I'm going to talk to cook about what else we can make."

Ketet headed out alone to the herb gardens. "Happy hunting, Huntress," she called over her shoulder, giving Diana a big smile.

Everyone in the community called Diana "Huntress" because when she pulled her hair back and armed up with knives and her bow and arrows, she had an uncanny resemblance to the painted statue of the goddess of the hunt in an old shrine at the base of the mountain.

Because of Hannibal, trading in the region had dried up, as had visits from gift-bearing pilgrims. Fortunately, the Sibyl's community was self-sustaining thanks to its small farms and orchards. Diana and the other hunters added to the cooking pots whenever they could, as did the fishermen who traversed secret tunnels to the abundant fresh waters of Lake Avernus. Even though Hannibal had never ventured in their direction, they were always on guard.

In the woods, Diana stopped by a makeshift altar she'd created for her namesake goddess, even though she no longer believed. But old habits die hard. As she did every time she visited, Diana added another tiny acorn top to the pile she'd accumulated over the months. The small tops reminded her of the little knitted caps mothers lovingly put on their newborns to keep them warm. She left one whenever she paid homage to her childhood friend Prisca still in Rome. Diana would never have made it to the compound without her help. She had no way of knowing whether Prisca survived the birth of her first child but laying another little acorn on the altar reminded her to be grateful for her friend's courage.

When they finally set off, Useless yipped in excitement and bounded into the woods ahead of her.

Attius

On a bend in the mountain road, Marcus stopped abruptly. "Do you hear that?" he whispered.

"Something is moving through the brush," Marcus murmured, freezing at Attius' warning touch.

Attius pulled his bow and arrow. At least it would be a boon for Marcus to arrive with game.

Silently he pulled his bow. But then he paused. It didn't sound like an animal. They'd been living off the land long enough now that he could tell the difference. It was a person. His heart raced. Someone was tracking them. They were good too. Hannibal's scouts?

Attius aimed his arrow in the direction of the noise. Only one person, he realized. Not a group of scouts. Perhaps one of the hunters they had met earlier had returned to guide them into the compound. He lowered his bow but cautiously reached for his hunting knife just in case.

A young woman jumped out from behind a bush, arrow drawn straight at his face. "What business do you have on this mountain?" she demanded.

Attius was struck dumb. She was dressed like the goddess Diana— tunica tucked up under her belt so she could run. A leather headband around braided hair, curls escaping in the breeze. A bow primed with an arrow ready to shoot him between the eyes. The sight of the woman was so incongruous, so unexpected, Attius stayed frozen in his defensive crouch, knife at the ready, unable to breathe let alone move.

The woman immediately unnotched her arrow. "I am sorry. You must be the travelers. Is one of you Marcus?"

That voice. He knew that voice. But that couldn't be right. His brain refused to register the possibility.

She'd been killed in Rome. Everyone said so.

The woman's eyes went to the man who waggled his head with excitement and grinned. "That is me," he cried. "Are we at the Sibyl's village?"

"Nearly so," she said. "You sister Marcia sent me out to check the traps to make your favorite—"

"Hare stew," he laughed and made a strange sound in his throat, heavy with mingled relief and joy. Still, Attius could not make sense of the person in front of them. He sheathed his knife with shaking fingers and returned to Marcus' side out of habit, half protecting him, half needing to push against his shoulder to ground himself. He rubbed his face and squinted at the young woman. "Who are you?" he asked, then mumbled, "I am losing my mind."

Marcus snorted. "I have known that for a long time, friend. Kind lady, excuse my friend's rudeness. We are much fatigued and would be extraordinarily grateful if you would guide us to my sister."

"Of course," she said. "But I am sorry to say your celebratory meal will not contain your favorite stew. The traps were empty."

"That is the least of my concerns," Marcus said. "Now tell us, what is your name?"

"Diana," she said, head down as she replaced the arrow in its quiver. "Like the huntress."

Attius made a choking sound in his throat. He wondered if perhaps he had died of thirst on this journey and was actually walking through the fields of Asphodel. He hadn't expected such bright sunlight in the afterworld, though. But it made sense that a vision of Mia would come to him as Diana.

"Are you alright?" the specter said to him. She looked down at her belt, pointing to a goatskin bladder. "Do you need water?"

Attius shook his head. He could barely breathe. He wondered if he would pass out. Could one pass out in the underworld? But why was Marcus here too?

"By the gods, what is wrong with you?" Marcus said, bumping his shoulder. He turned in the direction of the young woman's voice. "You must be quite beautiful for I've never before heard him have so much difficulty speaking. You already know I am Marcus. This here is Attius."

The woman froze then she blinked rapidly several times.

Attius colored as he was flooded with shame over his appearance: the rags of his ruined military tunic. The patchy beard on his dirty, sunburnt face. His peeling skin and knotted, overlong hair over his near skeletal frame. The jagged purple scars on his leg and shield arm. The tatters of military boots that were nothing more than flaps of leather held together with frayed found rope. He knew he reeked of sweat and smoke and misery and felt as if he'd aged twenty years.

Her eyes widened. "Attius of Capua? But I was told…I thought…"

Attius' mouth was so dry he was not sure he could speak. "Mi-Mia?" he croaked.

"It is you," she cried, covering her mouth.

"I think I am dreaming," Attius groaned, feeling dizzy.

"What is happening," Marcus asked. "I thought you said your name was Diana."

"It is," she said quickly, still staring wide-eyed at Attius. Then mouthed the word, '*Now.*'

A large barking dog burst through brush and nearly knocked Attius over. Whining and jumping in a frenzy of recognition, the dog scrabbled at Attius' feet, crying piteously.

"Useless, stop!" Diana cried. The dog ignored her. "Useless!"

Wide-eyed, Attius stared at the dog, then back up at Diana. At the sound of the dog's name, a great surge of suppressed grief crashed through Attius' chest, even as he struggled to believe what he was seeing. Even as he touched the dog he loved as a boy. He began to laugh at the dog's antics, but another wave of emotion overwhelmed him and he dropped his head into his hands and wept. Still-fresh horror and grief burst through his entire body in agonizing waves.

"What is happening?" Marcus repeated. "Attius, tell me!"

Diana dropped her bow and gathered the wrecked young man into her arms, intermittently laughing and sobbing herself. The dog ran in circles around the pair, barking and yelping as they whispered broken words, trying to understand.

Cannae. Survived. Trial. Fire. Escaped. New name. Helping Marcus. Starting over. And again and again, *Is this real? How is this possible?*

Attius held Diana out by the shoulders so he could examine her face. He touched her cheek in wonder.

"Against all the odds, Diana and Orion—" whispered Diana.

"Found each other in the woods," finished Attius.

Author's Note

The idea for this book came from years of witnessing the erosion of women's rights in the United States and abroad, and its connection to a religious obsession with sexual purity in girls and women. Year after year, religious leaders claim God sent disasters (hurricanes, floods, tsunamis, and so on) to punish whole nations over the sexual activity of a few (either gay or trans individuals or of women having sex outside of marriage).

In America, evangelicals such as Pat Robertson, Franklin Graham, Jerry Falwell Jr., Mike Huckabee, Ken Hamm, and others have publicly blamed hurricanes, floods, earthquakes, and other disasters on wanton behavior by gays and/or women. They were not alone—Catholic priests, Orthodox Jews, fundamentalist Muslim clerics, and even some Hindu and Buddhist leaders have claimed that disasters were sent by God or the gods or karma in divine anger over the sexual lives of LGBTQ individuals and/or women.

How was that any different, I wondered, than Rome blaming Vestal virgins for breaking their vows of chastity when disaster struck in ancient times, as they did numerous times throughout Rome's history?

I couldn't shake the question: Why does this kind of Bronze Age thinking persist in an age when we are capable of sending robots into space and onto the surface of Mars? It occurred to me, after watching interviews with deeply religious leaders, that many seemed to actually believe that God's judgment/wrath did or would rain down upon them or the nation because certain people were having sex. Realizing that the fear was real for them—or at least for their followers—changed everything for me. It led me to want to understand why and how they came to internalize this primitive, Bronze-age thinking that related the sexual activity of a few to the punishment of whole nations.

Around the same time, I was reading about the wars between Carthage and Rome, specifically the Second Punic War, when Hannibal (the North African general of Carthage) brought his entire army over the Alps with his elephants and rampaged throughout Italy for years. During this period, two Vestal virgins were accused of having sex after a devastating loss at the Battle of Cannae. The death of forty to fifty thousand Roman men in one day was so devastating, priests claimed there had to have been a supernatural reason for it. And that reason seemed indisputably clear to them: two of their most sacred virgins must have broken their vows of chastity. Nothing else could have outraged the gods to that extent.

Two priestesses—Floronia and Opimia (we have no more information about them than their names)—were accused and faced a religious court. Both died as a result, Floronia by suicide and Opimia by being buried alive (after being whipped first), as was the traditional punishment. Soon after their deaths, the Romans buried alive four more individuals—a Greek man and woman, and a Gaul man and woman (notably not Roman citizens, but foreigners and/or immigrants and most likely slaves).

Yes, the Romans performed human sacrifice. During the Second Punic War—arguably Rome's lowest point—Rome sacrificed six human beings in a frenzy of terror and in a desperate attempt to appease their angry gods.

Some have quibbled with the contention that Vestal punishments were human sacrifices. The proper term in some scholarly circles has been that these Vestals were victims of "ritual murder." Either way, it was indisputable that their elimination was designed as a "cleansing" or to appease wrathful gods. And as a punishment for having sex.

It was in the stories of these virgins that I saw the primal roots of our persistent tendency to blame the sexual activity of certain people as the "reason" why bad things happened to entire nations (i.e., god was angry because "those" people had sex).

I also noticed something else. Whenever I spoke about writing a novel about an accused Vestal, the knee-jerk reaction was a snigger and a wink, an almost automatic assumption that I would be writing about Vestals *actually* having sex. In reality, Vestals' lives were so constrained, the stakes so high, it seemed to me far likelier that most of the women put to death were innocent. After all, they were taken into the order as young children, separated from the world of men, and deeply indoctrinated/threatened with what would happen to Rome if they stepped out of line. To imagine that a Vestal would cavalierly break her vows in order to have "some fun" ignored the reality and burden of a *lifetime* of fear-based indoctrination. We know of at least twenty-one Vestals who were accused and killed throughout Roman history. Likely more women died in this manner though their deaths were never recorded. Every accusation correlated to a disaster—battles lost, plagues sweeping the city, widespread famine.

The fear that a supernatural entity would smite countless innocents because of the sexual behaviors of a targeted people has woven itself into the fabric of our unconsciousness. Religious education, especially in the Abrahamic religions, reinforces these fears, particularly in literalist interpretations of ancient sacred texts. So primal, so ancient is this belief, it continues in today's honor killings, endless slut shaming, and continual scapegoating of people in the LGBTQ community.

From a novelist's point of view, I became fascinated by how an intelligent, strong-willed woman might cope in this world. What did it do to the psyche of a woman who had been told from early childhood that she must behave a certain way or a god/the gods would make everyone—including every person she cared about—suffer in agonizing ways? And what shifts would be required for her to overcome those beliefs after they had been internalized?

Most importantly, I wanted to imagine a world where Mia survived and escaped her death sentence. After all, that is the fiction part of historical fiction.

In the end, I hope that Opimia's story holds a mirror up to our own ancient habits of thinking so that we may consciously decide whether they serve us or should be deposited into the bins of history as we have done with the idea of using leeches to remove "bad" humors in medicine. At the very least, my hope is that we can understand the ancient dynamics behind targeting groups and individuals to shame, blame, and scapegoat for the reality and inevitability of human suffering. And renounce such impulses once and for all.

Historical Notes

The Cleansing is based on the historical events of 216 BCE in Rome during the Second Punic War. The ancient sources include Polybius, Livy, and Arrian. Rome fought three wars against Carthage for dominance in the region. The First Punic War ended about twenty-three years before Opimia's story. The Second Punic War began in 218 BCE when Hannibal crossed the Alps to invade Roman-held territories. Two years after Hannibal began his rampages, 216 BCE, was the lowest point of the war for Rome. The Hannibal war lasted another fifteen years after the deaths of Opimia and Floronia. The third and final war took place about seventy years later, though it was more of a Roman act of aggression against an old enemy than a war. Carthage was completely destroyed in 146 BCE, and all its citizens either killed or taken as slaves.

It was during the Second Punic War, however, thanks to Hannibal, that Rome came closest to utter defeat and destruction. After a third devastating loss at the Battle of Cannae (the first two being at Trebia and Lake Trasimene), a panicked Rome sought a "reason" for why the gods had abandoned them. The priests of Rome claimed two Vestal virgins had broken their sacred vows of chastity, thus "causing" the carnage.

Real historical characters:

Opimia and Floronia: After being accused of breaking their Vestal vows of chastity in 216 BCE, Floronia committed suicide and Opimia was found guilty and buried alive, according to Livy. No additional information is recorded about these women or the religious court that indicted them. We do not even have their full names, let alone any details of their ages or personalities. According to historical accounts, Opimia was buried alive, but I chose a fictionalized path of freedom for her because I couldn't bear to write a scene of her slow asphyxiation inside a dark, underground tomb—abandoned and blamed for the mistakes of men and the horrors of war.

Lucius Cantilius: Cantilius was the man accused of debauching Floronia and Opimia. He was whipped to death. Livy identified him as a secretary to the Pontifex Maximus. I invented the familial relationship to the head priest.

Cornelius Lentulus: The Pontifex Maximus was the greatest/most powerful priest of Rome during this period. The pontiff oversaw the Vestal Order and was in charge of overseeing the flogging of his secretary and the deaths of Floronia and Opimia.

The Virgo Maxima: While the Virgo Maxima was the title of the senior leader of the six Vestal priestesses, we do not have the name of the Virgo Maxima during this period. The name Gegania Macerina is fictional, though her existence and power were very real. She was the only female member of the powerful Collegium of Priests.

Quintus Fabius Maximus Verrucosus, aka "Cuncator" ("the Delayer"): Quintus Maximus was a real Roman general who served as consul and dictator in 221 and 217 BCE. His strategy of not engaging in pitched battle against Hannibal but staying just out of reach, harassing foragers and small parties, and targeting supply lines worked for more than a year. However, his prudent, cautious approach grew unpopular and was labeled "un-Roman" and "unmanly." The abandonment of this strategy led to the disaster at Cannae. Many modern military scholars assert that had Rome held fast to Fabius' strategy, they would have starved Hannibal out and eventually destroyed their enemy within the year. Instead, the war went on after Cannae for another fifteen years on Italian soil. The Second Punic War ended when the young Roman general Scipio (later named Africanus in honor of his victory over Carthage) defeated Hannibal in the Battle of Zama in Carthage in 202 BCE.

Lucius Aemilius Paullus: Paullus was elected as consul twice (a consul was the highest elected political office during the Republic). He also served as general alongside co-consul and general Gaius Terentius Varro. Because of constant infighting, the Senate decreed that they would take turns leading the legions. Varro chose to engage in pitched battle at Cannae against Paullus' wishes on his day of rule. Paullus died in battle. Varro continued leading the remaining forces in Rome while Floronia and Opimia were blamed for the losses at Cannae.

Gaius Terentius Varro: He survived Cannae and returned to Rome to try to reassemble the legions. According to some sources, he was welcomed back to Rome after the defeat as a "hero" for the simple reason he did not commit suicide in shame for the devastation at Cannae, but instead returned to continue serving Rome. To me that smacks of ancient editorializing, of trying to paint the man as a hero despite his monumental mistake in engaging Hannibal on a field of his enemy's choosing and against his already proven superiority in pitched battle. Other sources say the disgraced general snuck inside the city in the dead of night to avoid the grief-maddened mob. To me, that seems more likely, which is why I chose that interpretation for the novel.

Fictional Characters:

Attius

Prisca

Melantho

Larce

The Sibyl's compound: There is no record of a compound or village near the cave of the Sibyl. I invented the idea that the Sibyl of Cumae represented a lasting remnant of those who continued a primal tradition of mother goddess worship. It seemed reasonable to assume that small, isolated pockets of worshippers of the "old ways" continued well into the Bronze Age and beyond.

Strange But True Facts About Ancient Rome In This Novel

Female Virginity

The ancient Romans did not have a concept of virginity that could be tested physically—i.e., by the presence of a hymen, a concept created in the Middle Ages. Perhaps ancient Romans understood, as medical experts do today, that the hymen's function is to serve as a barrier to keep the vagina clean during infanthood. As girls mature, the hymen can be stretched or torn in any number of ways and so was never considered proof of anything.

However, there was one test that was considered infallible—spending the night at the Temple of Juno with the sacred snakes. If the snakes took the girl's offering, her virginity was said to be affirmed by the goddess. This was often the "test" employed before marriage.

Why this test would be denied to a Vestal virgin seeking to prove her virginity is not clear, but it appears it was never employed in any of the Vestal trials. Every accusation against a Vestal was precipitated by a crisis—war, famine, plague etc. In the grip of religious panic, it is likely that the Pontifex Maximus would have ruled the test of Juno as invalid for the simple reason that he had the power to do so and that it was more important to contain the panic sweeping through the city in crisis by the ritual act of "removing" the impurity that caused the gods to turn from them in the first place—a choice I made for the novel.

Blood Sacrifices/Relationship with the Gods

Roman state religion was communal rather than personal and regularly involved the sacrifice of animals and other gifts such as plants, fruits, cakes, wine, oil, etc. Sacrifice was the primary means by which Romans connected to the divine and blood sacrifices in particular both beseeched for and ensured the peace of the gods.

It is hard for us to conceive just how drenched in blood ancient Rome was, particularly when one realizes that blood sacrifices also took place regularly in the home as well. Sacrifices were designed to appeal to the gods. It was transactional; the concept was *Do ut des*: I give so that you may give. And if the gods did not deliver, it meant there was something wrong in their offering. It provided a means of control in what likely felt like an out-of-control world. Sometimes, people sought out specialized priests to "divine" the god's will through examination of entrails of the sacrifice.

While Vestal virgins were forbidden from touching blood, they were present at every state sacrifice. They prepared the sacred salt cakes that were crumbled over the animal's head before the slitting of the throat and the catching of the first blood.

Romans feared that making a mistake during a sacrifice might insult or anger a god, so great care was taken to ensure all went as prescribed. If there was a problem of any sort, the rite would be repeated—including the sacrifice of another animal(s)—until it was deemed satisfactory to the gods.

As scholars of ancient Roman religion have pointed out, "*Terror* is an emotion that we seldom look for in Roman religion, but which recurs again and again." (Drs. L.G. Driediger-Murphy and E. Eldinow, *Ancient Divination and Experience*). The terror of war, of unexplained natural phenomena, of sickness, famine, etc., must have been strong and insistent in ancient times. Sacrificial/transactional religious practices likely served to provide a sense of order and control as well as safety in the face of that terror. During times of terror, Rome's streets ran with the blood of sacrificed animals.

Human Sacrifices

Romans regularly denounced "barbarians" for performing human sacrifice. They often accused the Carthaginians of sacrificing babies to their fire god, Ba'al. However, in truth, Rome sacrificed humans too. Vestal virgins have historically not been considered human sacrifices—some scholars called their live internments as "ritual murders"—but I fail to see the difference. Over recorded Roman history, nearly two dozen Vestal virgins were put to death for either having sex or allowing the Vestal fire to go out.

It is interesting to note too, that soon after the deaths of Floronia and Opimia in 216 BCE, the Romans buried alive four additional people—a Greek man and woman, and a Gaul man and woman—in the cattle market (Forum Borarium), an ancient site of human sacrifice. The sacrifice of Greek and Gaul couples occurred a total of three times that we know of (in 228, 216, and 114 BCE). There is every likelihood that it happened more often than that, especially during times of extreme stress.

Some scholars posit that the sacrifices of Greeks and Gauls—since all three recorded episodes took place after the deaths of Vestal virgins—represented their discomfiture and guilt over the deaths of likely innocent Vestal priestesses. In other words, they cleansed themselves of the guilt of killing Vestals by killing four additional people! All of the people buried alive after Vestal killings were identified as "outsiders" (i.e., Gaul and Greek, not Roman citizens and some assert that they were likely slaves, although the ancient accounts don't identify them as such). Whether slave, foreigner, or immigrant, Romans clearly excused the behavior by believing they were less than human.

The ritual of the Argei in the spring, mentioned in the novel, did indeed originally involve the ritual deaths of twenty-seven men thrown into the Tiber from Rome's oldest bridge in the early days of Rome. According to ancient sources, Hercules came to Rome—via Iberia—and instructed Romans to stop sacrificing living men and to replace them with straw effigies.

Prodigia

Many ancient peoples believed that strange or unusual natural phenomena were a form of divine communication (burning bush anyone?). The Romans were no different. Odd occurrences in nature served as warnings of imminent peril caused by divine wrath or divine abandonment. Prodigia warned of impending chaos, anarchy, and disorder. Anything that could not be explained or strange events in nature were called prodigia.

Many of the examples included in this book were taken directly from ancient sources. Lightning strikes were considered especially concerning as they were said to be a direct expression of Jupiter's anger. Lightning strikes hitting temples or statues or people were especially troubling.

Natural phenomena such as fires or plagues were prodigia. Just as alarming was the presence of unusual animals, such as owls or wolves entering a city, a swarm of bees in the forum, snakes inside a home, etc. Any strange, unexpected, or unexplainable event in the daily life of a Roman could be considered a prodigium and had the power to provoke religious panic.

On the political level, prodigia indicated divine will—usually divine wrath—and served as warnings of a future threat to Rome. They often pointed to some behavior or action of humans that caused the gods to withdraw their protection. Only by appeasement could Romans coax the gods back into their proper role of protecting Rome. Unfortunately for Vestal virgins, that appeasement usually required their executions.

Helvia, the Real Girl Struck by Lightning

In *The Cleansing*, I referenced the prodigium of a Roman girl struck by lightning and how the "indecent" state in which her body was found "meant" a Vestal virgin had broken her vows. This is a true story, though it took place in 114 BCE and not 216 BCE. As a result of this "sign from the gods," three Vestal virgins were accused of breaking their vow of chastity in 114 BCE. Two of the three virgins were acquitted and one was buried alive. But the people, caught in a religious panic over an impending war, insisted the religious judges had been wrong. A politician took the trial over, removed the panel of religious judges, installed his own judges and, unsurprisingly, found the other two Vestals guilty and they too were buried alive.

Slavery and the Torture of Slaves for Court Admittance

Slavery was ubiquitous throughout the ancient world. Scholars estimate that at various times in its history, one in three people were slaves in Rome. It is hard for us to imagine, but slavery as an institution was rarely questioned or considered a moral problem as a whole. Morally,

Romans were advised to treat their enslaved people well but they could punish and even kill their "property" with impunity. During most of Rome's history, slaves came primarily from Mediterranean people like themselves—from Greece and northern Italy primarily—and when they expanded the empire, from today's Germany, France, and Britain.

Slaves were indeed required to be tortured before their testimony could be used in court. Some scholars contend this was to discourage unhappy slaves/freedmen from frivolously using the court to avenge mistreatment by violent slave holders. However, the Romans seemed to understand that testimony taken under torture was unreliable. The practice continued nonetheless, likely a reflection of Roman anxiety at the sheer number of people enslaved in Rome.

Ghosts of Cannae/The Abandoned Survivors of the Battle of Cannae

As many as ten thousand Roman soldiers survived Cannae, but the Roman Senate inexplicably turned its back on them. They were deemed cowards for "running from the battlefield" and were barred from ever entering Rome again. A great many injured survivors limped their way out of the battlefield to nearby cities to recover. The cruelty of abandoning injured warriors and barring them from returning home is hard to fathom and no explanation has ever been found. The shame of the defeat may have played a factor but unfortunately, we have no record explaining why the Roman Senate made this decree.

The Romans, however, were deeply superstitious and there is a good chance that they saw the survivors of Cannae, as somehow "tainted" with defeat. They likely feared that they might bring a miasma of loss with them and infect the new legions charged with trying to protect the now exceedingly vulnerable Rome. As one Roman warrior reenactor explained to me one day, "We seriously underestimate the level of religiosity and superstition in Rome and in the Roman military."

Cannae survivors who could still fight were garrisoned in Sicily where they stayed for more than a decade. Publius Cornelius Scipio folded these veterans into a reformed army that took the Second Punic War to its conclusion eleven years later when Scipio defeated Hannibal at Zama in Carthage. *The Ghosts of Cannae: Hannibal and the Darkest Hour of the Roman Republic,* by Robert L. O'Connell, is an excellent resource on both the war and Rome's treatment of Cannae survivors.

No One Knows Why Hannibal Bypassed Rome after Cannae

Military historians continue to ponder why Hannibal did not take Rome right after his remarkable victory at Cannae. Rome was without its legions and in chaos. It seemed like easy pickings. According to Livy, after Cannae, Hannibal's Numedian general Maharbal told him they would be celebrating their victory over Rome in the fabled city in a matter of days. When Hannibal told him he was undecided about immediately marching on Rome, Maharbal reportedly said, "You know how to win, Hannibal, but you don't know how to use a victory."

So why didn't Hannibal invade right after Cannae? Although we will never know what the Carthaginian general was thinking, several factors likely influenced his decision:

1) Rome's adamant, "No!" to a demand of surrender suggested a level of stubbornness and intransigency that likely gave him pause.

2) To lay siege on a city like Rome—with its high and deep walls—Hannibal would have needed siege-equipment such as battering rams, catapults, ladders, towers, etc. He did not have this specialized equipment. Even if he'd had them, it would have taken months of continual attack to break through. How would he feed his men over the winter?

3) Hannibal's army was made up of mercenary soldiers (primarily Numedian, Iberian, and Gaulish forces). They fought for pay and plunder while the Romans fought for home and hearth.

4) Carthage was also suffering under the financial strain of paying for an army on foreign land, and Hannibal was likely unsure how much he could squeeze out of his home state to cover the cost of a long siege.

Bypassing Rome and attacking wealthy and undefended Capua gave Hannibal's mercenaries the opportunity to loot and pillage without opposition while they rested over the winter. Many scholars believe that it was that winter's occupation of Capua that began the undoing of Hannibal's amazing successes over Rome. They believe his mercenaries grew fat and complacent with the riches of Capua and never again experienced the hunger for destruction that had previously driven them. The Romans fought against Hannibal for another fourteen years before Hannibal was finally defeated on his own turf in Zama, North Africa.

The Three Vestal Miracles

I focused on three well-known legends about Vestal virgins—the first being about Tuccia who proved her innocence and purity by carrying water from the Tiber to the Forum in a sieve. The idea that glass was used to perform the trick was my own invention. Aemelia was the Vestal who accidentally let the fire go out but was redeemed when a piece of her dress reignited the fire. The final story of Claudia Quinta (she may or may not have been a Vestal), who pulled a ship off a sand-bar, actually took place after the deaths of Floronia and Opimia, during the Second Punic War. However, I included it in the novel as those three "miracles" are often grouped together as "proof" of divine favor for female obedience.

Laws to Control Women During the War

The Senate enacted several laws designed to control the behavior of women, particularly elite women, during the Second Punic War. Starting in 216 BCE, with the devastation at Cannae, the Senate decreed women were to be kept "off the streets" and in their own homes and that they should refrain from "public lamentation." In other words, women were to be silenced and prevented from grieving in public. The new law also restricted mourning to thirty days.

However, this was nothing new—a law of the Roman Twelve Tables prohibited "excessive female lamentation." After Cannae, the sheer scale of grieving mothers, wives, daughters, sisters, and grandchildren must have been immense and threatening, therefore considered "dangerous" enough to be managed by decree.

After controlling the expression of grief came controlling women's money. The growing financial crisis of the war resulted in a number of measures that affected women: money allotted to widows and orphans was put on "irregular deposit," which meant the men in charge could withhold payments as they saw fit. They also could control how much they could extract from remaining citizens, namely women. In other words, they confiscated wealth from widows and orphans.

The control over women's wealth increased with the *Lex Oppia,* enacted in 215 BCE, which restricted how much gold a woman could have and/or wear in public. It also limited what women were allowed to wear (no multi-colored cloth, especially purple), and forbade women from riding in carriages outside of religious festivals.

Women were banned from participating in foreign religious rites as well. Their sexual independence was also curtailed. With the loss of so many Roman men after Cannae, many women were no longer under a Roman man's "hand" or manus, making them legally autonomous, which disturbed the deeply conservative Romans.

In addition, as the state took funds meant for widows and orphans, many women were forced into prostitution to survive. Many were charged with sexual misconduct. Punishments for prostitutes, though, escalated over time from fines, to exile, and to, in some cases, execution. Most of these laws were enacted soon after the events depicted in this novel.

The Sibyl of Cumae

According to legend, there was a "prophetess of Apollo" in Cumae, which was originally a Greek colony. While there are legendary references to the Sibyl, we know very little about her. I invented the idea that the prophetess in Italy was actually a holdover from ancient/primal mother goddess worship to illustrate the evolution of women's slow erasure in religion.

It is true that Fabius the Delayer went to Greece to consult with the Delphic Oracle in order to determine how to appease the gods during the wars with Hannibal. Why, I wondered, would a Roman dictator travel over the sea rather than consult with the prophetess of their own homeland?

I also made up the idea of a nearby self-sustaining community serving the Sibyl. There is no evidence of such a community. But then again, there is no evidence that one did not exist either.

Roman Pederasty and the Cursus Honorum

The ancients did not have concepts of heterosexuality or homosexuality. In Rome's highly hierarchical and conservative culture, what mattered was who was doing what to whom. To maintain his virtus, dignitas, and manliness, an adult male could have penetrative sex with anyone he wished—woman or man, girl or boy, as long as he was the penetrator and of greater status than the penetrated. Adolescent boys were often pursued as love objects and taken as lovers as part of the process of climbing the ladder of offices into the highest levels of Roman political power (the Cursus Honorum).

Once a young man's beard came in, though, he was no longer considered a boy, but a man, and the rules changed. He was obligated to marry and must never be penetrated again, though it was expected he would, in turn, penetrate women, girls, or boys as he desired.

Although pederasty (an organized arrangement between an adult male with an adolescent boy) originated in Greece, the upper classes in Rome during the early Republic incorporated the spirit of the practice into relationships meant to steer adolescent boys along the path to political success. Not all of these mentoring relationships were sexual, but many were. Older men often courted boys and it was claimed that these boys held a great deal of power since they chose the older man. However, as only one party (the adult) had the power to destroy a young man's future prospects, it is hard to see how this could be so, and was likely used as an excuse to dismiss accusations against abusers.

In practice, these unions often began earlier than what I portrayed in this novel—sometimes with boys as young as twelve. Once a boy grew a beard and gave up his bulla, charm of protection, he was considered a man and could no longer be penetrated.

Interestingly, the Roman law Lex Scantinia forbade male sexual intercourse with a free-born Roman youth, but it is unclear whether the law pertained only to rape and not to pre-arranged political alliances.

The Roman preoccupation with status and the revilement of grown men who continued to enjoy being penetrated seems to me an outgrowth of deeply entrenched misogyny. The disgust was deep—and just as it continues today, the greatest insult you could make to a man was to accuse him of acting like a woman. The accusation of not just being penetrated but "liking it" was regularly hurled against political enemies to demean them. Even Julius Caesar was accused of this "crime" by his enemies.

Fascinus/Penis Charms to Avert Evil

Everywhere you turned in ancient Rome, you would likely come face to face with an image of an erect phallus—either in statuary, mosaics, paintings, lamps, windchimes, and graffiti. Boys wore tiny phalli in their bullas (traditional charms of childhood) as protection from evil. Phalluses were carved into walls and doors and business signs all throughout the city as both a means to avert evil and invite luck. The proliferation of phalluses in Rome and in the ancient world in general is somewhat shocking to our modern sensibilities, especially as their use was frequently tied to signals of fertility and/or abundance, but also as wards against the evil eye and for overall general protection. A common motif of protection was the erect phallus with wings.

Acknowledgments

A huge thanks to Ian Gregg-Shecter who helped edit this book and to Bruce, Aliya, and Matthew who patiently listened to all my writing woes on this project. Many of my friends—including Ash Parsons and Elizabeth O. Dulemba—waited for me to outgrow my obsession with this subject matter and didn't complain or roll their eyes when I could not. A special thanks to Michael Alvear for encouraging me to not give up on this story.

Also, I am very grateful to my editors, David G. McAfee and Rae McAfee, at Hypatia Press for believing in this book and supporting me. I am also grateful for Rob Johnson at Ockham Publishing.

A huge thank you to Ruth Osier, Latin teacher extraordinaire, for checking my use of Latin in the story. Any mistakes in Latin use or in interpretation of the ancient sources are mine and mine alone. Also thank you to Antonio R. Garcia who created the map based on public domain images of the Republican era Forum.

Finally, a big hug of gratitude to any reader who shares my obsession with how history—no matter the time period—always reflects our current challenges and forces us to examine how we can and must, "do better."

Victoria Alvear is the author of multiple award-winning books about the ancient world, including *A Day of Fire: A Novel of Pompeii* and *A Song of War: A Novel of Troy*. Her books for children, under the name Vicky A. Shecter, includes the young adult novels, *Cleopatra's Moon* and *Curses and Smoke*, and the nonfiction titles, *Warrior Queens*, *Cleopatra Rules!*, *Hades Speaks!* and others.

Find out more at: www.vickyalvearshecter.com